The Ghost Camp
Or The Avengers

by

Rolf Boldrewood

Double 9
BOOKS

The Ghost Camp
Or The Avengers
by Rolf Boldrewood

ISBN: 978-93-61423-28-4

Published by

DOUBLE 9 BOOKS

2/13-B, Ansari Road
Daryaganj, New Delhi – 110002
info@double9books.com
www.double9books.com
Tel. 011-40042856

ABOUT THE AUTHOR

Thomas Alexander Browne, an Australian author, wrote many of his novels under the pseudonym Rolf Boldrewood. Robbery Under Arms, a novel about bushranging from 1882, is his best known work. Browne was born in London, the eldest child of Captain Sylvester John Brown, a former shipmaster for the East India Company, and his wife Elizabeth Angell, nee Alexander. His mother was his "earliest admirer and most indulgent critic, to whom is chiefly due whatever meed of praise my readers may hereafter vouchsafe" (Dedication Old Melbourne Memories). Thomas added the letter 'e' to his surname in the 1860s. After his father's barque Proteus delivered a cargo of convicts in Hobart, the family relocated to Sydney in 1831. Browne spent approximately twenty-five years as a squatter and almost the same amount of time as a government official, but his third profession as an author lasted forty years. While recovering from a riding accident in 1865, he published two articles for the Cornhill Magazine about pastoral life in Australia, and he started contributing articles and serial stories to Australian weeklies. One of these, Ups and Downs: A Story of Australian Life, was published as a book in London in 1878. It was well reviewed, but received little attention. In 1890, it was reissued under the title The Squatters Dream.

CONTENTS

CHAPTER I

A wild and desolate land; dreary, even savage, to the unaccustomed eye. Forest-clothed hills towering above the faint, narrow track leading eastward, along which a man had been leading a tired horse; he was now resting against a granite boulder. A dark, mist-enshrouded day, during which the continuous driving showers had soaked through an overcoat, now become so heavy that he carried it across his arm. A fairly heavy valise, above a pair of blankets, was strapped in front of his saddle.

He was prepared for bush travelling—although his term of "colonial experience," judging from his ruddy cheek and general get-up, had been limited. A rift in the over-hanging cloud-wrack, through which the low sunrays broke with a sudden gleam, showed a darksome mountain range to the south, with summit and sides, snow-clad and dazzling white.

The wayfarer stood up and stared at the apparition: "a good omen," thought he, "perhaps a true landmark. The fellows at the mail-change told me to steer in a general way for the highest snow peak, which they called 'the Bogong,' or some such name. Though this track seems better marked, these mountain roads, as they call them—goat paths would be the better name—for there is not a wheel mark to be seen—one needs the foot of a chamois and the eye of our friend up there." Here he looked upward, where one of the great birds of prey, half hawk, half eagle, as the pioneers decided, floated with moveless wing above crag and hollow. Then rising with an effort, and taking the bridle rein, he began to lead the weary horse up the rocky ascent. "Poor old Gilpin!" he soliloquised, "you are more knocked up than I am—and yet you have the look of a clever cob—such as we should have fancied in England for a roadster, or a covert hack. But roads *are* roads there, while in this benighted land, people either don't know how to make them, or seem to do their cross-country work without them. I wonder if I shall fall in with bed and board to-night. The last was rough, but sufficing—a good fire too, now I think of it, and precious cold it was. Well, come along, John! I must bustle you a bit when we get to the top of this everlasting hill— truly biblical in that respect. What a lonesome place it is, now that the sun has gone under again! I suppose there's no one within fifty miles—Hulloa!"

This exclamation was called forth by the appearance of a horseman at no great distance—along the line of track. Man and horse were motionless, though so near that he wondered he had not observed them before. The rider's face, which was towards him, bore, as far as he could judge, an expression of keenest attention.

"Wonder if he is a bushranger?" thought the traveller; "ought to have brought one of my revolvers; but everybody told me that there were none 'out' now; that I was as safe as if I was in England—safer, in fact, than 'south the water' in the little village. However, I shall soon know."

Before he had time to decide seriously, the horseman came towards him. He saw a slight, dark, wiry individual, something above the middle height, sunburned, and almost blackened as to such portions of his neck and face as could be perceived for an abundant beard and moustache. The horse, blood-looking, and in hard condition, presented a striking contrast to his own leg-weary, disconsolate animal. The traveller thought him capable of fast and far performances. His sure and easy gait, as he stepped freely along the rocky path, stamped him as "mountain-bred," or, if not "to the manner born," having lived long enough amid these tremendous glens and rocky fastnesses, to negotiate their ladder-like declivities with ease and safety.

"Good evening!" said the stranger, civilly enough. "Going to 'Haunted Creek?'—a bit off the road, ar'n't you?"

"I *was* doubtful about the track, but I thought it might lead there. I was told that it was only eight miles."

"It's a good fourteen, and you won't get there to-night. Not with that horse, anyhow. But look here! I'm going to my place, a few miles off, with these cattle—if you like to give me a hand, I can put you up for the night, and show you the way in the morning."

"Thanks very much, really I feel much obliged to you. I was afraid I should have had to camp out, and it looks like a bad night."

"All right," said the bushman, for such he evidently was; "these crawlin' cattle are brutes to straggle, and I'm lost without my dog. I'll bring 'em up, and if you'll keep the tail going, we'll get along easy enough."

"But where are they?" inquired the tourist, looking around, as if he expected to see them rise out of the earth.

"Close by," answered the stranger, laconically, at the same time riding down the slope of the mountain with loose rein, and careless seat, as if the jumble of rocks, tree-roots, and rolling stones, was the most level high road in the world. Looking after the new acquaintance he descried a small lot of cattle perched on a rocky pinnacle, partly covered by a patch of scrub. The grass around them was high and green—but, with one exception, that of a cow munching a tussac in an undecided way, they did not appear to care about the green herbage, or tall kangaroo grass which grew around them. Had he known anything about the habits of cattle, he would have seen by their appearance that these fat beasts (for such they were) had come far and fast; were like his horse, thoroughly exhausted, and as such, indifferent to the attractions of wayside pasture.

However, with the aid of a hunting crop, which he flourished behind them, with threatening action, the bushman soon managed to get them on to the track, and with the aid of his newly-made comrade induced them to move with a decent show of alacrity. That some were footsore, and two painfully lame, was apparent to the new assistant, also that they were well-bred animals, heavy weights, and in that state and condition which is provincially alluded to as "rolling fat."

"Nice meat, ar'n't they?" said the bushman; "come a good way too. Beastly rough track; I was half a mind to bring them by Wagga—but this is the shortest way—straight over the ranges. I'm butchering just now, with gold-mining for a change, but that's mostly winter work."

"Where do you buy your cattle?" asked the Englishman—not that he cared as to that part of the occupation, but the gold-mining seemed to him a romantic, independent way of earning a living. He was even now turning over in his mind the idea of a few months camping among these Alpine regions, with, of course, the off-chance of coming upon an untouched gold mine.

"Oh! a few here and there, in all sorts of places." Here the stranger shot a searching glance, tinged with suspicion, towards the questioner. "I buy the chance of stray cattle now and then, and pick 'em up as I come across 'em. We'd as well jog along here, it's better going."

The track had become more marked. There were no wheel marks, the absence of which had surprised the traveller, since the beginning of his day's march, but tracks of cattle and unshod horses were numerous; while the ground being less rocky, indeed commencing to be marshy, no difficulty was found in driving the cattle briskly along it. His horse too, having "company," had become less dilatory and despondent.

"We're not far off, now," said his companion, "and it's just as well. We'll have rain to-night—may be snow. So a roof and a fire won't be too bad."

To this statement the tourist cheerfully assented, his spirits rising somewhat, when another mile being passed, they turned to the north at a sharp angle to the road, and following a devious track, found themselves at the slip-rails of a small but well-fenced paddock, into which the cattle were turned, and permitted to stray at will. Fastening the slip rails with scrupulous care, and following the line of fence for a hundred yards, they came to a hut built of slabs, and neatly roofed with sheets of the stringy bark tree (Eucalyptus obliqua) where his guide unsaddled, and motioned to the guest to do likewise. As also to put the saddle against the wall of the hut, with the stuffing outward. "That'll dry 'em a bit," he said; "mine's wet enough anyhow. Just bring your horse after me."

Passing through a hand gate, he released his horse, first, however, putting on a pair of hobbles; "the feed's good," he said, "but this moke's just out of the bush, and rather flash—he might jump the fence in the night, so it's best to make sure. Yours won't care about anything but filling his belly, not to-night anyhow, so he can go loose. Now we'll see about a fire, and boil the billy for tea. Come along in."

Entering the hut, which though small, was neat and clean; it was seen to contain two rooms, the inner one apparently used as a bedroom, there being two bed-places, on each of which was a rude mattress covered with a blanket. A store of brushwood and dry billets had been placed in a corner, from which a fire was soon blazing in the rude stone chimney, while a camp kettle (provincially a "billy") was on the way to boil without loss of time.

A good-sized piece of corned beef, part of a round, with half a "damper" loaf being extracted from a cupboard or locker, was placed on the rude slab table; after which pannikins and tin plates, with knives and forks, provided from the same receptacle, were brought forth, completing the preparations for a meal that the guest believed he was likely to relish.

"Oh! I nearly forgot," said the traveller, as his entertainer, dropping a handful of tea into the "billy," now at the boil, and stirring it with a twig, put on the lid. "I brought a flask, it's very fair whisky, and a tot won't hurt either of us, after a long day and a wet one." Going to his coat, he brought out a flask, and nearly filling the tin cup which was closed over the upper part, offered it to his host. He, rather to the surprise of the Englishman, hesitated and motioned as if to refuse, but on second thoughts smiled in a mysterious way, and taking the tin cup, nodded, and saying "Well, here's fortune!" tossed it off. Blount took one of the pannikins, and pouring out a moderate allowance, filled it up with the clear spring water, and drank it by instalments.

"I must say I feel better after that," he observed, "and if a dram needs an excuse, a long, cold ride, stiff legs, and a wetting ought to be sufficient."

"They don't look about for excuses up here," said his new acquaintance, "and some takes a deal more than is good for them. I don't hold with that, but a nip or two's neither here nor there, particular after a long day. Help yourself to the meat and damper, you see your supper."

The traveller needed no second invitation; he did not, like the clerk of Copmanhurst, plunge his fingers into the venison pasty, there being neither venison nor pasty, but after cutting off several slices of the excellent round of beef which had apparently sustained previous assaults, he made good time, with the aid of a well-baked "damper," and an occasional reference to a pannikin of hot tea, so that as their appetites declined, more leisure was afforded for conversation.

"And now," he said, after filling up a second pannikin of tea, and lighting his pipe, "I'm sure I'm very much obliged to you, as I hear the rain coming down, and the wind rising. May I ask whose hospitality I'm enjoying? I'm Valentine Blount of Langley in Herefordshire. Not long out, as I dare say you have noticed. Just travelling about to have a look at the country."

"My name's John Carter," said the bushman, with apparent frankness, as he confronted Blount's steady eye, "but I'm better known from here to Omeo, as 'Little River Jack'; there's lots of people knows me by that name, that don't know me by any other."

"And what do you do when you get gold—take it to Melbourne to sell?"

"There's no call to do that. Melbourne's a good way off, and it takes time to get there. But there's always gold buyers about townships, that are on for a little business. They give a trifle under market price, but they pay cash, and it suits us mountain chaps to deal that way. Sometimes I'm a buyer myself, along with the cattle-dealing. Look here!" As he spoke, he detached a leather pouch from his belt, looking like one that stockriders wear for carrying pipe and tobacco, which he threw on the table. The grog had inclined to confidences and relaxed his attitude of caution. Blount lifted it, rather surprised at its weight. "This is gold, isn't it?"

"Yes! a good sample too. Worth four pound an ounce. Like to look at it?"

"Very much. I don't know that I've ever seen gold in the raw state before."

"Well, here it is—the real thing, and no mistake. Right if a chap could only get enough of it." Here he opened the mouth of the pouch, which seemed three parts full, and pouring some of it on a tin plate, awaited Blount's remarks.

As the precious metal, partly in dust, partly in larger fragments, rattled on the plate, Blount looked on with deep interest, and then, on being invited so to do, handled it with the air of a man to whom a new and astonishing object is presented for the first time.

"So," he said musingly, "here is one of the great lures which have moved the world since the dawn of history. Love, war, and ambition, have been subservient to it. Priests and philosophers, kings and queens, the court beauty and the Prime Minister, have vainly struggled against its influence. But—" he broke off with a laugh, as he noted his companion's look of wonder, "here am I, another example of its fascination, moralising in a mountain hut and mystifying my worthy entertainer."

"And now, my friend!" he inquired, relapsing into the manner of everyday life, "what may be the market value of this heavy little parcel?"

"Well—I put it at fifty ounces, or thereabouts," said Mr. "Little River Jack," carefully pouring back the contents of the pouch, to the last grain; "at, say four pound an ounce, it's worth a couple of hundred notes, though *we* sha'n't get that price for it. But at Melbourne mint, it's worth every shilling, maybe a trifle more." Before closing the pouch, he took out a small nugget of, perhaps, half an ounce in weight, and saying, "You're welcome to this. It'll make a decent scarf pin," handed it to Mr. Blount.

But that gentleman declined it, saying, "Thanks, very much, but I'd rather not." Then, seeing that the owner seemed hurt, even resentful, qualified the refusal by saying, "But if you would do me a service, which I should value far more, you might introduce me to some party of miners, with whom I could work for a month or two, and learn, perhaps, how to get a few ounces by my own exertions. I think I should like the work. It must be very interesting."

"It's that interesting," said the bushman, all signs of annoyance clearing from his countenance, "that once a man takes to it he never quits it till he makes a fortune or dies so poor that the Government has to bury him. I've known many a man that used a cheque book as big as a school slate, and could draw for a hundred thousand or more, drop it all in a few years, and be found dead in a worse 'humpy' than this, where he'd been living alone for years."

"Strange to have been rich by his own handiwork, and not to be able to keep something for his old age," said Blount; "how is it to be accounted for?"

"By luck, d—d hard luck!" said John Carter, whom the subject seemed to have excited. "Every miner's a born gambler; if he don't do it with cards, he puts his earnings, his time, his life blood, as one might say, on the chance of a claim turning out well. It's good luck, and not hard work, that gives him a 'golden hole,' where he can't help digging up gold like potatoes, and it's luck, bad luck, that turns him out a beggar from every 'show' for years, till he hasn't got a shirt to his back. Why do I stick to it, you'll say? Because I'm a fool, always have been, always will be, I expect. But I like the game, and I can't leave it for the life of me. However, that says nothing. I'm no worse than others. I can just keep myself and my horse, while there's an old mate of mine living in London and Paris, and swelling it about with the best! You'd like to have a look in, you say? Well, you stop at Bunjil for a week, till I come back from Bago; it's a good inn, clean and comfortable, and the girl there, if I tell her, will look after you; see you have a fire too, these cold nights. Are you on?"

"Yes! most decidedly," replied Blount, with great heartiness. "A mountain hotel should be a new experience."

"Then it's a bargain. I'm going down the river for a few days. When I get back, I'll pick you up at Bunjil, and we'll go to a place such as you never seen before, and might never have dropped on as long as you lived, if you hadn't met me, accidental like. And now we'd as well turn in. I expect some chaps that's bought the cattle, and they won't be here later than daylight."
Accepting another glass of whisky as nightcap, and subsequently removing merely his boots and breeches, both of which he placed before the fire, but at a safe distance, Mr. "Little River Jack" "turned in" as he expressed it, and was shortly wrapped in the embrace of the kind deity who favours the dwellers in the Waste, though often rejecting the advances of the luxurious inhabitants of cities. Mr. Blount delayed his retirement, as he smoked before the still glowing "back log" and dwelt upon the adventures of the day.

"How that fellow must enjoy his slumbers!" thought he. "In the saddle before daylight, as he told me; up and down these rocky fastnesses—fifteen hours of slow, monotonous work, more wearying than any amount of fast going—and now, by his unlaboured breathing, sleeping like a tired child; his narrow world—its few cares—its honest, if sometimes exhausting labours, as completely shut out as if he was in another planet. Enviable mortal! I should like to change places with him."

After expressing this imprudent desire, as indeed are often those of men, who, unacquainted with the conditions surrounding untried modes of life, believe that they could attain happiness by merely exchanging positions, Mr. Blount undressed before the fire, and bestowed himself upon the unoccupied couch, where he speedily fell asleep, just as he had imagined himself extracting large lumps of gold from a vein of virgin quartz, in a romantic fern-shaded ravine, discovered by himself.

From this pleasing state of matters, he was awakened by a sound as of horse hoofs and the low growl of a dog. It was not quite dark. He sat up and listened intently. There was no illusion. He went to the hut door and looked out. Day was breaking, and through the misty dawnlight he was enabled to distinguish his host in conversation with a man on horseback, outside of the slip-rails. Presently the cattle, driven by another horseman, with whom was a dog, apparently of more than ordinary intelligence, came to the slip-rails. They made a rush as soon as they were through, as is the manner of such, on strange ground—but the second horseman promptly "wheeled" them towards the faint dawn line now becoming more distinct, and disappeared through the forest arches. Mr. Blount discerning that the day had begun, for practical purposes, proceeded to dress.

Walking over to the chimney, he found that the smouldering logs had been put together, and a cheerful blaze was beginning to show itself. The billy, newly filled, was close to it, and by the time he had washed the upper part of his body in a tin bucket placed on a log end, outside the door, his friend of the previous night appeared with both horses, which he fastened to the paddock fence.

"Those fellows woke you up, coming for the cattle? Thought you'd sleep through it. I was going to rouse you when breakfast was ready."

"I slept soundly in all conscience, but still I was quite ready to turn out. I suppose those were the butchers that you sold the cattle to?"

"Two of their men—it's all the same. They stopped close by last night so as to get an early start. They've a good way to go, and'll want all their time, these short days. Your horse looks different this morning. It's wonderful what a good paddock and a night's rest will do!"

"Yes, indeed, he does look different," as he saddled him up, and, plucking some of the tall grass which grew abundantly around, treated him to a partial rub down. "How far is it to Bunjil, as you call it?"

"Well, not more than twenty miles, but the road's middlin' rough. Anyhow we'll get there latish, and you can take it easy till I come back. I mightn't be away more than three or four days."

Misty, even threatening, at the commencement, the day became fine, even warm, after breakfast. Wind is rarely an accompaniment of such weather, and as the sun rode higher in the cloudless sky, Blount thought he had rarely known a finer day. "What bracing mountain air!" he said to himself. "Recalls the Highlands; but I see no oat fields, and the peasantry are absent. These hills should rear a splendid race of men—and rosy-cheeked lasses in abundance. The roads I cannot recommend."

Mr. John Carter had admitted that the way was rough. His companion thought he had understated the case. It was well nigh impassable. When not climbing hills as steep as the side of a house, they were sliding down bridle tracks like the "Ladder of Cattaro." These Mr. Carter's horse hardly noticed; a down grade being negotiated with ease and security, while he seemed, to Blount's amazement, to step from rock to rock like a chamois. That gentleman's own horse had no such accomplishments, but blundered perilously from time to time, so that his owner was fain to lead him over the rougher passes. This rendered their progress slower than it would otherwise have been, while he was fain to look enviously at his companion, who, either smoking or discoursing on local topics, rode with careless rein, trusting implicitly, as it seemed, to his horse's intelligence.

"Here's the Divide!" he said at length, pointing to a ridge which rose almost at right angles from the accepted track. "We leave the road here, and head straight for Bunjil mountain. There he stands with his cap on! The snow's fell early this season."

As he spoke he pointed towards a mountain peak of unusual height, snow-capped, and even as to its spreading flanks, streaked with patches and lines of the same colour. The white clouds which hung round the lofty summit—six thousand feet from earth, were soft-hued and fleecy; but their pallor was blurred and dingy compared with the silver coronet which glorified the dark-hued Titan.

"Road!" echoed Mr. Blount, "I don't see any; what passes for it, I shall be pleased to leave. If we are to go along this 'Divide,' as you call it, I hope it will be pleasanter riding."

"Well, it is a queerish track for a bit, but after Razor Back's passed, it's leveller like. We can raise a trot for a mile or two afore we make Bunjil township. Razor Back's a narrer cut with a big drop both sides, as we shall have to go stiddy over."

"The Divide," as John Carter called it, was an improvement upon the track they quitted. It was less rocky, and passably level. There was a gradual ascent however, which Mr. Blount did not notice until he observed that the timber was becoming more sparse, while the view around them was disclosing features of a grand, even awful character. On either side the forest commenced to slope downwards, at an increasingly sharp gradient. Instead of the ordinary precipice, above which the travellers rode, on one or other side of the bridle track, having the hill on the other, there appeared to be a precipice of unknown depth on *either hand*. As the ascent became more marked, Blount perceived that the winding path led towards a pinnacle from which the view was extensive, and in a sense, dreadful, from its dizzy altitude—its abysmal depths,—and, as he began to realise, its far from improbable danger.

"This here's what we call the leadin' range; it follers the divide from the head waters of the Tambo; that's where we stopped last night. It's the only road between that side of the country and the river. If you don't strike this 'cut,' and there's not more than a score or so of us mountain chaps as knows it, it would take a man days to cross over, and then he mightn't do it."

"What would happen to him?" asked Blount, feeling a natural curiosity to learn more of this weird region, differing so widely from any idea that he had ever gathered from descriptions of Australia.

"Well, he'd most likely get bushed, and have to turn back, though he mightn't find it too easy to do that, or make where he come from. In winter time, if it come on to snow, he'd never get home at all. I've known things happen like that. There was one poor cove last winter, as we chaps were days out searchin' for, and then found him stiff, and dead—he'd got sleepy, and never woke up!"

While this enlivening conversation was proceeding, the man from a far country discovered that the pathway, level enough for ordinary purposes, though he and his guide were no longer riding side by side, was rapidly narrowing. What breadth it would be, when they ascended to the pinnacle above them, he began to consider with a shade of apprehension. His hackney, which Mr. Jack Carter had regarded with slightly-veiled contempt as a "flat country horse, as had never seen a rise bigger than a haystack," evidently shared his uneasiness, inasmuch as he had stopped, stared and trembled from time to time, at awkward places on the road, before they came to the celebrated "leading range."

In another mile they reached the pinnacle, where Blount realised the true nature and surroundings of this Alpine Pass. Such indeed it proved to be. A narrow pathway, looking down on either side, upon fathomless glens, with so abrupt a drop that it seemed as if the wind, now rising, might blow them off their exposed perch.

The trees which grew at the depths below, though in reality tall and massive eucalypts, appeared scarce larger than berry bushes.

The wedge-tailed eagles soared above and around. One pair indeed came near and gazed on them with unblenching eye, as though speculating on the duration of their sojourn. They seemed to be the natural denizens of this dizzy and perilous height, from which the vision ranged, in wondering amaze over a vast lone region, which stretched to the horizon; appearing indeed to include no inconsiderable portion of the continent.

Below, around, even to the far, misty sky-line, was a grey, green ocean, the billows of which, through the branches of mighty forest trees, were reduced by distance to a level and uniform contour. Tremendous glens, under which ran clear cold mountain streams, tinkling and rippling ever, mimic waterfalls and flashing rivulets, the long dry summer through diversified the landscape.

Silver streams crossed these plains and downs of solemn leafage, distinguishable only when the sun flashed on their hurrying waters. These were rivers—not inconsiderable either—while companies of snow-crowned Alps stood ranged between, tier upon tier above them and the outlined rim, where earth and sky met, vast, regal, awful, as Kings of the Overworld! On guard since the birth of time, rank upon rank they stood—silent, immovable, scornful—defying the puny trespassers on their immemorial demesne. "What a land! what a vast expanse!" thought the Englishman, "rugged, untamed, but not more so than 'Caledonia stern and wild,' more fertile and productive, and as to extent—boundless. I see before me," he mused, "a country larger than Sweden, capable in time of carrying a dense population; and what a breed of men it should give birth to, athletic, hardy, brave! Horsemen too, in the words of Australia's forest poet, whom I read but of late. 'For the horse was never saddled that the Jebungs couldn't ride.' Good rifle shots! What sons of the Empire should these Australian highlands rear, to do battle for Old England in the wars of the giants yet to come!"

This soliloquy, and its utterance in thought came simultaneously to a halt of a decisive nature, by reason of the conduct of Mr. Blount's horse. This animal had been gradually acquiring a fixed distrust of the highway—all too literally—on which he was required to travel. Looking first on one side, then on the other, and apparently realising the dreadful alternative of a slip or stumble, he became unnerved and demoralised. Mr. Blount had ridden a mule over many a *mauvais pas* in Switzerland, when the sagacious animal, for reasons known to himself, had insisted on walking on the outer edge of the roadway, over-hanging the gulf, where a crumbling ledge might cause the fall into immeasurable, glacial depths. In that situation his nerve had not faltered. "Trust to old 'Pilatus,'" said the guide; "do not interfere with him, I beseech you; he is under the immediate protection of the saints, and the holy St. Bernard." He had in such a position been cool and composed. The old mule's wise, experienced air, his sure and cautious mode of progression, had been calculated to reassure a nervous novice. But here, the case was different. His cob was evidently *not* under the protection of the saints. St. Bernard was absent, or indifferent. With the recklessness of fear, he was likely to back—to lose his balance—to hurl himself and rider over the perpendicular drop, where he would not have touched ground at a thousand feet. At this moment Jack Carter looked round. "Keep him quiet, for God's sake! till I get to you—don't stir!" As he spoke he slid from his horse, though so small was the vacant space on the ledge, that as he leaned against the shoulder of his well-trained mount, there seemed barely room for his feet. Buckling a strap to the snaffle rein, which held it in front of the saddle, and throwing the stirrup iron over, he passed to the head of the other horse, whose rein he took in a firm grasp. "Steady," he said in a voice of command, which, strangely, the shaking creature seemed to obey. "Now, Boss! you get off, and slip behind him—there's just room." Blount did as directed, and with care and steadiness, effected a movement to the rear, while Jack Carter fastened rein and stirrup as before.

Then giving the cob a sounding slap on the quarter, he uttered a peculiar cry, and the leading horse stepped along the track at a fast amble, followed by the cob at a slow trot, in which he seemed to have recovered confidence.

"That's a quick way out of the difficulty," said Blount, with an air of relief. "I really didn't know what was going to happen. But won't they bolt when they get to the other side of this natural bridge over the bottomless pit?"

"When they get to the end of this 'race,' as you may call it, there's a trap yard that we put up years back for wild horses—many a hundred's been there before my time. Some of us mountain chaps keep it mended up. It comes in useful now and again."

"I should think it did," assented his companion, with decision. "But how will they get in? Will your clever horse take down the slip-rails, and put them up again?"

"Not quite that!" said the bushman smiling—"but near enough; we'll find 'em both there, I'll go bail!"

"How far is it?" asked Blount, with a natural desire to get clear of this picturesque, but too exciting part of the country, and to exchange it for more commonplace scenery, with better foothold.

"Only a couple of mile—so we might as well step out, as I've filled my pipe. Won't you have a draw for company?"

"Not just yet, I'll wait till we're mounted again." For though the invariable, inexhaustible tobacco pipe is the steadfast friend of the Australian under all and every condition of life, Blount did not feel in the humour for it just after he had escaped, as he now began to believe, from a sudden and violent death.

"A well-trained horse! I should think he was," he told himself; "and yet, before I left England, I was always being warned against the half-broken horses of Australia. What a hackney to be sure!—fast, easy, sure-footed, intelligent—and what sort of breaking in has he had? Mostly ridden by people whom no living horse can throw; but that is a disadvantage—as he instinctively recognises the rider he *can* throw. Well! every country has its own way of doing things; and though we Englishmen are unchangeably fixed in our own methods, we may have something to learn yet from our kinsmen in this new land."

"I suppose there have been accidents on this peculiar track of yours?" he said, after they had walked in silence for a hundred yards or more.

"Accidents!" he replied, "I should jolly well think there have. You see, horses are like men and women, though people don't hardly believe it. Some's born one way, and some another; teaching don't make much difference to 'em, nor beltin' either. Some of 'em, like some men, are born cowards, and when they get into a narrer track with a big drop both sides of 'em, they're that queer in the head—though it's the *heart* that's wrong with 'em—that they feel like pitching theirselves over, just to get shut of the tremblin' on the brink feelin'. Your horse was in a blue funk; he'd have slipped or backed over in another minute or two. That was the matter with *him*. When he seen old Keewah skip along by himself, it put confidence like, into him."

"You've known of accidents, then?"

"My word! I mind when poor Paddy Farrell went down. He and his horse both. He was leadin' a packer, as it might be one of us now. Well, his moke was a nervous sort of brute, and just as he got to the Needle Rock, it's a bit farther on before the road widens out, but it's terrible narrer there, and poor Paddy was walking ahead leadin' the brute with a green hide halter, when a hawk flies out from behind a rock and frightened the packer. He draws back with a jerk, and his hind leg goes over the edge. Paddy had the end of the halter round his wrist, and it got jammed somehow, and down goes the lot, horse and pack, and him atop of 'em. Three or four of us were out all day looking for him at the foot of the range. We knew where we'd likely find him, and sure enough there they were, he and his horse, stone dead and smashed to pieces. We took him back to Bunjil, and buried him decent in the little graveyard. We managed to fish up a prayer-book, and got 'Gentleman Jack' to read the service over him. My word! he *could* read no end. They said he was college taught. He could drink too, more's the pity."

"Does *every one* drink that lives in these parts?"

"Well, a good few. Us young ones not so bad, but if a man stays here, after a few years he always drinks, partickler if he's seen better days."

"Now why is that? It's a free healthy life, with riding, shooting, and a chance of a golden hole, as you call it. There are worse places to live in."

"Nobody knows why, but they all do; they'll work hard and keep sober for months. Then they get tired of having no one to talk to—nobody like theirselves, I mean. They go away, and come back stone-broke, or knock it all down in Bunjil, if they've made a few pounds."

"That sounds bad after working hard and risking their lives on these Devil's Bridges. How old was this Patrick Farrell?"

"Twenty-four, his name wasn't Patrick. It was Aloysius William, named after a saint, I'm told. The boys called him 'Paddy' for short. At home, I believe they called him 'Ally.' But Paddy he always was in these parts. It don't matter much now. See that tall rock sticking up by the side of the road at the turn? Well, that's where he fell; they call it 'Paddy's Downfall,' among the country people to this day. We've only a mile to go from there."

When Mr. Blount and his companion reached the Needle Rock, a sharp-edged monolith, the edge of which unnecessarily infringed on the perilously scanty foothold, he did not wonder at the downfall of poor Aloysius William or any other wayfarer encumbered with a horse. He recalled the "vision of sudden death" which had so nearly been realised in his own case, and shuddered as he looked over the sheer drop on to a tangled mass of "rocks and trees confusedly hurled."

"We've got Bunjil Inn to make yet," said the bushman, stepping forward briskly; "we mustn't forget that, if we leave my old moke too long in the yard, he'll be opening the gate or some other dodge."

In a hundred yards from the Needle Rock the track became wider, much to Mr. Blount's relief, for he was beginning to feel an uncanny fascination for the awful abyss, and to doubt whether if a storm came on, he should be able to stand erect, or be reduced to the ignoble alternative of lying on his face.

"They've passed along here all right," said the guide, casting a casual look at the path; "trust old Keewah for that, he's leadin' and your moke following close up."

Mr. Blount did not see any clear indication, and would have been quite unable to declare which animal was foremost. But he accepted in all confidence Little-River-Jack's assurance. The track, without gaining much breadth or similarity to any civilised high road, was yet superior in all respects to the chamois path they had left behind, and when his companion exclaimed, "There's the yard, and our nags in it, as safe as houses," he was relieved and grateful. The loss of a horse with a new saddle and bridle, besides his whole stock of travelling apparel, spare shoes, and other indispensable matters, would have been serious, not to say irreparable.

However there were the two horses with their accoutrements complete, in the trap yard aforesaid. The yard was fully eight feet high, and though the saplings of which it was composed were rudely put together, they were solid and unyielding. The heavy gate of the same material showed a rude carpentry in the head and tail pieces, the former of which was "let into the cap" or horizontal spar placed across the gate posts, and also morticed into a round upright below, sunk into the ground and projecting securely above it.

"They must have come in and shut the gate after them," remarked Blount; "how in the world did they manage that?"

"Well, you see, this gate's made pretty well on the balance to swing back to the post, where there's a sort of groove for it. It's always left half, or a quarter open. A prop's put loose agen it, which any stock coming in from that side's middlin' sure to rub, and the gate swings to. See? It may graze 'em, as they're going in, but they're likely to jump forward, into the yard. The gate swings back to the post, and they're nabbed. They can't very well open it *towards* themselves, they haven't savey for that. So they have to wait till some one comes."

This explanation was given as they were riding along a decently plain road to Bunjil township, the first appearance of which one traveller descried with much contentment.

The "Divide," before this agreeable change, had begun to alter its austere character. The ridge had spread out, the forest trees were stately and umbrageous, the track was fairly negotiable by horse and man. A fertile valley through which dashed an impetuous stream revealed itself. On the further bank stood dwellings, "real cottages," as Mr. Blount remarked, "not huts." These were in all cases surrounded by gardens, in some instances by orchards, of which the size and girth of the fruit trees bore witness to the richness of the soil as well as of the age of the township.

The short winter day had been nearly consumed by reason of their erratic progress; so that the evening shadows had commenced to darken the valley, while the clear, crisp atmosphere betrayed to the experienced senses of Mr. Carter, every indication of what he described as "a real crackin' frost."

"We're in luck's way," he said, in continuation, "not to be struck for a camp out to-night. It's cold enough in an old man frost hereabouts, to freeze the leg off an iron pot. But this is the right shop as we're going to, for a good bed, a broiled steak for tea, and if you make friends with Sheila (she's the girl that waits at table) you won't die of cold, whatever else happens to you. Above all, the house is clean, and that's more than you can say for smarter lookin' shops. We'd as well have a spurt to finish up with." Drawing his rein, and touching his hack with careless heel, the bushman went off at a smart canter along the main street, apparently the only one in the little town, Mr. Blount's cob following suit with comparative eagerness, until they pulled up at a roomy building with a broad verandah, before which stood a sign-board, setting forth its title to consideration, as the "Prospector's Arms" by William Middleton.

Several persons stood or lounged about the verandah, who looked at them keenly as they rode up. A broad-shouldered man with a frank, open countenance, came out of a door, somewhat apart from the group. He was plainly, by appearance and bearing, the landlord.

"So you're back again, Jack," said he, addressing the bushman with an air of familiar acquaintance; "didn't know what had come o'yer. What lay are ye on now?"

"Same's usual, moochin' round these infernal hills and gullies ov yours. There's a bit of a rush Black Rock way. I'm goin' to have a look in to-morrow. This gentleman's just from England, seein' the country in a gineral way; he'll stay here till I get back, and then we'll be going down river."

"All right, Jack!" replied the host. "*You* can show him the country, if any one can—the missus'll see he's took care of," and as he spoke he searched the speaker with a swift glance as of one comprehending all that had been said, and more that was left unspoken. "Here, take these horses round, George, and make 'em right for the night."

An elderly individual in shirt sleeves and moleskins of faded hue here came forward, and took the stranger's horse, unbuckling valise and pack, which the landlord carried respectfully into an inner chamber, out of which a door led into a comfortable appearing bedroom; where, from the look of the accessories, he augured favourably for the night's rest. Mr. Carter had departed with the old groom, preferring, as he said, to see his horse fed and watered before he tackled his own refreshment; "grub" was the word he used, which appeared to be fully understood of the people, if but vaguely explanatory to Mr. Blount.

That gentleman, pensively examining his wardrobe, reflected meanwhile by how narrow a chance the articles spread out before him had been saved from wreck, so to speak, and total loss, when a knock came to the door, and a feminine voice requested to know whether he would like supper at six o'clock or later. Taking counsel of his inward monitor, he adopted the hour named.

The voice murmured, "Your hot water, sir," and ceased speaking.

He opened the door, and was just in time to see a female form disappear from the room.

"We are beginning to get civilised," he thought, as he possessed himself of the hot water jug, and refreshed accordingly. After which he discarded his riding gear in favour of shoes and suitable continuations. While awaiting the hour of reflection, he took out of his valise a pocket edition of Browning, and was about to glance at it when the clock struck six.

Entering the parlour, for such it evidently was, he was agreeably surprised with the appearance of affairs. A clean cloth covered the solid cedar table, on which was a hot dish—flanked by another which held potatoes. A fire of glowing logs was cheerful to behold, nor was the "neat-handed Phyllis" wanting to complete the tableau. A very good-looking young woman, with a complexion of English, rather than Australian colouring, removed the dish covers, and stood at attention.

Here the wayfarer was destined to receive fresh information relative to the social observances of Australian society. "You have only laid covers for one," said he to the maid. "My friend, Mr. Carter, is not going to do without his dinner surely?"

"Oh! Jack!" said the damsel, indifferently; "he won't come in here, he's at the second table with the coachman and the drovers. This is the gentlemen's room."

"How very curious!" he exclaimed. "I thought every one was alike in this part of the world; all free and equal, that sort of thing. I shouldn't the least mind spending the evening with er—John Carter—or any other respectable miner."

The girl looked him over before she spoke. "Well, Mr. Blount (Jack said that was your name), *you* mightn't, though you're just from England, but other people might. When the police magistrate, the Goldfields Warden, and the District Surveyor come round, they always stay here, and the down river squatters. They wouldn't like it, you may be sure, nor you either, perhaps, if the room was pretty full."

He smiled, as he answered, "So this is an aristocratic country, I perceive, in spite of the newspaper froth about a democratic government. Well, I must take time, and learn the country's ways. I shall pick them up by degrees, I suppose."

"No fear!" said the damsel. "It'll all come in time, not but there's places at the back where all sorts sit down together and smoke and drink no end. But not at Bunjil. Would you like some apple-pie to follow, there's plenty of cream?"

Mr. Blount would. "Apple-pie reminds one of Devonshire, and our boyhood—especially the cream," thought he. "What fun I should have thought this adventure a few years ago. Not that it's altogether without interest now. It's a novelty, at any rate."

CHAPTER II

Mr. Blount, as he sat before the fire, enjoying his final pipe before retiring for the night, was free to confess that he had rarely spent a more satisfactory evening—even in the far-famed, old-fashioned, road-side inns of old England. The night was cold—Carter's forecast had been accurate. It was a hard frost, such as his short stay in a coast city had not acquainted him with. The wide bush fire-place, with a couple of back logs, threw out a luxurious warmth, before which, in a comfortable arm-chair, he had been reading the weekly paper with interest.

The well-cooked, juicy steak, the crisp potatoes, the apple-pie with bounteous cream, constituted a meal which a keen-edged appetite rendered sufficient for all present needs. The difficult ride and too hazardous adventure constituted a fair day's work—being indeed sufficiently fatiguing to justify rest without bordering on exhaustion. It was a case of *jam satis*.

He looked forward to an enjoyable night's sleep, was even aware of a growing sense of relief that he was not required to take the road next morning. The cob would be better for a few days' rest, before doing more mountain work. He would like also to ramble about this neighbourhood, and see what the farms and sluicing claims were like. And a better base of operations than the Bunjil Hotel, no man need desire.

He had gone to the stable with Carter, as became a prudent horse-owner, where he had seen the cob comfortably bedded down for the night with a plenteous supply of sweet-smelling oaten hay before him, and an unstinted feed of maize in the manger.

"They're all right for the night," said Carter. "Your nag will be the better for a bit of a turn round to-morrow afternoon, just to keep his legs from swellin'. I'll be off about sunrise, and back again the fourth day, or early the next. They'll look after you here, till then."

Mr. Blount was of opinion that he could look after himself from what he had seen of the establishment, and said so, but "was nevertheless much obliged to him for getting him such good quarters." So to bed, as Mr. Pepys hath it, but before doing so, he rang the bell, and questioned Sheila—for that was her name, as he had ascertained by direct inquiry—as to the bath arrangements.

"I shall want a cold bath at half-past seven—a shower bath, for choice. Is there one?"

"Oh, yes—but very few go in for it this time of year. The P.M. does, when he comes round, and the Goldfields Warden. It's one of those baths that you fill and draw up over your head. Then you pull a string."

"That will do very well."

"All right—I'll tell George; but won't it be very cold? It's a hard frost to-night."

"No—the colder it is, the warmer you feel after it."

"Well, good-night, sir! Breakfast at half-past eight o'clock. Is that right? Would you like sausages, boiled eggs and toast?"

"Yes! nothing could be better. My appetite seems improving already."

The Kookaburra chorus, and the flute accompaniment of the magpies in the neighbouring tree tops, awakened Mr. Blount, who had not so much as turned round in bed since about five minutes after he had deposited himself between the clean lavender-scented sheets. Looking out, he faintly discerned the dawn light, and also that the face of the country was as white as if it had been snowing. He heard voices in the verandah, and saw Little-River-Jack's horse led out, looking as fresh as paint. That gentleman, lighting his pipe carefully, mounted and started off at a fast amble up the road which skirted the range, and led towards a gap in the hills. Mr. Blount thought it would be as well to wait until Sheila had the fire well under way, by which he intended to toast himself after the arctic discipline of the shower bath, with the thermometer at 28 degrees Fahrenheit.

The bi-weekly mail had providentially arrived at breakfast time, bringing in its bags the local district newspaper, and a metropolitan weekly which skimmed the cream from the cables and telegrams of the day. This was sufficiently interesting to hold him to the arm-chair, in slippered ease, for the greater part of an hour, while he lingered over his second cup of tea.

His boots, renovated from travel stains and mud, standing ready, he determined on a stroll, and took counsel with Sheila, as to a favourable locality.

The damsel was respectful, but conversed with him on terms of perfect conversational equality. She had also been fairly educated, and was free from vulgarity of tone or accent. To him, straight from the old country, a distinctly unfamiliar type worth studying.

"Where would you advise me to go for a walk?" he said. "It's good walking weather, and I can't sit in the house this fine morning, though you have made such a lovely fire."

"I should go up the creek, and have a look at the sluicing claim. People say it's worth seeing. You can't miss it if you follow up stream, and you'll hear the 'water gun' a mile before you come to it."

"'Water gun?' What ever is that?"

"Oh! it's the name of a big hose with a four-inch nozzle at the end. They lead the water for the race into it, and then turn it against the creek bank; that undermines tons of the stuff they want to sluice—you'll hear it coming down like a house falling!"

"And what becomes of it then?"

"Oh! it goes into the tail-race, and after that it's led into the riffles and troughs—the water keeps driving along, and they've some way of washing the clay and gravel out, and leaving the gold behind."

"And does it pay well?"

"They say so. It only costs a penny a ton to wash, or something like that. It's the cheapest way the stuff can be treated. Our boys saw it used in California, and brought it over here."

So, after taking a last fond look at the cob, and wishing he could exchange him for Keewah, but doubting if any amount of boot would induce Carter to part with his favourite, he set out along the bank of the river and faced the uplands.

His boots were thick, his heart was light—the sun illumined the frost-white trunks, and diamond-sprayed branches of the pines and eucalypts—the air was keen and bracing. "What a glorious thing it is to be alive on a day like this," he told himself. "How glad I am that I decided to leave Melbourne!" As he stepped along with all the elasticity of youth's high health and boundless optimism, he marked the features of the land. There were wheel-tracks on this road, which he was pleased to note. Though the soil was rich, and also damp at the base of the hills and on the flats, it was sound, so that with reasonable care he was enabled to keep his feet dry. He saw pools from which the wild duck flew on his approach. A blue crane, the heron of Australia (*Ardea*) rose from the reeds; while from time to time the wallaroo (the kangaroo of the mountain-side) put in appearance to his great delight.

The sun came out, glorifying the wide and varied landscape and the cloudless azure against which the snow-covered mountain summits glittered like silver coronets. Birds of unknown note and plumage called and chirped. All Nature, recovering from the cold and darkness of the night, made haste to greet the brilliant apparition of the sun god.

Keeping within sight of the creek—the course of which he was pledged to follow—he became aware of a dull monotonous sound, which he somehow connected with machinery. It was varied by occasional reports like muffled blasts, as of the fall of heavy bodies. "That is the sluicing claim," he told himself, "and I shall see the wonderful 'water gun,' which Sheila told me of. Quite an adventure!" The claim was farther off than he at first judged, but after climbing with stout heart a "stey brae," he looked down on the sluicing appliances, and marvelled at the inventive ingenuity which the gold industry had developed. Before him was a ravine down which a torrent of water was rushing with great force and rapidity, bearing along in its course clay, gravel, quartz, and even boulders of respectable size.

He was civilly received by the claim-holders; the manager—an ex-Californian miner—remarking, "Yes, sir, I'm a 'forty-niner,'—worked at Suttor's Mill first year gold was struck there. This is a pretty big thing, though it ain't a circumstance to some I've seen in Arizona and Colorado. This water's led five hundred feet from these workings. See it play on the face of the hill-side yonder—reckon we've cut it away two hundred feet from grass."

Mr. Blount looked with amazement at the thin, vicious, thread of water, which, directed against the lower and middle strata of the mass of ferruginous slate, had laid bare the alluvium through which ran an ancient river, silted up and overlaid for centuries. The course of this long dead and buried stream could be traced by the water-worn boulders and the smoothness of the rocks which had formed its bed. Where he stood, there had been a fall of forty feet as shown by the formation of the rocky channel.

The manager civilly directed the "gunner" to lower the weapon, and aim it at a spot nearer to where Blount was standing. He much marvelled to see the stones torn from the "face" and sent flying in the air, creating a fair-sized geyser where the water smote the cliff. In this fashion of undermining hundreds of tons are brought down from time to time, to be driven by the roaring torrent into the "tail-race," whence they pass into the "sluice-box," and so on to the creek, leaving the gold behind in the riffle bars.

"I suppose it's not an expensive way of treating the ore in the rough?" queried Blount.

"I reckon not. Cheapest way on airth. The labour we pay at present only comes to one man to a thousand yards. This company has been paying dividends for fifteen years!"

Mr. Blount thanked the obliging American, who, like all respectable miners, was well-mannered to strangers, the sole exception being in the case of a party that have "struck gold" in a secluded spot, and naturally do not desire all the world to know about it. But even they are less rude than evasive.

He looked at his watch and decided that he had not more than enough time to get back to Bunjil in time for lunch. So he shook hands with Mr. Hiram Endicott and set out for that nucleus of civilisation.

Making rather better time on the return journey, he arrived much pleased with himself, considering that he had accomplished an important advance in bush-craft and mineralogy.

Sheila welcomed him in a clean print dress, with a smiling face, but expressed a faint surprise at his safe return, and at his having found the road to the sluice-working, and back.

"Why! how could I lose the way?" he demanded, justly indignant. "Was not the creek a sufficiently safe guide?"

"Oh! it can be done," answered the girl archly. "There was a gentleman followed the creek the wrong way, and got among the ranges before he found out his mistake; and another one—he was a newspaper editor— thought he'd make a near cut, found himself miles lower down, and didn't get back before dark. My word! how hungry he was, and cross too!"

"Well, I'm not very hungry or even cross—but I'm going to wash my hands, after which lunch will be ready, I suppose?"

"You've just guessed it," she replied. "You'll have tea, I suppose?"

"Certainly. Whether Australia was created to develop the tea and sugar industry, or tea to provide a portable and refreshing beverage for the inhabitants to work, and travel, or even fight on, is not finally decided, but they go wondrous well together."

After an entirely satisfactory lunch, Mr. Blount bethought him of the cob—and knowing, as do all Englishmen, that to do your duty to your neighbour when he is a horse, you must exercise him at least once a day, he sent for George, and requested that he should be brought forth. In a few moments the valuable animal arrived, looking quite spruce and spirited, with coat much smoother and mane tidied; quite like an English covert hack, as Mr. Blount told himself. His legs had filled somewhat, but the groom assured Blount that that was nothing, and would go off.

Taking counsel of the landlord on this occasion, that worthy host said, "Would you like to see an old hand about here that could tell you a few stories about the early days?"

"Like?" answered Mr. Blount with effusion, "nothing better." It was one of his besetting virtues to know all about the denizens of any place—particularly if partly civilised—wherever he happened to sojourn for a season. It is chiefly a peculiarity of the imaginative-sympathetic nature whereby much knowledge of sorts is acquired—sometimes. But there is a reverse side to the shield.

"George! Ge-or-ge!" shouted the landlord, "catch the old mare and bring her round. Look slippy!"

George fled away like the wind, with a sieve and a bridle in his hand, and going to the corner of a small grass paddock, under false pretences induced an elderly bay mare to come up to him (there being no corn in the sieve), then he basely slipped the reins over her head and led her away captive.

The landlord reappeared with a pair of long-necked spurs buckled on to his heels, and getting swiftly into the saddle, started the old mare off at a shuffling walk. She was a character in her way. Her coat was rough, her tail was long, there was a certain amount of hair on her legs, and yes! she *was* slightly lame on the near fore-leg. But her eye was bright, her shoulder oblique; and as she reined up at a touch of the rusty snaffle and stuck out her tail, Arab fashion, she began to show class, Mr. Blount thought.

"She'll be all right, directly," said the landlord, noticing Mr. Blount's scrutiny of the leg, "I never know whether it's rheumatism, or one of her dodges—she's as sound as a bell after a mile." To add to her smart appearance, she had no shoes.

They passed quickly through cornfields and meadow lands, rich in pasture, and showing signs of an occasional heavy crop. The agriculture was careless, as is chiefly the case where Nature does so much that man excuses himself for doing little. A cottage on the south side of the road surrounded by a well-cultivated orchard furnished the exception which proves the rule. Mr. Middleton opened the rough but effective gate, with a patent self-closing latch, without dismounting from his mare, who squeezed her shoulder against it, as if she thought she could open it herself. "Steady!" said her owner—"this gate's not an uphill one—she'll push up a gate hung to slam down hill as if she knew who made it. She does know a lot of things you wouldn't expect of her." Holding the gate open till Mr. Blount and the cob were safely through, he led the way to the cottage, from which issued a tall, upright, elderly man, with a distinctly military bearing.

"This is Mr. Blount, Sergeant," said the host, "staying at my place for a day or two—just from England, as you see! I told him you knew all about this side, and the people in it—old hands, and new."

"Ay! the people—the people!" said the old man meditatively. "The land's a' richt—fresh and innocent, just as God made it, but the people! the de'il made *them* on purpose to hide in these mountains and gullies, and show what manner of folk could grow up in a far country, where they were a law unto themselves."

"There was wild work in those days before you came up, Sergeant, I believe!" asserted the landlord, tentatively.

"Ay! was there," and the old light began to shine in the trooper's eyes. "Battle, murder, and sudden death, every kind of villany that the wicked heart of man could plan, or his cruel hand carry out. But you'll come ben and tak' a cup of tea? The weather's gey and cauld the noo."

Mr. Blount would be only too pleased. So the horses were "hung up" to the neat fence of the garden, and the visitors walked into the spotless, neat parlour.

"Sit ye doon," said the Sergeant—"Beenie, bring in tea, and some scones." A fresh-coloured country damsel, who presently appeared bearing a jug of milk and the other requisites, had evidently been within hearing. "My wife and bairns are doon country," he explained, "or she would have been prood to mak' you welcome, sir. I'm by ma lane the noo—but she'll be back next week, thank God; it's awfu' lonesome, when she's awa."

"You knew Coke, Chamberlain, and Armstrong, all that crowd—didn't you, Sergeant?" queried the landlord.

"That did I—and they knew *me* before I'd done with them, murdering dogs that they were! People used to say that I'd never die in my bed. That this one or that had sworn to shoot me—or roast me alive if they could tak' me. But I never gave them a chance. I was young and strong in those days—as active as a mountain cat in my Hieland home, and could ride for twenty-four hours at a stretch, if I had special wark in hand. Old Donald Bane here could tell fine tales if he could talk"—pointing to a grand-looking old grey, feeding in a patch of lucerne. "The General let me have him when he was cast, that's ten years syne. We got our pensions then, and we're just hanging it out thegither."

"I suppose there are no bad characters in this neighbourhood now, Sergeant?" said Blount. "Everything looks very quiet and peaceful."

"I wouldna say that," answered the veteran, cautiously. "There's many a mile of rough country, between here and the Upper Sturt, and there's apt to be rough characters to match the country. Cattle are high, too. A dozen head of fat cattle comes to over a hundred pound—that's easy earned if they're driven all night, and sold to butchers that have one yard at the back of a range, and another in the stringy-bark township, to take the down off."

"Yet one wouldn't think such things could be carried on *easily* in this part of the country—where there seem to be so many watchful eyes; but I must have a longer ride this lovely morning, so I shall be much obliged if you and our host here will dine with me at seven o'clock, when we can have leisure to talk. You're all by yourself, Sergeant, you know, so there's no excuse."

The Sergeant accepted with pleasure; the host was afraid he would be too busy about the bar at the dinner hour, but would look in afterwards, before the evening was spent. So it was settled, and the recent acquaintances rode away.

"What a fine old fellow the Sergeant is!" said Blount; "how wonderfully neat and trim everything inside the house and out is kept."

"You'll generally notice that about a place when the owner has been in the police; the inspector blows up the troopers if there is a button off, or a boot not cleaned. You'd think they'd let a prisoner go, to hear him talk. Barracks—stable—carbine—horse—all have to be neat and clean, polished up to the nines. Once they get the habit of that they never leave it off, and after they settle down in a country place, as it might be here, they set a good example to the farmers and bush people."

"So the police force promotes order in more ways than one—they root out dishonesty and crime as well—they're a grand institution of the country."

"Well, yes, they are," assented the landlord without enthusiasm, "though they're not all built the way the Sergeant is. I don't say but what they're a trifle hard on publicans now and again for selling a drink to a traveller on a Sunday. But if it's the law, they're bound to uphold it. We'd be a deal worse off without them, and that's the truth."

Blount and the landlord rode down the course of the stream with much interest, as far as the Englishman was concerned. For the other, the landscape was a thing of course. The rich meadow land which bordered the stream—the far blue mountains—the fat bullocks and sleek horses feeding in the fields—the sheep on their way to market, were to him an ancient and settled order of things, as little provocative of curiosity as if they had existed from the foundation of the world. He had been familiar from childhood with them, or with similar stock and scenery.

But the stranger's interest and constant inquiry were unceasing. Everything was new to him. The fences, the crops, the maize, of which the tall stems were still standing in their rows, though occasionally stripped and thrown down by the pigs which were rooting among them and gleaning the smaller cobs left behind in the harvest plucking. A certain carelessness of husbandry was noticed by the critic from over sea. The hedges were mostly untrimmed, the plough too often left in the furrow; the weeds, "thick-coming carpet after rain," untouched by the scarifier; the fences broken, hedges indifferently trimmed.

"This sort of farming wouldn't go down in England."

"Perhaps not. Never was there," replied the Australian Boniface; "but these chaps are mostly so well off, that they don't mind losing a trifle this way, rather than have too many men to pay and feed. Labour's cheap in England, I'm told; here it's dear. So the farmer crowds on all he can get till harvest and shearin's past, then he pays off all hands, except an old crawler or two, to milk cows and draw wood and water. Afterwards he hires no more till ploughing begins again."

"There does seem to be a reason for that, and other things I have observed," assented Mr. Blount. "I suppose in time everything will be nearer English, or perhaps American ideas. More likely the last. Machinery for everything, and no time for decent leisurely country work."

"Yes, sir—that's about it," said Mr. Middleton, looking at his watch, "and now we've just time to get back for your lunch, and to tell my old woman that the Sergeant's coming to dine with you."

"Doesn't your mare trot?" said Blount, as they moved off, "it seems to me that Australian horses have only two paces, walk and canter. She doesn't seem lame now."

"I think sometimes it's only her villany; she's going as sound as a bell now. Yes! she can trot a bit when she likes."

The cob, a fair performer, had just started, when Mr. Middleton gave the mare's left ear a gentle screw, which induced her to alter her pace from a slow canter to a trot. "Trot, old woman!" he said, and settling to that useful pace, she caught up the cob. Mr. Blount gradually increased his pace—the old mare kept level with him, till after a dig with the spurs, and a refresher with the hunting crop, it became apparent that the cob was "on his top," in stable phrase, doing a fair ten or eleven miles an hour.

"Are ye trotting now?" said the landlord, taking the old mare by the head.

"Yes! oh, yes—and pretty fair going, isn't it?"

"Not bad, but this old cripple can do better." On which, as if she had heard the words, the old mare stretched out her neck and passed the cob "like a shot!" as her owner afterwards stated when describing the affair to an admiring audience in the bar room.

The cob, after an ineffectual attempt to keep up, was fain to break into a hand gallop, upon which the old mare was pulled up, and the rider explained that it took a professional to beat old "Slavey"; but that owing to her uncertain temper, he had been unable to "take on" aspiring amateurs, and so missed good wagers.

"You might have 'taken me on' for a pound or two," said Mr. Blount, "if you had cared to back her, for I certainly should not have thought she could have beaten my cob. She doesn't seem built for trotting—does she?"

"She is a bit of a take down," admitted Mr. Middleton, "but I don't bet with gentlemen as stays in my house. Though her coat's rough, she's a turn better bred than she looks. Got good blood on both sides, and you can drive her in single or double harness, and ride her too, as far and as fast as you like. There's no doubt she's a useful animal, for you can't put her wrong."

"You wouldn't care to sell her?"

"No! I couldn't part with her. My wife and the children drive her. She's so good all round, and quiet too; and though there's lots of horses in the district, it's wonderful what a time it takes to pick up a real good one."

"Quite Arab like! I was told people would sell anything in Australia, especially horseflesh. There's the luncheon bell! Well, I've had a pleasant morning, and even with the prospect of dinner at seven o'clock, I feel equal to a modest meal, just to keep up the system. It's wonderful what an appetite I've had lately."

Mr. Blount fed cautiously, with an eye to dinner at no distant period. Sheila was much excited at the idea of the Sergeant coming to dine with him.

"He's a splendid old chap," said she. "Such tales I used to hear about him when I was a kiddie at school. Many a day when he's been out after cattle-stealers, and bushrangers, people said he'd never come back alive. He was never afraid, though, and he made them afraid of *him* before he was done."

"By the way, where did you go to school, Sheila? You speak excellent English, and you haven't any twang or drawl, like some of the colonial girls."

"Oh! at She-oak Flat. There was a State school there, and mother kept us at it pretty regular, rain or shine, no staying at home, whatever the weather was like or the roads, and we had three miles to walk, there and back."

"So you didn't go to Melbourne, or Sydney?"

"No! Never been away from Bunjil. I suppose I shall see the sea some day."

"*Never seen the sea—the sea?* You astonish me!"

"Never in my life. Do I look different or anything?"

"You look very nice, and talk very well too. I begin to think the seaside's overrated; but I must take another walk, or the landlord will think I don't do his dinner justice. What's it to be?"

"Well, a turkey poult for one thing; the rest you'll see when the covers are taken off."

"Quite right. It's impertinent curiosity, I'm aware."

"Oh! not that, but we're going to astonish you, if we can."

Upon this Mr. Blount put on his boots again; they had been splashed in the morning, and required drying. Crossing the creek upon a rustic bridge, which seemed to depend more upon a fallen tree than on any recognised plan of engineering, he turned his steps up stream, and faced the Alpine range. The afternoon, like the morning, was golden bright, though a hint of frost began to be felt in the clear keen air. The road was fairly good, and had been formed and macadamised in needful places.

It lay between the rushing creek on one side, towards which there was a considerable drop, and the line of foot-hills on the other, leaving just room for meeting vehicles to pass one another, though it needed the accurate driving of bush experts to ensure safety. Water-races, flumes, and open ditches crossed the road, testifying to the existence of gold-workings in the neighbourhood, while an occasional miner on his way to the township of Bunjil emerged from an unfrequented track and made towards, what was to him, the King's Highway. Once he heard the tinkling of bells, when suddenly there came round a corner a train of thirty or forty pack-horses, with all manner of sacks and bags, and even boxes on their backs. There were a few mules also in the drove, to whom was accorded the privilege of leadership, as on any block or halt taking place, they pushed their way to the front, and set off up or down the track with decision, as if better instructed than the rank and file.

"Ha! 'Bell-horses, bell-horses, what time o' day? One o'clock, two o'clock, three and away,' as we used to say at school. Puts one in mind of Devonshire," murmured the tourist. "Many a keg of smuggled spirits was carried on the backs of the packers, with their bells. I daresay an occasional breach of custom-house regulations has occurred now and then if the truth were told. I wouldn't mind being quartered here at all. It's a droll world!" Mr. Blount's rambles and reveries came to an end half an hour after sunset, which just left him time to get back to his hostelry, make some change for dinner, and toast himself before the fire, in anticipation of the arrival of his guest. The Sergeant arrived with military punctuality, a few minutes before the hour, having donned for the occasion a well-worn, well-brushed uniform, in which he looked like a "non-com." recommended for the Victoria Cross.

He greeted Sheila cordially and expressed a favourable opinion as to her growth, and development, since she used to play hockey and cricket with the boys at She-oak Flat. "And right weel did she play," he continued, addressing himself to his entertainer, "she won the half-mile race too, against all comers, didn't you, Sheila?"

"I was pretty smart then, wasn't I, Sergeant? Do you remember fishing me out of the creek, when I slipped off the log?"

"I mind weel, I thocht you were a swimmer, till I saw ye go down, head under; so I was fain to loup into ten feet of snow water and catch a cold that was nigh the deeth o' me. I misdooted gin ye were worth it a'! What think ye?"

The girl shook her head at him, her dark, grey eyes bright with merriment, as she tripped out of the room, to reappear with the turkey poult before referred to. "She's a grand lassie!" said the Sergeant, looking after her admiringly, "and as guid as she's bonnie. The men and women that are reared among these hills are about the finest people the land turns out! The women are aye the best, it's a pity the lads are not always sae weel guided. If there was a Hieland regiment here to draft some of thae lang-leggit lads into ilka year, it would be the making of the haill countryside."

"Very likely there will be, some day, but do you think they would stand the discipline?"

"Deevil a doot on't, they're easy guided when they have gentlemen to deal with as offishers; as for scouting, and outpost duty, they're born for it. Fighting's just meat and drink to them, ance they get fair started."

"English people don't think so," said the tourist. "They've always opposed the idea of having a naval reserve here, though everybody that's lived in the country long enough to know will tell me that Sydney Harbour lads are born sailors, and if there are many of the mountain boys like my friend 'Little-River-Jack,' they should make the best light cavalry in the world."

The Sergeant bent a searching eye on the speaker. "'Little-River-Jack,' ay, I ken the callant brawly. Ride, aye, that can he, and he's a freend, ye say?"

"Well, I came here with him. He showed me the way, an I wouldn't swear he didn't save my life, coming over that Razor-back pinch, on the Divide, as he called it."

"And so ye cam' on the Divide wi' him, ou, ay? And ye're gangin' awa' wi' him to see the country?"

"Yes! I hear he knows every inch of it from the head of the Sturt to the Lower Narran, besides the mountain gold diggings. I'm going to see one of them, with him, when he comes to-morrow. There's nothing strange about that, is there?"

"I wadna say; he joost buys gold in a sma' way, and bullocks, for the flesher-folk, aboot the heid o' the river. There's talk whiles that he's ower sib with the O'Hara gang, but I dinna ken o' my ain knowledge."

"Not proven, I suppose—the Scottish verdict, eh! Sergeant?"

The dinner was a success. The soup was fair. The fish represented by a Murray cod, about five pound weight, truly excellent. The turkey poult, like most country-bred birds, incomparably plump and tender, was roasted to a turn. The other adjuncts in strict keeping with the *pièce de résistance*.

The guest declined to join his entertainer in a bottle of Reisling, preferring a glass of whisky and water. Towards the close of the entertainment the landlord was announced, who took neither wine nor whisky, excusing himself on the ground that he had already been compelled "for the good of the house" to drink with more than one customer.

"I shall have to take to a decanter of toast and water, coloured to look like sherry. This 'What'll you have, Boss?' business, is getting too hot for me lately, and the men don't like to see you afraid to taste your own liquor. But, as long as it's something, they don't seem to care what it is. I'll take a cigar, though, sir, so as to be good company."

One of the tourist's extra quality Flor de Habanas being lighted the conversation grew more intimate, and bordering on the confidential. The

Sergeant was prevailed upon to mix a tumbler of toddy, the night being cold, and the landlord, whose tongue had been previously loosened, among the choice spirits in the second dining-room, incited the Sergeant to give the company the benefit of his reminiscences.

"It's cold enough, and a man that came in late," said he, "could feel the frozen grass as stiff as wire. But the Sergeant's been out many a night as bad, with nothing but his coat to sleep in, and afraid to make a fire for fear of giving away where his camp was."

"Ay!" said the Sergeant, and his face settled into one of grim resolve, changing not suddenly, but, as it were, stage after stage.

"I mind one chase I had after an outlawed chiel that began wi' horse-stealing, and cattle 'duffing' (they ca' it in these parts), and ended in bloodshed maist foul and deleeberate. Ye've heard of Sub-Inspector Dayrell?"

"Should think I had," said the landlord. "It was before I took this house; I was at Beechworth then, but every one heard of the case. He was the officer that 'shopped' Ned Lawless, and a young swell from the old country. There was a girl in it too. Eumeralla was where he arrested them, and everybody knew there was something 'cronk' about it."

"The verra mon! He's gane to his accoont, and Ned's serving his sentence. I aye misdooted that the evidence against Lance Trevanion (that was his name, he cam' of kenned folk in Devon,) was 'cookit,' and weel cookit too, for his destruction, puir laddie."

"Then you think he was innocent?"

"As innocent as the lassie that brocht in the denner."

"What sentence did he get?"

"Five years' imprisonment—wi' hard labour. But he didna sairve it. He flitted frae the hulk *Success* where they sent him after he nigh killed Warder Bracker. He was a dour man and a cruel; he'd made his boast that he'd 'break' Trevanion, as he called it, because he couldna get him to knuckle doon to him like ither convicts, puir craters! So he worked him harder and harder—complained o' him for insolence—got him to the dark cell—once and again insulted him when there was nae ither body to hear—and one day gave him a kick, joost as he'd been a dog in his road.

"That was mair than enough. Clean mad and desperate, Trevanion rushed at him, had him doon, and him wi' his hands in his throttle, before he could cry on the guard. His eyes were starting out of his head—he was black in the face and senseless, when a warder from outside the cell who heard the scuffle, pulled him off. Anither ten seconds, and Bracker would have been a dead man—as it was, he was that lang coming to, that the doctor gave him up."

"What sentence did he get? They'd have hanged him long ago?" queried the host.

"He'd have got 'life,' or all the same twenty years' gaol; but Bracker had been had up for cruelty to prisoners in another gaol before, and Mr. Melrose the Comptroller and the Visiting Justice were dead against a' kinds o' oppression, so they ordered a thorough inquiry. Some of the prisoners swore they'd seen Bracker knocking Trevanion about. He'd been 'dark-celled' for weeks on bread and water. When he came out he could hardly stand up. They'd heard him swear at Trevanion and call him a loafing impostor— and other names. The evidence went clear against him. Mr. McAlpine said Bracker ought to have had a year in gaol himself, and recommended his dismissal. So he left the service, and a good thing too. I'm no sayin' that some of the convicts o' the early fifties were not desperate deevils, as ever stretched halter. But they were paying for their ineequities—a high price too, when they're lockit up night and day, working the whiles with airn chains on their limbs. And they that would make *that* lot harder and heavier, had hearts like the nether millstane."

"What became of Trevanion, after all?"

"He was sent to the hulk *Success*. No great relief, ane would think. But it was better than stone walls. He had the sea and the sky around him day and night. It made a new man of him, they say. And before the year was oot (he had plenty money, ye see), he dropped into a boat through the port hole, one dark night, just before the awfullest storm ye ever saw. Horses were waitin' on him next day, and ye'll no hinder him frae winning to the New Rush at Tin Pot Flat Omeo, where he worked as a miner and prospector, for twa year and mair, under the name of 'Ballarat Harry.'"

"Could not the police find him?" queried the tourist. "They were said to be awfully smart in the goldfields days."

"Yes!" said the old Sergeant solemnly, "they did find him, but they could do naething till him."

"You don't say so! Well, this is a strange country. He was identified, I suppose?" said the stranger. "Why was that?"

"Because he was deid, puir laddie! We pulled him up from a shaft saxty feet deep, wi' a bullet through him, and his head split with an axe. It was Kate Lawless that found him—her husband, Larry Trevenna and the murdering spawn o' hell, Caleb Coke, had slain him for his gold—and it may be for ither reasons."

"Good God! what a tragedy! Did the scoundrels escape?"

"Coke did by turning King's evidence. But Trevenna's wife rode near a hundred miles on end to give Dayrell the office. He ran Trevenna down in Melbourne, just as he had taken his passage to England under a false name. He was found guilty, and hanged."

"Then Trevenna's wife worked the case up against her own husband? How was that?"

"Weel, aweel, I'll no deny the case was what may be tairmed compleecated—sair mixed up. Lance Trevanion had been her sweetheart, and when she jaloused, owing to Dayrell's wiles, that he had thrown her over, she just gave the weight o' her evidence against him, on his trial for having a stolen horse in his possession, knowing it to be stolen. Then in rage and desperation, for she repented sair, when she saw what her treachery had brought on him, she married Trevenna, who used her like a dog, they say, and was aye jealous of Lance Trevanion. And her cousin Tessie Lawless, it was her that got him frae the hulk."

"Oh! another woman!" murmured Blount; "as you say, Sergeant, it is a trifle mixed up. Who was she in love with?"

"Just Lance, and nae ither. She was true as steel, and never ceased working for him night and day till she got a warder in the hulk weel bribit, and persuadit twa gentlemen that lived in Fishermen's Bend by wild-fowling to tak' him awa' in their dinghy and find a guide and twa horses that brought him to Omeo. A wild, uncanny spot it was then, I warrant ye. Then the young lady, his cousin that came frae England to marry him—"

"What do I hear, Sergeant? *Another woman* in love with the ill-fated hero; that makes *three*—in love with the same man at the same time. It sounds incredible. And were they *really* fond of him?"

"Woman's a mysterious crea-a-tion, I've aye held, since she first walkit in the gairden o' Eden," quoth the Sergeant impressively. "Either of the Lawless girls would have died for him—and gloried in it. Kate, that was his ruin, wild and undeesciplined as she was, but for the poison that Dayrell insteeled into her, wad ha' laid her head on the block to save his. Puir Tessie *did* die for him, as ye may ca' it, for she went into Melbourne Hospital when the fever was at its fiercest, and cried that they should give her the warst cases. The puir sick diggers and sailors called her 'The Angel of the Fever Ward,' and there she wrought, and wrought, day after day, and night after night, until she catchit it hersel', and so the end came. The doctors and the ither attendants said she hadna the strength to strive against it."

"A jewel of a girl!" quoth the Englishman; "why didn't he marry her?"

"She wouldn't marry *him*," said the Sergeant. "She kenned he was promised to his cousin, a great leddy frae the auld country, who came all the way to Australia to find him, and she said he must keep his troth."

"Women seem to differ in Australia much as they do elsewhere," mused the stranger.

"And what for no?" queried the old trooper; "there's bad and good all over the world—men as weel's women—and the more you see of this country, the more you'll find it oot. If they're born unlike from the start, they're as different from one another as your cob (as ye ca' him) frae 'Little-River-Jack's' Keewah that can climb like a goat, or from Middleton's auld 'Slavey' that can gallop twenty miles before breakfast, or draw a buggy sixty miles a day at a pinch. But if we get talking horse, we'll no quit till cockcraw."

CHAPTER III

"You will tell us about Dayrell, Sergeant?" said Mr. Blount. "Is it a tale of mystery and fear?"

"It was God's judgment upon the shedding of innocent blood," said the Sergeant solemnly; "they're in their graves, the haill company, the betrayer and the betrayed. The nicht's turned dark and eerie. To say truth, I wad as lieve lay the facts before ye, in the licht o' day. It's a dark walk by the river oaks, and a man may weel fancy he hears whisperings, and voices of the deid in the midnight blast. I'm at your sairvice ony day before ye leave Bunjil, but I'll be makin' tracks the noo, wi' your permeession, sir, and my thanks to ye. Gude nicht!"

The veteran had made up his mind, and wrapped in a horseman's cloak such as the paternal Government of Victoria still serves out to the Mounted Police Force, he marched forth into the night. The landlord parted from him on the verandah, while Blount walked up and down for an hour, watching a storm-cloud whelming in gathering gloom the dimly outlined range, until the rain fell with tropical volume necessitating a retreat to the parlour, where the logs still sent out a grateful warmth. "The old man must have missed that downpour," he said. "He was wise to depart in good time."

Another meeting was arranged. "Little-River-Jack" sent word by a "sure hand," as was the wording of a missive in pre-postal days, that he would arrive in Bunjil on the next ensuing Saturday, ready for a daylight start on Sunday morning, if that would suit Mr. Blount's convenience.

Pursuant to his promise, the Sergeant arrived to lunch at the Bunjil Hotel on the day specified. He did not make demand for the groom, but riding into the yard, opened the stable door and put up his ancient steed, slipping the bridle back over his ears, however, but leaving it ready to be replaced at short notice.

"It's an auld habit o' mine," he said to the landlord, who now made his appearance with apologies for the absence of the groom, who was "out, getting a load of wood," he explained. "We burn a lot here in the winter — it's just as well we haven't to pay for it — but it takes old George half his time drawing it in."

"You've got some fresh horses here," said the Sergeant, his keen eye resting on three well-conditioned nags at one end of the row of stalls; "are ye gaun to have races—the Bunjil Town Plate and Publican's Purse—and are the lads that own thae flyers come to tak' pairt? Yon grey's a steeplechaser, by his looks, and the two bays are good enough for Flemington."

The landlord fidgeted a little before answering.

"They're some digging chaps that have a camp at Back Creek. They buy their beef from 'Little-River-Jack,' and he takes their gold at a price. They do a bit of trade in brumbie-shooting now and then, the hides sell well and the horse-hair—I'm told. Between that and digging they knock out a fair living."

"Nae doot," replied the Sergeant, slowly and oracularly. "If there's aught to be won by a guid horse and a bould rider, these are the men that'll no lose it for want of a sweater or twa. What names have they?" And here the old man fixed his eye searchingly on the host.

"Two O'Haras and a Rorke," answered the host, haltingly. "So they tell me—'Irish natives,' from Gippsland way they call themselves."

"I wadna doot," quoth the Sergeant. "Eldest brother Jemmy O'Hara, a fell chiel. But let byganes be byganes. It's ill raking up misdeeds of fouk that's maybe deid or repenting, repenting in sa-ack-cloth and ashes. It'll be one o'clock, joost chappit. I'll awa ben."

"Ay!" said the Sergeant, lunch being cleared away, and both men sitting before the replenished fire, which the proximity of Bunjil to the snow line, as well as the frost of the night before, rendered grateful, "it's e'en a tale of vengeance long delayed, but the price of bluid was paid—ay, and mair than paid, when the hour cam', and the man. I was stationed at Omeo, I mind weel, years after Larry Trevenna was hangit for the crime, as well he desairved. If one had misdooted the words of Holy Writ, there was the confirmation plain for a' men to see. 'Be sure thy sin will find thee out.' They were half brithers, it was weel kenned, word came frae hame to that effect, and little thought the author of their being that the bairn o' shame, the offspring of the reckless days of wild, ungoverned youth, was born to slay the heir of his ancient house, in a far land; to die by the hangman's cord, amid the curses of even that strange crew amang whom his life was spent. But he was fain to 'dree his weird,' as in auld Scottish fashion we say; all men must fulfil their appointed destiny. It's a hard law maybe, and I canna agree with oor Presbyterian elders, that ae man is foredoomed to sin and shame, the tither to wealth and honours, and that neither can escape the lot prepared for him frae the foundation of the warld! But whiles, when ye see the haill draama played oot, and a meestery made clear, the maist careless unbeliever must acknowledge that Heaven's justice is done even in this warld o' appairent contradeections. Weel, aweel, I'm gey and loth to come to the tale deed o' bluid, o' the fearsome eend. Things had settled doon at Omeo after the events ye ken o'. There was a wheen duffing and horse-stealing to contend wi'! But siccan lifting of kye will there be, amang these mountains and glens, I had a'maist said till the Day of Judgment— but no to be profane, the country was quieter than it had been for years, when word came to heidquarters that Ned Lawless had broken gaol; had been seen makin' across by Talbingo to the table-land, aboot Long Plain and Lobb's Hole. There was an 'auld gun' (as we ca' confairmed creeminals) in the lock-up, as the news came; a Monaro native, and haun and glove with a' the moss-troopers and reivers south of the Snowy River.

"'D'ye know where Inspector Dayrell is now, Sergeant?' says he, quite free and pleasant. He was only in for 'unlawfully using'—a maitter o' six months' gaol at the warst.

"'Maybe I do, maybe I don't; what call have ye to be speirin'?'

"'He'll never trouble me again, Sergeant, I'm full up of anything like a big touch now; this bit of foolishness don't count. But if you want to do Dayrell a rale good turn, tell him to clear out to New Zealand, the Islands, San Francisco—anywhere.'

"'Why should I?' says I. 'And him to lose his chance of being made a Superintendent.'

"'Superintendent be hanged!' (it was not in Court, ye ken), and he put his heid doon low, and spak' low and airnest.

"'Is a step in the service worth a man's life? You tell him from me, Monaro Joe, that if Ned Lawless isn't dead or taken within a month, his life's not worth a bent stirrup iron.'

"'And the Lawless crowd broken up?' says I. 'Man! ye're gettin' dotty. Ned's a dour body, waur after these years' gaol. I wadna put it past him, but he's helpless, wantin' mates. Coke's a cripple with the rheumatics. Kate's awa, naebody kens where.'

"'Ye're a good offisher, Sergeant,' says he, 'but you don't know everything. You want a year's duffing near Lobb's Hole to sharpen you up. But if I lay you on to something, will you get the Beak to let me down easy about this sweating racket, a bloomin' moke, worth about two notes! I never offered him for sale, the police know that. A rotten screw, or I shouldn't have been overhauled by that new chum Irish trooper. I was ashamed of myself, I raly was.'

"'If ye give information of value to the depairtment as regards this dangerous creeminal,' says I, 'I'll no press the case.'

"'Well—this is God's truth,' says he, quite solemn. 'His sister Kate's been livin' at Tin Pot Flat for months, under another name. They say she's off her head at times, never been right since she lost her child.'

"'Lost her child!' says I. 'Ye don't say so—the puir crater, and a fine boy he was. How cam' that?'

"'Well, the time Kate rode to White Rock and started Dayrell after Larry Trevenna, just as he was goin' to clear out for the old country, passin' hisself off for Lance (that *was* a caper, wasn't it?), she left her boy with the stockrider's young wife at Running Creek. The girl (she was a new chum Paddy) was away for a bit, hangin' out clothes or somethin'; the poor kid got down to the creek and was drowned. Kate was stark starin' mad for forty-eight hours. Then she took the kid in front of her on the little roan mare, and never spoke till after the Coroner come and orders it to be buried.'

"'And she at Tin Pot Flat, and me nane the wiser! Any mair of the crowd?'

"'You remember Dick?—the young brother—he that was left behind when they cleared for Balooka—he's a man grown, this years and years; well, she lives with him. And they say she goes to the shaft every day that Lance was hauled out from, to kneel down and pray. What for, God only knows. Dick's quiet, but dangerous; he's the best rider and tracker from Dargo High Plain to Bourke, and that's a big word.'

"'I ken that; I'll joost ride round, and tak' a look—he'll need watchin', and if he's joined Ned, and Kate's makin' a third, there'll be de'il's wark ere lang.'

"That evening the tent was doon, Kate and the younger Lawless chiel gane—and nane could say when, how, or where.

"For a week, and the week after that, the wires were going all day and half the nicht. Every police station on the border of New South Wales and Victoria from Monaro to Murray Downs was noticed to look up their black tracker, and have their best horses ready. As for Dayrell, they couldna warn him that the avengers o' bluid, as nae doot they held themselves to be, were on his trail. He was richt awa amang the 'snaw leases,' (as they ca'd them—a country only habitable by man or beast frae late spring to early autumn;) on the trail o' a gang o' horse and cattle thieves that had defied the police of three colonies. They had left a record in Queensland before they crossed the New South Wales border.

"Noted men among them—ane tried for murder! A mate, suspect o' treachery, was found in a creek wi' twa bullets in's heid—there were ither evil deeds to accoont for.

"Ay, they were a dour gang—fightin' to the death. So Dayrell took five of his best men and volunteered for the capture. 'He was getting rusty,' he said, 'but would break up this gang or they should have his scalp.' These were the very words he used.

"Omeo diggings were passed on the way up. There was sure to be some one that knew *him*, wherever he went in any of the colonies.

"A tall man put his head out of a shaft on 'Tin Pot' as he rode through the Flat at the head of his troopers, and cursed him with deleeberate maleegnity until they were out of sight. 'Ride on, you bloody dog!' he said—grinding his teeth—'you won't reign much longer now that Ned and I can work together again, and we have your tracks. I know every foot of the road you're bound to travel now—once you're as far as Merrigal there's no get away between Snowy Creek and the Jibbo. It was our rotten luck the day we first set eyes on you. We were not such a bad crowd if we'd been let alone. Tessie had half persuaded Ned to drop the cross work after we got shut of the Balooka horses. The day afore he told me he'd two minds to let 'em go on the road. Then he couldn't have been pulled for more than illegal using, which isn't felony. But *you* must come along and spoil everything. Lance was copped, as innocent as a child: Ned gets a stretch—it was his death sentence. I know what it's turned *him* into. Kate's gone mad, what with losin' the kid—a fine little chap, so he was (I cried when I heard of it)! Larry's hanged—serve him right.

"'Lance is dead and buried, poor chap! I don't know what'll become of me. And what's more I don't care; but I'll have revenge, blast you! before the year's out, if I swing for it!'

"He didna ken Dick Lawless again in his digger's dress, and there were few that he didna remember either, if it was ten years after. So he joost gaed alang blithe and gay. The sun was abune the fog that aye hangs o'er the flat till midday, or maybe disna lift at a' like a Highland mist. He touched his horse's rein, and the gey, weel-trained beastie gave a dance like, and shook his heid, till bit and curb chain jingled again.

"Ah! me, these things are fearsome at the doing and but little better in the telling. He wadna hae been sae blithe had he seen anither face that peered o'er the shaft just as he turned at the angle of the road and struck into a canter with his troopers ahint him. It was the face of a haggard, clean-shaved man, with hair cut close to the head, and a wild, desperate look like a hunted beast—only one miner on the field knew who the strange man was, and he would never have kent him, but for hearin' a whisper the night before of a 'cross cove' having come late at night to 'Mrs. Jones's' tent.

"Dead beat and half starved to boot was he, but word went round the little goldfield that it was Ned Lawless, the famous horse and cattle 'duffer' who'd been arrested by Inspector Dayrell, and 'put away' for five years.

"Miners are no joost attached to thae kind o' folk, and for this one, believed to have stolen wash-dirt cart-horses at Ballarat, they certainly had no love, but, as for layin' the police on the hunted wretch, even though the reward was tempting, not a man, working as they were on a poor field, but would have scorned the action, and been vara unceevil to him that suggested it. No! that was the business of the police—they were paid for it—let them run him down or any other poor devil that was 'wanted,' but as for helping them by so much as raising a finger, it was not in their line.

"Anyhow, an hour before dawn, one man who had reasons for airly rising thought he saw Dick with his sister, 'Mrs. Jones,' and the stranger, ride down the gulley which led towards Buckley's Crossing; the woman was on a roan pony mare, which she brought with her when she came on 'Tin Pot,' a year ago. The stranger had an old grey screw Dick had bought for a note, which would let any one catch him, night or day. The fog was thick, and he couldn't say on his oath which way they went, but they took what was called the 'mountain track.'"

"A nice crowd, as they say in these parts," said Mr. Blount. "Where did they go and what did they do, Sergeant?"

"They were ready for any de'il's wark, ye may believe," said the old man, impressively, "and, as I heard frae one that daurna speak me false, they were no lang ere they were at it.

"The day after they were seen leaving 'Tin Pot,' they called at a small settler's place and took his twa best horses. He was a man that had good anes, wad win races at sma' townships.

"The wife and her sister were at hame, the man was awa'.

"They loaded up a packhorse with rations, more by token a rug and twa pairs blankets. The younger man told them the horses wad maybe stray back. He paid for the rations and the blankets, but said they must have them. It was a lonely place. The woman sat on her horse, and wadna come ben, though they asked her to have a cup of tea. She shook her head; they couldna see her face for a thick veil she wore.

"This information didna come in for some days later, when the man won hame; the women were afraid to leave the place, ye may weel believe.

The raiders rode hard, maistly at nicht, keepit aff the main road, and took 'cuts' when they could find them. Dick Lawless knew them a', could amaist smell them, his mates used to say.

"They got the Inspector's trail and never lost it; if they were off it for a while, they could always 'cut' it again. *They* had telegraphs plenty (bush anes) but there were nane to warn Dayrell o' them that thirsted for his life-bluid, and were following on through the snaw, like the wolves on a Russian steppe, as the buiks tell us. He was joost 'fey,' in the high spirits that foretell death or misfortune, as we Hielanders believe. He had the chance o' a capture that would ring through three colonies. It did that, but no in the way he expeckit.

"He heard tell frae a bushman, a brither o' the man that the gang shot before he had time to do more than threaten to 'give them away,' that they were to be at the 'Ghost Camp' aboot the twentieth o' the month. An auld fastness this, at the edge o' broken, mountainous country, where the wild blacks cam' to hide after killing cattle or robbing huts, when Queensland was first ta'en up by squatters. A place no that easy to ride to, maist deeficult to discover, amang the great mountain forests o' the border. Battles had there been, between the black police and the wild native tribes that were strong and bold in the pioneer days, no kenning, puir bodies, the strength o' ceevilised man. It was there they halted after the massacre of Wild Honey Bank, where they killed after nightfa' the haill family, men and women, wives and weans, an awfu' spectacle they were as they lay deid in the hot sun, unshaded, uncovered. I was tauld it by a man, was ane of the pairty that helped bury them. The pursuers slew and spared not. Wha shall judge them after the fearsome sights they saw? There's but few of that tribe left alive, and sma' wonder.

"An eerie, waesome spot, they tell me. The gunyahs hae na been leeved in this mony a year. The few fra-agments o' the tribe conseeder it to be haunted, and winna gang near. It's a' strewed wi' skulls, and skeletons of whites and blacks mingled, nane having been at the pains to bury them. The grass grows rank abune the mouldering relics o' baith races. The banes gleam white when the moon is at her full, lying matted thegither amaist concealed by the growth of years.

"Weel, aweel! I'm just daundering on toward the eend, the sair, sorrowfu' eending o' a fearsome tale. The twa pairties, that wad be the Queensland gang, and the Sydney-side lot, were nigh hand to the 'Ghost Camp' aboot the same time.

"That's sayin' the three Lawless bodies had ridden night and day— picking up fresh horses for the men, as they came along. Kate rode the roan pony mare all through, a grand little crater she was, and weel she earned her name 'Wallaby,' sae ca'ed after the kangaroo beastie that wad hop frae rock to rock, like ony goat o' the cliffs.

"The Inspector reckoned that Bradfield's gang wad show up in the gloaming o' the appointed day. No kenning that they had been betrayed, they wad camp careless like. Dayrell's tracker creepit oot and lay ahint a rock while they unsaiddled and turned loose their horses. Bradfield he knew—a tall powerfu' chiel, with a big beard, a Sydney-side native, and if he wasna the best bushman in Queensland, he wasna that far aff. Of the four men with him, twa had 'done time,' and were worse after they cam' oot o' gaol, than when they gaed in. They had grog in them; they made a fire—not a black fellow's one—and talked and laughed and swore, as they didna care wha might hear them.

"So far, a' went weel. Dayrell's party lay close—made no fire—prepared to deleever attack at dawn, when dootless Bradfield's men wad be asleep or all unsuspeecious. But were they? By no manner of means. The twa Lawless brithers and Kate had won to Wandong Creek i' the nicht—Ned and Kate had lain them doon, joost dead beat and like to dee wi' sheer exhaustion. Dick stowed the horse away in the gulley. It's deep, and amaist covered in wi' trees and fern. Then being a tireless crater and in hard work and training, he thocht he would tak' a wee bit look oot, to make a' safe. It was weel thocht on—though not for the police party. It wasna lang ere he heard a horse whinnie. Not the nicher o' a brumbie, either. Then cam' the tramp o' anither and the jingle o' a hobble chain. Could it be the police? He would soon know. Creeping frae tree to tree, he came on the mob. Six riding horses, and two 'packers' all with the Crown brand on. Dayrell's dark chestnut, he knew *him* again. And a light bay with two white hind fetlocks. Police horses all, well fed and groomed. Now where was the camp?

"Keeping wide and crawling from log to log, like a night-wandering crater o' the forest, he thought he saw a glimmer o' a fire—not a small one either. What d—d fool had lighted that, with a hot trail so close? So he walkit, ye ken, till what suld ail him to come ram-sham on six sleeping men. Police in plain clothes? Never! It was Bradfield's gang, believing that Dayrell was no within a colony o' them. And now to get speech. Their revolvers were under their hands, their rifles handy ye ken. If an alarm was given it might spoil the whole plan. With two other rifles, not counting Kate (and she was a fair shot at short range), they might turn the tables on Dayrell and his blasted police.

"Keen and ready witted as are the de'il's bairns at their master's wark, Dick Lawless wasna lang in conseedering the pairt he was to play. Crawling on hands and knees, he got as near Bradfield as was wise like without awaking him. He then gave a low whistle, such as stockriders give to tell of cattle in sight.

"'Who the hell's that?' growled Bradfield, awake and alert.

"'All right, Jim, only Dick Lawless. Cattle going to break camp. (They had been droving in old days.) Quite like old times, isn't it?'

"'Wish I was back again behind a thousand Windorah bullocks,' said the bushranger.

"'I wouldn't mind either, Jim. But all that's behind us now—worse luck! Where do you think Dayrell is? Give it up? D'ye see that black ridge, with three pines on it? Well, he's there, waiting for daylight. He's not fool to make a fire you can see miles off. You've nearly been had, Jim. He came up on purpose to collar you. T'other side the black ridge, he's planted men and horses, six of 'em and a packer.'

"'Who's with you?'

"'Just Ned and Kate. They're lying down in Wandong Creek. Kate's goin' dotty now, poor thing, but she would come with us. Thinks she'll see the last of Dayrell.'

"'Strikes me it's a case of "Just before the battle, mother,"' said Bradfield. 'I'll wake these chaps. We must have a snack and fix up the Waterloo business. It's an hour to daylight yet.'

"Thus speaking he touched the man on his left, who awoke and touched the next. Without a spoken word the five men were aroused.

"'Now, chaps!' said the leader, in low but distinct tones, 'Dick Lawless is come to give in the office. He's on the job too. Dayrell's behind the black ridge, with his five fancy troopers. He's come to collar us. Dick here and Ned have come to pay off old scores. With us to help he's like enough to do it. We're nigh about equal members, not countin' Kate, but the surprise they'll get's as good as two men.'

"'How's that?' asked one of the gang.

"'It's this way, we'll have first go. He thinks we don't know he's here. We'll take cover, and as soon as he shows out to surprise us, we roll into him. Dick here, Ned and Kate, go at him from Wandong Creek side. That'll put the stuns on him. Ned and Dick, both dead shots, will account for Dayrell. If he goes down the other traps won't stand long. Dick, you'll have a snack? No? Then, so long.'

"The faint line of clearer sky was slowly making itself veesible in the east as Dayrell at the head of his troopers moved towards Bradfield's camp. The black tracker had showed him the position. The glimmering fire did the rest. 'Now for a rush, men, we'll catch them asleep.' Saddles and swags were strewn around the fire, billy and frying-pan were there, not a man to be seen. But from five rifles at short range came a volley at the troopers, well-aimed and effective, and Dayrell's right arm fell to his side broken or disabled.

"Three shots immediately followed from the Wandong Creek timber, on the left flank of the police. Confused at finding themselves between two fires, their leader wounded—for Dayrell's right arm still hung useless—the troopers, after a second ineffectual volley, wavered. Just then three figures appeared, standing on a rock which ran crossways to the narrow outlet by which alone could the police party mak' retreat.

"At the second volley two troopers dropped, one mortally, the other severely, wounded. 'Hold up your hands, if you don't all want to be wiped out,' shouted Bradfield.

"'By the Lord! that's Kate Lawless,' said one of the troopers, pointing to a tall woman who waved a rifle and shouted defiance after the first volley was fired.

"'And that's Ned, or his ghost,' said another. 'I thought he was safe in Ballarat Gaol. How the h—l did they get here?'

"As he spoke, the two men on the rock took deliberate aim and fired, the Inspector in return firing his revolver with the left hand.

"The clean-shaved man dropped dead, wi' a bullet through his head; Dayrell staggered for a few seconds and making an attempt to recover himself, sank to the earth. The woman sprang down from the rock, and rushing across the line of fire raised the dying man's head from the ground and gazed into his face, in which the signs of fast-coming death were apparent.

"'So this is the end of Inspector Frank Dayrell,' she said, 'trapped like a dingo by the poor devils he was hunting down. I told you you'd repent it, if you didn't let us alone. And now my words have come true; the Lawless family gang's broke up, but the bloodhound hasn't much life in him neither. I sha'n't last the year out, the old lot's close up dead and done for, that was so jolly, and worked hard and straight, when we first came on Ballarat. Pity we took to 'cross' work, wasn't it? Love—as they call it—' here she smiled a strange, sad smile, 'then jealousy, revenge, false swearing, murder—Poor Lance! I *did* him cruel wrong, and but for you, you, Francis Dayrell, I'd never have sworn a word to harm him. It's driven me mad—mad! do you hear, Frank Dayrell? Good-bye, till we meet in—in—the other place!'

"The firing was o'er, Dick Lawless now showed himself between the rock and the clear space where lay the dead trooper and Dayrell. The Inspector raised himself on one arm and with the last glimmer o'licht in his glazing e'en, looked full in the woman's face, as he drawled out the words, 'Au revoir! Kate, pleasant journey, inner circle of mine with the left, eh?' The light faded out of his eyes with the last word, and falling back, he was dead when his head touched the ground. The woman gazed for one moment on the still face; then in obedience to a sign from her brother, walkit over to him, and, mounting their horses, they rode away into the forest thegither. The police couldna but see they were ootnummered. Their leader and one trooper dead; anither was badly wounded. Four men—one barely able to sit on a horse—were no match for six.

"'See here, men,' said Bradfield, a tall, powerful native chiel wi' a black beard, a grand bushman, too; 'this here battle's over, you're euchred, your boss expected to catch us on the hop, and he's been took himself. He was a game chap, and we don't owe him no grudge, nor you either, though he went a bit out of his way in leavin' his own district to collar another officer's game. He didn't reckon on Ned and Dick Lawless, and it's them that knocked over his wicket. A fair fight's righto, but it don't do even for a policeman to get hisself disliked.'

"'I say, Jim, the horses are up; are yer goin' to preach here till the military's called out?'

"'All right, Jack, there's no hurry. What's to be done with the dead men? There's Inspector Dayrell, our poor cove, and Ned Lawless. We can't leave 'em here.'

"'The police must pack their mates,' said the second in command, 'we'll take away ours. Where's the nearest township, or graveyard, if it comes to that?'

"'We can make Warradombee in twenty mile'; here spoke one of the police troopers. 'It's close to Grant's head station.'

"'All right, you've got your packers; strap on the Inspector, and that Goulburn native, and let 'em be buried decent. We're not black fellows. We'll carry our man, and bury him first chance. Ned must stay where he is—he's better there than under the gaol yard. Like as not Dick and Kate'll come back to him. They've not gone far. Well, you'd better load, and clear—we'll give you a lift, as you're short handed. Don't sing a bigger song than you can help. Give us a day's law, and then we don't care what you do. We haven't acted so bad to you.'

"'No, by George, you haven't,' said the senior constable, 'except killin' the two of us, and you couldn't help that, seein' you was fightin' for your lives, as the sayin' is.'

"So the enemies (as I'm tauld) helped to raise the fallen men, and fasten them on their horses. It was a sad-looking troop, as they moved off, with their dead legs tied underneath, and at the knees, to the saddles, their heads bowed low on the horses' necks, so that they couldna fall off. But the upper bodies, with heids swaying aboot in that dreadful guise, lookit awfu' ghaistly. Little thocht Frank Dayrell that he wad ride his last ride in siccan a fashion. But nane can foretell his eend, nor the manner o't.

"Bradfield's lot cleared without loss o' time, carrying with them their dead and wounded, until a convenient burial place was reached. This duty completed, they separated, to meet in the 'Never Never Country,' between Burke Town and 'The Gulf,' a 'strange, vain land' (as one has written) where 'night is even as the day,' and the decalogue is no that sariously regairded, as in longer settled communities.

"Although the tither ootlaws wadna chairge themselves with Ned Lawless' funeral, it is no' to be infaired that he was buried without a prayer, or that tears werena shed o'er his lonely unhallowed grave. As had been surmeesed, Kate and the younger brother returned after nightfall.

"It was nearly midnight, the moonrays lighted up the weird shadows of the 'Ghost Camp,' lately throbbing wi' gunshots, oaths, cries and exclamations. Blood had been shed; life had been taken; now all was still and deserted looking.

"Tribe had met tribe in the old, old days, and with spear-thrust, nulla nulla and boomerang, had fought oot their conflicts, waged for pride, ambition or revenge. And always to the bitter end! Then came the white invader, with his iron axes, fine clothes and magical weapons, which slew before they touched. The sheep and cattle, such delicate morsels but which except a price was paid, too often that o' bluid—they dared na' take. Battles then were fought in which their bravest warriors fell; or if by chance they slew stockrider or shepherd, a sair harryin' o' the tribe followed.

"Those days were past; and now, how strange to the elders of the tribe, the white strangers fought amang themselves, wounding, killing, and carrying away captive their brithers in colour and speech. These things were hard to understand. The rays of the lately risen moon lit up the sombre glades of the battlefield as a man and woman rode in frae the forest track, and tied up their horses. They came to the rock where the dead man lay. He had fallen back when Dayrell's bullet pierced his brain, and was lying with upturned face and dreadful staring eyes. The woman knelt by his side, and while she closed them, said, 'Poor old Ned! I never thought to lay you out in a place like this. God's curse on them that drove you to it; but *he's* gone that we have to thank for our ruin; that debt's paid, anyhow! You were always a soft-hearted chap, and none of us, when we were little, had a hard time with you. Not like some brothers, who'd knock about the poor kiddies as if they were dingo pups.'

"'I've nothing to say agen him,' said the man, 'he was always good to me, I'd 'a done anything for him. It's hard to see him here lying dead, and with that infernal prison crop, not even a beard on his face, and what a jolly one he used to have. Here's where the irons hurt him; I expect he tried to break out afore, and they made him work in these.'

"'My God!' cried the woman, passionately; 'don't talk of it any more. I shall scream out directly, and go more off my head than I am now, and that's bad enough. To think of him that used to come out of a morning so fresh and jolly, well dressed, and always with a good horse under him, and couldn't he ride? And now to see him lying here, starved and miserable, like a beggar; it's enough to break a heart of stone—'

"'It's too late now, Kate, too late; but we'd better have taken Tessie's warning and started a square trade, carrying or something, when the digging broke out,' said the man. 'We were all strong and full of go. I could do a man's work, young as I was; the money would have run into our pockets— yes, regular run in—if we'd made a square start and stuck to it. Look at Benson and Warner, see where they are now! They couldn't read and write neither, no more than us. Then there was that infernal Larry Trevenna. Poor Lance! I *was* sorry for him. They did us all the harm in the world; Larry with his gambling ways, and Lance setting you up to think you were good enough to marry him, and putting Dayrell's back up agen the family. Our luck was dead out from start to finish, and now they're all gone except you and me. I'd better set about the grave.'

"'Where'd ye get the pick and shovel?'

"'Some fossicker left them outside his camp. I saw them when I went to the spring for a drink.'

"'For God's sake take them back, no use making more enemies than we can help. There'll be a row if he misses 'em!'

"'All right! I'll drop them as we pass,' said her brother, as he drove the pick into the hard, stony soil.

"The woman took the short mining shovel, and with feverish energy cleared the narrow shaft as often as required. An hour's work showed a cavity of the necessary width and depth, wherein the brother and sister laid the wasted body of the eldest son of the family—once its pride as the best horseman, shearer, reaper, cricketer, stockrider, and all-round athlete of the highland district of New South Wales. The pity of it, when misdirected energies hurry the men along the fiend's highway, leading to a felon's doom, a dishonoured grave!

"The pity of it! The man now lowered into the rude sepulchre, amid that ill-omened, blood-stained wild, might, under happier circumstances, and at a later day, have been receiving the plaudits of his countrymen, the thanks of his Sovereign, as the fearless, resourceful scout, whose watchful eye had saved a squadron, or whose stubborn courage had helped to block an advance until the reinforcement came up.

"It was not to be. Sadly and silently, but for the exclamation of 'Poor Ned! good-bye! God have mercy on your soul!' from the woman, the brother and sister rode away into the night.

"A rude cross had been fashioned and placed in a cairn of stones piled upon the grave. 'The moonbeam strook, and deepest night fell down upon the heath' as the hoofstrokes died away in the distance, deepening the sombre solitude of the spot, which had long worn the appearance of a place accursed of God and man!"

The far back, and by no means busy township of Dumbool was, if not enlivened, aroused from its normal apathy (when a race meeting, or a shearer's carouse was not in full operation), by the return of a party of mounted police. The leading inhabitants, always well informed in such matters, had received notice of them passing through the district, heading towards the border. The township was not so insignificant or the two hotels so unimportant, as not to provide "Our Own Correspondent" of the *Weekly Newsletter*. This gentleman, who was Rabbit Inspector, Acting Clerk of the Bench, Coroner, and Honorary Magistrate, held all the minor appointments, not incompatible with the ends of justice, and the dignity of the Post Office, of which he was the present acting head, the Government Official of the branch being away on leave. He performed these various duties fairly well, delegating the Postal work to the leading storekeeper, and the Bench work to a neighbouring squatter, who, coached by the senior constable, was capable of getting through a committal without blundering. But the work of Special Correspondent was the one which he really enjoyed, and on which he chiefly prided himself.

He had often murmured at the poverty of the journalistic resources of his surroundings, which afforded no field for literary ability. Even when Nature seemed kindly disposed, by reason of abnormal conditions, he was restricted in efforts to improve the occasion by the vigorously expressed local censorship of the pastoralists. Did he draw a harrowing picture of the stricken waste, denuded of pasture, and strewn with dead and dying flocks, and herds, every one was "down on him," as he expressed it, for taking away the character of the district. Did he dilate on the vast prairies waving with luxuriant herbage, after a phenomenal rainfall, he was abused as "inviting every blooming free-selector in the colony to come out and make a chess-board of their runs, directly they had a little grass." There was no pleasing them. Even the editor of the *Weekly Clarion*, mindful of influential subscribers, had admonished him to be careful in good seasons, as well as bad.

He was at his wits' end, between the agricultural Scylla, and the pastoral Charybdis, so to speak. It may be imagined with what gratitude he hailed the "Tragedy of Ghost Camp," as his headline described it, in which he was likely to offend nobody excepting the Police Department, for whose feelings his public had no great consideration.

Extract from the *Weekly Newsletter and Down River Advertiser*.

"It is long since the site of this celebrated locality, once notorious for tribal fights, and dark deeds of revenge, not always stopping at cold-blooded murder, if old tales be true, has resounded with the echo of rifle shots, the oaths of the victors, the groans of the dying! Yet such has lately been the case. But a few days since a deed of blood, of long-delayed vengeance, has been enacted, recalling the more lurid incidents of pioneer days.

"We had received information of the passing of Inspector Francis Dayrell, with a party of picked troopers, on a back track, running parallel to our main stock route. They carried a light camp equipment, not halting at stations or townships and apparently desirous to avoid observation. We have in another place expressed our disapproval of this practice, holding that the ends of justice are better served by forwarding information to the local press. Had that been done in the present case, the fatal finale might have been averted.

"Be that as it may, the *cortège* that was descried approaching our principal street at an early hour this morning, presented a very different appearance from that of the well-accoutred police party that our informant noticed but two days earlier heading for the broken mountainous country at the head of the Wandong Creek. The troopers detailed for this dangerous service were led by that well-known, and, we may say, dreaded police officer, the late Inspector Francis Dayrell, the greatest daredevil, the most determined officer of the Victorian Mounted Police.

"It was quickly noted by a sharp-eyed bushman, in the neighbourhood of Host Parley's well-kept and commodious hotel, which commands the approach to our township from the north-east, that something was wrong with the body of police now approaching the town at a funeral pace.

"The trooper who rode in front led Inspector Dayrell's well-known charger, a matchless hackney, perfect in the *manège* in which all troop horses are trained. The inspector was badly wounded and nearly insensible, from the manner in which he bowed himself on the horse's neck, while he swayed helplessly in the saddle. The second trooper also led a horse on which was a wounded man. Behind rode two men, one evidently so badly hurt, that he sat his horse with difficulty.

"'They've been cut up bad,' said one of the bushmen. 'Let's ride up and meet 'em, Jack!' Two men waiting for the mail mounted their horses, and met the little party; from which, after a word or two with the Sergeant, they came back full speed to the hotel, and thus imparted the melancholy news.

"'Police had a brush with Bradfield's gang from Queensland, as they thought they were going to take. Some other chaps had joined them along with Dick Lawless, and double-banked 'em. Dayrell's killed, and a trooper — they're the two first; Doolan's wounded bad. The Sergeant wants a room to put the dead men in till the Coroner's inquest's held; he'll have 'em buried as soon as it's over.'

"Great excitement was naturally evoked by this statement.

"In a few minutes the police arrived at the Hotel, where they were met by Mr. Clarkson, J.P., who obligingly undertook all necessary arrangements. The Inspector and the dead trooper were laid side by side in the best bedroom, the landlord resenting a suggestion to place the corpses in an outhouse — 'He'd have had the best room in the house if he was alive. He always paid like a prince, and I'm not going to treat him disrespectful now he's been killed in the discharge of his duty. Them as don't care about sleeping there after him and poor Mick Donnelly, may go somewhere else. They'll be buried decent from *my* house, anyway.'

"The Coroner impanelled a jury without unnecessary delay; and after the Sergeant and his men had necessary rest and refreshment, that official elicited evidence which enabled him to record a verdict of 'Wilful murder against Edward James Bradfield and Richard Lawless in the cases of Inspector Francis Dayrell of the Victorian Mounted Police Force, and trooper Michael Joseph Donnelly, then and there lying dead.' This formality concluded, preparations were made for the funeral to take place next morning in the graveyard appertaining to the township, which already held a number of occupants, large in proportion to the population.

"Word had been sent to the neighbouring stations, so that by noon—the hour appointed—nearly as large a concourse as at the annual race meeting had assembled. There being no resident clergyman, the service was read over both men by the Coroner, who, by the way in which he performed the duty, showed that he was not new to this sad ceremony. We have repeatedly urged upon the Government the necessity of providing increased police protection for this important and scantily defended district. May we trust now that local wants will be more promptly attended to.

"The last offices being paid to the dead the surviving troopers rode slowly away leading the spare horses, and bearing the arms and effects of their comrades with them.

"Kate Lawless and her brother had disappeared. Whether they had made for the farthest out settled districts of Queensland, or had found a hiding place nearer home, was not known, though rumours to either effect gained circulation."

"And noo ye hae the haill history o' Frank Dayrell, late Inspector o' the Mounted Police Force o' Victoria, no forgetting the death of Ned Lawless, who died by his hand.

"And, as the sun's low, and we've, I winna say wasted the afternoon—maybe expended wad be a mair wise-like expression—I'll just say good e'en to you, gentlemen, and gae me ways hame. The nicht's for frost, I'm thinkin'," and so saying, the worthy Sergeant declining further refreshment marched off along the meadow.

An early breakfast next morning, in fact, before the frost was off the ground, awaited Mr. Blount. In some inns it would have been a comfortless repast; a half-lighted fire struggling against a pile of damp wood, and producing more smoke than heat; a grumbling man cook, not too clean of aspect, who required to know "why the blank people wanted their grub cooked by candlelight," and so on—"he'd see 'em blanked first, if there was any more of this bloomin' rot." Such reflections the guest has been favoured with, in the "good old days," before the gold had settled down to a reasonable basis of supply and demand, and the labour question—as it did subsequently—had regulated itself. Waiting, too, for half an hour longer than was necessary for your hackney to eat his oats.

Far otherwise was the bounteous, well-served repast which sent forth Blount in fit order and condition to do his journey creditably, or to perform any feats of endurance which the day's work might exact.

Sheila had been up and about long before daylight. She had consulted the favoured guest through his chamber door, as to which of the appetising list of viands he would prefer, and when the adventurous knight sallied forth in full war paint, he found a good fire and a tempting meal awaiting him.

"I tell you what, Sheila," he said, regarding that praiseworthy maiden with an approving smile, "this is all very fine and you ought to get a prize at the next Agricultural Show, for turning out such a breakfast, but how am I to face burnt steak and sodden damper at the diggers' camp to-morrow morning?"

The girl looked at him earnestly for a moment or two without speaking, and then with an air of half warning, half disapproval, said, "Well—if you ask me, sir, the cooking's not the worst of it in those sort of places, and I can't see for my part why a gentleman like you wants going there at all. They're very queer people at the head of the river, and they do say that the less you have to do with them the better."

"But I suppose there *are* all sorts of queer characters in this new country of yours. I didn't come from England to lead a feather-bed life. I've made up my mind to see the bush, the goldfields, and all the wild life I could come across, and I suppose Mr. Little-River-Jack is about the cleverest guide I could have."

"Well—ye—es! he's *clever* enough, but there *are* yarns about him. I don't like to tell all I've heard, because, of course, it mightn't be true. Still, if I were you, sir, I'd keep a sharp look out, and if you spotted anything that didn't look square, make some excuse and clear."

"But, my dear girl, what *is* there to watch? Do he and his friends steal cattle or rob miners of their gold? Any highway business? Why can't you speak out? I see you're anxious lest I should get into a scrape; on account of my innocence, isn't that it? And very kind of you it is. I won't forget it, I promise you."

"I can't say any more," said the girl, evidently confused. "But be a bit careful, for God's sake, and don't take all you're told for gospel;" after which deliverance she left the room abruptly and did not appear when Mr. Blount and his guide, both mounted, were moving off. They were in high spirits, and the cob dancing with eagerness to get away. As they left the main road at an angle, Blount looked back to the hotel towards a window from which the girl was looking out. Her features wore a grave and anxious expression, and she shook her head with an air, as it seemed to him, of disapproval.

This byplay was unobserved by his companion, who was apparently scrutinising with concentrated attention the track on which he had turned.

Throwing off all misgivings, and exhilarated by the loveliness of the weather, which in that locality always succeeds a night of frost, he gave himself up to an unaffected admiration of the woodland scene. The sun now nearly an hour high had dispelled the mists, which lay upon the river meadows, and brought down in glittering drops the frost jewels sparkling on every bush and branch.

The sky of brightest blue was absolutely cloudless, the air keen and bracing; wonderfully dry and stimulating. The grass waved amid their horses' feet. The forest, entirely composed of evergreens, from the tallest eucalypt, a hundred feet to the first branch, to the low-growing banksia, though partly sombre, was yet relieved by an occasional cypress, or sterentia. The view was grand, and apparently illimitable, from the high tableland which they soon reached. Range after range of snow-clad mountains reared their vast forms to the eastward, while beyond them again came into view a new and complete mountain world, in which companies of snow peaks and the shoulders of yet loftier tiers of mountains were distinctly, if faintly, visible. What passes, what fastnesses, what well-nigh undiscoverable hiding-places, Blount thought, might not be available amid these highlands for refugees from justice—for the transaction of secret or illegal practices!

He was aroused from such a reverie by the cheery voice of his companion, who evidently was not minded to enjoy the beauty of the morning, or the mysterious expanse of the landscape in silence. "Great country this, Mr. Blount!" he exclaimed, with patronising appreciation. "Pity we haven't a few more men and women to the square mile. There's work and payin' occupation within sight"—here he waved his hand—"for a hundred years to come, if it was stocked the right way. Good soil, regular rainfall, timber, water no end, a bit coldish in winter; but look at Scotland, and see the men and women it turns out! I'd like to be Governor for ten years. What a place I'd make of it!"

"And what's the reason you people of Australia, natives of the soil, and so on, can't do it for yourselves, without nobles, King or Kaiser—you've none of *them* to blame?"

"Haven't we? We've too many by a dashed sight, and that's the reason we can't get on. They call them Members of Parliament here, and they do nothing but talk, talk, talk."

"Oh! I see; but they're elected by the people, for the people, and so on. The people—you and your friends, that is—must have been fools to elect them. Isn't that so?"

"Of course it is. And this is how it comes; there's always a lot of fellers that like talking better than work. They palaver the real workers, who do all the graft, and carry the load, and once they're in Parliament and get their six pound a week it's good-bye to honest work for the rest of their lives. It's a deal easier to reel out any kind of rot by the yard than it is to make boots and shoes, or do carpentering, or blacksmith's work."

"H—m! should say it was. Never tried either myself; but when they get into Parliament don't they do anything?"

"Well, in a sort of way, but they're dashed slow about it. Half the time, every law has to be altered and patched and undone again. They're in no hurry, bless you!—they're not paid by the job; so the longer they are about it the more pay and 'exes' they rake in."

"What's wrong with the law about this particular neighbourhood?"

"Well, they're allowed to take up too much land for one thing. I wouldn't give more than a hundred acres, if I had my way, to any selector," said this vigorous reformer. "The soil's rich, the rainfall's certain, and the water-supply's everlastin'. What's wanted is labour—men and women, that means. It'll grow anything, and if they'd keep to fruit, root crops, and artificial grasses, they could smother theirselves with produce in a year or two. Irrigate besides. See that race? You can lead water anywhere you like in this district."

"Well, why don't they? One would think they could see the profit in it. Here it is, under their feet."

"It's this way; a man with a couple of thousand acres can keep a flock of sheep. They don't do extra well, but they grow a fleece once a year, and when wool's a decent price the family can live on it—with the help of poultry, eggs and bacon, and chops now and then. It's a poor life, and only just keeps them—hand to mouth, as it were."

"Still, they're independent."

"Oh! independent enough—the ragged girls won't go out to service. The boys loaf about on horseback and smoke half the time. If they had only a hundred acres or so, they couldn't pretend to be squatters. The men would dig more and plough more, the greater part of the area would be cultivated, they could feed their cows in winter (which *is* long and cold in these parts), fatten pigs, have an orchard (look at the apple-trees at the last place we passed), do themselves real well, and have money in the bank as well."

"We must have a republic, and make you first Dictator, I see that. Now, where does this tremendous ravine lead to?"

"It leads through Wild Horse Gully, down to the Dark River—we'd better get off and walk the next mile or two—there's a big climb further on."

"I shouldn't wonder," said the traveller. "How wild horses or any other travel about here, astonishes me. Where do they come from? There were none in Australia when the first people came, I suppose?"

"Not a hoof. They've all been bred up from the stray horses that got away from the stations, long ago. They're in thousands among these mountains. It takes the squatters at the heads of the rivers all their time to keep them under."

"Do they do much harm?"

"Well, yes, a lot. They eat too much grass for one thing, and spoil more than they eat, galloping about. Then they run off the station horses, especially the mares. Once they join the wild mob, they're never seen again. Get shot by mistake, too, now and again."

"Why! do they shoot horses here?"

"Shoot 'em, of course! The hides and hair fetch a fairish price. Some men live by it. They make trap yards, and get as many as a hundred at a time. The squatters shoot them now and again, and pay men to do it."

"It seems a pity. A horse is a fine animal, wild or tame, but I suppose they can't be allowed to over-run the country."

The Wild Horse Gully, down which they were proceeding at a slow and cautious pace, was a tortuous and narrow pathway, hemmed in by rugged precipitous mountain sides. From its nature it was impracticable for wheeled vehicles, but the tracks of horses and cattle were recent and deeply indented. These his companion scrutinised with more than ordinary care. The horse tracks were in nearly all instances those of unshod animals, but as he pointed out, there were two sets of recent imprints on the damp red loam, of which the sharp edges and nail heads told of the blacksmith's shop as plainly as if a printed notice had been nailed to one of the adjacent tree trunks; also that a dozen heavy cattle had gone along in front of them at rather a fast pace. These last had come in on a side track, their sliding trail down the face of the mountain showing plainly how they had arrived, and, as nearly as possible, to the experienced eye of one horseman, at what hour.

The day had been tedious, even monotonous, the pace necessarily slow; the chill air of evening was beginning to be felt, when the bushman, with a sigh of relief, pointed to a thin wreath of smoke. On an open, half-cleared spot, a hut built of horizontal logs was dimly visible; a narrow eager streamlet ran close to the rude dwelling, while at their approach a pair of cattle dogs began to bark as they walked in a menacing manner towards the intruders.

CHAPTER IV

"Down, Jerry! Down, Driver!" said the bushman, "that'll do, you're making row enough to frighten all the cattle in the country." By this time the guardians of the outpost had left off their clamour, and one of them, by jumping up and fawning on Blount, showed that he had gained their friendship. The older dog, not so demonstrative, had stains of blood on his mouth and chest. "Ha! Driver, you old villain, been behind those cattle yesterday? Now lie down, and let's see if we can raise a fire and get some tea under weigh, before the boys come in."

After unsaddling, and turning out their horses, they entered the hut, which, though not differing materially from the bush structures which Blount had already visited, was seen to be neater than usual in the internal arrangements. "Little-River-Jack" proceeded at once to business. By lighting twigs from a store of brush-wood, laid ready for such an emergency, and adding another to the smouldering logs at the back of the huge chimney he secured a cheerful blaze, calculated to warm through his shivering companion, and to provide him speedily with the comforting, universal beverage. Opening a rude locker, he took from it a tin dish containing corned beef and "damper," also a couple of tin plates with knives and forks of democratic appearance, and a butcher's knife which did duty for a carver.

"You see your dinner, Mr. Blount," said he. "I daresay you've got an appetite this cold day; I know I have. Help yourself, the billy's boiling, I'll put in the tea." Suiting the action to the word, he took a handful of tea out of a bag hanging by a nail in the wall, and placing a pannikin of sugar on the table, invited his guest to help himself and fall to.

"It's not quite up to the breakfast we had this morning," he said; "but I've had worse many a time; tucker like this will carry a man a long way when he's on the road or at regular work."

This statement, more or less correct, was confirmed by the performance of both wayfarers, Mr. Blount plying a remarkably good knife and fork, besides disposing of a wedge of damper, and washing the whole down with a couple of pints of hot tea.

The fire was by this time in steady glow. Stretching his legs before it, and indulging in a luxurious smoke, the tourist expressed his opinion that he had known more artistic cookery, but had never enjoyed a meal more.

Mr. John Carter, the while, had washed and replaced the plates and pannikins; also rearranged the beef and bread with a deftness telling of previous experience. This duty concluded, they awaited the return of the gold-diggers.

"They don't come in while there's light to work by," he explained; "the days are that short now, that unless you're at it early and late there ain't much to show for it."

The twilight had faded into all but complete darkness when the dogs growled in a non-committal way, as though merely to indicate human approach without resenting it. "It's my pals comin'," the bushman observed; and, closely following the words, footsteps were heard, and a big, bearded, roughly-dressed man entered the hut. "Hullo! Jack, you're here, and this is the gentleman from England," he continued, fixing a bold, penetrating glance upon Blount. "Glad to see you, sir! This is a rough shop; but we've got fair tucker, and firewood's plenty. We'll soon show you the ins and outs of gold-digging, if that's what you want to see. Jack got you a feed, I expect; fill up the billy, old man, while we get a wash."

Seizing a handful of rough towels, and a bag which hung near the head of the bunk in the corner to the right of the speaker, he went out into the night; while certain splashing noises told that face and hands' cleaning was in progress.

Little more than ten minutes had elapsed, when the speaker, accompanied by three other men, re-entered the hut, and after an informal mention of names to the stranger, sat down to the table, where they went to work at the beef and damper, with strict attention to business. Mr. Blount had an opportunity while they were thus engaged of a complete inspection. Though roughly dressed, there was nothing unpleasing to the educated eye about their appearance.

They wore red or blue woollen shirts, rough tweed or moleskin trousers, and heavy miners' boots. All had beards more or less trimmed, and wore their hair rather short than long.

Three of the party were tall, broad-shouldered, and muscular; the fourth was middle-sized, slight and active-looking. He wore only a fair moustache, and seemed younger than the others. Commencing to make conversation at once, he was evidently regarded as the wit of the party.

"So you're back again, Jack, old man!" he said, addressing the guide with a half-humorous, half-cynical expression. "Goin' to and fro on the earth, seekin' what you might—well, not devour exactly, but pick up in a free and easy, genteel sort o' way, like the old chap we used to be so frightened of when we were kiddies. Don't hear so much about him now, do we? Wonder why? He ain't dead, or played out, what d'ye make of it?"

"You seem to take a lot of interest in him, Dick," said the guide. "Been readin' sermons, or beginnin' to think o' your latter end? Lots of time for that."

"Well, not so much that way, but I'm seriously thinkin' o' clearin' out o' this part o' the country and tryin' another colony. It's too dashed cold and wet here. I'm afraid of my precious health. I hear great talks of this West Australian side—Coolgardie, or something like that—where it never rains, hardly, and they're getting gold in buckets' full."

"You're doin' middlin' well here, Dick," said one of the other men in a dissuasive tone of voice. "The lead's sure to widen out as it gets deeper and junctions with the Lady Caroline. Why don't you have patience, and see it out?"

"Well, haven't I been waitin' and waitin', and now I'm full up; made up my mind to sell out. If any one here will give me twenty notes for my fourth share of the claim after this divide, I'm up to take it."

"I'll buy it," said Mr. Blount impulsively. "I should like to have a turn at real mining, and this seems a fair chance."

"Done with you, sir; we can write out an agreement here now. You'll have a fourth share in the hut and tools, won't he, mates?"

The men nodded assent. "Going cheap, Jack, isn't it?"

"Dirt cheap, and no mistake. Mr. Blount never made a better bargain. I'll cash his cheque on Melbourne, so you can clear to-morrow, Dick, though I think you're a fool for your pains. We'll witness the agreement here, and he can hold your miner's right till he gets a transfer from the Registrar at Bunjil."

This transaction, concluded with ease and celerity, seemed to meet with general approbation. Mr. Blount was charmed with his business insight, which had enabled him to seize upon an opportunity of joining a "bona fide going concern" in regular work.

"How's the 'Lady Julia' been behaving lately?" inquired Jack Carter.

"Well, here's the fortnight's clean up, close on twelve ounces, I should say. Might be better, but it's more than tucker, three ounces a man, say £40 for two weeks' work. The month before it was £60, and of course, there's a chance of a nugget, or a make in the lead, any day!"

"A nugget's a lump of gold, isn't it? What size are they?" queried the new partner.

"Any size from a pound to a hundredweight. A Chinaman turned up one worth £230 just after we came, at Back Creek," answered the big miner; "in old ground, too. Of course, they're not everyday finds. But there's always a chance. That's what makes digging so jolly excitin', a party can always keep themselves if they work steady, and then there's the off-chance of a big slice of luck comin' their way."

"I should think it did,", assented the stranger, heartily. "A free life, perfect independence, healthy occupation. It will suit me down to the ground."

"Early to bed and early to rise is another of the advantages given in with the honest miner's business," said the young man called Dick. "A feller's so jolly tired if he's been amusin' himself with a pick and shovel all day, or even the cradle, that by the time he's had tea, and a smoke, he's glad to get to his bunk for fear he should go to sleep, like a trooper's horse, all standin'. So Mr. Blount had better collar my bunk, which I hereby make over to him, along with my share of the 'Lady Julia' claim and tools, cradle, and one-fourth interest in the perlatial residence, as the auctioneers say. I'll doss near the fire along with Jack. Mr. Blount's got his own blankets, so that'll be all right."

Suiting the action to the word, Dick dragged his blankets and a few articles of attire from the bunk indicated, including a weather-worn leather valise into which he stuffed the smaller matters.

Arranging his blankets near the fire, he made a pillow of the valise, and removing his boots and coat, lit his pipe, and lay down on the earthen floor, pulling the blankets over him, and apparently quite prepared for a sound night's rest. "Good-night all!" were his parting words.

"I'll say good-night, too," said Little-River-Jack, undoing the swag, which he had carried in the front of his saddle during the day's journey, and which seemed chiefly composed of a pair of serviceable blue blankets. "Dick and I'll take the claim by the chimney. I'll put on a back log, to keep us all warm, and do to boil the billy to-morrow morning. So I'll say good-night, Mr. Blount, and wish you luck now, as I'll be off before daylight. I'd not get up, if I was you, it's shivering cold till the sun's up."

The three men who were now Mr. Blount's "mates" (or partners) in the claim lost no time in depositing themselves in their separate sleeping places, removing only the more necessary articles of clothing.

Mr. Blount sat before the fire for half an hour, lost in thought, before arraying himself in a suit of pyjamas, which would have excited the admiration of his companions had they been awake. Their regular breathing, however, denoted that such was not the case, and he, too, after a decent interval, abandoned his unwonted environment for the land of mystery and enchantment which men call sleep.

Next morning the clatter of tin plates, and other accompaniments, upon the literal "board" which stood for the table and all appurtenances, aroused the new partner from a profound slumber.

The dim light of a cloudy dawn was struggling with the smoky flame of a tallow lamp of rude shape. The "billy" full of hot tea had just been placed upon the table by the acting cook, who had previously disposed a tin dish containing fried beef steaks beside it.

Snatching up his towel and sponge bag, the stranger made a rush for the creek bank, where a rude stage permitted him to indulge in a copious sluicing of his head, neck and shoulders.

Ice-cold as was the water, he achieved a glow after a vigorous application of his rough towel, and dressing in haste, was able to dispose of his share of the meal more or less creditably.

With more consideration than might have been expected, the dish of steaks had been put down by the fire and kept warm in his absence.

"I shall not over-sleep myself another morning," he said, apologetically, "but I suppose the long day *did* tire me a bit. It was awfully slow too, stumbling over those rocky tracks. I shall be in better trim shortly."

"Expect you will," said the big digger, "a man's always soft for the first week, specially if he hasn't been used to the life. We'll start for the claim, soon's you're through with breakfast; Jack and Dick's off hours ago. There were cattle to take back, left here for the butcher." He now remembered as in a dream having heard a dog bark, and a whip crack, in the middle of the night, as it seemed to him.

"Early birds," he remarked sententiously; after which, finishing his second pannikin of tea, he expressed himself as ready for the road.

The mists were clearing from the mountain-side, which lay dark and frowning between the little party and the East, but ere long the curving shoulders of the range became irradiated. A roseate glow suffused the pale snow crown, transmuting it gradually into a jewelled coronet, while the mountain flanks became slowly illumined, exhibiting the verdant foot-hills, in clear contrast with the sombre, illimitable forest. As the sun's disc became fully apparent, all Nature seemed to greet with gladness the triumph of the Day-god. The birds chirped and called in the dense underwoods through which the narrow path wound.

Flights of water-fowl high overhead winged their way to distant plains and a milder air. A rock kangaroo, cleared the streamlet with a bound and fled up the hillside like a mountain hare. A cloud of cockatoos flitted ghost-like across the tree-tops, betraying by an occasional harsh cry the fact that a sense of harmony had been omitted, when their delicately white robes were apportioned to them. As the sun gained power and brilliancy, Mr. Blount found the path easy to follow and his spirits began to rise.

"How far to the claim?" he asked.

One of the miners pointed to a hillock of yellow and red earth by the side of which a rude stage had been erected, and a rope wound around, from which depended a raw hide bucket.

Moving up, he was aware of a shaft sunk to a depth of fifty or sixty feet; from appearances, the precious metal had been extracted by rude appliances on the bank of the creek, still running briskly through the little flat.

"I'm the captain of this claim," said the big miner, "elected by a majority of the shareholders, so, till I'm turned out, I'll have all the say." The other diggers nodded. "You're new to the game, mister, so I'll give you the easiest show to begin with. Later on, you can tackle the pick and shovel. We three go below, one at a time, you see how it's done, and be middlin' careful: there's a man's life on the rope every time, and if you let the windlass run away with you, out he goes! Next man in."

Sitting down on the "brace," the miner took hold of the hide rope above his head with both hands, while one of the others at the windlass began to lower him slowly down, a short strong piece of pointed timber, referred to as the "sprag," being inserted into the roller, through which the hide rope ran, in order to check its velocity, and give the man at the windlass control.

Blount looking down, saw him gradually descend, until the bottom of the shaft was reached. The second man was lowered. When the third with his foot in a bight of the rope prepared to descend, he felt a little nervous, which the miner was quick to observe. "Don't be afraid of killin' me, mate! just hold on to the windlass-handle like grim death. It'll come easy after a bit." He laughed as he commenced to descend, saying, "When you hear this tin arrangement clap together, it means 'haul away.'"

Mr. Blount was most careful, and finding that he could manage the windlass easily, with the help of the "sprag" aforesaid, became more confident. The next excitement was when the clapper sounded, and he began to haul up. But the weight below seemed to be too great. The rope refused to draw up the bucket. Then he noticed that the "sprag" was still in the roller.

Smiling at his mistake he took it out, and immediately began to haul up. Though a good pull it was not a difficult task for an athletic young man, in high health and spirits. So he bent his back to the work, and presently the hide bucket, filled with yellow and red clay, came to the surface; this he drew on one side, and tilted over on to the "tip" or "mullock" heap, having to that extent been instructed. Lowering it again he continued the somewhat monotonous work, without cessation, till noon, when a double note on the clapper warned him that his mates desired to revisit upper air. This ascent accomplished safely, the billy was boiled, and dinner, so called, notwithstanding the early hour, was disposed of.

"My word! you're gettin' on fine, mate," said the big miner, "and that reminds me, what are we to call you? You needn't trouble about your real name, if you want to keep it dark. Many a good man's had to do that hereabouts. Anyway, on a goldfield it's no one's business but the owner's, but we must call you somethin'!"

"Call me Jack Blunt. It's near enough for the present."

"All right, Blunt; now you're christened," said the big miner. "Phelim O'Hara's mine, and these other chaps are my brother Pat and George Dixon; we're all natives, only as he's Lancashire by blood we call him 'Lanky' for short; we may's well go down now, and you can do a bit of pick and shovel work for a change."

Mr. Blount considered it to be a change in the fullest sense of the word when he found himself dangling between earth and sky, with his leg in the loop of a rope, having a great inclination to turn round and round, which he combated by thrusting his leg against the side of the shaft. He realised a feeling akin to that of being lowered over a cliff, which he had read of in boyhood, reflecting, too, that he had no more *real* security than a man in that embarrassing position. Still the narrow shaft had an appearance of safety, which in his case prevented vertigo. The pick and shovel work was not hard to comprehend. He did his best, though easily outpaced by his mates.

In a week's time he found himself quite *au fait* at the work, while improving daily in wind and muscle. "Capital training for a boat-race," he said, "only there's no water hereabouts, except this little brook, but we don't seem to be getting rich very fast, do we, George?"

George was sententious. He had been a navvy. The best worker of the party, he was slow of speech, and disinclined to argue on abstract matters.

"Forty or fifty pound a fortnight for four of us ain't so bad," he growled out.

Not only was Mr. Blount himself becoming accustomed to this unfamiliar mode of life, but his cob, though he did not take kindly to the mountaineering work, as we have seen, became familiarised to being turned out with the claim horses and foregathered with them amicably. However, one afternoon, when they were brought in for a ride, as it was too wet to work, the cob, now fat and frolicsome, was reported missing.

His master was much annoyed and alarmed at this state of affairs. However, Phelim O'Hara volunteered to stay at home, and moreover to lend him his horse on which to search for the defaulter. Mr. Blount eagerly accepted the offer, and lost no time in going off to hunt for "John Gilpin" as the cob was facetiously named. Unlike a bushman, he rode hither and thither, not troubling himself about tracks, or keeping a course in any given direction.

The consequence was that towards nightfall he found himself several miles from camp, or indeed any landmark which he had passed in the early part of the day. He was, however, sensible enough to follow a creek, which eventually led him to the river; between which and the hilly country he had been traversing, he saw a piece of level country on which several wild horses were grazing.

He was attracted by the appearance of a handsome grey stallion, who appeared to be the leader and, so to speak, commander of the "manada," around which he trotted or galloped, driving in the mares and colts, and indeed, with open mouth and threatening heels, forcing them to keep within bounds.

Suddenly there was the sound of a rifle shot from the side of the forest nearest to the troop. The leader gave a sudden bound forward, then dropped on his haunches. He made several unavailing attempts to rise.

Struck in the region of the spine, he was evidently paralysed. He reared himself on his fore-legs but was unable to move forward, more than once neighing piteously. The mares and foals had fled like a herd of deer at the sound of the gun, but following the habit of these steeds of the mountain parks, though "wild as the wild deer, and untamed," came timidly back, and stood near their lord and master. As the hinds and fawns are unwilling to leave the death-stricken stag, so these descendants of man's noblest servant refused to quit the spot where the monarch of their kingdom lies wounded to the death. They circled around him until another shot from the invisible marksman pealed forth, and a fine black mare, with a young foal, dropped dead near the wounded sire.

They scattered afresh at this new stroke of fate; Mr. Blount wondering much whether they would return. But the grey whinnied from time to time, making frantic efforts to reach the dead mare—all vainly. He swung round on his fore-legs but was unable to do more.

His struggles became tremendous, his agonised distress piteous to behold. Bathed in sweat and foam he seemed ready to succumb with terror and exhaustion, as he sunk sideways till his head, lying prone upon the grass, nearly touched that of his dead mate. Then again the deadly weapon rang out, and another victim, this time a frolicsome chestnut filly, fell to the unerring aim of the marksman, as before, invisible. Mr. Blount felt a disinclination to move from his position, not knowing exactly how near he might be to the concealed hunter's line of fire.

At length, as nearly all the "mob" were down, a tall man in a Norfolk jacket of tweed with knickerbockers and gaiters to match, walked forth from behind an immense eucalyptus. He was plainly dressed, though Mr. Blount discerned a distinction in his air and bearing which convinced him that the man was no stockrider. He carried a Winchester magazine rifle, from which he sent a bullet into the head of the wounded horse, thus putting an end to his sufferings, and leaving him lying dead amid the females of his court.

The accost of the hunter was not markedly cordial as Mr. Blount stated that it was a lovely morning, and that the scene before him reminded him of a battlefield.

"Indeed!" he replied, with a certain amount of hauteur. "May I ask the favour of your name? and also what you are doing on this part of my run?"

"Your run! I was led to believe that I was on the area of Crown land, open, as such, to all travelling on lawful business. My name is Blount. May I ask in return for yours? As to my business, I am at present looking for a strayed horse."

"Was he a bay cob with a short tail and hogged mane, a letter and number on the near shoulder?"

"That is his exact description."

"Then he is safe," said the stranger. "He had joined the station horses and was run in with them this morning. He is now in my paddock, as I assumed that he had strayed from his owner, and was making his way down to the river. My name is Edward Bruce of Marondah, which is not more than fifteen miles distant. You had better come home with me; I shall be happy to put you up for the night, and you can take your horse back in the morning."

The day was drawing to a close. It was a long way to the claim, and Blount was by no means sure that he could find his way back or even pick up his own tracks.

"I think," he replied, "that I can't do better than accept your offer, for which I feel most grateful."

"There is no real obligation, believe me," said Mr. Bruce.

"But where is your horse?" said Blount, looking at the stranger's serviceable leggings.

"Not far, you may be sure, and in safe keeping; my gillie is pretty handy." Putting two fingers to his mouth, he gave the drover's whistle, with such volume and shrillness that it might have been heard at a considerable distance. After a short interval, a high wailing sort of cry (the Australian aboriginal call) came floating through the forest, and a black boy galloped up, riding one horse, and leading another of such superior shape and action that Blount thought it criminal to run the risk of injuring him in such rough country.

The black boy led the horse to his master, but did not offer to dismount, or hold the stirrup, as an English groom would have done. Nor did such attention appear necessary, as Mr. Bruce mounted with alacrity, and motioning the boy to ride ahead followed at a brisk trot through the forest and along the rocky cattle tracks, which, though occasionally running in different directions, converged, and appeared to lead almost due south. All the while, the son of the forest sitting loose-reined and carelessly on his horse, never deviated apparently from his course, or was in doubt for a moment.

In less than two hours, when the light was becoming uncertain, and the chill evening air of these Australian highlands apparent, a chorus of baying dogs of all ages, sizes and descriptions announced the vicinity of the homestead. At the same time, the winding course of a full fed mountain stream was revealed.

On a promontory which seemed to have dissociated itself from the forest glades, and been arrested just above the broad river meadow, stood a roomy bungalow protected by wide verandahs from sun and storm.

"This is Marondah!" said Mr. Bruce, not without a certain air of dignity—"allow me to welcome you to my home." A black girl came running up at the moment, who showed her enviably white and regular teeth in a smile of greeting, as in a matter-of-fact way she unstrapped the guest's valise, and led off his horse.

"You put 'em yarraman longa stable," commanded the squatter—for such he was. "Your horse will be all right. Polly is as good a stable hand as Paddy—a turn better, I sometimes think. She's a clever 'gin' all round. Ah! I see Mrs. Bruce."

As they walked forward, a lady came through the garden gate, and met them—receiving the guest with cordiality—then turning to her husband.

"You're rather late, Ned! What kept you? I'm always nervous when you're out at that end of the run!"

"Well, if you must know, I found the grey horse's mob, which I've been tracking for some time—and got them all—a real bit of luck. Then I fell in with Mr. Blount, who was looking for that smart cob that came in with our horses this morning. Luckily for him, as it turns out."

"So it was. Did you shoot the poor things? I always feel so sorry for them."

"Of course I did; they're more trouble than all the other 'brumbies' on the run, galloping about, smashing fences, destroying dams, and wasting grass, for the use of which I pay the Crown rent."

"Yes, a farthing an acre!" laughed the lady. "All the same, it's very cruel—don't you think so, Mr. Blount? What would they say in England of such barbarous work?"

"It would raise a scandal, Mrs. Bruce; but everything depends on the value of the animal, apart from the sentiment."

Thus conversing, they walked through the garden, which was encompassed by an orchard of venerable age. It stretched to the river bank, along which a line of magnificent willows partly over-arched the stream with graceful, trailing foliage, while the interlaced roots performed valuable service in supporting the banks in time of flood.

Passing along the broad verandah, vine and trailer-festooned, they entered a hall, of which the door seemed permanently open.

The walls were garnished with whips, guns on racks (where Mr. Bruce carefully placed his redoubtable Winchester), the great wings of the mountain eagle, the scarlet and jet tail-feathers of the black macaw, and the sulphur-coloured crests of his white relative. These, and other curios of the Waste, relieved the apartment of any appearance of bareness, while avoiding incongruity of ornamentation. Passing into a large, comfortably-furnished room, where preparations for the evening meal were in evidence, the host pointed to a spirit-stand on the sideboard, and suggesting that a tot of whisky would not be inappropriate after a long day, invited his guest to join him. This offer Mr. Blount frankly accepted, as, besides being tired with a long, dragging ride, he felt nearly as cold as if he had been deer-shooting in the Scottish Highlands, instead of this southern mountain land.

He had donned the riding-suit in which he had arrived at Bunjil, and had also packed necessaries of travel in his valise, in case he might have to stay a day at a decent house. This sensible precaution (never needless in the wildest solitudes of Australia) now stood him in good stead. And he felt truly thankful, after being ushered into a comfortable bedroom, that he had resisted the temptation to start off without them. He was enabled, therefore, to issue forth reasonably fitted for the society of ladies, and the enjoyment of the hospitality of the period. So that, when shown into another room smaller than the first he had entered, but more ornate as to furniture, he felt comparatively at ease, notwithstanding the roughness of his late surroundings.

Mrs. Bruce was already there, and, rising from a sofa, said—

"Allow me, Mr. Blount, to introduce you to my sister Imogen."

A tall girl had at this moment arisen, not previously referred to by his host or the lady of the house.

It was not an introduction—it was a revelation, as Blount subsequently described the interview. Mrs. Bruce was a handsome woman, tall and stately, as are many Australians, possessing, withal, fine natural manners improved by travel, and she might reasonably have been expected to possess a good-looking sister. For so much Blount stood prepared. But this divinity of the waste—this Venus Anadyomene—was above and beyond all expectation, all imagination or conception. He gazed at her, as he confessed to himself, with an expression of unconventional surprise; for Imogen Carrisforth was, indeed, a girl that no man with the faintest *soupçon* of taste or sentiment could behold without admiration.

Mrs. Bruce was dark-haired, with fine eyes to match, distinctly aristocratic as to air and carriage; her sister was fair, with abundant nut-brown hair shot with warmer hues, which shone goldenly as the lamplight fell across it. It was gathered in masses above her forehead and around her proudly-poised head, as she smiled a welcome to the stranger with the hospitably frank accost which greets the guest so invariably in an Australian country home. While looking into the depths of her brilliant hazel eyes, Blount almost murmured "O, Dea certe!" while doubting if he had ever before beheld so lovely a creature.

Mrs. Bruce attributed his evident surprise to the fact of his not having been informed of the fact of a second lady being at the house. "Ned ought to have told you," she said, "that my sister was staying with us. She has just come from town, where she has been at school. She is so tall that really it seemed absurd to keep her there any longer."

"You forget that I am eighteen," said the young lady under observation. "My education should be finished now, if ever."

"Indeed, I'm afraid you won't learn much more," said her brother-in-law, paternally, "though I'm not sure that another year under Miss Charters would not have been as well."

"Oh! but I *did* pine so for the fresh air of the bush—the rides and drives and everything. I can't bear a town life, and was growing low-spirited."

"How about the opera, balls, the Cup Day itself, at your age too?" interposed Blount.

"All very well in their way. But society in town seems one unmeaning round with the same people you meet always. One gets dead tired of it all. I must have gipsy blood in me, I think, for the gay greenwood has a fascination, which I feel, but can't explain."

During dinner, Blount found Mrs. Bruce most agreeable, and, indeed, entertaining. He learned something too about the neighbours, none of whom were nearer than ten miles. Some, indeed, much farther off. It was also explained to him that the region of the Upper Sturt was not all rock and forest, swamp and scrub, but that there were rich tablelands at "the back," which might be north or north-east. Also that the country became more open "down the river," as well as, in a sense, more civilised, "though we don't call ourselves *very* barbarous," she added, with a smile.

"Barbarous, indeed!" repeated the guest, with well-acted indignation. "You seem to me to have all the accessories, and more of them than we in that old-fashioned country called England. Here you have books, papers, all the comforts and many of the luxuries of the Old Land, besides a free, unfettered existence, independence, and no earthly annoyance or danger."

"I am not so sure about the last items," said Mrs. Bruce. "Ned has been worrying himself lately about a gang of men who call themselves miners, but are more than suspected to be cattle-stealers. He has missed valuable animals lately."

"You surprise me!" replied Blount, with a shocked expression. "The bush people whom I have come across have appeared to be such simple, hard-working fellows. But surely Mr. Bruce doesn't apprehend danger from gold-diggers or drovers? They are so civil and well-mannered too."

"Their manners are good enough; better, people tell us, than those of the same class at home. But they are not always to be trusted, and are revengeful when thwarted in their bad practices. Edward has more than once been warned to be more careful about riding alone near their haunts in the ranges, though he always goes armed."

"But surely none of the 'mountain men,' as I have heard them called, would lie in wait for Mr. Bruce, or any other proprietor, even if he was unpopular, which I feel certain Mr. Bruce is not?"

"There is no saying. Blood has been shed in these mountains before now, peaceful as they appear. However, Edward never stirs out in that direction without his rifle, and you have seen him shoot. He has no fear, but I cannot feel free from anxiety myself. And now I think we must go into the drawing-room, or wrap up and sit in the verandah while you men smoke; what do you say, Imogen?"

"I vote for the verandah. There's no wind, and the moon is nearly full. It's tolerably cool; but dry cold never hurts any one. Indeed, it's said to be the new cure for chest ailment at Davos Platz, isn't it, Edward?"

"They say so. Doctors are always changing their theories. I prefer a climate that's moderately cosy myself. But we must have our smoke, and you girls can talk to us, if you keep to low tones and modulated expressions."

Blount would have vowed to renounce tobacco for the rest of his natural life if but Miss Imogen would sit by him. The moon had risen, flooding the dark woods and river pools with silver radiance. Could they but continue to listen dreamily to the rhythmic murmur of the stream, the softly-sighing, complaining sound of the trailing willows as from time to time the river current lifted them—what had life to compare with such sensations? However, this idyllic joy was in its nature fleeting, as it became apparent that the frosty air "was really too keen for reasonable people who had colds to consider and babies." So Mrs. Bruce, thus remonstrating, arose, and with two words, "Come, Imogen!" made for one of the French windows which opened from the drawing-room to the verandah. When they entered that comfortable, well-furnished apartment—a handsome Blüthner piano stood open, with music conveniently close—Mr. Bruce quasi-paternally ordered Imogen to sing, in order that he might judge what progress she had made during the half year.

So they had a song, another, several indeed to finish up with. Mr. Blount admitted a slight knowledge of music, and even took a creditable second in one of Miss Carrisforth's songs. The night wore on, until just before ten o'clock, a neat maid brought in a tray with glasses, and the wherewithal to fill the same. The ladies declining refreshment, said good-night, and left Mr.

Bruce and his guest to have their final smoke, hoping that they would not sit up too late, as they must feel tired after their long day's ride.

The night was glorious, the moon, nearly at its full, had floated into the mid-heaven. The cloudless, dark blue sky seemed to be illumined with star clusters and planets of greater lustre than in ordinary seasons. As they smoked silently, Blount listening to the river gurgling and rippling over its pebbly shallows, the sharp contrast of his surroundings with those he had so lately quitted, indeed even with those during the penultimate sojourn at Bunjil, struck him so forcibly that he could hardly repress a smile.

However he merely remarked—"Australia is certainly a land of wonders—my friends in England will not believe half my adventures when I tell them."

"I can quite understand that," replied his host. "When I returned to my native place, after ten years' absence, mine showed signs of utter disbelief in my smaller experiences, while hazardous tales were swallowed without hesitation."

Mr. Blount rose early and was rewarded by a view of the dawnlight suffusing the eastern horizon with pale opaline tints, gradually increasing in richness and variety of colouring. Roseate golden clouds were marshalled around the summit of the snow-crowned alp, and even the darksome forest aisles responded to the divine informing waves of light and life.

He was aroused from reverie as he gazed upon the wondrous apparition by resounding whips and the roll of hoofs, as the station horses were being run into the yard. The cob was easily distinguished by his cropped tail and mane, while, refreshed by rest and freedom, he galloped and kicked up his heels, as if he had been reared in the bush, instead of in a suburban paddock. Mr. Blount also witnessed his being caught and conveyed to the stable, in company with Mr. Bruce's favourite hackney, and another distinguished-looking animal. With respect to the last-named, Paddy said that one "belong'n Miss Immie," volunteering further information to this effect.

"My word! that one missy ride fustrate." Storing this encomium in his mind, Mr. Blount repaired to his apartment, where he made all ready for departure, resolving not to remain longer away from his associates in the "Lady Julia," however great the temptation.

This came at breakfast time, when Mrs. Bruce invited him to stay a few days, when they would show him their best bits of scenery and otherwise try to amuse him. There was a muster of fat cattle coming on, which was always held to be an interesting spectacle to visitors from the other side of the world. Mr. Bruce was convinced that he would acquire more colonial experience in a week at this particular time, than half a year would show him at a different season. A few neighbours would come over—very decent fellows, and fair specimens of Australian country gentlemen. It would be a regular "house-party," as they say in England. The opportunity should not be lost.

Miss Imogen did not join in the endeavour to tempt Mr. Blount from the path of duty, but she looked as if such a deflection from the narrow way would meet with her approval. After his very courteous, but distinct expression of regret, that he was compelled by a business engagement to decline—with how much reluctance, he could hardly say—their most kind and flattering invitation, the request was not pressed, and the remainder of the breakfast passed off in a lively interchange of the pleasantries proper to the occasion.

"We are going to speed the parting guest, if he will not honour our abode any longer," said Mrs. Bruce, playfully; "but we must do it after our own fashion. My husband, Imogen and I, will ride with you for part of the way—indeed nearly as far as where you met Ned yesterday, if you don't mind?"

"Mind," replied the guest, with a look of surprised gratitude, which caused Miss Imogen to smile and blush. "Nothing could possibly give me greater pleasure."

"So that's settled," said Bruce. "I'll order the horses round; we'll take Paddy with us, who may as well lead your cob till we part company, and I'll mount you on one of the best hacks in this district, or any other. It will save your horse, and as you're likely to have a long day that's a consideration."

"How you are adding to my load of obligation; I shall never be able to repay half the debt."

"Time enough when we meet again," said the host, "but we've none to spare at present. So, Imogen, ten minutes and no more to put on your habit."

"Five will do," said the girl, as she laughingly ran out of the room, to reappear gloved, hatted, and turned out in a most accurately-fitting habit as the horses were led up.

Her brother-in-law put his hand under her dainty foot, and lifted her lightly into the saddle, while the bright chestnut mare sidled, and arched her neck, as she felt the lightest of hands on her bridle rein. Mr. Bruce guaranteed that the hunter-looking bay detailed for his guest's use was "prompt in his paces, cool and bold" like Bevis, upon whom the spectre knight's night-ride had such an unfortunate effect, while he himself mounted the favourite steed which his guest had remarked at their first meeting, saying: "You don't often see a better-looking lot together; as good, too, as they are good-looking." Mr. Blount was convinced of the justice of this valuation, and thought that the statement might even be applied to the riders. Paddy, on a veteran stock horse, brought up the rear leading the cob, whose short tail and hogged mane excited Polly's unmeasured ridicule: "Mine thinkit, that one pfeller brother belongin' to pig," and seized with the comicality of the idea, she exploded in fits of laughter, as casting lingering looks of regret at the receding cavalcade, she walked soberly back to the huts.

"These two horses are the fast walkers of the party, Mr. Blount," began the fair Imogen, as the clever hackney she rode started off at so fast a pace as to incur the suspicion of ambling. "Ned and his henchman, Paddy, will go rambling ahead or on a parallel, looking for strange tracks, denoting trespassers on the run, strayed cattle, indeed found sometimes before they are lost, that is by the lawful owners. The life of the owner of a cattle station is often 'not a happy one.' It is surprising how many kinds of annoyances, risks and anxieties, he may suffer from."

"Mr. Bruce doesn't look as if he suffered from any of the ills of life," said Blount, gazing at his fair companion, as who should say, "How *could* any man be unhappy who has such a charming sister-in-law, not to mention a delightful wife and a nice baby?" However he did not wish for a catalogue of his host's annoyances. He wanted to hear his companion's appreciation of the grand scheme of colour, tone, light and shadow, just opening out before them, as the "glorious sun uprist" amid clouds which had recently rolled away, leaving full in view the forest-clothed uplands, the silent gorges, and the glittering summit of the majestic alp.

Right joyous are the pastimes connected with horse and hound in the older land whence our fathers came, amid the wide pastures, the hedge-bordered fields of green England.

With the hog-spear and rifle on the dusty plains and sudden appearing nullahs of Hindostan, Arab and Waler, by riders of world wide fame, are hard pressed in rivalry. In equestrian tournaments, in the polo gymkhana, and other military contests, there are trials of skill and horsemanship, with a suspicion of danger, to stir a man's blood. But a gallop through the glades of an Australian forest, in the autumnal season of the year, or even in the so-called mid-winter under the cloudless skies and glowing sun of the southern hemisphere, yields to no sport on earth, in keenness of enjoyment or the excitement generated by the pride of horsemanship.

When the company is illumined by a suitable proportion of dames and demoiselles, right royally mounted, and practised in the *manège*, the combination is perfect.

CHAPTER V

And, in the joyous days of youth, the glorious, the immortal, the true, the ever-adorable deity of the soul's childhood, unheeding, careless of the future, thinking, like charity, no evil, revelling in the purely sensuous enjoyment of the fair present, which of the so-called pleasures of the future can claim equality of richness or flavour, with those of that unsurpassable period of the mysterious human pageant! "Carpe Diem!" oh! fortunate heir of life's richest treasure-house, is the true, the only true philosophy. Enjoy, while the pulse is high, the vigour of manhood untouched by Time, the spirit unsaddened by distrust of the future.

For you, glows that cloudless azure; for you the streams murmur, the breezes sigh, the good horse bounds freely over the elastic sward; for you shine the eyes of the beauteous maiden with a fore-taste of the divine dream of love. Thank the kind gods, that have provided so bounteous a feast of soul and sense! Oh! happy thou, that art bidden to such a banquet of the immortals; quaff the ambrosia, while the light still glows on Olympus, and Nemesis is as yet an unimagined terror.

In the days which were to come, in the destiny which the Fates were even then weaving for him, Valentine Blount told himself that never in his whole life had so many conditions of perfect enjoyment been combined as in that memorable riding party.

The sun rays prophetic of an early summer, for which the men of a thousand shearing sheds were even now mustering, were warm, yet tempered by the altitude of the region and the proximity of the snow fields. All nature seemed to recognise the voice of spring. The birds came forth from their leafy coverts, their wild but not unmusical notes sounding strangely unfamiliar to the English stranger. An occasional kangaroo dashed across their path, flying with tremendous bounds to its home on the mountain side. A lot of half-wild cattle stood gazing for a few moments, then "cleared," as Miss Imogen expressed it, for more secluded regions.

"I wonder if I could 'wheel' them," she said, as her bright glance followed the receding drove; "I see Ned and Paddy on the other wing; Mr. Blount, you can follow, but don't pass me, whatever you do;" and in spite of Mrs. Bruce's prudential "Oh! Imogen, don't be rash!" away went the wilful damsel, through the thickening timber, at a pace with which the visitor, excellently mounted as he was, on a trained stock-horse, found it no easy task to keep up. Directly this enterprising movement on the part of the young lady was observed by the watchful Paddy, he called to Mr. Bruce, "Miss Immy wheel 'em, my word. Marmy! you man'em this one piccanniny yarraman, me 'back up.'" Paddy's old stock horse dashed off at speed, little inferior to that of the young lady's thoroughbred, and appeared on the "off side wing" just as the fair Diana had wheeled (or turned) the leaders to the right. Paddy riding up to them on the left and menacing with his stockwhip, caused them to turn towards Imogen. This manœuvre persevered with, was finally crowned with success; inasmuch as the two protagonists, working together and causing the drove to "ring" or keep moving in a circle, finally persuaded them to stop and be examined, when with heaving flanks they bore testimony to the severity of the pace.

Mrs. Bruce, with instinctive knowledge of the points of the situation, had kept quietly behind her guest, who so far from passing his fair pilot, found that it gave him enough to do to keep sight of her.

He did service however, if unconsciously, by keeping at a certain distance behind Imogen, which prevented the cattle from "breaking" or running back behind her. Mrs. Bruce had ridden quietly behind the rear guard, or "tail" (as provincially expressed), and as Mr. Bruce, though hampered with the cob, which he had caught and led along, kept his place between Mrs. Bruce and Paddy, the disposition was theoretically perfect, also successful, which in battles as well as in the lesser pursuits of the world is *the* great matter, after all.

"Upon my word, Imogen!" said Mr. Bruce, "you have given us a pretty gallop, and as these bullocks are fat, it can't have done them much good. However," riding round as he spoke, "it gives me a chance to look through them, and, Hulloa! By Jove! it's as well I came here to-day, somebody has put a fresh brand on that black snail-horned bullock, J. C. just over the E. H. B.; I never sold that beast, I swear! And who the dickens has put those two letters on? Been done in a pen. You can see it's put on from above."

"Me see um fresh brand on one feller cow," stated Paddy, with gravity and deliberation; "me thinkum might 'duff' bullock alonga Wild Horse Gully, me seeum track shod horse that one day marmy shootem brumbie."

"All right, Paddy," said his master, "you lookem out track nother one day."

"My word!" replied Paddy, "me track um up jolly quick."

Mr. Bruce seemed disconcerted by the discovery just made. It was not unimportant. He had suspected that he was losing cattle at this "end of the run," among the ranges and broken country. He had not too good an opinion of the honesty of the small parties of miners who worked the gullies and creeks which led to the river. He supposed that they got a beast now and then, but was loath to believe that there was any organised system of plunder. Now, it was as plain as print that cattle were yarded in small numbers and branded, before they were delivered to the buyers, whoever they were. How many had been taken he could hardly venture to guess at. Cattle being worth from eight to twelve pounds a head, it would not take so many to be worth a thousand pounds. It made him look grave, as he said—

"I'm afraid, after this pleasant ride of ours, that it's time for these ladies to get home. It will be past lunch-time when they sight Marondah, and Mrs. Bruce has family responsibilities, you know. However, I'll send Paddy on with you till he puts you on a track which will lead to your destination."

Mr. Blount was profuse in thanks, and exhausted himself in statements that he had never enjoyed himself so much in his life, and had a glorious gallop into the bargain; that it had given him quite a new idea of Australia, that he had been slow to believe the romantic tales he had heard about Australian bush-riders and their cross-country work. He was now in a position to confirm any such statement made, and to declare that Australian ladies, in science, coolness and courage, were equal to any horsewomen in any country in the world. He should never forget the hospitality he had received, nor the lessons in bushmanship. He trusted to revisit Marondah again before long, when he might, perhaps, be permitted to taste a more leisurely enjoyment of their fascinating country life.

Dismounting, he took leave of the ladies, assuring Mrs. Bruce that he should never forget her kindness and that of Mr. Bruce. If he was less diffuse in his explanations to Miss Imogen, it may have been that there was a warmth of his final hand-clasp, or an expression as their eyes met, before she turned her horse's head and rejoined her friends, which was comparatively satisfactory.

The return stage was short, as Blount did not desire to take the hawk-eyed aboriginal too near the claim, much less within tracking distance of the stockyard. The fresh tracks of the unwilling cattle, forced into a strange and small enclosure, would be like a placard in large letters to the wildwood scout. Hence, as soon as he had land-marks to guide him, he dismissed his Hiberno-Australian attendant, who handed over the cob and departed with a cheerful countenance and a couple of half-crowns.

Left to himself, Mr. Blount rode slowly and heedfully along what he conceived to be the way to the claim, much exercised in his mind as to his line of conduct.

Putting together various incidents and unconsidered trifles, the conviction flashed across his mind that he had been involuntarily an associate of cattle-stealers, and it might well be believed an accomplice.

What position would be his if the whole gang were arrested, and he himself included in the capture? Could it be, during that ride with Little-River-Jack, that he had assisted to drive certain fat cattle afterwards sworn to be the property of Mr. Bruce of Marondah, and bearing his well-known brand "E. H. B."? Could he deny that he had heard cattle put into the stockyard near the "Lady Julia" claim late in the evening, by John Carter (*alias* "Little-River-Jack"), and taken away before daylight?

He had received his share of the money for which the gold won in the claim where he had worked was sold, or *said to be sold*. How could he prove that it was not a part of the price of the stolen cattle? And so on. He felt like many another man innocent of evil, or thought of evil, that, with absurd credulity, and want of reasonable prudence, he had, to a certain degree, enmeshed himself—might, indeed, find it difficult, if not impossible, to get free from the consequences of a false accusation.

Perhaps it might have been his duty, in the interests of justice, to have acquainted Mr. Bruce with the circumstances of his sojourn at the claim with the O'Haras and Dixon (otherwise Lanky); also of the suspicious cattle-dealing. This would have simply amounted to "giving away" the men whose bread he was eating, and who were, however unfortunate the position, his "mates" and comrades. Mr. Bruce would, naturally, lose no time in setting the police to work. Then, Little-River-Jack had certainly saved his life on the "Razor-Back" ridge; another second or two and the cob with his rider would have been lying among the rocks below. One such accident *did* happen there, when man and horse went over, and were found dead and mangled. As for the two O'Haras and George Dixon, he had no sort of doubt now of their being mixed up with the taking of Mr. Bruce's cattle—possibly of those of other squatters in his neighbourhood. Of the men who brought the cattle to the yard, he, of course, had no knowledge, and could have none. In the half-darkness of the winter dawn he could only dimly discern a couple of horsemen, one of whom appeared to ride on with Jack Carter, the other returning.

He was glad now that he had not seen them near enough for identification. He was close to the claim now, having hit upon the track, which he remembered was only a few miles distant.

What was he to say to his late companions, and what would be their feelings towards him, if they heard of the police being after them so soon after his trip down the river? Would they be persuaded that he had not betrayed, or at any rate attracted suspicion towards them, which came to the same thing?

He was in their power, he could not but feel that. What chance could he have against three determined men, with perhaps as many more who might be members of the outside gang, the men who were heard, but not seen, for now he remembered to have heard the lowing of driven cattle more than once, and the guarded voices of drovers. There was, of course only one thing to do. He must face the position squarely and tell the truth, whatever might be the consequences. He would warn them that Mr. Bruce suspected the miners in the locality of being in league with cattle-stealers, who were selling his fat cattle to the butchers on the smaller diggings, of which there were not a few between the heads of the rivers and the foothills of the mountain range. They knew Mr. Bruce, a determined, fearless man, who would show them no mercy. They had better "clear," to use one of their own expressions, before the pursuit was too hot.

Revolving these thoughts in his mind, he rode briskly on. He had remounted the cob, now very fresh, and led the borrowed horse, who, as he thought, deserved all reasonable consideration. When within half a mile of the camp he saw a man walking along the track towards him. It was Phelim O'Hara, the big miner, whom he had always admired as a fine specimen of an Australian. He was a good-natured giant, possessing also a large share of the rollicking, reckless humour which is the heritage of the Milesian Celt. Phelim was a native-born Australian, however, and on occasion could be sufficiently stern, not to say savage. Now he did not look so pleasant as usual.

"Safe home, Mr. Blount," he said. "I see you've found that cob of yours, bad cess to him! I've lost a day through him, and maybe more than that. But I'm dealin' with a gentleman, lucky for all consarned."

"I hope so, Phelim," said the Englishman; "but what's the matter, the camp seems deserted?"

"The meaning's this, Mr. Blount." Here his voice became rough, if not menacing. "The police are after us. There's some yarn got up about Little-River-Jack and us duffing cattle and selling them on the small diggings. Pat and Lanky have cleared. I stayed behind to get this horse of mine and give you the office. There's some says you gave us away to Mr. Bruce, and we know what *he* is when he thinks he's being robbed."

"I've heard your story, Phelim, now for mine. I met Mr. Bruce, who'd been shooting wild horses. He asked me what I was doing *on his run*—he spoke rather shortly. I told him I was looking for my cob, and that I believed it was Crown land, open to all. He then asked me to describe the cob, and telling me it was in his paddock, invited me to stay at Marondah all night, where I was most hospitably treated. He proposed to ride part of the way back with me, and for Mrs. Bruce and his sister-in-law to accompany us."

"That's Miss Imogen," said O'Hara. "Isn't she the beauty of the world? And ride! There isn't a stockrider from this to Omeo that she couldn't lose in mountain country. Mrs. Bruce rides well too, I'm told."

"Yes, indeed; we rounded up a mob of cattle. Miss Imogen 'wheeled' them at the start. Black Paddy, who had been brought to lead the cob, was on the other wing. After that they began to 'ring,' and stopped. Then Mr. Bruce, looking through them, unfortunately saw one of the 'E. H. B.' bullocks with a strange brand newly put on. 'That bullock's been yarded,' he said, 'and the brand "J. C." has been put on in a crush.' I said nothing. Paddy came with me as far as the cattle track, by the creek that leads to the claim. I remembered that. Then he gave me the cob, and I came on. Now you have the whole story. I did not say where I had come from, nor did Mr. Bruce question me. Of course I put two and two together about the fat cattle. But I said nothing. I have eaten your salt, and Little-River-Jack certainly saved my life."

"Then you didn't give us away," said O'Hara, "or say where we was camped, or tell our names? O'Hara's not a good one, more's the pity," and here the big mountaineer looked regretful, even repentant over the past.

"No! not by a word. As luck would have it, Mr. Bruce did not ask me where or with whom I had been living."

"And what brought you back here? Wouldn't it have been easy enough to clear away down the river, and get shut of us, for good and all?"

"Easy enough, and to have gone down river by steamer. But I wanted to warn you in time. I knew Mr. Bruce suspected that there were diggers hereabouts that knew about the fat cattle he missed. So I came to give you fair warning. Where are the others?"

"They've cleared out. I don't think they'll be seen in a hurry, this side anyhow. They've packed all they wanted, and sent word to some of their pals to come and collar the rest. They can't be pulled for that. There's a few ounces of gold coming to you, and the 'clean up' was the best we've had. Here it is." And suiting the action to the word, he pulled out from a leather pouch a wash-leather bag which, for its size, felt heavy.

"Keep it, Phelim, I won't take a penny of it. I learned a good deal while I was with you, and shall always be pleased to think that I worked with *men*, and could hold my own among them."

"You're a gentleman, sir, and we'll always uphold you as one, no matter what happens to us. We're not bad chaps in our way, though things has gone against us. What'll you do now? Camp here to-night? No? Then I'll ride with you past 'Razor Back'; you'll have light then and the road's under your feet. You'd better take my horse till we pass 'Razor Back.' *He* won't boggle at it if it was twice as narrow."

It did not take long to pack all that was strictly necessary, which alone Mr. Blount decided to take with him. After which O'Hara boiled the billy, and produced a decent meal, which Mr. Blount, having tasted nothing since breakfast, did justice to. No time was lost then, and O'Hara leading off with the cob started at a canter, with which Blount on his horse found no difficulty in keeping up. The contract was performed, they safely negotiated the perilous pass, the mountain horse treading as securely and safely as on a macadamised high road, and the cob going very differently with a different rider. He was then bestridden by his lawful owner, who prepared to make good time into Bunjil. The moon was rising, when the men—so strangely met, and associated—parted. Blount held out his hand, which the other grasped with unconsciously crushing force. Then the mountaineer quitted the road, and plunging down the steep into the darksome forest, disappeared from sight.

Bunjil township was reached before midnight. There had been the local excitement of an improvised race meeting, the head prize being a bridle and saddle; the Consolation Stakes boasted a silver-mounted whip, generously presented by the respected host of the Bunjil Hotel. So that Mr. Blount, whose train of thought for the last hour or two wavered between encouragement and depression, as he dreaded the inn being shut, the ostler asleep, the fire out and the girl gone to bed, felt reassured as he heard voices and saw lights, indicative of cheery wakefulness. By good luck, too, the best bedroom and the parlour were unoccupied. Sheila promised a fire in the latter apartment and tea ready in less than no time. The ostler took the cob to a loose box, just vacated, while Mr. Blount having deposited his "swag" in the bedroom and made all ready for a solid meal, and a royal toasting of his person before the fire of logs, felt quite a glow of happiness.

On re-entering the parlour he was warmly welcomed by Sheila, who indeed was so unaffectedly cordial in hailing his safe return, that the guest concluded that there must have been reason for conjecturing that the reverse might have occurred.

As she greeted him with natural unstudied welcome, he could not resist taking both her hands in his, and shaking them with a warmth corresponding with her feeling of gratitude at his safe return from apparently unknown and mysterious dangers. The girl blushed and disengaged her hands, but showed no discomposure as she said, "We didn't know but something might have happened to you, out in that wild place, and Little-River-Jack said you had a narrow escape on 'Razor Back,' as your cob got frightened and might have gone over the downfall like Paddy Farrell. Then Dick came along, he sold out his share to you, didn't he? And he got on the spree for a day or two and let out a few things that he'd better have kept to himself. So taking it altogether, we're all glad, Mr. Middleton, the missis, and me too, that you're back safe and sound."

While the latter part of this dialogue was proceeding, Mr. Blount had seated himself at the table with his back to the fire, and made a frontal attack upon a broiled steak flanked by a dish of floury potatoes, which told of the sharpening effect on the appetite of a long day in the saddle, and the stimulation of a night journey with two degrees of frost.

"You had better take away these dishes, Sheila, or I shall never stop eating. I think, however, that I can hold out till breakfast, now we have got so far."

About this time the landlord appeared, blandly apologetic for delay, but pleading the necessity for being in the bar while there were so many "gents" round anxious to go home on good terms with themselves.

"More likely to run against a fence, or the bough of a tree," said Sheila, who had now rejoined the party, "that's the sort of 'good terms with themselves,' that's the fashion, Bunjil way. I wonder there's not more legs and arms broken than there are."

"Why, it's a good month since you left us, Mr. Blount," said the landlord, cheerily unheeding the maid's moral reflections. "The Sergeant was here a day or two back, and asked after you—Little-River-Jack came last week, and talked of going away unless things mended. He billed Stubbins for a quarter of beef he owed him, and they had a row, and got to fighting over it."

"How did that come off?" queried the guest, dallying with his second cup of tea, and a plate of buttered toast. "Jack's rather a light weight."

"So he is—but he can use his hands, and he's that active he takes a lot of beating. Well, the butcher at Green Point is a couple of stone heavier, and fancies himself a bit. He says, 'You'd better summon me, Jack!' We all knew what that meant."

"You're takin' a mean advantage," says Jack, "it's a cowardly thing to do. But I'll tell you what, if you're man enough, I'll fight you for it—it's a matter of four notes—five and twenty shillings a hundred—are you on?"

"All right!" says the Green Point chap; "so they stripped to it, and had a regular ding-dong go in. The butcher seemed to have the best of it at first, but Jack wore him out, hittin' and gettin' away, and dancin' round him—all them tricks. At last he bunged up his eyes and nearly blinded him, they say. Then Jack went in and finished him; what with loss of wind, and the punishment he got, the butcher was clean knocked out afore the tenth round. So he didn't come to time, and the referee gave it against him. Jack got the four notes and cleared—the butcher paid up honourable—but he couldn't show outside the shop for a fortnight afterwards."

"A capital stand-up fight, I'm sure. I should like to have been there to see it. And now, I think I'll turn in. I'm a bit tired, and dead sleepy. Good-night, Mr. Middleton, good-night, Sheila! I'll have breakfast at nine o'clock, please, bacon and eggs is my present fancy. I'll stay in Bunjil a few days and loaf for a change."

If there is anything in life more conducive to happiness than waking at dawn in the country, assured of comfort, free from anxiety and relieved from duty, few people have experienced it.

And nowhere can the rare luxury of the conditions be more fully savoured than in Australia. Mr. Blount was firmly of this opinion, as in virtue of his late habitudes, the birds' wild melody awoke him, as the first dawnlight tinged the grey, reluctant East.

However, on reflection he decided to take another hour's repose, while all things were favourable to such indulgence.

Then, between sleeping and waking, he dozed deliciously until half-past seven, when he sallied forth, towel in hand, to the creek bank. In the garden was a rude, but competent bath-house, from which he was enabled to plunge into the ice-cold stream.

Truth to tell, he did not make a lengthened stay therein, the mercury being little, if anything, above freezing point, but devoted himself to a complete and conscientious scrubbing with the rough towel, at the conclusion of which, he found that a delicious glow had rewarded his efforts, and the praiseworthy self-denial of the cold-colder-coldest bath he had taken as a daily custom, ever since he could remember. It is the after taste, which, as in other matters, is so truly luxurious.

Running back to the house, he saw that his expectation of a full-sized, first-class fire in the breakfast room had been realised. After warming himself at this, he attacked the serious business of dressing for the day, which he pursued with such diligence that he was ready for the bacon and eggs, before referred to, as nearly as possible at the appropriate hour.

"Got you a good fire, you see," remarked Sheila, who, smiling and rosy as the morn, stood in attendance. "Hope you slept well. My word! we got an awful start, didn't know what was going to happen, when Senior Constable Moore came here the day before yesterday to get warrants for Little-River-Jack (*alias* John Carter), Phelim O'Hara, his brother Patrick, and also a man working in the claim, known as Jack Blunt, and one 'Tumberumba Dick.' Asked me and Mr. Middleton a lot of questions."

"And what did you say?"

"We didn't know much, or say much either, if it comes to that. Yes! knew that Little-River-Jack passed through here now and again. Where he went to—couldn't say—hadn't seen him lately. Heard the O'Haras were working miners from Queensland or Gippsland—only seen them once. Tumberumba Dick stayed a day or two here last week, and got on the spree rather. Said he'd sold his share to Jack Blunt, and was clearing out for West Australia. Little-River-Jack was a butcher, and supplied the small diggings."

"What did they ask about Jack Blunt, eh?"

"Oh! a lot. What was he like?—how was he dressed?"

"Tall and dark" (I said), "not bad-looking." Here Mr. Blount bowed. "Dressed like any other gentleman travelling for pleasure. Rough tweed suit and leggings. Left a few things here. Went away a month ago, with Little-River-Jack."

"What for—did he say?" the Senior Constable asked.

"Yes! he talked quite free and open. Said he wanted to see the country— what gold-diggings were like, and all that. Jack promised to show him a regular mountain claim—the 'Lady Julia.' Tumberumba Dick when he came by, said 'he'd sold his share to him for £20. He was full up of mountain claims, was clearing out for West Australia, where there were big rises to be made.'"

"Why didn't they serve warrants, then?"

"The Senior Constable had a long talk with our old Sergeant—he's retired now, but everybody puts great faith in him."

"Did you hear what he said?"

"No—but it came out that the Sergeant told him to be careful about arresting men on suspicion—there was no direct evidence (those were the words) against any of the men named. Nobody could swear to their having been seen taking or branding cattle. Those who knew the O'Haras spoke of them as hardworking diggers—who sold their gold to Little-River-Jack or got him to sell it for them. As for Jack Blunt they said—" here the speaker hesitated.

"Well, what did they say about him?"

"I hardly like to tell you, sir."

"Oh! come, out with it. What does it matter?"

"Well, sir"—the girl smiled mischievously—"they said—(that is Tumberumba Dick told some one, who told some one else), that you were a harmless 'New Chum,' that hardly knew a cow from a calf, and couldn't have 'duffed' a bullock off a range, if you'd tried for a year."

"Very complimentary indeed, I must say. So everybody's honest in this country who can't ride—eh?"

"Well, yes, sir—about cattle; with sheep it's different."

"I see—never struck me before. I'm glad my honesty is undoubted in a cattle district, because I can't gallop down a range. They don't fine or imprison for bad riding, I suppose—*yet*. And so you stood up for me, Sheila, didn't you?"

"How did you know that, sir?"

"Why, of course you did. I knew you would because we've always been friends. Besides, I saw you looking after me warningly the day I went away with Jack Carter."

"I know I did," said the girl, impetuously. "I had a great mind to say all I knew, and tell you to have nothing to do with him or his mates."

"And why didn't you?"

"Well, you were so set upon going, and it wasn't for a girl like me to advise a gentleman of your sort."

"I don't see why you shouldn't. Every one is as good as any one else in Australia. So the papers say, at any rate."

"Nothing of the sort. A gentleman is a gentleman, and a servant girl a servant in Australia; all over the world, if it comes to that. I don't hold with this democratic rot. All the same, there's nothing to prevent you and me having a talk now and then, as long as we keep our places."

"I should think not," he rejoined, "and though I might have got into a serious difficulty through Carter's introductions, I'm not sorry, on the whole, that I went with him, the experience was most interesting."

"That means you saw somebody. Who was *she*, I wonder? Men are all alike, gentle and simple. I believe I could give a guess, as we heard you went down the river."

To this day Blount declares that he never enjoyed a better meal; he certainly never had a better appetite. And as the sun rising higher in the heavens irradiated the meadows, the hurrying water of the creek, the brilliant green of the opening buds of the great elms and poplars that fringed that streamlet, he admitted that the landscape was almost worthy of the memorable meal.

After a leisurely assimilation of the journals of the day, and a smoke in the verandah, he ordered the cob to be brought round, being of opinion that gentle exercise would be advantageous to his legs, which the last day's work might have tried unfairly. They certainly had puffed, but there was no sign of lameness, and his owner decided that daily exercise would meet the complaint. Hearing that the Sergeant was at home he resolved to look up that gallant officer, and gather from him what rumour had asserted as to Little-River-Jack, the O'Haras, Mr. Bruce, and lastly himself, if rumours there were.

He found the ex-guardian of the peace, and, so to speak, warden of the marches, weeding his garden, a trim, well-ordered plot, which, like the remainder of his little property, was a standing object lesson to the surrounding homesteads. Putting down his hoe, the veteran advanced with an air of great cordiality, and welcomed him.

"Sae you have won back frae the Debatable Land, as they ca'ed Nicol Forest in my youth. There have been wars, and rumours o' wars, but the week past; warrants to be issued for Phelim and Patrick O'Hara, and one Little-River-Jack (went by the name of John Carter), forbye 'Tumberumba Dick,' and a man known as Jack Blunt (*alias* Valentine Blount) seen in company with the above on the 20th of August last. Ay! it was openly said, and I was lookin' to see you arrive, maybe with the bracelets on. What think ye of that?"

"That I should have had good cause of action for false imprisonment," answered the tourist. "But why didn't they issue the warrants?"

"Maybe they were no that sure aboot the evidence. There's neecessity, ye ken, that there should be full and aample proof in thae 'duffing' cases, as the country people ca' them. A bush jury winna convict as lang's there a link short o' the Crown Prosecutor's chain o' evidence."

"And was there? I feel personally much obliged to the Department of Justice for their scruples, which do them honour."

"Weel, ye ken, though Mr. Bruce o' Marondah deposed on aith that he saw an E.H.B. bullock, his property, with a J.C. brand put freshly on, there was nae witness who saw John Carter or any ither carle do it or the like. He missed cattle, sure enough, and Black Paddy led him and two troopers to a deserted claim known as the 'Lady Julia,' near which was a stockyaird wi' fresh cattle tracks baith in and oot. They didna gang in their lane. A'body kens that. But wha saw them gang in or gang oot? Strong presumption, clear circumstantial evidence, but next to nae proof. Sae the airm of the law was stayed—a great peety, wasna it?"

"Really, it seems like it. Fine paragraphs, lost to the local press. Capture of cattle-stealers, a leading butcher implicated. A gentleman lately from England arrested. Damages laid by him for false imprisonment at £10,000. Really, I might have bought a station with the money, and been rich and respected. Many a big squatter, Dick told me, had begun that way, but he *had* stolen the cattle or sheep, and served sentence for it, before he turned his talents to better purpose."

"Dick's no to lippen to," replied the Sergeant, "nor nane o' thae kind o' folk. They'll tell lees by the bushel, gin ye stay to believe them. When a's said and done, laddie, ye're well oot o' it. Ye'll maybe tak' heed o' chance companions anither time."

"Very possibly, Sergeant. It does appear as if I had been a trifle imprudent. I must curb my spirit of adventure, which has led me astray before now. I nearly got shot in Spain through joining a band of smugglers, they were such joyous dogs; and Manuela—ah! what eyes! what a figure! It was rash, no doubt, I must ask for references, another time. Ha! Ha!"

Mr. Blount treated the escape which he perceived he had narrowly missed of being hauled before the bar of justice, with apparent levity, but in his own mind, he was conscious that affairs might have taken a permanently disagreeable turn, and seriously compromised him socially, however it ended. What would the Bruce family think of him? What could Imogen believe? Either that he shared the ill-gotten gains of the O'Haras and their associates, or that he was so inconceivably dense, and unsuspicious that any amount of dishonesty might go on before his face, without his being aware of it. On either assumption, he was between the horns of a dilemma. Adjudged guilty of folly, or dishonesty. His vexation was extreme. However, he exhibited no outward signs of remorse, and concluded his visit by thanking the Sergeant for his information, and begging him to join him at dinner if he had no lingering suspicion of his moral character.

"Na! na! I'd pit ma haill trust in thee, if matters luikit as black again. The glint in thae grey 'een werena given thee for naught; we'll hae mair cracks before a's said and done; the spring's to be airly, I'm thinking."

The season was more advanced than when Blount first entered Bunjil, the warmer weather had made it apparent that "the year had turned." The meadow grasses had grown and burgeoned, the English trees always planted near the older settlements in Australia, many of them the growth of half a century, were nearly full leaved, putting to shame with their brilliant colouring, and opulent shade, the duller hues of the primeval forest. The water-fowl in flocks flew and dived and swam in the great lagoons, which marked the ancient course of the river. The cattle and horses browsing in the lanes and vacant spaces, were sleek of skin, and fair to behold. All nature spoke of abundance of pasture. In this fertile valley there was no hint of the scarcity, which once, at any rate, within the recollection of men then living had been known to overspread the land: when this very spot, now running over with plenteousness, the vine, the olive, the fig, peaches, and plums, apples, and pears, in full leaf and promise of fruit, was bare and adust, the creek even dry, between the great water-holes, for half a mile at a stretch.

Mr. Blount on returning from his ride found a large assortment of letters and newspapers awaiting him. Among them was a telegram marked *Urgent*. This bore the postmark of a neighbouring colony and had been forwarded by private messenger, at some expense. Thus ran the magic message:—"Hobart, 20th. Come over at once. No delay. Great news. Credit unlimited, Imperial Bank, Melbourne."

Walking straight into his bedroom, he threw the letters on to the counterpane of his bed, and drawing forward a chair, proceeded to open his correspondence seriatim. After noting date and signature, he returned the greater portion of them to their envelopes, postponing fuller examination to a more convenient season. The last two, which bore the postmark of the nearest post-office to Marondah, he retained. Of its name he was aware, having heard the ladies asking that the post-bag should be delayed for a few minutes on account of their unfinished letters.

He did not linger over the first, addressed in a strong, clear, masculine hand. There was no difficulty in mastering its tone and tenor.

"Sir,—I feel justly indignant that I should have extended hospitality to a person who, while assuming the outward appearance of a gentleman, has proved by his conduct to be unworthy of recognition as such.

"As an associate of the O'Hara brothers and two others, who, under pretence of mining, have in concert with a well-known gang of cattle stealers, preyed on my herd and those of neighbouring stations, for the last two years, you have laid yourself open to grave suspicion. I cannot be expected to believe that you were, although a new arrival, so unsuspicious as to have no knowledge of their dishonest ways. In a stockyard near the claim, branding as well as concealment of stolen cattle had been carried on.

"You were present when I pointed out my E. H. B. bullock, on which a new brand had been recently placed. You knew that I suspected dishonesty in that neighbourhood. Was it not your plain duty to have informed me of any suspicious proceedings? Not only did you fail to do so, but, while accepting my hospitality, you suppressed the fact of your living as a mining mate with the O'Hara brothers, and other suspicious characters, as well as that the notorious 'Little-River-Jack' was a member of the same precious company. I believe that warrants have been applied for at the instance of one of my neighbours. Should you find that you are included in the arrest, you will only have yourself to thank for incredible folly, or criminal carelessness, as to the distinction between *meum* and *tuum*.

"I remain, faithfully yours,

"E. Hamilton Bruce."

"Very faithfully, indeed," quoth the recipient of this plain-spoken epistle. "Under the circumstances I don't wonder at the wrath of this Squire of the South. It is but too natural. Fancy a game-preserving English country gentleman, discovering that a recent guest, free of croquet and morning walks with his charming wife and daughters, had been sojourning with poachers—partaking, peradventure, of his host's own stolen pheasants! 'Six months' hard' would have been the least, and lightest penalty, that he would have dropped in for, and but for having a friend or two at court, or out of it, Valentine Blount, late of Her Majesty's F.O., by courtesy the Honourable, and so forth, might have 'done time' for the heinous offence of having concealed on his person certain beefsteaks and portions of the 'undercut' for the possession of which he could give no reasonable account—moreover defied the peace officer to take them from him. This of course is bordering upon a joke, and a very keen jest it was like to have been. Maybe yet, for all I know. What d—d fools men are sometimes! This I take to be a feminine superscription—the contents less logical, and perhaps—*perhaps* only—more emotional, and less lenient of sentence. I wonder what Mrs. Bruce and the fair Imogen think of the agreeable stranger (I have been thus described, ere now), who tarried within their gates. I feel distinctly nervous, however."

Here Mr. Blount carefully opened the envelope, and was slightly reassured by the "Dear Mr. Blount" which introduced the subject-matter.

"We are afraid, Imogen and I, that Edward has written you an extremely disagreeable, not to say threatening letter. He was furiously angry, would hear neither reason nor explanation, when the O'Hara stockyard mystery was unveiled. You *must* confess that explanation *was* difficult, not to say embarrassing for your friends. *We* are certain that there has been some great mistake which needs clearing up without delay. It will never do for you to lie under this accusation—false as we believe it to be—of living with dishonest people, and with the knowledge of their malpractices; of course, you may not know that no men are more artful in hiding their true characters than our bush cattle and horse thieves (or 'duffers') to use a vulgar expression. They are *not* coarse ruffians—on the contrary very well-mannered, hospitable, even polite, when compared with the labourers of other lands; good-natured, and most obliging, outside of their 'profession.' Indeed I heard a story from a nice old priest, that visited our station, when I was a girl, which explains much. A bushman was dilating on the noble qualities of a comrade. 'Jack's the best-hearted chap going; good-natured? why, he'd lend you his best horse, if you was stuck for one on the road. If he hadn't a horse handy, why, he'd *shake* one for you, rather than let you leave the place afoot!' Of course the situation *looks* bad, on the face of it, but Imogen and I will *never* believe anything against your honour. You have a friend at court, perhaps two." Besides this—there was a tiny scrap inside the envelope, apparently pushed in *after* the letter had been closed.

"Don't believe you *knew* anything.—Imogen."

Mr. Blount read this soothing epistle twice over and put away the scrap in his pocket-book very carefully. Having done this, he sat down and wrote hard until summoned to lunch, after which he packed up carefully all his belongings, leaving out only such as might be wanted for an early morning start. He was more grave than usual at that comfortable meal, and it was with an effort that he replied to Sheila's query whether he'd received bad news.

"Not bad, no! only important, which comes almost to the same thing. You have to think over plans and make up your mind, perhaps, to start off at a moment's warning, which is always distressing."

"Oh! nonsense," said Sheila, who seemed in better spirits than usual. "I often wish I were a man; how I would wire in when there was anything to do, even if it was only *half* good. Men do too much thinking, I believe. If they'd only ride hard at the fence, whatever it is, they'd get over, or through it, and have a clear run for their money."

"But suppose they came a cropper and broke a leg, an arm, or their neck, as I see one of your steeplechase riders did at Flemington the other day, what then?"

"Oh! a man must die some time," replied the cheerful damsel, who looked indeed the personification of high health, abounding spirits, and as much courage as can be shown by a woman without indiscretion, "and you get through nine times out of ten: the great thing is to go at it straight. 'Kindness in another's woes, courage in your own,' that's what Gordon says."

"Who is Gordon, may I ask?"

"Why, Adam Lindsay, of course, our Australian poet. Haven't you heard of him? I thought everybody had."

"And do you read him?"

"Yes. Every Australian man, woman, and child, if they're old enough, knows him by heart."

"I think I've caught the name. Was he born here?"

"Is he dead? Perhaps you've heard of Mark Twain?" said Sheila scornfully, who seemed to be in rather a reckless humour. "Well! he is. No! he was not born here, more's the pity, for he knows us cornstalks better than we know ourselves. He was the son of a British officer, the family's Scotch. I'm half Scotch, that's partly why I am so proud of him. But it would have been all the same whatever country owned him. I find my tongue's running away with me, as usual—the unruly member, as the Bible says. But you take my tip, Mr. Blount, 'never change your mind when you pick your panel' (that's Gordon again), it's the real straight griffin, with horse or man."

"This *is* a wonderful country, and you're a wonderful young woman. I haven't time to analyse you, just now, for my affairs, which I had intended to treat to a short holiday, are conspiring to hurry me up. At what hour can I leave in the morning?"

"To-morrow?" said the girl, and her face changed. "You don't mean to say you're going away to-morrow?"

"Sorry to say I must; you saw that I got a telegram, and if I don't *clear*, as your people say, I may lose thousands, perhaps a fortune."

"The coach goes at six, sharp; and gets to the railway-station at the same hour the next morning. You'd like breakfast first, I suppose?"

"It's too early to ask you to have it ready—anything will do."

"Oh! I daresay. You've had some decent meals here, haven't you?"

"Never better in my life."

"Well, you'll go away to-morrow, fit and ready for as long a day's work as ever you did. It's almost a pity you're having the Sergeant to dine. However, he'll not stay late. I'll send over and take your coach tickets. You'd better have everything packed and ready this afternoon. Cobb and Co. wait for nothing and nobody."

"There's no doubt (Mr. Blount told himself) that the conditions of life in Her Majesty's colonies tend to the development of the individual with a completeness undreamed of in our narrow and perhaps slightly prejudiced insular life. What a difference there is between this young woman and a girl of her rank of life in any part of Britain. What energy, intelligence, organising power she has; I feel certain that she could rally a wavering regiment on a pinch, drive a coach, ride a race, or swim a river, in fact do all sorts of things, as well as, ay, better than, the ordinary man. This is going to be a great country, and the Australians a great people—arts of war and peace, and so on. How good-looking she is, too," concluding his reflections with this profound observation, which showed that in spite of his subjective turn of mind, the primary emotions still held sway.

Mr. Blount betook himself to his packing with such concentration, that by the time he had finished his letters, nothing remained of his impedimenta, but such as could be easily carried out and packed in the coach, while he was finishing a distinctly early breakfast.

These said letters required much thought and preparation, it would appear. First there was a vitally necessary answer to Mr. Bruce's warlike communication. To this he concluded to reply as follows:

"Bunjil Hotel, *September*—.

"Dear Sir,—While fully admitting that appearances are against me, I think that you might with propriety have suspended judgment, if not until the offences charged against me were proved, or, at least, until you had heard my explanation, which I give seriatim.

"No. 1. As a matter of fact, I did live with the O'Haras and two other men on the 'Lady Julia' claim. They were hardworking, and well-conducted miners. For all that I saw, they might have been the most honest men in Australia. I knew that cattle were brought to the stockyard late, and taken away early. I judged it to be the custom of the country, and accepted their statement that they were bought and sold in the ordinary way. I was cautioned not to go near the yard for fear of frightening them. I did not see a brand, or look for one—nor should I have known its significance if I had. As to the O'Haras, and their 'mates,' whatever might have been their previous history, no men could have worked harder, or more regularly; they could not have *actively* assisted in the cattle trade without my noticing it.

"No. 2. That I did not inform you of my position in the claim.

"It would certainly appear to have been my duty so to do under ordinary circumstances, after I knew of your suspicions. But the circumstances were *not* ordinary.

"And the question arises, Should I have been justified in betraying—for that would have been the nature of the act—the *suspicious*, merely suspicious circumstances, which I observed during my involuntary comradeship with these men? I had eaten their salt, been treated with respect, and in all good faith shared their confidences. Moreover—and this is the strongest point in my defence—the man known as Little-River-Jack—of his real name, of course, I am ignorant—certainly *saved my life*, on the dizzy and narrow pass, known locally as 'Razor Back'—of that I feel as certain as that I am writing at this table. In another moment, my frightened horse, unused to mountain travelling, would have assuredly fallen, or thrown himself over the precipice, which yawned on either side of him, while I was equally unable either to control him or to dismount. By this bushman's extraordinary quickness and resource, I was enabled to do both. Was I to give information which would have driven him into the hands of the police?

"As a citizen, I may have been bound to assist the cause of justice. But as a *man*, I felt that I could not bring myself to do so.

"3. For the rest, I dissociated myself without more delay than was absolutely necessary to collect my effects, and return the borrowed horse, from such compromising company. I was offered my 'share'—not a very small amount—of the last gold won, but declined it, and riding late, reached this hotel at midnight of the day we parted. I heard that the senior constable of the nearest police station had instructions to take out warrants for the persons referred to, including *myself*, but, from some alleged defect in the evidence, that course was not persevered with.

"Circumstances (wholly unconnected with this unfortunate affair) compel me to leave to-morrow morning for Tasmania. I have entered fully into the 'case for the defendant.' If the jury consisting of yourself, with your amiable wife and her sister—whose kindness I can never forget, and on whose mercy I rely—do not acquit me of all evil intent, I can only hope that time may provide the means of my complete rehabilitation. Meanwhile I can subscribe myself with a clear conscience,

"Yours sincerely,

"Valentine Blount."

Having with much thought, and apparent labour, concocted this conciliatory epistle, of which he much doubted the effect, he commenced another which apparently did not need the same strain upon the mental faculties. This was addressed to Mrs. E. Hamilton Bruce, Marondah, Upper Sturt, and thus commenced:

"Dear Mrs. Bruce,—To say that for your kind and considerate letter I feel most deeply grateful, would be to understate my mental condition lamentably. After reading Mr. Bruce's letter, it seemed as if the whole world was against me; and, conscious as I was of entire innocence, except of an act of egregious folly (not the first one, I may confess, which a sanguine temperament and a constitutional disregard of caution have placed to my account), my spirits were lowered to the level of despair. There seemed no escape from the dilemma in which I found myself.

"I stood convicted of egregious folly, or dishonour, with the sin of ingratitude thrown in. I could not wonder at the harsh tone of your husband's letter. What must he—what must you all—think of me? was the inexorable query. Suicide seemed the only refuge. Moral *felo-de-se* had already been committed.

"At this juncture I re-read your letter, for which I shall never cease to bless the writer, and, may I add, the probable sympathiser? Hope again held up her torch, angel bright, if but with a wavering gleam. I regained courage for a rational outlook. I think I gave a sketch of my imminent peril and the rescuer to Miss Imogen, as we rode away from Marondah on that lovely morning. Her commentary was that it was not unlike an incident in *Anne of Geierstein*, except that the heroine was the deliverer in that case. We agreed, I think, in rating the book as one of the best in the immortal series.

"I have fully explained the position in which I stand, to Mr. Bruce in my letter, which you will doubtless see, so I need not recapitulate. I have been recalled on important business (unconnected with this regrettable affair) to Hobart, for which city I leave early to-morrow. Meanwhile, I trust that all doubts connected with my inconsistent conduct will be cleared up with the least possible delay.

"In which fullest expectation,

"I remain,

"Very gratefully yours,

"Valentine Blount."

The writer of these important letters, after having carefully sealed them, made assurance doubly sure by walking to the post-office, and placing them with his own hands in the receptacle for such letters provided. He further introduced himself to the acting postmaster, and ascertained that all correspondence—his own included—which were addressed to the vicinity of Bunjil, would be forwarded next morning soon after daylight, reaching their destination early on the following morning. "It's only a horse mail," said that official, "the bags are carried on a pack-horse. But Jack Doyle's a steady lad, and always keeps good time—better, for that matter, than some of the coach-contractors."

The rest of Mr. Blount's correspondence was apparently easily disposed of, some being granted short replies, some being placed in a convenient bag, and others unfeelingly committed to the flames. About the time when the Sergeant and dinner arrived, Mr. Blount held himself to be in a position of comparative freedom from care, having all his arrangements made, and, except Fate stepped in with special malignity, everything in train for a successful conclusion to a complicated, unsatisfactory beginning. His city address was left with the acting postmaster aforesaid; all letters, papers, &c., were to be forwarded to Valentine Blount, Esq., Imperial Club, Melbourne.

He would probably return in three weeks or a month; if not, full directions would be forwarded by his agent.

The dinner was quite up to the other efforts of the Bunjil Hotel *chef*, an expatriated artist whom advanced political opinions had caused to abandon "la belle France." So *he* said, amid the confessions, indirect or otherwise, made during his annual "break-out." But his cookery was held to confirm that part of his statement, as well as a boast that he had been *chef* at the Hôtel du Louvre in Paris. Whatever doubt might be cast on his statements and previous history, as related by himself, no one had ever dreamed of disparaging his cookery. This being the case, and the time wanting nearly three months to Christmas, which was the extreme limit of his enforced sobriety, neither Mr. Blount nor any one else could have complained of the banquet.

Nor was "the flow of soul" wanting. The Sergeant was less didactic than usual; he drew on his reminiscences more and more freely as the evening grew late, and the landlord contributed his quota, by no means without pith or point, to the hilarity of the entertainment. The Sergeant, however, completely eclipsed the other *convives* by a choice experience drawn from his memory wallet, as he turned out that receptacle of "tales of mystery and fear," which decided the landlord and his guest to "see him home" at the conclusion of the repast.

This duty having been completed, Mr. Blount was moved to remark upon the fineness of the night. It was certainly curiously mild and still. "Quite like spring weather."

Mr. Middleton looked up and expressed himself doubtfully as to its continuance. "It's too warm to be natural, sir," he said, "and if I was asked my opinion, I'd say we're not far from a burst up, either wind or rain, I don't say which, a good way out of the common. If you're in a hurry to get to Melbourne, you were right to take your passage by Cobb and Co., or you might not get away for a week."

"I wouldn't lose a week just now for a hundred pounds."

"Well, of course, it's hard to say, but if the creeks and rivers come down, as I've seen 'em in a spring flood, and we're close on the time now, there'll be no getting to Warongah in a week, or perhaps a fortnight on top of that. But I think, if you get off to-morrow morning, you'll just do it, and that's all."

When they returned all traces of the symposium had been removed, and the cloth laid ready for the early breakfast, which Blount trusted nothing would occur to prevent him from consuming.

On the plate at the head of the table, near the fire-place, was a half-sheet of notepaper, on which was written in bold characters:

"Dear Sir,—The groom will call you at five sharp, breakfast at 5.30. Coach leaves at six. I've got you the box seat.

"Yours truly,

"Sheila."

"That's a fine girl," said the landlord, "she's got 'savey' enough for a dozen women; and as for work, it's meat and drink to her. The missus is afraid she'll knock herself out, and then we'll be teetotally ruined and done for. I hope she won't throw herself away on some scallowag or other."

"Yes! it would be a pity. I take quite an interest in her. But she has too much sense for that, surely?"

"I don't know," answered the landlord, gloomily, "the more sense a woman has, the likelier she is to fancy a fool, if he's good-looking, that's my tip. Good-night, sir. I'll be up and see you off. Old George will call you."

"Oh! I shall be up and ready, thank you."

The landlord, however, having exceptional opportunities of studying human nature, warned old George to have the gentleman up at 5 a.m. sharp, which in result was just as well. For Blount being too excited from various causes to sleep, had tossed and tumbled about till 3 a.m., when he dropped into a refreshing slumber, so sound that George's rat-tat-tat, vigorous and continued on his bedroom door, caused him to dream that all the police of the district, headed by Mr. Bruce and Black Paddy, had come to arrest him, and were battering down the hotel in order to effect a capture.

CHAPTER VI

A dip in the creek, and a careful if hasty toilet, produced a complete change of ideas. The morning was almost too fine, the leaves of the great poplars were unstirred, which gave an unnaturally calm and eerie appearance to the landscape. This was not dispelled by the red sun shedding a theatrical glare over the snow-peaks and shoulders of the mountain range.

"My holiday's over, Sheila!" said he, moving from the fire front to the table upon which was such an appetising display that he wished he had gone to bed a little earlier. However, the savour of the devilled turkey reassured him, and he felt more drawn towards the *menu* which was to form the sustaining meal of the day. "Now, what do *you* think of the weather? Shall I have a safe journey to the station?"

"Well, you may, and you may not, sir. We all think there's a big storm coming; if it's wind, it may blow a tree down on the coach and horses; if it rains hard, there'll be a flood, which will rise the Kiewah and the Little River in a few hours, so as they can't be crossed under a week."

"That's a bad look out!" said the traveller, making good time with the scrambled eggs and toast, which succeeded the devilled turkey, "but we'll have to go straight at it, as your friend and philosopher, Gordon, has it. By the way, I bought a copy at the post-office store, so I can read it on the way down and think of you when I come to the lines 'Kindness in another's trouble,' and so on."

"Oh! I daresay," replied the girl, "a lot you'll think about me when you're on the road to Melbourne and wherever else you're bound for. But we'll all remember *you* here, never fear! And if you ever come back, you'll see how glad all hands will be to welcome you."

"*You're* only too good to me, but why should the other people have this sort of feeling towards me?"

"Well, one reason is that you never put on any side, as they call it. You've been free and easy with them, without being too familiar. The country people hereabouts, and in the bush generally, may be rough, and haven't seen much, but they know a gentleman when they see one, and besides, there's another reason—" And here she seemed to hesitate.

"And what might that be?"

"Well, it came out somehow, I don't know how, that when you were 'pinched' (that is, nearly arrested and tried for being 'in' with the O'Haras and Little-River-Jack in the cattle racket), that you wouldn't give them away; never let on that you'd been with them in the claim, or seen cattle in their yard or anything."

"But, my dear Sheila! I heard nothing and saw nothing that the town-crier at the market-place (is there one in this droll country, I wonder?) might not have proclaimed aloud. I didn't know there was any 'cross' work (is that right?) going on. I certainly guessed after I visited Mr. Bruce that I might just as well not advertise the O'Haras, and as Little-River-Jack certainly saved my life on Razor Back, how *could* I give him up to the law? Now, could I?"

"Not as a gentleman, sir, I should say. I suppose Mr. Bruce is pretty wild about it, after you being at his house and all that. He's a fine man, Mr. Bruce; all he's got he's earned. His brother and he worked like niggers when first they came from home. Now they're well off, and on the way to be richer still. But no man likes to be robbed, rich or poor. He'll have Jack yet for this if he don't mind, sharp as he is."

"Well, I suppose it serves him right."

"I suppose it does," said the girl, hesitatingly; "but I can't help feeling sorry for him, he's so pleasant and plucky, and such a bushman. He can find his way through those Wombat Ranges, they say, the darkest night that ever was, and drive cattle besides."

"''Tis pity of him, too, he cried,

Bold can he speak, and fairly ride,'

as the Douglas said about Marmion, who, though more highly placed than poor Jack, was but indifferent honest after all. Do you read Walter Scott?"

"Well, I've read bits of the *Lady of the Lake* and *Marmion* too. We had them to learn by heart at school. Only I haven't much time to read now, have I? It's early up and down late. But you'd better finish your breakfast; it's getting on to six o'clock, and I see Josh walking down to the stable."

"So I will; but tell me, how do you write out a receipt for a horse when you've sold him?"

"Oh! easy enough. 'This is to certify that I have sold my bay horse, branded "J. R." (or whatever he is) to Job Jones for value received.' That's enough; you've only to sign your name and put a stamp on."

"Nothing could be simpler. Get the landlord to receipt my bill while I write out a cheque, and ask George if he's put my saddle and bridle into the coach."

The girl ran out. He wrote the cheque for the account, which he had seen before breakfast. Then more carefully, a receipt for the cob in the name of Sheila Maguire, in which he enclosed a sovereign. "Isn't that your side-saddle? Where's your horse? You haven't got one, eh? Why, I thought every girl in this country had one."

"Mine got away; I'm afraid I'll never see him again."

"What will you give me for the cob? he's easy and safe if you don't try the Razor Back business with him?"

"I wouldn't mind chancing a tenner for him, sir."

"Would you, though? Well, I'll take it. There's the receipt. You can pay me when I ask for it."

At that moment, the coachman having drawn on his substantial gloves, mounted the box and called out "All aboard!" Mr. Blount pressed the receipt and the sovereign into the girl's reluctant hand, who came out of the room with rather a heightened colour, while the driver drew his lines taut as the passenger mounted the box and was whirled off, if not in the odour of sanctity, yet surrounded with a halo (so to speak) of cheers and good wishes.

Once off and bowling along a fairly good road behind a team of four fast horses, specially picked for leaving or approaching towns, a form of advertisement for the great coaching firm of Cobb and Co. (then, as now, famed for speed, safety and punctuality throughout the length and breadth of Australasia), Mr. Blount's spirits began to improve, keeping pace, indeed, with the rising of the sun and his own progress. That luminary in this lovely month of early spring was seen in his most favourable aspect.

The merry, brawling river, now rushing over "bars" gleaming with quartz pebbles, the boom of the "water-gun," the deep, reed-fringed reaches, in which the water-fowl dived and fluttered, alike engaged the traveller's alert interest. The little river took wilful, fantastic curves, as it seemed to him through the broad green meadows. Sometimes close-clinging to a basaltic bluff, over which the coach appeared to hang perilously, while on the other side was the mile-wide, level greensward, thickly covered with grazing kine and horses. The driver, a wiry native from the Shoalhaven gullies, was cheerful and communicative.

He was in a position to know and enlarge upon the names and characters of the different proprietors of the estates through which they passed. The divisions were indicated by gates in the fences crossing the roads at right angles, at which period Mr. Joshua Cable requested his passenger to drive through while he jumped down and opened the gates and shut them after the operation was concluded. As this business was only necessary at distances varying from five to ten miles apart, the stoppages were not serious; though in one instance, where the enclosure was small and the number of gates unreasonably large, his temper was ruffled.

"D—n these gates," he said; "they're enough to ruin a chap's temper. They put up a new cross fence here—wire, too—since I was here last. This is a bother, but when a man is driving by himself at night it's worse. And they can summons you, and fine you two pounds and costs for leaving a gate open, worse luck!"

"How do you manage then?" asked the passenger, all unused to seeing a coach and four without groom or guard.

"Well, it's rather a ticklish bit of work, even with a pair, if they're at all touchy, as I've had 'em, many a time. You drive round before you come to the gate and tie your leaders to the fence as close as you can get 'em. I carry halters, and that's the best and safest way; but if you haven't 'em with you, you must do the best you can with the lead reins. You're close enough to jump to their heads and muzzle 'em if they're making a move. No chance to stop four horses *after* they're off. When you've opened the gate and driven through, you have to turn your team back and let 'em stand with the leaders' heads over the fence till you've shut the gate. If it's a gate that'll swing back to the post, and you've only a pair, you may manage to give it a shove just as it clears the hind wheels, but it's a chance. It's a nuisance, especially at night time and in rainy weather, but there's nothing else for it, and it's best always to keep sweet with the owners of the property the road runs through. Now we've five miles without a gate," said Josh Cable as he led his horses out and proceeded to make up time, with three horses at a hand gallop, and the off-wheeler, a very fast horse, trotting about fourteen miles an hour; "the road's level, too. We'll pull up in another hour at the Horse and Jockey for dinner." It may be explained that in Australian road-travel, whatever may be the difference of climate, which ranges indeed from sunshine to snow, the "dinner" so called, is the meal taken at or about mid-day—an hour or two, one way or another, not being regarded of importance. The evening meal at sundown, allowing for circumstances, is invariably "tea," though by no means differing in essentials from the one at mid-day. It is at the option of the traveller to order and pay extra for the orthodox "dinner," with wine, if procurable, as an adjunct.

The Horse and Jockey Hotel was duly reached, the half-hour dinner despatched, and, at sunrise, the railway station at Warongah reached, into which, after a hurried meal, Mr. Blount was enabled to hurl himself and luggage, the train not being crowded. Long before this hour he had ample time to admire the skill used in driving on a road never free from stumps and sidelings, creeks, and other pitfalls. Certainly the *seven* lamps, which he had never seen before on a coach, assisted the pilot's course, with the light afforded by the great burners, three on high above the roof of the composite vehicle, a sort of roofed "cariole" defended as to the sides by waterproof curtains; while four other lamps gave the driver confidence, as they enabled him to see around and for some distance ahead as clearly as in the day.

In sixteen hours from the terminus Mr. Blount was safely landed per cab at the Imperial Club, Melbourne, in which institution he enjoyed the privileges of an honorary member, and was enabled to learn that the *Pateena* would leave the Queen's Wharf at four o'clock p.m. next day for Launceston. Here he half expected to have one or more letters in answer to his appeal to the mercy of the Court as represented by Mrs. Bruce and Miss Imogen, or its justice, in the shape of Edward Hamilton Bruce of Marondah, a magistrate of the Territory. But none came. Other epistles of no importance, comparatively; also a fiery telegram from Hobart, "Don't lose time. Your presence urgently needed." So making arrangements for his correspondence to follow him to the Tasmanian Club, Hobart, he betook himself to the inter-colonial steamship, and at bed-time was sensible that a "capful" of wind was vexing the oft-turbulent Straits of Bass.

Hobart—the peaceful, the picturesque, the peerless among Australian summer climates, whether late or early. Hither come no scorching blasts, no tropical rains. Nestling beneath the shadow of Mount Wellington, semi-circled by the broad and winding Derwent, proving by old-fashioned—in many instances picturesquely ruinous—edifices, it claims to be one of Britain's earliest outposts. Mr. Blount, from the moment of his landing, found himself in an atmosphere about as peacefully secluded as at Bunjil.

From this Elysian state of repose, he was routed immediately after breakfast by the tempestuous entrance of Mr. Frampton Tregonwell, Mining Expert and Consulting Engineer, as was fully set forth on his card, sent in by the waiter.

"Bless my soul!" called out this volcanic personage, as soon as he entered the door which he shut carefully behind him. "You are a most extraordinary chap! One would think you had been born in Tasmania, instead of the Duchy of Cornwall, whence all the Captains of the great mining industry have come from since the days of the Phœnicians and even earlier. Lucky you picked up a partner who is as sharp, excuse me, as you are—ahem—Blount!"

"When I'm told what all this tirade is about, ending with an atrocious pun, perhaps I may be able to reply," answered the object of the attack, complacently finishing his second cup of tea.

"Did you get my telegram? Answer me that, Valentine Blount."

"I did, and have come over to this tight little island at great personal inconvenience, as you may have observed, Mr. Tregonwell!"

"Have you any recollection of our buying a half share in a prospecting silver claim, of four men's ground, in the West Coast?"

"I do seem to recall some such transaction, just before I left for Australia. All the fellows I met in the Hobart Club told me it was a swindle, and advised me not to put a pound in it."

"That was the reason that you *did* invest in it, if I know you."

"Precisely, I've rarely taken advice against my own judgment that I haven't regretted it. Did it turn out well?"

"Well! Well? It's the richest silver lode in the island, in all Australasia—" almost shouted Tregonwell—"fifty feet wide; gets richer, and richer as it goes down. I've been offered twenty thousand pounds, cash down, for my half; you could get the same if you care to take it."

"I've a great mind to take it," said Blount languidly "—mines are so uncertain. Here to-day, gone to-morrow."

"Take it?" said his partner, with frenzied air, and trembling with excitement, "*take* it! Well!"—suddenly changing his tone—"I'll give you a drive this afternoon, capital cabs they have here, and the best horses I've seen out of England. The way they rattle down these hills on the metal is marvellous! We can't start for the mine till to-morrow morning; I suppose you'd like to see it? But if you're determined to sell, I'd like you to see a friend of mine first. He has a magnificent place a few miles out. He'd be charmed to meet you, I'm sure."

"Certainly, by all means. What's your friend's name? Is he a squatter or a fruit-grower? They seem to be the leading industries over here."

"Neither; he's a medical man in large practice. His name is Macandrew. Medical superintendent of the new Norfolk lunatic asylum."

"Well, really, Tregonwell, this is too bad," answered the other partner, roused from his habitual coolness. "Has it escaped your memory that *you* wished to sell out before I left for Australia, that I stuck to the claim, and have been paying my share of expenses ever since?"

"Quite true, old fellow; it was your confounded obstinacy and luck combined, a sheer fluke, which has landed us where we are, not a particle of judgment on either side; and now, then, let's get through business detail before lunch. I have it all here."

Mr. Tregonwell was a thoroughbred Cornishman, short, square set, and immensely powerful. His coal-black, close-curled hair, with dark, deep-set eyes, short, upright forehead, and square jaw proclaimed him a "Cousin Jack" to all who had ever rambled through the picturesque Duchy, or heard the surges boom on castle-crowned Tintagil. In one way or other he had been interested in mines since his boyhood; had, indeed, delved below sea level in those stupendous shafts in his native place of Truro.

An off-shoot of a good old Cornish family, he had worked up to his present position from a penniless childhood and a youth not disdaining hard manual labour as a miner, when none better was to be had. This gave him a more thorough knowledge of the underground world and its inhabitants than he could otherwise have obtained. As a mining "Captain" therefore, his reputation had preceded him from the silver mines of Rio Tinto in Mexico and the great goldfields of California. A noted man in his way, a type worthy of observation by a student of human nature, like Valentine Blount, who, having added him to his collection, had drifted into friendship, and a speculative partnership which was destined to colour his after life.

As there remained a couple of hours open to such a task before lunch, the partners settled down to a "square business deal," as Mr. Tregonwell (who had possessed himself of trans-Atlantic and other idioms) phrased it; in the course of which the following facts were elicited. That the stone, in the first place accidentally discovered as an out-drop in one of the wildest, most desolate, regions of the West Coast of Tasmania, was the richest ever discovered in any reefing district "South of the Line," as Mr. Tregonwell magniloquently expressed it. On sinking, even richer ore came to light, "as much silver as stone" in some of the specimens. He, Tregonwell, had taken care to comply with the labour conditions, and the necessary rules and regulations, according to the Tasmanian Mining Act, in such case made and provided. He had satisfied the Warden of their *bona fides*, and this gentleman had supported him in all disputes with the "rush crowd" which, as usual under such circumstances, had swarmed around the sensational find, as soon as it was declared. Everything, so far, had been plain sailing, but there was sure to be litigation, and a testing of their title on some of the technical points of law which are invariably raised when the claim is rich enough to pay the expenses of litigation. The great thing now was to float the discovery into a company, exhibit the specimens in the larger cities and in England, and offer half the property in shares to the public. This was agreed to. Tregonwell, with practised ease, drew out the prospectus, explaining the wondrous assays which had already been made, the increasing body of the lode, its speculative value and unrivalled richness as it descended to the hundred and fifty feet level. The prospectors had invited tenders for a fifty head stamp battery to be placed on the ground. Abundance of running water was within easy reach; timber also, of the finest quality, unlimited in quantity. Carriage, of course, in a rough, mountainous country, must be an expensive item. The directors were anxious not to minimise the cost in any way, and all statements might be regarded as absolutely truthful. The stone, if it kept up quality and output, would pay for *any* rate of carriage and the most up-to-date machinery. When a narrow-gauge railway had been completed to the Port, where the Company had secured wharf accommodation, the transit question would be comparatively trifling.

Mr. Blount retired for lunch to the hotel in which Tregonwell had engaged rooms—a quiet, old-fashioned house of highly conservative character, selected by his partner as specially adapted for privacy. The family had inherited the business and the house from the grandfather, who had made the business, and built the house in the early days when the island was still known as Van Diemen's Land. Mr. Polglase, whose portrait in oils still ornamented the dining-room, in company with that of Admiral Rodney, in whose flagship he had been a quartermaster, had reached Tasmania in a whaler from New Zealand.

The *Clarkstone* having made a successful voyage, and Mr. Polglase's "lay" as first mate amounting to a respectable sum, he decided to quit the sea, and adopt the more or less lucrative occupation of hotel-keeping. In those days when the convict population outnumbered the free, in the proportion of fifty to one, when the aboriginal tribes and far more savage convict outlaws terrorised the settlers at a comparatively short distance from Hobart, it was not altogether a peaceful avocation. But Mark Polglase, a man of exceptional strength and courage, who had enforced discipline and quelled mutiny among the turbulent whaling crews hailing from Sydney Cove, was not the man to be daunted by rioters free or bond. The small, but orderly, well-managed inn soon came to be favourably known both to the general public and the authorities, as a house where comfortable lodging was to be procured, and, moreover, where a strict system of orderliness was enforced. When the coaching system came to be developed, for many years the best in Australasia, after admirable roads had been formed by convict labour, the Lord Rodney was the headquarters of the principal firm. From the long range of stabling issued daily in the after-time the well-bred, high-conditioned four-horse teams, which did the journey between Hobart and Launceston (a hundred and twenty miles) in a day. To be sure the metalled road was perfect, the pace, the coaches, the method of driving, the milestones even, strictly after the old English pattern. So that the occasional tourist, or military traveller, was fain to confess that he had not seen such a turn-out or done such stages since the days of the Cottons and the Brackenburys.

The pace was equal to that of the fastest "Defiance" or "Regulator" that ever kept good time on an English turnpike road. Here the erstwhile Cornish sailor settled himself for life. To that end he wrote to a young woman to whom he had become engaged before he left Truro on his last voyage, and sent her the wherewithal to pay her passage and other expenses. She was wise enough to make no objection to a home on "the other side of the world," as Jean Ingelow puts it, and had no reason to regret her decision. Here they reared a family of stalwart sons, and blooming lasses—the latter with complexions rivalling those of Devonshire. They married and spread themselves over the wide wastes of the adjoining colonies, with satisfactory results, but never forgetting to return from time to time to their Tasmanian home, where they could smell the apple blossoms in the orchards and hear the bee humming on the green, clover-scented pastures.

The parents in the fulness of time had passed away, and lay in the churchyard, near the Wesleyan meeting house, which the old man had regularly attended and generously supported. But his eldest son, lamed through an accident on a goldfield, reigned in his stead. He too had a capable wife—it seemed to run in the family. So the name and fame of the Lord Rodney remained good as of old.

The prospectus and plan of operations being now regarded as "shipshape" by Mr. Tregonwell, he proceeded to sketch the locality. "It's an awfully rough country—nothing you've ever seen before is a patch on it. We shall have to walk the last stage. A goat could hardly find footing, over not *on*, mind you, the worst part of the track. How Charlie Herbert, who discovered the show, got along, I can't think. He was more than half starved, 'did a regular perish,' as West Australians say—more than once. However it was a feat to brag about when he *did* come upon it, as you'll see when we get there."

"Herbert's in charge now, I suppose?"

"Yes! he and his mate. You won't find him far off, unless I'm handy. It doesn't do to leave such a jeweller's window to look after itself. There are two wages men, Charlie takes one and Jack Clarke the other, when they work. They get lumps and lumps of 'native silver' worth £50 and £60 apiece."

"Is it as rich as all that?"

"Rich! bless your heart, nothing's been seen like it since Golden Point at Ballarat, and that was alluvial. This is likely to be as rich at 200 feet as on top—and ten years afterwards—as it is now."

"We may call it a fortune, then, for us and the other shareholders."

"A fortune!" said Tregonwell, "it's a dozen fortunes. You can go home and buy half a county, besides marrying a duke's daughter, if your taste lies in the direction of the aristocracy."

"H—m—ha! I'm not sure that one need go out of Australia for the heroine of this little romance."

"What! already captured!—that's rapid work," said his partner, throwing himself into a mock heroic attitude. "You're not a laggard in love, whatever you may be in practical matters. However, it's the common lot, even I—Frampton Tregonwell—have not escaped unwounded." Here he heaved a sigh, so comically theatrical, that Blount, though in no humour to jest on the subject, could not forbear laughing.

"Whatever you may surmise," he replied, "we have something more serious to think about at the present time. After I have handled this wonderful stone of yours, and knocked a few specimens out of the 'face'—you see I have gained some practical knowledge since we parted—then we can discuss the plan of the future. In the meantime, I am with you to the scaling of the 'Frenchman's Cap,' if that forms any part of the programme."

The journeying by land or sea to Hobart had been comparatively plain sailing. From Hobart to the west coast of Tasmania inaugurated a striking change. The tiny steamer, *Seagull*, to which they committed themselves for a thirty hours' trip, was dirty, and evil smelling. The shallow bar at Macquarie Harbour forbade a larger boat. Crowded also, her accommodation was necessarily restricted. The twelve male passengers had one cabin allotted to them. The women shared another, where berths like those at a shearer's hut were arranged at the sides. On a coast, by no means well lighted, where no shelter from the fierce gales is found nearer than the South Pole, the passage, performed at night, is invariably a rough one. All honour is due to the hardy seamen commanding the small coast fleet. They lose no time on the trip—overladen with freight, more also to follow—full passenger lists for a month in advance. That there are not more accidents seems a miracle to the passenger, as they thread their course in and out, among the numberless islands and frequent reefs, with marvellous accuracy. Tregonwell, who was half a sailor, by reason of his manifold voyages, was loud in admiration.

"The skipper *must* chance it, now and then," he remarked, "but he doesn't show it, and certainly will not confide in the ordinary passenger." They bumped on the bar at Macquarie Harbour, and also had a narrow escape at "Hell's Gates," formed by the rocky point which runs abruptly northward. They touched bottom in the double whirlpool formed by the island in the very jaws of the current, where the heavy seas breaking over the tiny *Seagull* would not have taken long to turn her into matchwood. Here the skipper showed himself resourceful in such trifling matters. Rough though the water, and dark the night, a man would dash along a spar, laying out a sail to keep her head straight, or bring her round, if broadside on and steering way was lost. Then "full speed astern" perhaps, when not being jammed in too tightly, she glided back into smooth water, ready for another attempt. In an hour, however, the tide rose until the requisite depth of water, in the harbour bar, enabled them after the grim, ghostly night, to glide up the smooth surface of Macquarie Harbour.

It was early morning. They looked out on a sea of mist, walled in by basaltic cliffs, wherein Mounts Heemskirk and Zeehan kept watch over that dreary, wreck-lined coast.

Declining breakfast on board, Messrs. Blount and Tregonwell made for the chief "hotel" of the Macquarie Harbour township, where on a clean white beach, a friendly host, with comely daughters, made them welcome to an excellent meal.

What a change from the days when a few fishermen or prospectors constituted the entire population!

Strahan was now crowded with eager, anxious men, all of whom had money to spend. Vessels were arriving all day long—sailing craft, as well as steamers, loaded with supplies of all kinds, for the "silver field" of Zeehan, so named after one of the vessels of Abel Tasman.

It was a scene of hopeless confusion, as far as the freighting was concerned. Mining machinery, groceries, drapery, blankets, axes, picks and shovels were all dumped upon the sand, with scant ceremony and no regularity.

Day after day they had been passing historic landmarks, were actually on the scene of Marcus Clarke's great novel, *His Natural Life*. They could afford to wait: "Hell's Gates" lay behind them.

In the distance rose "The Isle of the Dead," to which they promised themselves a visit some day, with a ramble among the ruined prison-houses, where so many tortured souls had languished.

One pictured the wretched officers in charge. How dull and aimless their lives! Small wonder if they grew savage, and vented the humours, bred of *ennui* and isolation, upon the wretched convicts.

The walls of the little stone church are standing still. Tregonwell had camped there for a few days once, with some fishermen, shooting ducks at night, and fishing in the long, still, silent days. What a lonely place for men to be stationed at! The interminable forest walled it in on all sides, to the very shore. They pulled for miles up the Gordon River, a grand and picturesque stream, but the land on either bank was absolutely barren of herbage. Nothing grew for miles but the unfriendly jungle of undergrowth, above which waved the mournful pines and eucalypts of the dark impenetrable forest. The distracted owners toiled and wrangled to separate their goods from the ill-assorted mountain of heterogeneous property.

After that, came the more important question of carriage to the rich, but ill-ordered mining camp of Zeehan, where, of course, showy wooden edifices, of calico, or hessian architecture were being erected. The land transit was wholly dependent upon pack horses and a few mules. Drays and waggons were then unknown on that coast. The roads were bad for pedestrians, utterly impassable for wheel traffic. The busiest men were the Customs officers, stationed to watch the goods shipped from other colonies, and to collect the duties exacted thereon. Forwarding agents also had a careworn look. In the midst of the turmoil, a pretentious two-storied hotel was being run up. Stores and warehouses rose like mushrooms from the rain-soaked, humid earth, while town allotments were sold, and resold, at South Sea Bubble prices.

By dint of Mr. Blount's persuasive powers, now fully exerted, and Tregonwell's abnormal energy, conjoined with reckless payments, they saw their personal luggage strapped on to a horse's back, and confided to a packer, who started with them, and contracted to deliver it when they arrived on the following day.

They thus commenced the fifteen mile walk to Trial Bay. This was the nearest port. It lacked, however, any description of harbour, shelter, or roadway. Small craft could deliver freight in fine weather.

The pedestrians carried their blankets and a change of underclothing. That was the recognised fashion on the West Coast. If men didn't start in the rain, they were certain to be wet through before long. Mr. Blount was pleased to admit that their day of commencement was fine; more grateful still to see Trial Bay the same night. Their condition was fairly good, the walking distinctly heavy. A few miles of sandy beach, then came the track through the bush proper.

Now commenced the stern realities of the expedition, necessary before Mr. Blount could have personal cognisance of his strangely acquired property. After some experience of the forests which lay between Bunjil and the "Lady Julia" claim, he had thought himself qualified to judge of "rough country." To his astonishment, he found that all previous adventure had given him no conception of the picture of dread and awful desolation which the Tasmanian primeval wilderness presented. The gigantic, towering trees, (locally known as Huon River pines), the awful thickets, the rank growth of a jungle more difficult to pass through, than any he had known or realised, contributed an appalling *carte du pays*. The peculiarity of this last forest path was, that without a considerable amount of labour being expended upon it, it was impassable for horses, and not only difficult but dangerous for men. The "horizontal scrub," locally so termed, was the admixture of immense altitudes of forest timber, with every kind of shrub, vine, and parasitic undergrowth. Stimulated by ceaseless rain it hid even the surface of the ground from the pedestrian's view. For centuries, the unimpeded brush-wood beneath the gigantic forest trees, which, shooting upwards for hundreds of feet, combined by their topmost interlacing of branches to exclude the sunlight, had fallen rotted, and formed a superincumbent mass, through which the traveller, passing over a filled up gully, once falling through the upper platform, so to speak, might sink to unknown depths. From these indeed, a solitary wayfarer might find it difficult, if not impossible, to return.

"What a track!" exclaimed Blount, toilsomely wading through waist-high bracken, and coming to a halt beside a fallen forest giant, eight feet in diameter, and more than two hundred feet to the first branch. "It ought to be a prize worth winning that tempts men to penetrate such a howling wilderness. Hardly that indeed, for there's an awful silence: hardly a bird or beast, if you notice, seems to make known its presence in the ordinary way."

"I heard this region described by an old hand as exclusively occupied by shepherds, blacks, bushrangers, tigers and devils," replied Tregonwell. "The blacks killed the shepherds, who in their turn harboured the bushrangers, when they didn't betray them for the price set on their heads. The 'tigers' and 'devils' (carnivorous marsupials) killed the sheep and occasionally the sheep-dogs. They were the only other inhabitants of this quasi-infernal region."

"*Facilis descensus*, then, is another quotation which in this land of contradictions has come to grief. I suppose we ought to try and cross this sapling which bars our path?"

"I will go first," said Tregonwell, "and report from the other side," and he prepared to climb the huge and slippery trunk.

The outward appearance of Mr. Blount had undergone a striking and material change, from the days of Bunjil, and even of the "Lady Julia" alluvial claim. A blue serge shirt, considerably torn, even tattered from encounters with brambles, had replaced the Norfolk jacket and tweed suit. His gaiters were mud-covered to the knees. His boots, extra-strong and double-soled, were soaked and wrenched out of shape. To add to his "reversal of form," he carried on his back a heavy "swag," in which under a pair of coarse blue blankets, all his worldly goods immediately indispensable were packed.

"This is something like 'colonial experience,'" said he. With a slight twist of the shoulders, and a groan expressive of uneasiness, he shifted the weight of the burden. "I never carried a swag before, though now I come to think of it, our knapsacks of the old days on walking tours were much the same thing, though more aristocratically named. This confounded thing seems to get heavier every mile. There is a touch of John Bunyan about it also."

The partners found Trial Bay in a worse muddle than Strahan. Tents had been pitched everywhere; men were working hard to get their own and other peoples' loading away.

The small inn was in the usual independent state that obtains when there is too much custom. "They could sleep there, if they had luck," said the landlord airily, but "he didn't know as there was any beds vacant." Accommodation for the travelling public was a secondary matter, in his estimation. The bar paying enormous profits, was filled to overflowing the whole day through—the night also. Here Tregonwell's colonial and other experience stood him in good stead—an all-round "shout" or two, combined with an air of good fellowship, and judicious *douceurs* to the maid-servants, resulted finally in permission to sleep in No. 5—which haven of rest, after a South African sort of meal, largely supported by "bully beef," the tired partners bestowed themselves. After forcibly ejecting several volunteer bedfellows, they slept more or less soundly until daylight.

Certainly no fitter habitat could have been chosen for the desperate irreclaimable convicts, who alone were exiled there. The dense, gloomy, barren forests provided sustenance neither for man nor beast.

No birds—no animals—with one exception, the so-called "badger" (or wombat) which was snared, and eaten by the convicts. The endless rain, priceless in other lands, was valueless here, save to change the mood of the outcast from depression to despair.

The Gordon River pine is the most valuable of the enormous growth of timber in proximity to its banks; a beautiful, soft, red wood, not unlike the cedar of Australia. It can be split into excellent palings and will, fortunately, burn well, either in a wet or dry state. The dense undergrowth, closely intertwined with climbers, renders it impossible even for a man to get through, unless with an axe to clear his way before him. And the locally named "horizontal scrub" is a study in forestry.

It is possible to progress for a quarter of a mile at a stretch, without being nearer the ground than eighteen or twenty feet. This curious shrub, growing as it does at a considerable angle less than forty-five degrees, with its intertwined branches made the jungle all but impenetrable. A stage of fifteen miles was no child's play therefore, and meant a hard day's work for strong men, if unused to walking. Even slow walking on the Corduroy, demoralised by the heavy traffic, was exasperating. Many logs were missing altogether. This meant extra danger for the pack-horses and mules. These horses were wonderfully sure-footed and sagacious. Though carrying two hundred pounds (dead weight too) they were fully as clever at this novel species of wayfaring as the mules. The pack tracks were cleared just wide enough for the animals to travel in single file—and with the exception of a few places they could not get off them, as the forest timber, with dead wood and undergrowth, was impossible for any horse to get through, until a track was cut.

No deviations were possible; in a climate where the rainfall was ninety inches per annum, one could imagine into what a condition these tracks would get.

From time to time a pack horse would sink down behind, irretrievably bogged. In such a case he would wait patiently, knowing that struggling made matters worse, until the packer and his mate came to his assistance. They would lever him up with poles, and whenever they shouted, he would make his effort.

Sometimes they would unload, to give him a chance to extricate himself. Then the packs were put on again, and a general start made. Such men would probably have ten or twelve horses and mules walking loose—often with not even a bridle on.

The charge made was at the rate of threepence a pound—roughly twenty-five pounds a ton—from Strahan to the "field," in those early days.

The only variation from the dense forest was that of the "button grass" country. This was composed of open flats covered with a tufted plant, similar to the Xanthorrhea or grass tree—only wanting the elongated spear-like seed stalk. No animal eats the button grass; it is worthless for fodder alive or dead.

What sights on the road they saw! Men and boys, with an odd woman or two, struggling through the mud in the soaking, drizzling rain! Men wheeling barrows with their tools, swags and belongings generally. Men harnessed to small carts, tugging them along. Four Germans drew a small wheeled truck, which they had made themselves, and a staunch team they were. So practised had some of the early prospecting parties become that (Tregonwell said) they plied a paying trade of packing on *their own backs* to outside claims, where pack tracks for horses had not yet been cut. These men would carry from eighty to a hundred pounds, walking the journey of thirty miles in two days. The charge was a shilling a pound. They would walk back "empty" in one day. If it seemed high pay, it was hard work. Climbing hills of fifteen hundred feet and going down the other side with that crushing weight of bacon or flour taxed a man's strength, condition and pluck. Tregonwell said you could always pick out the packers in a crowd after they had been a year or two at it. They invariably "stood over" at the knees, like old cab horses, from the strain of steadying themselves down hill with heavy weights up.

"Many a time, when the field first opened" (said Tregonwell), "have I walked beside one of these men the day through, carrying only my blankets and a change, not weighing more than fifteen pounds; my packer companion would carry his fifty to eighty pounds up the long hills with comparative ease, passing me, if I didn't look out, pulling up, too, quite fresh at night, while I could scarcely stagger into camp; yet I could outdo, easily, any other amateur on the field."

Some original inventions Blount noted outside of his gradually extending colonial experience. Each camp had a "fly" pitched permanently over the fire-place to keep the endless rain from putting it out. "Kindling" wood was kept under this fly, so that it was always in readiness. After the fire was well started, green or wet wood could be put on and would burn well.

Tregonwell, having once started, said that he soon got into form, improving in pace and condition daily. He expatiated on the keen enjoyment of the hot meal at the end of the day's journey, rude as might be the appliances and primitive the cookery. The meal was chiefly composed of tinned meat, stewed or curried, with bacon added for flavour; and freshly-made damper, or "Johnny cakes," to follow. The change of garments was to dry pyjamas, with a blanket wrapped round the wearer.

It was, he stated, a luxurious, half-tired, languorous but fully-satisfied feeling, the sensation of mind and body essential to the fullest enjoyment of tobacco. Then the yarns of the old prospectors, grizzled, sinewy, iron-nerved veterans! Where had they not been? California in '49, Ballarat in '51, pioneers of Lambing Flat, at the big rush, Omeo, Bendigo, New Zealand, West Coast, 25,000 men on the field in a week; those were the times to see life! Queensland, Charters Towers, Gympie, New Guinea, the Gulf, ah! "This Zeehan racket's a bit of a spirt; but talk of mining! It's dead now, dead, sir, and buried. Those were the days!" The dauntless pioneer fills another pipe and falls into a reverie of cheap-won gold, reckless revelry, wherein perils by land or sea, danger, ay, and death, would seem to have been inextricably mingled.

A strange race, the prospectors, *sui generis*. Hardly a spot on the globe was there which these men had not searched for the precious metals. Distance, climate, are nothing, less than nothing, in their calculations, once let the fact be established of a payable silver or gold "field." Landing in Australia in the early fifties, they had worked on every field before mentioned, and are still ready to join the rush for any country under heaven should gold happen to "break out." Klondyke, Argentina, South Africa, all equally eligible once the ancient lure is held out. They often put together a few thousand pounds in the early days of a rich goldfield, their wide experience and boundless energy making some measure of success certain. They may not drink, but all live luxuriously, even extravagantly, while the money lasts, possibly for a few years, then go back to their roving, laborious life. They generally make enough on each field to carry them to the ends of the earth, if necessary, and it is mostly so from their point of view. When funds are low, they can, and do, live cheaply; will work hard and do long journeys on the scantiest fare. Natural bushmen, often Australian-born; from this type of man, above all others, a regiment might be formed of "Guides" or "Scouts," ready to fight stubbornly in any war of the future; would hunt, harry, and run to earth De Wet, or other slippery Boer, if given the contract and a "free hand."

Harking back to his experiences—"That wild West Coast," continued Tregonwell, "was a place to remember—the wooded ranges piled one upon another, as far as eye could reach, in shape, height, timber, or colouring hardly differing in any essential particular; yet the noted prospectors never lost themselves. Stopping for weeks at a likely 'show,' as long as the bacon and flour held out, they avoided all settlements or mining centres on the way. The first prospector, George Bell, carried a lump of galena of forty pounds' weight in his swag right through from Zeehan to Mount Bischoff.

For a distance of fifty miles he went straight between the two points without a road or track being cut for him."

When the partners arrived at Zeehan, it certainly appeared to Mr. Blount a place of peculiar and unusual characteristics. The excitement was naturally great; stores, hotels, dwellings, lodging-houses going up in all directions. Timber was plentiful to excess, luckily such as split into slabs and palings easily.

Tents were beginning to be voted hardly equal to so vigorous a climate. No one, however, stayed under cover for that reason. They were wet all day and every day, but the rule was to change into dry things at night. No harm, strange to say, came to anybody. There was less sickness, certainly less typhoid, on that field than any since reported.

Less, certainly, than at Broken Hill and the West Australian Goldfields. The hotels, quickly run up, were rough both in appearance and management. About fifty men slept in the billiard room for the first few nights. Then, as their importance as "capitalists" began to be recognised, beds were allotted. Over these they had to mount guard for an hour or more before bedtime, as a rule, or else to "chuck out" the intruder. Here the personal equation came in. The landlord had no time to support the legal rights of his guests. He merely went so far as to allot each man a bed. He had to keep it and pay for it.

The term "capitalist" on a mining field is understood to apply to people with money of their own, or substantial backers who are prepared to pay down the deposit on mines, sufficiently developed or rich enough to "float"; worth securing the "option" of purchase for a month, so as to give time to raise the necessary funds.

The Tregonwell party had secured the "fancy show" of the field (*i.e.*, the next richest in reputation to the Comstock) by promptness in agreeing to all the owner's conditions, as he named them, thus giving him no chance to change his mind. Other offers had been made from Hobart and elsewhere. However, they paid a liberal deposit, and, after thoroughly sampling and examining the ore body, agreed to float the mine in a fortnight. Very short terms! Also to place £10,000 to its credit as a working capital, and to give the owner £5,000 cash as well as a certain number of shares.

They knew the market, however, and their business. Tregonwell *walked* to Strahan in a day and a half, being then in high condition, and got off to Hobart by steamer that night. Had the transfers signed and registered in the Mines Department in his name, subject to the conditions being fulfilled. Wired to their Melbourne brokers, and in twenty-four hours the shares were applied for three times over, and the stock quoted at a premium. It seems easy, but such is not always the case. The boom must be on. The buyers must be well known to the public as having the necessary experience, and being reliable on a cash basis.

A shout from a tall, well-dressed man—comparatively, we may say—greets them at the long-desired camp. He comes forward and shakes hands with Tregonwell, more heartily than even the occasion demands, it would seem.

"By Jove! old fellow. I *am* so glad to see you. Would have sent a line to Hobart to hurry you up, if I could have found a man to take it. But most of the fellows have gone to Marble Creek, so we're a small community. But we're forgetting our manners. Introduce me."

"Mr. Valentine Blount, permit me to present Mr. Charles Herbert, one of our partners. You mustn't swear at the place, the roads, the climate, the people, or anything belonging to Tasmania, as it's his native land, to which he is deeply attached. In all other respects he may be treated as an Englishman."

"He certainly looks like one," said Blount, glancing over the fine figure and regular features of the tall, handsome Tasmanian. "If the other gentleman who makes up the syndicate is a match for him, we should be an efficient quartette."

"Clarke is a light-weight," said Tregonwell, "but as wiry as a dingo, besides being the eminent mining expert of the party (of course, when I'm away); but he's perhaps more up to date, as when he went to California he learned the latest wrinkles in silver-mining. He's rather an invalid at present, having jarred his right hand with a pick, and sprained his left ankle in taking a walk through this 'merry greenwood,' as old writers called the forest."

"I thought I had seen some rough country in New South Wales," said Blount, "but this tops anything I have ever seen or indeed heard of, except an African jungle."

"Climate not quite so bad, no fever yet," replied Herbert, "but can't say much for the Queen's Highway. However, the silver's all right, and where that's the case, anything else follows in good time. But, come inside—no horses to want feeding, luckily, as the oats which came in advance, cost a guinea a bucket."

So saying, he led the way to a small but not uncomfortable hut, at one side of which a fire of logs was blazing in a huge stone chimney. The walls of this rude dwelling were composed of the trunk of the black fern tree, placed vertically in the ground, the interstices being filled up with a compost of mud and twigs, which formed a wind and waterproof wall, while it lasted. On one of the rude couches lay a man, who excused himself from rising on the score of a sprained ankle.

"It's so confoundedly painful," he said, "that even standing gives me fits. Of all the infernal, brutal, God-forsaken holes, that ever a man's evil genius lured him into, this is the worst and most villanous. In California, the Tasmanians and Cornstalks were looked on as criminals and occasionally lynched as such, but you *could* walk out in daylight and were not made a pack-horse of. If I were this gentleman, whom I see Tregonwell has enticed here under false pretences, I should hire a Chinaman to carry me back to Strahan, and bring an action against him as soon as I reached Hobart."

"I'm afraid he's delirious, Mr. Blount," said Herbert, soothingly, "and as he's lost a leg and an arm, so to speak, we can't hammer him at present, but he's not a bad chap, when he's clothed and in his right mind. In the meantime, as a fellow-countryman, I apologise for him."

"Don't believe a word these monomaniacs tell you, Mr. Blount," said the sufferer, trying to raise himself on one arm, and subsiding with a groan. "Herbert's an absurd optimist, and Tregonwell—well, we know what Cousin Jacks are. However, after supper, I daresay I shall feel better. Do you happen to have a late paper about you?"

"Several," said Blount, "which I hadn't time to read before we left, including a *Weekly Times*."

"In that case," said the pessimist, "I retract much of what I have said. I have read everything they have here, and thought I was stranded in the wilderness without food, raiment, or *pabulum mentis*. Now I descry a gleam of hope."

"I brought a packet of wax candles," observed Blount. "Thought they might be useful."

"Useful!" cried the invalid, "you have saved my life, they are *invaluable*. Fancy having to read by a slush lamp! Mr. Blount, we are sworn brothers from this hour."

"For Heaven's sake let us have supper," interposed Tregonwell. "Is the whisky jar empty? I feel as if a nip would not be out of place, where two tired, hungry, muddy travellers are concerned."

"Not quite so bad as that," replied Herbert, who had been spreading tin plates and pannikins over the rude table on trestles, with corned beef in a dish of the same material, and baker's bread for a wonder. A modicum of whisky from the jar referred to was administered to each one of the company, prior to the announcement of supper.

When the primitive meal had been discussed with relish, Mr. Jack Clarke considered himself sufficiently restored to sit up against the wall of the hut, and begin at Mr. Blount's newspapers with the aid of one of that gentleman's wax candles in a bottle, by way of candlestick. The others preferred to sit round the fire on three-legged stools provided for such purpose, and smoke, carrying on cheerful conversation the while.

The discovery of the Comstock as a deeply interesting subject, commended itself to Mr. Blount; so Tregonwell persuaded Herbert, who was the pioneer, to sketch the genesis of this famous property, destined to exercise so important an influence on their future lives.

"Come, Charlie," said he, "you're the real prospector, Clarke wouldn't have gone into it but for you, and I shouldn't have taken a share but for Blount, who knew nothing about mines, having just come from England. I wanted to chuck it, but Blount, who is obstinate (not a bad virtue, in its way), determined, for that very reason, to stick to it.

"So he paid his share of the expenses, went away, met all kinds of adventures and all sorts and conditions of men—with, of course, a girl or two, not wholly unattractive, and forgot all about it. I kept an eye on it, so did Charlie; complied with the labour condition, kept up the pegs, according to the Act, did a little work now and then. And now, Charlie! it's your turn."

Mr. Herbert put down his pipe carefully and began the wondrous tale. "You know I was always fond of mooning about—wallaby-shooting, fishing, and collecting birds and plants in mountain country. We had a sheep station on the edge of this horizontal scrub country in old times; and I used, when I had leave, to get away and spend a week or two of my Christmas holiday there. One of the shepherds was a great pal of mine. Like many of the prisoners of the Crown in old days, he had been transported wrongfully, or for very slight offences (as much to get rid of Britain's surplus population as for any other reason it really would seem). He was fairly educated, and was a very decent, well-behaved old chap, with a taste for geology and minerals.

"When his sheep were camped in the middle of the day I would find out his flock, and we would boil the billy and have lunch, with ever so much talk.

"'Look here, Master Charles!' he said one day, as he took out a dull, grey-looking stone from his 'dilly bag,' 'do ye know what that is?' I did not, and like most youngsters of my age, looked upon it as rubbish, and showed that I would rather have had a shot at one of the 'tigers' or 'devils' that came every now and then and killed the sheep at the stations than all the silver ore in the country.

"'It's silver ore,' said he in a solemn voice; 'and there's enough where that came from to buy all your father's stations ten times over, if I could only find my way back to the place where I found it.'

"'And why can't you?' said I; 'you know all the country round here.'

"The old man looked very sad, and pointed out towards the Frenchman's Cap, which was just being covered with mist, while a heavy shower began to fall, and a thunderstorm roared and echoed among the rocks and caves of the 'Tiers,' at the foot of which we managed to get shelter.

"'It was a strange day and a strange sight I saw when I picked up this slug,' he said. 'I was never nearer losing my life!—but I'll tell you all about it another day. You'd better get back to the station now, or you'll get wet through, and maybe catch cold, and then the master won't let you come here again.'

"So I was obliged to leave the telling of the story to another day. I forgot all about the silver ore, and, chiefly remembering the strange part of the story, was determined to hear about it from the old man another day.

"It was the late spring-time when we had this talk, old Chesterton and I; but a month or so afterwards I got a holiday, and as the weather was warm and fine I cleared out to his out station, and never rested till I bailed up the old man for another yarn. It is sometimes hot in the island, though you mightn't think so."

"Don't believe him," growled Mr. Clarke; "it's a popular error. The seasons have changed. Listen to that!" The rain was certainly falling with a sustained volume, which discredited any references to warmth and sunshine.

"However," continued Herbert, paying not the slightest attention, "remember, it was at the end of the Christmas holidays, and the rocks felt red hot; there had been bush fires, but the young feed, such as it was, was lovely and green. The air was clear, the sky for once hadn't a cloud on it, and the old man was in a wonderful good humour for a shepherd.

"'Well, Master Charles,' he said, 'if ye must have it, ye must. I don't know that it can do you any harm, though it kept me awake for weeks afterwards, and every time the dog barked I felt my heart beat like, and would wake me up all of a tremble. Well, to come to the story, I was sitting on a log half asleep with the sheep camped quiet and comfortable under a big pine, when I heard my old dog growl. He never did that for nothing, so

I looked up, and the blood nearly froze in my veins at what I saw. It wasn't much to scare the seven senses out of me, but I knew how I stood.

"'A man and a woman were coming down a gully from the direction of the mountain; they were near enough to see me, and it was no use making a bolt of it. I should only lose my life. Anyhow, I couldn't leave the flock. I should get flogged for that. No excuse was taken for anything of that sort in those days. Following the man was a young gin with a lot of things on her back as if they had been shifting camp. She was much like any other black girl of her age, sixteen or thereabouts, maybe less; they grow up fast and get old fast, too, specially when they are worked hard, beaten, and brutally treated, as most of them are, and this one certainly was. Poor Mary! The man had no boots, and his trousers were ragged, he was mostly dressed in kangaroo skins, and had a fur cap on.

"'He had a long beard down to his chest; his black hair fell in a mat over his shoulders. He carried a double-barrelled gun, and had a belt with a pouch in it round his waist. He looked like the pictures of Robinson Crusoe, but I didn't feel inclined to laugh when he came close up and stared me in the face. I had seen, ay, lived with criminals of all sorts since I first came to Tasmania, but such a savage, blood-thirsty-looking brute as the man before me, I had never come across before. He saw that I was afraid; well I might be—if he had shot me there and then, it was only what he had done to others. With a fiendish grin that made him, if possible, more beast-like in appearance, he said: "Did ye ever see Mick Brady afore? No! Well, ye see him now. Maybe ye won't live long enough to forget him!"

"""I've heard of you," I said, "of course." I tried to look cool, but my teeth chattered, for all the day was so hot. "I'm a Government man, like yourself. I've never done you any harm that I know of."

"""No harm!" he shouted, "no harm! Aren't ye one of old Herbert's shepherds—a lot of mean crawlers that work for a bloody tyrant, and inform on poor starving brutes like me that's been driven to take to the bush by cruelty and injustice of every kind. I came here to shoot you, and shoot you I will, and your dog too; the dingos and the tigers may work their will on the flock afterwards. He'll feel that a d—d sight more than the loss of a shepherd. I know him, the hard-hearted old slave-driver!" God forgive him for miscalling a good man and a kind master.

"""Don't shoot the dog," I said, "he's the best I ever had—a prisoner's life's not much in this country, but a dog like him you don't see every day."

"""Kneel down," he said, "and don't waste time; ye can say a short prayer to God Almighty, or the devil, whichever ye favour most. Old Nick's given *me* a lift, many a time."

"'He stood there, with the death-light in his red-rimmed, wolfish eyes, and no more mercy in them than a tiger's, lapping the blood of a Hindoo letter-carrier. When I was a soldier I'd seen the poor things brought in from the jungle, with their throats torn out, and mangled beyond knowing. Surely man was never in a worse case or nearer death. Strangely, I felt none of the fear which I did when I saw him first. I had no hope, but I prayed earnestly to God, believing that a very few moments would suffice to place me beyond mortal terrors.

"'The girl meanwhile had crept closer to us and stood with her large eyes wide open, half in surprise, half in terror—as she leaned her laden back against one of the rock pillars which stood around. She murmured a few words in her own language—I knew it slightly—against bloodshed, and for mercy. But he turned on her with a savage oath, and made as though he would add her murder to the long list of his crimes.

CHAPTER VII

"'At that moment, the last I ever expected to see on earth, the black girl uttered a sudden cry. The report of a gun was heard, as a bullet passed between me and Brady, flattening itself against the rock where I had been leaning just before. At the same time four men dashed across the gully and made for him. He looked at me with devilish malignity for a moment, but I suppose, wanting the charge in his gun for his own defence, turned and fled with extraordinary speed towards the forest, the police—for such they were—with a soldier and the informer, firing at him as he went. Their guns were the old-fashioned tower muskets; they were bad shots at best—so the girl and he disappeared in the thick wood, unhurt as far as I could see. I fell on my face, I know, and thanked God before I rose—the God of our fathers, who had answered my prayer and delivered me out of the hand of the "bloody and deceitful man," in the words of the Psalmist. I took my sheep home early, and put them in the paling yard—dog proof it was—and needed to be, in that part of the country. Just as it was getting dark, the men came back, regularly knocked up, with their clothes torn to rags and half off their backs. They hadn't caught Brady. I didn't expect they would—he was in hard condition, and could run like a kangaroo. He got clean out of sight of them in a mile or two after they left us. What astonished me was, that they brought back the black girl, with a bullet through her shoulder, poor thing!

"'"I suppose that was a mistake," said I, "you didn't fire at the poor thing, surely?"

"'"We didn't," said the soldier, "but who d'ye think did?"

"'"You don't say?" said I.

"'"But I do. It was that infernal villain and coward, Brady himself, that shot her. She couldn't keep up with him, and for fear she'd fall into our hands, and give away his 'plants,' he fired at her, and nearly stopped her tongue for ever. But he's overdid it this time—she's red hot agen 'im now, and swears she'll go with any party to help track him up."

"'"Serve the brute right. Let's have a look at the poor thing's shoulder, I wonder if the bullet's still in it?"

"'We washed off the blood, and between us, managed to get it out. It was wonderful how many people in those days knew something about gunshot wounds. After we'd shown Mary the bullet, we bound it up, and the poor gin thanked us, and lay down on her furs by the fire, quite comfortable. We kept watch and watch, you may be sure, for fear Brady might come in the night, and shoot one of us, but nothing happened, and after breakfast the party went back to Hobart, taking the girl with them.

"'I was in fear for weeks afterwards that he might come and pay me out. But he didn't do that either. He was taken not long after, and when he was, it was through that same girl, Mary, whom he tried to shoot. He met his fate through his own base bloodthirsty act, and if any one brought it on his own head, and deserved it thoroughly, Mick Brady was that man.

"'Now this happened a many years ago, before you were born, or thought of, as the saying is. Often and often, when I could leave the flock safe, did I try to find out the place where this stone came from, but I never could drop on it again. When I found it first and saw that there was a regular lode, and plenty more "slugs" as rich as this, which is nearly pure silver, mind you, I was in such a hurry to get back to the sheep, that I'd only time to mark two or three trees, and drive in a stake, before I started for home.

"'I was sure I could find it again. But I never did. It was hot weather, and a bush fire started that day, and burned for weeks, sweeping all that side of the country.

"'You'll remember reading of Black Thursday, Master Charles? it burned all Port Phillip, Victoria as they call it now, from Melbourne town to the Ottawa range. So I expect my marks were burnt out. For I never could find the way to it again: what with the fallen timber that covered over the ground, and the ashes that was heaped up a foot deep in some places, the whole face of the country was altered past knowing. You might have heard tell that ashes fell on board some of the coasting craft miles from the shore, and a black cloud hung over the coastline, for days afterwards. But, take my word for it, Master Charles, the word of a dying man, for I'm not long for this world, that whoever finds the gully where this stone came from, and takes up a prospecting claim, will own the richest silver mine, south of the line. Your father's always been a good master to his prisoner servants, that Mick Brady told a lie when he said he wasn't, and there's none of 'em that wouldn't do him a good turn, if they could; and I have known you and loved you ever since you was the height of a walking stick. So here's the silver "slug," and the wash-leather bag of specimens, there's gold and copper besides, and I hope there'll be luck with them.'

"The poor old chap didn't live long after that. He was comfortable enough for the last year or two of his life, for my father pensioned his old servants, and his old horses too, for that matter. He couldn't bear to think that after they'd worked well all their lives, they should be allowed to drag out a wretched existence, starved, or perhaps ill-treated, till death came to their relief. So the silver 'slug' was bequeathed to me, this is a bit of it on my watch-chain, with the malachite colouring showing out. It always comes with time, they say. Anyhow it brought me luck in the end, though it was a precious long time coming about."

"As you've brought us so far," said Jack Clarke, "and Mr. Blount seems interested (he hasn't been asleep more than twice), I think it would be a fair thing to give us the last chapter. For, I suppose you *did* find the old man's marked tree, and if so, how? as lawyers say."

"As you have deduced, with your usual astuteness, that I must have found it, or we shouldn't be here, I suppose, I may lay aside my modesty, and enlighten the company. The 'Comstock' has a well-marked track now, if there's nothing else good about it. Old Parkins gave me the bearings of the 'Lost Gully,' as he always called it. Once a year, I always took a loaf round the locality after Christmas, poking about doing a little fishing, when there was any: shooting wallaby or anything worth while that I came across. Got an old man kangaroo bailed up at the head of a gully, one day after a big fight with my dogs. I had fired away my cartridges, and was looking round for a stick to hit him on the head with, when I backed on to a stump of an upright sapling, as I thought, out of a 'whip stick scrub,' which had grown up since the fire.

"It did not give way, as I expected, and putting back my hand to feel it, I found it was a *stake*! It was charred all round, but still sound, and hard to the core. Lucky for me, it was stringy bark timber. I pulled it up, and tried it on the old man's skull, which it cracked like an egg shell. It had been pointed with a tomahawk, and driven well into the ground. That clinched the matter. It *was the old man's peg*! The next thing was to clear the ground round about of timber and ashes, with all the accumulation of years. This I did next day, carefully, and it was not long before I discovered a couple of tomahawk marks on a big 'mess-mate' not far off. The bark had partly grown over it. It was in the form of a cross. Underneath the new bark the marking was perfect, as I had often seen surveyors' marks, years and years after they had been done. Then I came upon the cap of the lode, broke off some rock, fifty per cent. ore, no mistake. Blazed my track and cleared for Hobart. Took up a prospector's claim next morning at 10 a.m. Registered in due form. Met Clarke and accidentally Messrs. Blount and Tregonwell, new—er—that is to say, newly arrived from England, and the great silver property, known to the world as the 'Tasmanian Comstock, Limited,' and so on was duly launched."

"Well done, Charlie, my boy! No idea you'd so much poetry in your composition! You were not regarded as imaginative at the old 'Hutchins Institute,' where we both had 'small Latin and less Greek' hammered into us. But you were a sticker, I will say that for you. Now that I'm *hors de combat*, I seem to see that quality in a new light. Main strength and stupidity we used to call it in your case."

"I've no doubt; you were horribly ill-mannered, even without a sprained ankle," retorted Herbert, "but we make allowances for your condition as an invalid. By the time we get that corduroy track finished, and traffic other than 'man-power' restored, we shall look for improvement."

The next day, being bright with sunshine, dispersed some of the gloom which wet, cold and unwonted fatigue had imposed upon the partners. The shafts of sunlight, flashing through the endless glades and thickets of the primeval forest, formed a thousand glittering coruscations of all imaginable forms and figures.

The pools of water reflected the glimpses of cloudless sky, framed in sombre but still burnished shades of green. Birds called and twittered in approval of the change, while strings of water-fowl, winging their way to the great mountain lakes, told of a happier clime, and the undisturbed enjoyment in which the tribes of the air might revel.

The obvious primary duty after breakfast was to get to the mine itself. The distance was not great, but the task was less easy than might be supposed. The track through the jungle of scrub and forest was necessarily narrow, as the labour necessary for clearing it was great and, therefore, expensive. The tremendous rainfall had turned the adjoining country into a quagmire, the only means of crossing which was by a corduroy road.

On this inconvenient makeshift the friends stumbled along until they came to a collection of huts and tents, the usual outcrop of a mining township, which springs up, mushroom-like, at the faintest indication of proved, payable gold, silver or copper in any part of Australia. Of course there was a "store," so called, from which proudly flaunted a large calico flag, with "Comstock Emporium" rudely painted thereon, while a few picks and shovels, iron pots and frying-pans, with a half-emptied case of American axes outside the canvas door, denoted the presence of the primary weapons used in the war with nature.

A score or more of shafts, above which were the rude windlasses with rope and bucket of the period, disclosed the beginning of mining enterprise, advertising the hope and expectation of a subterranean treasure-house—the hope invariable, the expectation, alas! so often doomed to barren disappointment and eventual despair.

However, when the prospectors' claim was reached, within the area of which no intrusion was allowed, the dull grey rock from which Mr. Blount was urged to break down a few fragments disclosed a perfect Aladdin's cave of the precious metal. His enthusiasm, slow to arouse, became keen, stimulated by this "potentiality of boundless wealth." His more emotional partner was loudly enthusiastic upon the immense value of the discovery.

"See that stone," he said, knocking off a corner of the "face," "it's all fifty per cent. stuff—when it's not seventy-five. Look at the native silver and the malachite! I've been on the 'Comstock,' and the 'Indian Chief' in Denver, and can make affidavit that in their best days they never turned out better stone than that—most of it was less than half the percentage, indeed. The ore bodies were larger, you say? No such thing. This lode widens out; the deeper you go, the more there is of it. Easy worked, too. Freight expensive? Wait till the corduroy's finished to the main road; we'll have stores and hotels, the electric light, hot and cold water laid on; a couple of clubs, with the last month's magazines, and *The Times* itself on the smoking-room table. You don't know how everything comes to 'a big field,' gold, silver or copper, as soon as the precious metal is proved—proved, mind you—to have a settled abode there. Fortune? There's a fortune apiece for every proprietor here to-day—even for Clarke, who's now in his bunk reading a yellow-back novel."

All this fairy-appearing relation turned out to be a sober and accurate statement of facts, as far as could be gathered from the survey made by the partners in the enterprise. The stone, which was of surpassing richness, was principally found in a well-defined lode, forty feet wide, increasing in volume as the shafts pierced more deeply into the bowels of the earth.

A mining expert of eminence turned up, who had, after many perils and disasters, found his way to Comstock. On being permitted a "private view," he confirmed Mr. Tregonwell's wildest flights of fancy.

"Nothing in the Southern Hemisphere as rich, or half as rich, has ever been discovered," he said. He doubted, as did Tregonwell, whether in all the mines from Peru to Denver such a deposit had ever been unearthed. He proved by reference to scientific geological treatises that it was so rare as to have been doubted as a possibility that such a find *could* occur, but if so, the most apocryphal yield of Peru and Chile would have paled before the size and richness of this Silverado of the Wilderness, so long hidden from the gaze of man.

Then an adjournment was made to the "Emporium," as it was proudly styled, the meagreness of its materials and adornments being in the inverse proportion to its imposing designation.

But the glory of the future, the assured development of the mine, and, as a natural sequence, of the "field," was shed around with irradiating effect and brilliancy of colouring. Upon this the proprietor proceeded to dilate, after an invitation to a calico shielded sanctum, sacred to the account books and documents of the establishment. In the centre of the compartment stood a table composed of the top of a packing case, placed upon stakes driven into the earthen floor. At one side was a stretcher with his blankets and bedclothes, surmounted by a gaily coloured rug, upon which the visitors were invited to sit, while the host after placing a bottle of whisky of a fashionable brand upon the festive board, cordially requested his guests to join him in drinking the health of the energetic and spirited proprietors of the Great Comstock Silver Mine.

"Not that it looks much now, gentlemen; no more does this stringy bark and calico shanty of mine. But that says nothing. I was at Ballarat in the 'fifties,' and Jack Garth, the baker, had just such a gunya as this. I brought up a load of flour for him, and was paid a hundred and fifty pound a ton for the carriage. The roads were bad certainly—puts me in mind of this hole, in that way; but you *could* travel, somehow. And look at Ballarat now, with trams, and town halls, and artificial lakes, and public gardens and statues—just like the old country. And Jack Garth, well, he's worth a couple of hundred thousand pounds, if he's worth a penny; owns farms and prize stock, and hotels, and everything a man can want in this world. How came that, gentlemen? Because he was a hardworking straightgoing chap? No! that wouldn't have done it, though he'd always have made a good living— any man of the right sort can do *that* in Australia. But *the gold was there!* It was there then, and it's there now. It floated the whole place up to fortune and fame, the diggers, the storekeepers, the publicans, the commissioners, the carriers, the very police made money: some of 'em saved it too. Didn't one of 'em own a whole terrace of houses afterwards? Well, the gold was there, and *the silver's here*; that's all that's wanted for miners to know, and they'll follow it up, if it was to the South Pole; and mark my words, gentlemen, this place'll go ahead, and grow and flourish, and make fortunes for us men standing here, and for the er—er—babe unborn." Concluding his peroration with this effective forecast, which showed that his connection, as member, with the Bungareeshire council had not been without effect on his elocution, Mr. Morgan replenished his glass, and invited his distinguished guests to do likewise.

Hobart, at length. Mr. Blount was unaffectedly pleased, even joyous, when for the second time he sighted the towering summit and forest-clothed sides of Mount Wellington, overlooking the picturesque city, the noble stretches of the Derwent, and the Southern main. Impatient of delay, and feverishly anxious to receive the letters which he had not cared to trust to the irregular postal service of Silverado; almost certain, as he deemed, of answers to his letters from Mrs. Bruce and Imogen, even if the master of the house had not relented, he had stayed a day to ensure the company of the mining expert, the road being lonely, the weather bad, and the conversation of a cultured companion valuable under the circumstances. Mr. Blount ran rapidly through the pile of letters and papers which he found awaiting him; indeed, made a second examination of these former missives.

A feeling of intense disappointment overcame him when no letters with the postmark of the village on the Upper Sturt turned up, nor did he discover the delicate, yet free and legible handwriting, which conveyed such solace to his soul at Bunjil.

Looking over the correspondence, mechanically, however, he came across the postmark of that comparatively obscure townlet, and recalling the bold, characteristic hand of Sheila Maguire, tore it open. It ran as follows:—

"Dear Mr. Blount,—You told me when you went away that cold morning, that if anything happened here that I thought you ought to know, I was to write and tell you. We all thought there would be a heavy fall of rain, and most likely a big storm that night. I expect you just missed it, but there must have been a waterspout or something, for the Little River, and all the creeks at the head of the water, came down a banker. It knocked the sluicing company's works about, above a bit, and flooded the miners' huts—but the worst thing it did was to drown poor Johnny Doyle the mailman. Yes! poor chap, it wasn't known for days afterwards, when the people at Marondah wondered why they didn't get their mail. He was never known to be late before. However, drowned he was, quite simple too. He could swim first-rate, but the pack-horse was caught in a snag, and he must have jumped in, to loose the bags, and got kicked on the head and stunned. So the packer was drowned, and him too, worse luck! His riding horse was found lower down—he'd swum out all right. They fished up the pack saddle with the mail-bags, but the letters were squashed up to pulp—couldn't be delivered.

"So, if you wrote to any one *down the river, she didn't get it.*

"I thought it as well to let you know, as you might be waiting for an answer, and not getting one, go off to foreign parts in *a despairing state of mind*. Bunjil's much the same as when you left, except that Little-River-Jack, the two O'Haras, and Lanky Dixon were arrested in Gippsland, but not being evidence enough, the P.M. here turned them up. A report came that you had struck it rich in Tasmania, so you may be sure of getting *all* your letters now and some over. I've noticed that. So long. I send a newspaper with the account in it of the flood.

"Believe me always,

"Your sincere friend and well-wisher,

"Sheila Maguire.

"P.S.—The cob goes first-rate with me. I'm learning him to jump. He's christened 'Bunjil.' I'm going to live in Tumut after Christmas, and he will remind me of the time you came here first."

"By Jove! Sheila, you're a trump!" was Mr. Blount's very natural exclamation, as he arose and walked up and down the room, after mastering the contents of the momentous epistle. "This clears up the mystery of their silence. No wonder they didn't write, Bruce thinking that I was willing to let judgment go by default. Mrs. Bruce and Imogen believing Heaven knows what? That I must be a shady character, at any rate, no gentleman, or I would have answered one or other of their letters—sent in the goodness of their hearts. So this is the explanation!"

The temporary relief accorded to the recipient of Sheila's letter encouraged him to hunt through the pile of newspapers for the unassuming *Bunjil, Little River, and Boggy Creek Herald*, which, presently descrying, he fastened upon the headlines, "Disastrous flood." "Great destruction of property." "Lamentable death by drowning."

"We regret deeply to be compelled to chronicle the melancholy and fatal accident by which Mr. John Doyle, a valued employé of the Postal Department, lost his life last week.

"The mail from the township to the Tallawatta Post-Office, by no means inconsiderable or unimportant, is carried on horseback, though we have repeatedly pointed out its inadequacy as a mode of transport. Our remonstrance has unfortunately been emphasised by the drowning of the mail-carrier, and the total loss of the letters and papers. Mr. Doyle was a fine young man, of steady habits, a good horseman and expert swimmer. It is surmised that in attempting to free the pack-horse, since discovered entangled in a sunken tree root, he was kicked by the struggling animal and stunned; the *post-mortem* examination before the inquest, made by Dr.

Dawson, M.D., who came over from Beechworth for the purpose, disclosed a deep cut on the temple and the mark of a horseshoe. The coroner, with a jury of six, brought in a verdict of 'Accidental death by drowning.' At the funeral, nearly a hundred persons attended, showing the respect in which the deceased was held by the neighbours. Father O'Flynn of the Presbytery at Hovell conducted the service. This occurrence has cast quite a gloom over our township and the surrounding district."

So much for poor Johnny Doyle, a game, active, hardworking son of the soil; sober and well conducted, the chief support of his widowed mother, with a brood of half-a-dozen young children.

There was some argument after the funeral upon the mystery of permitted evil, and the dispensation which allowed the sacrifice of poor Johnny, whose life was a benefit in his humble sphere, to all connected with him, while as to certain worthless members of the body politic, freely referred to by name, the invariable verdict upon an apparently charmed life was, "You couldn't kill 'em with an axe."

Though temporarily immersed in thought, Mr. Blount quickly came to the conclusion that, as his former letters had been prevented by fate from achieving their purpose, it would be the obvious course to write to the same persons at once, furnishing the same explanation. He devoted the evening to that duty solely, and after conveying to Mr. Bruce his regrets for the unavoidable delay which had occurred, and lamenting the injurious construction which might be put upon his silence, made an appeal to his sense of honour that he should be granted a hearing, and be permitted to explain personally the apparent inconsistency of his conduct.

To Mrs. Bruce he wrote with more freedom of expression, deploring the unkind fate which had denied him an opportunity of clearing away the aspersions on his character. As to his non-appearance, he had been called away by business of the *greatest urgency*, affecting not only his own but other people's interests. His future prospects had been deeply involved. Nothing short of prompt action could have saved the situation. Now, he was rejoiced to be able to assure her and Miss Imogen, that a fortune of no inconsiderable amount was actually within his grasp.

He forwarded a copy of the *Hobart Intelligencer*, a respectable journal, in which she would find a confirmation of his statement. Also, a detailed account of the rise and progress of the property, though more rose-coloured than he would care to assert. The value of the property, a mining expert of eminence had said, could hardly be over-estimated. It was his intention, without more delay than the consolidation of the directorate and other essential arrangements required, to return to New South Wales, and present himself before them at Marondah, no matter what the outcome might be. The result he felt would colour his future existence for happiness or misery, yet he was determined to undergo the ordeal. A final decision, however disastrous, would be more endurable than the condition of doubt and uncertainty under which he had existed for the last few weeks. Accompanying these letters was a packet containing letters of introduction to the Governors of more than one colony. They were from personages of high standing, even of great political influence. Not couched in the formal phraseology which the writers of such communications hold to be sufficient for the purpose, they spoke of the bearer as a young man of great promise, who had unusual opportunities of rising in the diplomatic or other official branches of the Civil Service, but had, somewhat inconsiderately, preferred to explore new and untried roads to fortune. The writers had no doubt but that he would distinguish himself in some form or other before his novitiate was ended.

A short but impassioned appeal had been enclosed in this letter to Mrs. Bruce. Her womanly compassion would, he trusted, impel her to deliver it to Imogen, whose sympathetic feelings, if not a warmer emotion, which he hardly dared to classify, he felt instinctively to be in his favour.

Having completed his task, he was not satisfied until he had posted the letters and packet with his own hands, and with an unuttered prayer that they would meet with no mischance similar to the last, he returned to the Tasmanian Club, where he slept soundly till aroused by the fully arisen sun and the hum of labour, combined with the ceaseless clatter of vehicles.

A man's mental turmoils and uncertainties doubtless act upon his physical constitution, but he must indeed be exceptionally framed who can withstand the cheering influence of a well-cooked breakfast and a fine day in spring. The surroundings of a first-class Australian Club are such as to cause the most fastidious arrival from Europe to recognise the social kinship of the cultured Briton to be worldwide and homogeneous. The conventional quietude of manner, the perfection of attendance, the friendliness towards the stranger guest, all these minor matters, differentiated from the best hotel life, tend to placate the traveller, much as he may be given to criticise all more or less foreign institutions, when distant from the "Mecca" of his race.

So it came to pass that, on forth issuing from that most agreeable caravanserai, his bruised and lacerated spirit felt soothed by the courtesy of the members generally, as well as of those immediately near to him at the table where he sat. He had drifted easily into conversation with several manifestly representative men: with one, indeed, an all-powerful mining investor (as he learnt subsequently), holding the fortunes of a mammoth copper syndicate in the hollow of his hand. Of this gentleman he took special heed, but neither from his appearance, manner nor conversation was he enabled to make a probable guess as to the nature of his occupation.

He might have been an *habitué* of cities, or a life-long dweller in the country, interested in commerce, in finance, pastoral or agricultural pursuits; in any one of these, or in all. But there was nothing to indicate it. A complete negation of the first person singular marked his conversation, yet he was apparently equally at ease in each and every topic as they arose. One thing, however, could not be mistaken—the massive frame and exceptional capacity for leadership, which would seem to be wasted on a city life.

Another of a widely different type had been his right-hand neighbour at the genial but conventional board—a young and fashionably-dressed man, "native and to the manner born," who seemed to be the recognised *arbiter elegantiarum*, as well as leader and referee of all sport and pastime. Secretary to the polo club, steward at the forthcoming Race-meeting and Hunt Club Cup, on the committee of the Assembly Ball, also imminent, he tendered an offer to our honorary member to procure seats, tickets, and introductions for himself and friends, with special facilities for joining or witnessing these annual celebrations. He also was not *affiché* to any known profession—at least, to none that could be gathered from looks or manner. Others of the ordinary denizens of club-land to whom he was introduced mentioned his partner, Mr. Tregonwell, as an out-and-out good fellow, and, as a mining expert, a benefactor to this island. He had evidently toned down his exuberance in the interests of conventionality. Mr. Blount, in contradistinction to the men who had extended the right-hand of friendship to him, was patently a *novus homo*—ticketed as such by dress and deportment, and assured of courteous entertainment from that very circumstance.

It was early in the "season" for Hobart to be in full swing as the recuperating region for the exhausted dwellers in continental Australia, where from Perth to the Gulf of Carpentaria King Sol reigns supreme in the summer months. Still, there was no lack of hospitality, including agreeable *réunions*, which, more informal than in metropolitan Australian cities, are pleasanter for that circumstance. There was an old-fashioned air about the environs of Hobart, a pleasantly-restful expression, a total absence of hurry or excitement. Small farms with aged orchards abounded, the fruit from which, exceptionally well flavoured and plenteous, recalled the village homes of Kent and Devon. Unlike the dwellers on the continent, the yeomen—for such they were—seemed fully contented with a life of modest independence, which they were unwilling to exchange for any speculative attempt to "better themselves."

What better position could they hope to attain than a home in this favoured island, blessed with a modified British climate and a fertile soil, where all the necessaries of a simple yet dignified existence were within reach of the humblest freeholder?

No scorching droughts, no devastating floods, no destructive cyclones harassed the rural population. Mr. Blount amused himself with daily drives through the suburbs, within such distances as were accessible in an afternoon. Having been much struck with the action of a pair of cab-horses which he took for his first drive, he arranged for their services daily during his stay in Hobart. Of one—a fine brown mare, occupying the "near" side in the pair—he became quite enamoured; the way in which she went up the precipitous road to Brown's River, and down the same on the return journey, without a hint from the driver, stamped her, in his estimation, as an animal of exceptional quality.

The metalled road, too, was not particularly smooth, albeit hard enough to try any equine legs. On inquiring the price the owner put on the pair, he was surprised to find it was but £35. Twenty pounds for his favourite, and fifteen for her less brilliant companion—useful and stanch though she was, and a fair match for shape and colour. He immediately closed the bargain, and thought he should enjoy the feeling of setting up his own carriage, so to speak; a barouche, too, chintz-lined, as are most of the cabs of Hobart—obsolete in fashion, but most comfortable as hackney carriages.

Before the fortnight expired, to which he limited his holiday, he was sensible of a slight, a very slight, change of feeling, though he would have indignantly repelled any imputation of disloyalty to Imogen. But it was not in human nature for a man of his age, still on the sunny side of thirty, to live among bevies of, perhaps, the handsomest women in Australasia, by whom he found himself to be cordially welcomed, without a slight alleviation of the feeling of gloom, if not despair, into which the absence of any recognition of his letters from Bunjil had thrown him. Moreover, the reports of the richness of the Comstock mine, confirmed, even heightened, by every letter from Tregonwell, were in all the local papers.

"A gentleman, lately arrived from Europe and touring the colonies, now staying at the Tasmanian Club, was known to be one of the original shareholders. And if so, his income could not be stated at less than £10,000 a year. It was by the merest chance that Mr. Valentine Blount (such is the name, we are informed, of this fortunate personage) bought an original share in the prospecting claim, which must be regarded henceforth as the 'Mount Morgan', of Tasmania. Mr. Blount is a relative of Lord Fontenaye of Tamworth, where the family possesses extensive estates, tracing their descent, it is asserted, in an uninterrupted line from the impetuous comrade of Fitz Eustace, immortalised in *Marmion*."

Valentine Blount, it may well be believed, if popular before this announcement, became rapidly more so, reaching, indeed, the giddy eminence of the lion of the day. Rank he was declared to possess, heir-presumptive to a baronetcy, or indeed an earldom, as well-informed leaders of society claimed to know, with a large income at present, probably an immense fortune in the future. Of course he would leave for England at an early date. Handsome, cultured, travelled, what girl could refuse him? So without endorsing the chiefly false and vulgar imputation upon Australian girls that he was "run after," it may be admitted that he was afforded every reasonable opportunity of seeing the daughters of the land under favourable conditions.

With the more lengthened stay which the "millionaire" *malgré lui* (so to speak) made in this enchanting island, the more firmly was his opinion rooted that he had fallen upon a section of "old-fashioned England," old-fashioned, it may be stated, only in the clinging to the earlier ideals of that Arcadian country life, which Charles Lamb, Addison, Crabbe, and more lately, Washington Irving, have rendered immortal. In the orchards, which showed promise of being overladen with the great apple crop in the sweet summer time, now hastening to arrive; in the cider-barrels on tap in the wayside inns and hospitable farmhouses; in the clover-scented meadows, where the broad-backed sheep and short-horned cattle wandered at will; in the freestone mansions of the squirearchy, where the oak- and elm-bordered avenues, winding from the lodge gate, the ranges of stabling, whence issued the four-in-hand drags, with blood teams, coachmen and footmen "accoutred proper" at race meetings or show days, exhibited the firm attachment which still obtained to the customs of their English forefathers.

These matters, closely observed by the visitor, were dear to his soul, proofs, if such were needed, of steadfast progress in all the essentials of national life, without departing in any marked respect from the ancestral tone.

At Hollywood Hall, at Westcotes, and at Malahide, where he was made frankly welcome, he rejoiced in these evidences of inherited prosperity, but still more in association with the stalwart sons and lovely daughters of the land. "Here," he thought, as he mused at early morn, or rode in the coming twilight beneath the long-planted elms, oaks, walnuts and chestnuts, of the far land, so distant, yet home-seeming, "are the real treasures of old

England's possessions, not gold or silver, diamonds or opals (and such there are, as Van Haast assured me), but the men and women, the children of the Empire, of whom, in the days to come, we shall have need and shall be proud to lead forth before the world."

Here, and in other offshoots of the "happy breed of men" whom the parent isle has sent forth to people the waste lands of the earth, shall the Anglo-Saxon world hail its statesmen, jurists, warriors, poets, writers, singers—not, indeed, as feeble imitators of the great names of history, but bright with original genius and strong in the untrammelled vigour of newer, happier lands.

"And why is Mr. Blount so deeply immersed in thought," asked a girlish voice, "that he did not hear me coming towards him from the rose-garden, where the frost has tarnished all my poor buds? You are not going to write a book about us, are you? for if so, I must order you off the premises."

"Now what *can* be written but compliments, well-deserved praises about your delightful country, and its—well—charming inhabitants?" replied Blount, after apologising for his abstraction and shaking hands warmly with the disturber of his reverie.

"Oh! that is most sweet of you to say so. But so many Englishmen we have entertained have disappointed us by either magnifying our small defects, or praising us in the wrong place—which is worse."

"That I am not going to write a book of 'Tours and Travels in Search of Gold,' or anything of the sort, I am free to make affidavit. But if I were, what could I say, except in praise of a morning like this—of a rose garden like the one you have just left, of an ancient-appearing baronial hall like Hollywood, with century old elms and oaks, and the squire's daughter just about to remind an absent-minded visitor of the imminent breakfast bell? I saw it yesterday in the courtyard of the stables, and what an imposing pile it ornaments! Stalls for five and twenty horses—or is it thirty? Four-in-hand drag in the coach house, landau, brougham, dog carts, pony carriage—everything, I give you my word, that you would find in a country house in England."

"You are flattering us, I feel certain," said the young lady, blushing slightly, yet wearing a pleased smile at this *catalogue raisonné*; "of course I know that the comparison only applies to English country houses of the third or fourth class.

"Those of the county magnates, like Chatsworth and at Eaton, must be as far in advance of ours, as these are superior to the cottages in which people lived in pioneer days. However, there is the nine o'clock bell for breakfast; we are punctual also at one for lunch, which may or may not be needed to-day."

The big bell clanged for about five minutes, during which visitors and members of the household were seen converging towards the massive portico of the façade of the Hall. It was a distinctly imposing edifice, built of a neutral-tinted freestone, a material which throughout the ages has always lent itself easily to architectural development.

Hollywood Hall, standing as it did on the border of a river stocked with trout, and centrally situated in a freehold estate of thirty thousand acres of fertile land, might fairly be quoted as an object lesson in colonising experience, as well as an example of the rewards occasionally secured by the roving Englishman.

The breakfast room though large appeared well filled, as Blount and his fair companion joined the party. Certain neighbours had ridden over, after the informal manner of the land, in order to break the journey to Hobart and spend a pleasant hour in the society of the girls of Hollywood Hall. Truth to tell, the sex was predominant, the proportion of the daughters of the house being largely in excess of the men. Tall, graceful, refined, distinctly handsome, they afforded a notable instance of the favouring conditions of Australian life. They possessed also the open air accomplishments of their class. Hard to beat at lawn tennis, they could ride and drive better than the average man, following the hounds of a pack occasionally hunted in the neighbourhood.

The merry tones and lively interchange of badinage which went on with but little intermission during the pleasant meal proved their possession of those invaluable gifts of the budding maid—high health and unfailing spirits, with a sufficient, though not overpowering, sense of humour.

The squire, a well-preserved, fresh-looking, middle-aged man, sitting at the head of his table with an expression of mingled geniality and command, as the contest of tongues waned, thought it well to suggest the order of the day. "I feel sorry that I am obliged to drive to an outlying farm on business, which will occupy me the greater part of the day. So you will have, with the assistance of Mrs. Claremont, to amuse yourselves."

"I think we can manage that," said the youngest daughter, a merry damsel of sixteen. "Captain Blake is going to drive Laura and me over to Deep Woods. Mother says we can ask them to come over to dine, as we *might* have a little dance afterwards."

"So that's one part of the programme, is it? you monkey," said the host; "I might have known you had some conspiracy on foot. However, if your mother approves, it's all right. Now, does any one care about fishing, because the trout are taking the fly well, and I heard that snipe were seen at the Long Marsh yesterday; they're a week earlier this year" — this to the son and heir of the house; "what were you intending to arrange?"

"Well, sir, I thought of driving over to see Joe and Bert Bowyer — they're just back from the old country — been at Cambridge, too. I've got a fairish team just taken up. Mr. Blount with two of the girls, and Charlie could come. It's a fine day for a drive; perhaps the boys will come back with us."

"But won't you want some girls?"

"Oh! I think we shall do, sir! Mother sent a note to Mrs. Fotheringay early this morning. They'll come, I'm pretty sure."

"Aha! master Philip! *you* managed that, I can see. Well, quite right — have all the fun you can now; one's only young once. So you think I may go away with a clear conscience, as far as our guests are concerned?"

"I'll be responsible, sir! you may trust me and mother, I think," said the son and heir, a tall, resolute-looking youngster.

So the family council was concluded, and Mr. Blount being informed that the drag party would not start until eleven o'clock, rested tranquil in his mind. Miss Laura, his companion of the morning, let him know that for household reasons her society would not be available until the drag was ready to start — but that he would find a good store of books in the library upstairs, also writing materials; if he had letters to answer, the contents of the post-bag in the hall would reach Hobart at six o'clock.

To this haven of peace Blount betook himself, satisfied that he would have a sufficiency of outdoor life before the end of the day, and not unwilling to conclude pressing correspondence, before commencing the round of gaiety which he plainly saw was cut out for him. There was a really good collection of books in the spacious library, from the windows of which an extensive view of wood and wold opened out. He felt tempted by the old records of the land, calf-bound and numbered with the years of their publication, but resolutely sat down to inform Tregonwell of his whereabouts, with the probable duration of his stay in the district; warning him to write at once if any change took place in the prospects of the Comstock. He also requested the secretary of the Imperial Club at Melbourne to forward to his Hobart address all letters and papers which might arrive. This done, he satisfied himself that he was outwardly fit to bear inspection, presented himself in the hall a few minutes before the time named for the start of the drag party, which he found was to be accompanied by a mounted escort. A distinguished looking neighbour whom everybody called "Dick," evidently on the most kindly, not to say affectionate terms with all present, was here introduced to him as Mr. Richard Dereker of Holmby—one of those fortunate individuals, who come into the world gifted with all the qualities which recommend the owner equally to men and to women of all ranks, classes, and dispositions. Handsome, gay, heir to a fine estate, clever, generous, manly, he was fortune's favourite, if any one ever was. He had already come to the front in the Colonial Parliament; there it was sufficient for him to offer himself, for society to declare that it was folly for any one to think of opposing his election. He had been invited to join the party, and as the idea of disappointing the company was too painful to contemplate, he agreed at once to join the mounted division. As, however, he had ridden twenty miles already, Philip Claremont insisted on handing over the reins of the drag to him, and sending for a fresh hackney, prepared to follow the drag on horseback. "Did Mr. Dereker drive well?" Mr. Blount asked his next neighbour—as he had noticed the four well-bred horses, in high condition, giving young Claremont enough to do to hold them, as they came up from the stables; the leaders, indeed, breaking into a hand gallop now and then.

"Drive? Dick Dereker drive?" He looked astonished—"the best four-in-hand whip in the island. Phil is a very fair coachman, but there's a finish about Dereker, that no other man can touch."

So, when the all-conquering hero, drawing on his neatly fitting doeskin gloves, lightly ascended to the box seat, the helpers at the leaders' heads released those fiery steeds: as Mr. Dereker drew the reins through his fingers, and sat up in an attitude of which Whyte Melville would have approved, every feminine countenance in the party seemed irradiated with a fresh gleam of brilliancy, while the team moved smoothly off. The roads of Tasmania in that day—formed chiefly with the aid of convict labour, of which an unlimited supply was available for public works—were the best in Australasia. Well-graded and metalled—with mile stones at proper distances—lined with hawthorn hedges, trimly kept for the most part—passing through quiet villages where the horses were watered, and the landlord of the inn stood with head uncovered, according to traditional courtesy, there was much to remind the stranger of the mother land; to support the intercolonial contention that Tasmania was the most English-appearing of all the colonies, and in many respects, the most advanced and highly civilised.

With this last opinion, Blount felt inclined to agree—although, of course, other evidence might be forthcoming. In conversation with Mr.

Dereker, between whom and himself Miss Laura Claremont was seated, he learned that the larger estates from one of which he was coming, and to another of which he was going, had been acquired by purchase or grant, at an early stage of the occupation of the colony. The area of fertile land being more circumscribed than in the colonies of New South Wales and South Australia, the home market good, and the Government expenditure during the transportation system immense, while labour was cheap and plentiful, it followed that agricultural and pastoral pursuits became for a succession of seasons most profitable.

Hence, the country gentlemen of the land, as in the old days of the West Indian planters, were enabled to build good houses—rear high-class horses, cattle and sheep—and, in a general way, live comfortably, even luxuriously. Owing to the high value of the land and the richness of the soil, the distances between the estates were not so great as in New South Wales; were therefore convenient for social meetings, for races, steeplechases, cricket, shooting and hunting; Reynard's place being supplied by the wild dog, or "dingo," who gave excellent sport, being both fast and a good stayer. Like his British prototype, he was a depredator, though on a more important scale: sheep, calves and foals falling victims to his wolfish propensities. So his pursuit answered the double purpose of affording excellent sport, and ridding the land of an outlawed felon.

With reference to hunting, of which old English pastime Mr. Dereker was an enthusiastic supporter, he explained that owing to the estates and farms being substantially fenced, horses that could negotiate the high and stiff rails were a necessity. The breeding of hunters and steeplechasers had been therefore encouraged from the earliest days of the colony. Hacks and harness horses for similar reasons. "So that," said Mr. Dereker, allowing his whip to rest lightly on his off side wheeler, "I don't think you will find a better bred, better matched team in an English county than this, or four better hackneys than those which are now overtaking us."

Certainly, Mr. Blount thought, there was no reason to dispute the assertion. The team they sat behind, two bays and two greys, driven chequer fashion, a grey in the near lead, and another in the off wheel, would be hard to beat. They were, perhaps, hardly so massive as the English coach horse, but while less powerful and upstanding, they showed more blood and were generally handsomer. This might account for the ease with which they accomplished the twenty mile stage in little over the two hours, and the unchanged form which they carried to the journey's end, with a fairly heavy load behind them. As for the hackney division, when Miss Dalton and her companion overtook the coach just before they turned into the drive at

Holmby, there was a general expression of admiration from the party, as the beautiful blood mare that she rode reined up, tossing her head impatiently, while her large, mild eye, full nostril, and high croup bore testimony to the Arab ancestry.

"Yes! Zuleika *is* a beauty!" said Miss Laura, looking with pardonable pride at the satin coat and delicate limbs of the high-caste animal, "and though she makes believe to be impatient, is as gentle as a lamb. She is my personal property—we all have our own horses—but I lent her to Grace Dalton to-day, for her palfrey, as the old romancers say, met with an accident. She is a fast walker, and will show off going up the drive."

"You appear to have wonderfully good horses of all classes in Tasmania," said the guest; "indeed in Australia generally, judging by those I saw in Victoria and New South Wales—but here the hackneys and harness horses seem to have more 'class.'"

"For many years," said Mr. Dereker, "we have had the advantage of the best English blood—with occasional high-caste Arab importations from India; so there is no reason why, with a favourable climate, and wide range of pasture, we should not have speed, stoutness and pace equal to anything in the world. But here we are at Walmer, so we must defer the treatment of this fascinating subject till after lunch, when the ladies have retired." As he spoke, he turned into the by road which led to the lodge gate, which, opened by an aged retainer, admitted them to a well-kept avenue shaded by oaks and elms, and lined by hawthorn hedges. The house was a large and handsome country home, differing in style and architecture from Hollywood Hall, but possessing all the requisite qualifications for hospitality needed by a manor house. As they drove up to the entrance steps, a fine boy of fourteen ran out and assisted Miss Claremont to descend, after which he nimbly climbed up beside the driver, saying, "Oh! Mr. Dereker, isn't it a jolly team?—won't you let me drive round to the stables; you know I can drive?"

"You drive very well, for your time of life, Reggie, but these horses pull, so be careful."

"I can hold them," said the confident youngster, who, indeed, took over the reins in a very workman-like manner, "besides they've done twenty miles with a load behind them. Aren't you going to stay all night?"

"Might have thought of it, Reggie, but the ladies are not prepared; we must get your sister to come instead—you too, if your father will let you. I suppose Joe and Bertie are at home? How does Tasmania strike them after the old country?"

"Oh! they're jolly glad to get back, though they've had a ripping time of it. Father says they must set to work now for the next few years. Who's the man that was next to you? Englishman, I expect!"

"Yes! Mr. Blount, only a year out. Seems a good sort, partner with Tregonwell in that new silver mine, the Eldorado."

"My word! he's dropped into a good thing, they say it's ever so rich, and getting better as they go down. I must get father to let me go to the Laboratory in Melbourne, and study up mineralogy. It's the best thing going, for a younger son. I don't want to be stuck at a farm all my life, ploughing and harrowing for ever. Joe and Bertie will have the old place, and I must strike out, to get anything out of the common."

"Quite right, Reggie, nothing like adventure, only don't go too fast. Here we are."

Reggie pulled up in the centre of a square, on all sides of which was a goodly number of stalls, loose boxes, cow houses, and all things suitable for a great breeding establishment, where pure stock of all kinds were largely reared. The horses were promptly taken out and cared for, while Mr. Dereker, admiringly gazed at by the whole staff, exchanged a few words of greeting with the head groom, and older stable men, before he accompanied Master Reggie to the great hall, which was evidently used for morning reception.

It had magnificent proportions, and was decorated, according to traditional usage, with the spoils of the chase—mostly indigenous, though the forest trophies gave evidence that the men of the house had not always been home-keeping youths. In addition to fine heads of red, and fallow deer, kangaroo skins, and dingo masks, "tigers" and "devils" (Australian variety) stuffed, as also the rarer wombat and platypus, there were trophies which told of hunting parties in the South African "veldt," and the jungles of Hindostan. Horns of the eland, and the springbok, alternated with lion and tiger skins, bears and leopards!

The sons of the first generation of landholders had gone far afield for sport and adventure before they decided to settle down for life, in the fair island which their fathers had won from the forest and the savage.

There was scant leisure to muse over these, or other gratifying developments, as the buzz of conversation, extremely mirthful and vivacious, which was in full swing when Mr. Dereker and his young companion entered the hall, was apparently accelerated by their arrival.

A certain amount of chaff had evidently been directed against the two collegians, so lately returned from their university. How did the men and maidens of the old country compare with their compatriots here—in athletics, in field sports, in looks (this related only to the feminine division), and so forth? Mr. Joe and Mr. Bertie Bowyer had been apparently hard set to hold their ground; beset as they were by sarcastic advice, adjured to keep to the strict line of truth on one side—but not to desert their native land on the other—they were in imminent danger of wreck from Scylla, or Charybdis. Their opinions were chiefly as follows:

In athletics and field sports the colonists held their own fairly well, with perhaps a trifle to spare. Notably in the hunting field; the small enclosures and high stiff fences of Tasmania giving them practice and experience over a more dangerous line of country than any in Britain. In horsemanship, generally, the colonists were more at home, from having been in youth their own grooms and horse-breakers. In shooting, and the use of the gloves, particularly in the art of self-defence, the Australians showed a disposition to excel. Already a few professionals from Sydney had shown good form and staying power. In boating there was a distinct and growing improvement, few of the Oxford and Cambridge boat-races being without a colonist in one or other crew. There was often one in both. This state of matters is hailed with acclamation. The great advantage which the old country possessed in the way of sport lay in the social environment. The difference between its pursuit here and in Britain consisted in the fact that the seasons were carefully defined, and the laws of each division strictly adhered to. Moreover, in whatever direction a man's tastes lay, hunting, fishing, shooting, or coursing, he was always sure of the comradeship of the requisite number of enthusiastic *habitués* and amateurs.

After lunch, which was a conspicuously cheerful reunion, it was decided that a start homeward was to be made at four o'clock sharp. In the meantime, the brothers Bowyer intimated their intention to drive over in a mail phaeton, which they had brought out with them, built by Kesterton of Long Acre, with all the newest improvements of the most fashionable style. One of the Misses Bowyer and her friend, Jessie Allan, an acknowledged belle from Deloraine, would join the party; Reggie might come too, as he was a light weight, and would be useful for opening gates. The intervening time was spent in exploring the orchard and gardens, both of which were on an unusually extensive scale. The fruit trees, carefully pruned and attended to, were of great age. Indeed Mr. Blount felt impelled to remark that apparently one of the first things the early settlers seem to have done, after building a house, not a mansion, for that came afterwards, was to plant a garden and orchard.

"Our grandfathers," said Mr. Joe Bowyer, "remind me of the monks of old, who, in establishing the abbeys, which I always examined in our walking tours, for I am an archaeologist in a very small way, always took care to choose a site not far from a trout stream, and with good meadow lands adjoining, equally suitable for orchard, corn or pasture. These estates mostly commenced with a Crown grant of a few thousand acres, such as were given at the discretion of the early Governors, to retired officers of the army and navy, many of whom decided to settle permanently in the island. The grantee had a certain time allotted to make his choice of location. This he employed in searching for the best land, with access to markets, &c. In a general way, the country being open, and there being at that time no system of sale by auction of bush land, the nucleus was secured of what has since become valuable freeholds."

"I should think they were," said the stranger guest, "and in the course of time, with the increase of population, as the country becomes fully settled, must become more valuable still. Do you look forward to spending the whole of your lives here, you and your brother, or retiring to England, where your rents, I should suppose, would enable you to live very comfortably?"

"We might have a couple of years in the old country," said the Tasmanian squire, "before we get too old to enjoy things thoroughly, but after a run over the Continent, for a final memory, this is our native land, and here we shall live and die."

"But the fulness of life in Britain, foreign travel, the great cities of the world, music, art, literature such as can be seen and enjoyed in such perfection nowhere else, why leave them for ever?"

"Yes, of course, all that is granted, but a man has something else to do in the world but merely to enjoy himself, intellectually or otherwise. This land has made *us*, and we must do something for it in return. Luxuries are the dessert, so to speak, of the meal which sustains life. They fail to satisfy or stimulate after a while. We are Australians born and bred; in our own land we are known and have a feeling of comradeship with our countrymen of every degree. The colonist, after a few years, has an inevitable feeling of loneliness in Europe, which he cannot shake off. It is different with an Englishman however long he has lived here. He goes home to his family and friends, who generally welcome him, especially if he has made a fortune. Even they, however wealthy and used to English life, often return to Australia. There is something attractive in the freer life, after all."

"Yes, I suppose there must be," and a half sigh ended the sentence, as he thought of Imogen Carrisforth's hazel eyes and bright hair, her frank smile and joyous tones, a very embodiment of the charm and graces of divine youth. A cloud seemed to have settled upon his soul, as his companion led the way to the entrance hall, where the whole party was collecting for the homeward drive. However, putting constraint upon his mental attitude, he took his seat with alacrity beside his fair companion of the morning.

CHAPTER VIII

The return drive was made in slightly better time than the morning journey, the English mail phaeton of the Messieurs Bowyer, with a pair of exceptional trotters, taking the lead. The mounted contingent followed at a more reasonable pace, as they had from time to time to put "on a spurt" to come up with the drag, harness work, as is known to all horsemen, keeping up a faster average pace than saddle. However, everybody arrived safely at the Hall in excellent spirits, as might have been gathered from the cheerful, not to say hilarious, tone which the conversation had developed. Mr. Blount, in especial, whose ordinary optimism had reasserted sway, told himself that (with one exception) never had he enjoyed such a delicious experience of genuine country life. There was no more time available than sufficed for a cup of afternoon tea and the imperative duty of dressing for dinner. At this important function the mistress of the house had exercised a wise forecast, since, when the great table in the dining-room, duly laid, flowered, and "decored with napery," met the eyes of the visitors, it was seen that at least double as many guests had been provided for as had assembled at breakfast. "Dick!" said the host to Mr. Dereker, "Mrs. Claremont says you are to take the vice-chair; you'll have her on your right and Miss Allan on your left—wisdom and beauty, you see—so you can't go wrong. Philip, my boy! you're to take the right centre, with Joe Bowyer and Miss Fotheringay on one side, Laura and Mr. Blount on the other. Jack Fotheringay fronts you, with any young people he can get. I daresay he'll arrange that. You must forage for yourselves. Now I can't pretend to do anything more for you. I daresay you'll shake down."

So they did. There was much joking and pleasant innuendo as the necessary shufflings were made, brothers and sisters, husbands and wives having to be displaced and provided with neighbours not so closely related. Nothing was lacking as far as the material part of the dinner was concerned—a famous saddle of mutton, home-grown from a flock of Southdowns kept in the park, descended from an early English importation; a grand roast turkey, upon which the all-accomplished Mr. Dereker operated with practised hand, as did the host upon the Southdown, expatiating at intervals upon the superiority of the breed for mutton purposes only. The red currant jelly was a product of the estate, superintended in manufacture by one of the daughters of the house; trout from the river, black duck from the lake, equal to his canvas-back relative of the Southern States; a haunch, too, of red deer venison, Tasmanian born and bred. For the rest, everything was well cooked, well served, and excellent of its kind. Worthy of such viands was the appetite of the guests, sharpened by the exercise and a day spent chiefly in the open air, the keen, fresh, island atmosphere.

The host's cellar, famous for age and quality in more than one colony, aided the general cheerfulness. So that if any of the fortunate guests at that memorable dinner had aught but praise for the food, the wines, the company, or the conversation, they must have been exceptionally hard to please. So thought Mr. Blount, who by and by joined the ladies, feeling much satisfied with himself and all the surroundings. Not that he had done more than justice to the host's claret, madeira, and super-excellent port. He was on all occasions a temperate person. But there is no doubt that a few glasses of undeniably good wine, under favourable conditions, such as the close of an admirable dinner, with a dance of more than common interest to follow, may be considered to be an aid to digestion, as well as an incentive to a cheerful outlook upon life, which tends, physicians tell us, to longevity, with health of body and mind.

It happened, fortunately, to be a moonlight night. The day had been one of those of the early spring, which warm, even hot, in the afternoon, presage, in the opinion of the weather-wise, an early summer, which prediction is chiefly falsified. But while this short glimpse of Paradise is granted to the sons of men, no phrase can more truly describe it. Cloudless days, warmth, without oppressive heat, tempered by the whispering ocean breeze, beseeching the permission of the wood nymphs to invade their secret haunts, all flower, and leaf, and herb life responsive to the thrilling charm — the witchery of the sea voices.

Such had been the day. That the drives and rides through the green woodland, the hill parks, the meadow fields, had been absolutely perfect all admitted. Now the evening air seemed to have gained an added freshness. When the French windows of the ballroom were thrown open it was predicted that many a couple would find the broad verandahs, or even the dry and shaded garden paths, irresistibly enticing after the first few dances.

Such, indeed, was the case. What with accidental and invited guests, the number had been increased to nearly twenty couples, all young, enthusiastic, fairly musical, and devoted to the dance.

The music, indeed, had been an anxiety to the hostess. The piano was a fine instrument, luckily in perfect tune. Half the girls present could play dance music effectively. But another instrument or two would be *such* an aid in support.

Then inquiry was made; Chester of Oaklands was a musical amateur, the violin was his favourite instrument, he was so good-natured that he could be counted upon. Then there was young Grant of Bendearg, who played the cornet. So, messengers with polite notes were despatched on horseback, and both gentlemen, being luckily found at home, were secured. The band was complete. Mr. Blount, with proper precaution, had secured the hand of Miss Laura Claremont at dinner, for two waltzes, a polka, and the after-supper galop; among her sisters and the late arrivals he had filled his card. These had been written out by volunteer damsels during the after-dinner wait.

He had, therefore, no anxiety about his entertainment for the evening. No time was lost after the conclusion of the dinner. The young ladies from Cranstoun and Deepdene had, of course, brought the necessary evening wear with them. Mr. Blount's English war-paint had been stored in Melbourne while he was learning something about gold-fields and cattle-lifting, this last involuntarily. He was "accoutred proper," and as such, not troubled with anxiety about his personal appearance. The Bowyers, of course, were resplendent in "the very latest" fashion; as to canonicals, the other men were fairly up to the standard of British evening toggery, and for the few who were not, allowances were made, as is always the case in Australia. People can't be expected to carry portmanteaux about with them, especially on horseback, and as they were among friends they got on quite as well in the matter of partners as the others.

It certainly was a good dance. The music kept going nobly. The young lady at the piano was replaced from time to time, but the male musicians held on till supper time without a break. When that popular distraction was announced half-an-hour's interval for refreshments was declared, after which a good-natured damsel stole in, and indulged the insatiable juniors with a dreamy, interminable waltz. Then the two men recommenced with the leading lady amateur, and a polka of irresistible swing and abandonment soon filled the room.

Certainly a dance in the country in any part of Australia is an object lesson as to the vigour and vitality of the race. All Australian girls dance well—it would seem to be a natural gift. Chiefly slender, lissom, yet vigorous in health, and sound in constitution, they dance on, fleet-footed and tireless, as the fabled Nymphs and Oreads of ancient Hellas. Hour after hour passed, still unwearied, unsated, were the dancers, until the arrival of the soup suggested that the closure was about to be applied. But the dawnlight was stealing over the summit of the mountain range when the last galop had come to an end, and a few couples were by way of cooling themselves in the verandah or the garden paths. Here, and at this hour, Mr. Blount found himself alone with Laura Claremont, who had indeed, in spite of faltering maiden remonstrance, completed her fifth dance with him. He was not an unstable, indiscriminate admirer, least of all a professional trifler with the hearts of women, but he had been strongly attracted (perhaps interested would be the more accurate word) by her quiet dignity, conjoined with refinement and high intelligence.

She had read largely, and formed opinions on important questions with greater thoroughness than is the habit of girls generally. Without being a recognised beauty, she had a striking and distinguished appearance. Her dark hair and eyes, the latter large and expressive, the delicate complexion for which the women of Tasmania are noted, in combination with a noble figure and graceful shape, would have given her a foremost position by looks alone in any society. The expression of her features was serious rather than gay, but when the humorous element was invoked a ripple of genuine mirth spread over her countenance, the display of which added to her modest, yet alluring array of charms.

Such was the woman with whom Blount had been thrown temporarily into contact for the last few days, and this night had shown him more of her inward thoughts and feelings, unveiled as they were by the accidents of the dance and the driving party, than he had ever dreamed of. Returning to the ballroom, the final adieus were made, and as he pressed her yielding hand he felt (or was it fancy?) an answering clasp.

On the following day he had arranged to leave for Hobart, as he expected to deal with propositions lately submitted for the amalgamation of the original prospecting claim with those adjoining, thus to include a larger area upon which to float a company to be placed upon the London market, with an increased number of shares.

This had been done at the suggestion of Mr. Tregonwell, whose energetic temperament was constantly urging him to cast about for improved conditions of management, and a more profitable handling of the great property which kind fortune had thrown into their hands.

"What is the sense," he had asked in his last letter from the mine, "of going on in the slow, old-fashioned way, just turning out a few thousand ounces of silver monthly, and earning nothing more than a decent income, this fabulously rich ore body lying idle, so to speak, for want of organisation and enterprise? The specimens already sent home have prepared the British investors for the flotation of a company, of which a large proportion of the shares will be offered to the public. I propose to call a meeting of the shareholders in Number One and Two, North, and South, and submit a plan for their consideration at once.

"With our property thrown in we can increase the shares to five hundred thousand one pound shares, resuming a hundred thousand paid up original shares from the prospectors. You and I, Herbert and Clarke, pool the lot and put them before the public, allotting so many to all applicants before a certain day—after which the share allotment list will be closed. With the increased capital, we can then carry out and complete such improvements as are absolutely necessary for the working of the mine on the most productive scale, ensuring a return of almost incredible profits within a comparatively short period. In a series of years, the price of silver may fall—the money market, in the event of European wars, become restricted, and in fact the future, that unknown friend or enemy to all mundane affairs, may blight the hopes and expectations which now appear so promising.

"Everything is favourable *now*, the mine, the output, the market—money easy, machinery available on fair terms. But we don't know how soon a cloud *may* gather, a storm—financial or political—may burst upon us. The directors in the great Comstock Mine in America looked at things in that light—doubled their capital, quadrupled their plant, built a railway, and within five years banked dollars enough to enable the four original prospectors (I knew Flood and Mackay well—worked with them in fact—when we were all poor men) to become and *remain* millionaires to the end of their lives. Meanwhile giving entertainments, and building palaces, which astonished all Europe, and America as well—a more difficult matter by far.

"Now, what do we want, you will ask, for all this development, this Arabian Night's treasure house? I say—and I am talking strict business—that we must have, presuming that the 'Great Tasmanian Proprietary Comstock and Associated Silver Mines Company, Limited,' comes off, and the shares will be over-applied for twice over—what do we want, I repeat? A battery with the newest inventions and improvements—a hundred stamps to begin with. It may be, of course, increased; we shall provide for such a contingency.

"Secondly, we must have a railway—from the mine to the port—to carry our men—materials, supplies generally. We can't go back to this Peruvian mode of transit-carrying—on men's backs, at a frightful waste of time and money. We can't afford the *time*—it's not a question so much of money as of *time*, which is wasting money at compound interest. We want a wharf at Strahan and a steamer of our own to take the ore to Callao. She'll pay for herself within the year. Is that all? I hear you asking with your cynical drawl, which you affect, I know you, when you're most interested.

"No, *sir*! as we all learnt to say in the States—the best comes last. We want a first-class American mining manager—a real boss—chock full of scientific training from Freiberg, practical knowledge gathered from joining the first crowd at Sutter's Mill—and more important than all, the knack of keeping a couple of thousand miners, of different creeds, countries and colours, all pulling one way, and him keeping a cool head in strikes and other devilries that's bound to happen in every big mine in the world, specially when she's doin' a heap better than common—see! His price is £5,000 a year, not a cent less—if you want the finished article!" Here, Mr. Tregonwell's fiery eloquence, albeit confined to cold pen and ink, led him into the mining American dialect, so easy to acquire, so difficult to dislodge—which he had picked up in his early experiences. In the class with which he had chiefly associated in earlier years, and to which he belonged in right of birth, he could be as punctiliously accurate in manner and speech, as if he had never quitted it. With a certain reluctance, as of one committing himself to a voyage upon an unknown sea, his more prudent, but less practical partner gave a guarded consent to these daring propositions, premising, however, that the company must be complete in legal formation and the shares duly allotted, before a cheque was signed by Frampton Tregonwell and Company, in aid of operations of such colossal magnificence.

Mr. Blount excused himself from accepting a pressing invitation to remain another week at this very pleasant reproduction of English country house life, on the plea of urgent private affairs, but he acceded to Mr. Dereker's suggestion that he should stay a night with him at Holmby, on the way to Hobart, where he would undertake to land him an hour or two before the coach could arrive. This was a happy conjunction of business and pleasure, against which there was no valid argument. So, with many regrets by guest and entertainers, and promises on the part of the former to return at the earliest possible opportunity, he after breakfast started in Mr. Dereker's dog-cart from the hospitable precincts of Hollywood Hall.

Holmby, the well-known headquarters of the sporting magnates of the island, was reached just "within the light," though, as the road was exceptionally good—metalled, bridged, and accurately graded all through—the hour of arrival was not of great consequence.

Mr. Dereker was a bachelor, and had mentioned something about bachelor's fare and pot luck generally, to which Mr. Blount, feeling equal to either fortune, had made suitable reply. Rather to his surprise, however, as his host had driven round to the stables they saw grooms and helpers busy in taking out the team of a four-in-hand drag.

The equipage and appointments arrested his attention, and caused him to utter an exclamation. They constituted indeed an uncommon turnout. An English-built coach—such as the Four-in-hand and the coaching clubs produce on the first day of the season, for the annual procession, so anxiously awaited, so enthusiastically watched,—complete with every London adjunct, from hamper to horn, etc. The horses had just been detached, and were, at Mr. Dereker's order, detained for inspection. Four flea-bitten greys, wonderfully matched, and sufficiently large and powerful to warrant their easy action in front of so heavy a drag, as the one in which they had been driven over. Their blood-like heads, and striking forehands, not less than their rounded back ribs, and powerful quarters, denoted the fortunate admixture of the two noblest equine families—the Arab and the English thoroughbred: of size and strength they had sufficient for all or any harness work, while their beauty and faultless matching would have graced any show-ground in England.

"This team was bred by a relative of mine, who is a great amateur in the coaching line, and is thought to be the best team in Australasia! His place, Queenhoo Hall, is only fifteen miles off. He is a connection by marriage: therefore we don't stand on ceremony. I suspect he is giving his team an airing before driving them to the Elwick Races next month, where he always turns out in great style. You will not have a dull evening, for his wife and a niece or two are sure to have accompanied him."

In passing through the outer hall, such an amount of mirthful conversation reached the ear, as led to the belief in Mr. Blount's mind, that either the number of the Squire's nieces had been under-stated, or that, according to the custom of the country, the coach had been reinforced on the way. So it proved to be—the hall was apparently half full of men and maidens, unto whom had been added a few married people, as well as a couple of subalterns from a regiment then quartered in Hobart. The chaperons were not noticeably older than their unmarried charges, so that the expectation of a dance was fully justified.

Mr. Blount was introduced to the "Squire," as he was universally called, as also to his nieces, two attractive-looking girls; and of course, to all the other people, civil and military. He felt as he once did in the west of Ireland, where he accepted so many invitations to spend a month, that the number of months would have had to be increased if he had not more than a year in which to keep holiday. He complimented the Squire, with obvious sincerity, on his wonderful team, and promised, strictly reserving compliance until after the flotation of the great mining company, to visit him at Queenhoo Hall in the summer time now approaching. The dinner and the dance were replicas of those he had enjoyed at Hollywood. Here he had another opportunity of admiring the lovely complexions, graceful figures, and perfect grace and fleetness of the daughters of the land in the waltz or galop, and when he started for Hobart soon after sunrise, the drive through the fresh morning air dispelled all feelings of weariness, which, under the circumstances, he might have felt, after hearing the cock crow two mornings running before going to bed.

"Heaven knows how long this sort of thing might have lasted, if that letter of Tregonwell's had not turned up last night," he told himself. "There is a time for all things—and if I do not mistake, it is high time now, as our pastors and masters used to say, to make a stern division between work and play—'poculatum est, condemnatum est,' so 'nunc est agendum' in good earnest."

Hobart, reached two hours before the coach could have drawn up before the post-office, reassured him as to Mr. Dereker's guarantee holding good. A cab from the nearest stand bore him and his luggage to the Tasmanian Club, where, freed from the distractions of country houses, he was able to collect his thoughts before attacking the great array of letters and papers, which met his eye when he entered his room.

A copy of the morning paper reposing on the dressing-table disclosed the fact in an aggressive headline that the Proprietary Tasmanian Comstock and Associated Silver Mines Company (Limited) was already launched upon the Australian mining world, and indeed upon that of Europe, and the Universe generally.

"The Directors of this magnificent silver property, which includes the original Comstock Claim—amalgamated with the Associated Silver Mines Company we understand"—wrote the fluent pen of the Editor of the *Tasmanian Times*—"have at length succumbed to outside pressure, and in the interest of the British and Colonial Public, consented to form these mines of unparalleled richness into a company. The Directors are Messrs. Valentine Blount, Frampton Tregonwell, and Charles Herbert and John Westerfield Clarke, names which will assure the shareholders of honourable and straightforward dealing at the hands of those to whom their pecuniary interests are committed. These names are well and favourably known in England, in Mexico, in the United States of America, and the Dominion of Canada. Comment is superfluous—they speak for themselves.

"Wherever gold or silver mining is carried on the names of Clarke and Tregonwell are familiar as 'household words' and always associated with skilled treatment and successful operations. That this enterprise will have a beneficial effect not only upon the mining, but on the commercial, and all other industries of Tasmania, lifting her, with her fertile soil, her equable climate, her adaptability for all agricultural and pastoral products to her proper place in the front rank of Australian colonies no sane man can henceforth doubt. A line of steamers from Strahan to Hobart, a short though expensive railway, and a metalled coach road, are among the indispensable enterprises which Mr. Tregonwell assured our representative would be commenced without delay. Advance, Tasmania!"

Looking hastily through the pile of unopened letters, but keeping private-and-confidential-appearing correspondence strictly apart, and relegating those in Mr. Tregonwell's bold, rapid handwriting, to a more convenient season, he started, and trembled, as his eye fell upon a letter in Mrs. Bruce's handwriting which bore the Marondah postmark. His heart almost stopped beating, when an enclosed note fell out, still more likely to affect his inmost soul. Yes! it was in the handwriting, so closely scanned, so dearly treasured in the past, of Imogen Carrisforth. For the moment, a spasm of regret, even remorse affected him painfully. He stood self-convicted by his conscience of having lingered in frivolous, social enjoyment, while uncertain of the welfare and feelings of one who had aroused the deepest emotions of his being, nor had he (with shame he reflected) taken all possible means to discover to what circumstance it was that his letters had been apparently treated with indifference or contempt.

Mrs. Bruce's letter gave an explanation which, though not fully comprehensive, cleared up a part of the mystery, as far as Imogen was concerned. It ran as follows:—

"Dear Mr. Blount,—I am afraid you must have thought us a very ill-mannered set of people, as it seems by your letter of — that you have not received *any answer* to your letters written the night before you left Bunjil for Melbourne. Yet, it was scarcely our fault. That poor lad who was drowned in the flood, which rose on the *very day* you left, carried answers from me and Imogen; these, I think, you would have considered friendly, and even in a sense apologetic for my husband's attitude in condemning you unheard. We both scolded him soundly for deciding your case so hastily, in disregard of the laws of evidence. *He* particularly, who is looked upon as the best magistrate on the Marondah bench. We got him to hear reason at last, and to write expressing regret that he had made no allowance for your ignorance of our bush population, and their ways with stock. This letter was in the bags of the mail coach to Waroonga, and *it also* was lost when two horses were drowned at Garlung: the bridge being six feet under water. None of the passengers were injured, but the coach was swept down the stream with the mail bags, which have not been recovered. It certainly was a most unlucky occurrence, for all concerned.

"When your letter from Melbourne arrived, poor Imogen was laid up with a bad attack of influenza, from the effects of which she was confined to bed for several weeks, her lungs having been attacked and pneumonia supervening; so that what with nursing her, and Mr. Bruce having left on a three months' trip to Queensland, all correspondence was suspended for a while. She was very nearly *dying*, and in fact was given up by two out of three of the doctors who attended her!

"Her good constitution pulled her through, and she has regained her former health, though not her spirits, poor girl!

"Then, after she was up, all these accounts of your wonderful success in Tasmania, and large fortune derived from the Tasmanian Silver Mine (I can't recollect its name) were circulated in the district. On account of this she did not write, as I wanted her to do, fearing (very foolishly, as I told her) lest you might think her influenced by your altered fortunes. She is not that sort of girl, I can safely assert. The man who touched her heart would remain there installed, for richer, for poorer, till death's parting hour.

"Whether you have said more to her than she has told me—she is very reserved about herself—I cannot say. I have written fully, perhaps too much so, as to which I trust to your honour, but my sole intention has been to clear up all doubts on your part, as to the feeling which actuates us as a *family*, about the past misunderstanding. I enclose a scrap which she gave me reluctantly.

"Yours sincerely,

"Hildegarde Bruce."

Mr. Blount picked up the half sheet of notepaper, which having kissed reverently, and indeed twice repeated the action, he read as follows. Very faint and irregular were the characters:—

"What a chapter of accidents since you left! Poor Johnny Doyle drowned! my letter and Hilda's lost. Your reply also never came.

"My illness, in which I was 'like to die' following closely.

"We thought you had left without troubling to answer our letters—at least, *they* did. My sister has written you *sheets*, so I need not enlarge upon matters. Edward is still in Queensland. The weather is lovely now, after the cold winter. If you can tear yourself away from Hobart, you might see what Marondah looks like in early summer.

"Yours truly,

"Imogen."

Mr. Blount's reply, *by telegram*, was sent with no unnecessary loss of time:—

"Leaving for Melbourne and Marondah by to-morrow's steamer."

Other letters, papers, circulars, requests, invitations in shoals lay ready for inspection. All the tentative appeals, complimentary and otherwise, which track the successful individual in war or peace, law, letters, or commerce. A large proportion of these were transmitted to the waste-paper basket—a piece of furniture now rendered necessary by the volume of Mr. Blount's correspondence.

He felt inclined to burn the whole lot, excepting those relative to the development of the Tasmanian Comstock and Associated Silver Mines Company (Limited), now stamped on a score of large and portentous envelopes.

Making a final search, a letter was detached from a superincumbent mass, the superscription of which had the Tumut and Bunjil postmarks. This was sufficient to arrest his attention. The handwriting, too, was that of Sheila Maguire, whose interest in his welfare did not seem to have declined.

"Dear Mr. Blount,—I little thought, when I used to get up at all hours to make you comfortable in our back block shanty, that this humble individual was ministering (that's a good word, isn't it? I've been reading up at odd times) to the wants of a Director of the Great Comstock Silver Mines Company. What a lark it seems, doesn't it? And you, that didn't know the difference between quartz and alluvial then!

"Shows what a fine country Australia is, when a gentleman may be nearly run in for 'duffing' one month, and the next have all the world bowing and scraping to him as a millionaire! That's not my line, though, is it? The money, if you had ten times as much, wouldn't make Sheila Maguire more your friend—your *real friend*—than she is now. The other way on, if anything. And there's a young lady down the river—not that I even myself with *her*, only she's a 'cornstalk'—one of the same brand, as the saying is. *She* don't mind the dirty money—any fool can come by that, or any man that's contented to live like a black-fellow, and save farthings till they mount up. He can't help it. But who'd take him, with his muck-rake?

"Great book, *Pilgrim's Progress*, isn't it? Just fell across it.

"'What the devil's the girl driving at?' I hear you say. That's not much of a swear for Bunjil, is it? Well, you'll see about it in the postscript, by and by.

"First and foremost, I want a hundred shares in the Great Comstock Associated. On the ground floor. *Original*, like the Broken Hill Proprietary.

"An uncle of mine, old Barney Maguire, of Black Dog Creek, died a month ago, and left us boys and girls five thousand apiece. *He* couldn't read and write, but he had ten thousand acres of good freehold land, river flats, too, and a tidy herd of cattle—every one knows the 'B. M.' brand. Some good horses, too. Comes of saving and screwing. He lived by the creek bank in an old bark hut with two rooms, never married, and never gave one of us boys and girls the value of a neck-ribbon or a saddle-strap while he was alive. I'm sending a cheque for the scrip, so make your secretary post them at once. As you're a director, you'll have to sign your *real* name, so I'll know what it is. I never was sure of the other. You're born lucky, and I'm going to back you right out. Perhaps I am, too, and might rise in life; who knows? I'm going to work up my education on the chance. What I learned at She-oak Flat'll stick to me. So we'll see. And now for the postscript. I looked it out—derived from *post scriptum (written after)*. Never thought what 'P.S.' meant before. Easy enough when you know, isn't it?

"Well, 'let me see!' says the blind man—oh! I forgot; that's vulgar—no more of that for Miss Sheila Maguire—one of the Maguires of Tumut. 'Fine gal, aw. Hear she's got money, don't yer know?' Ha! ha! they won't catch me that way. 'I've travelled,' though it's only on a bush track. False start; come back to the post, all of you! The straight tip is this—'a dead cert.' I had it from my cousin, Joe Macintyre, her that was maid to Mrs. Bruce. Miss Imogen *hadn't influenza*—only a bit of a cold; but she was real bad and low, all the same, after a certain gentleman went away. No word, and *no letters came back*. She'd sit and cry for hours. No interest in anything; not a smile out of her for days. Then she got ill, and no mistake; lower and lower—close up died. Doctors gave her up. Had to go to Sydney for change. I saw her in the train at Wagga. My word! I hardly knew her. She was that dog-poor and miserable, pale as a ghost, I nearly cried. Now she's home again, and looks better, Joe says.

"But if *some one* doesn't turn up before the summer's well on, I shall know what to think him who *was* a man and a gentleman, but that no one about here will call either the one or the other again, least of all,

"His friend and well-wisher,

"Sheila Maguire.

"P.S. No. 2.—Strikes me this isn't very different to the Church Service, which begins with 'Dearly beloved,' and ends with 'amazement.' What do you think?"

Mr. Blount couldn't help smiling at certain sentences in this frank and characteristic epistle. But he looked grave enough at the concluding one. This was the light then in which his conduct would appear to the rural inhabitants of the township and district of Bunjil.

Simple and chiefly unlettered they might be, but shrewd and accurate to a wonderful degree in their discernment of character.

It was evident that the false cavalier who "loved, and who rode away," would have small consideration shown him on the day when he might fall in with half a dozen Upper Sturt men at annual show or race meeting. There was a veiled threat in Sheila's closing sentence, and though, in his or any other defaulter's case, retributive justice might be stayed or wholly miscarry, yet it was not a pleasant thought that any act of his should bear the interpretation of bad faith; or that sentence of excommunication would, so to speak, be pronounced against him from one end of the river and the great Upper Sturt district to the other. By gentle and simple alike there would be unanimous agreement on that score. From the "mountain men" of the Bogongs and Talbingo, to the sun-burned plain-riders of the Darling, the vigorous English of the Waste would be searched for epithets of scorn and execration.

In the old Saxon days of the first Christian King, the epithet of "niddering" (worthless), which men committed suicide rather than endure, would have been decreed. Even the rude miners of the West would feel injured. From club to hotel, from the cool green, sunless forests of the Alpine chain, where the snow-fed rills tinkled and gurgled the long, bright summer through, to the burning, gold-strewn deserts of West Australia, he would be a marked man, pointed at as the coward who won a girl's heart and "cleared out," because he happened to "strike it rich" in another colony.

Luckily for his state of mind and the condition of his business prospects, Mr. Tregonwell happened to turn up a day earlier than he was expected, so that by sitting far into the night in council with that experienced though fervid operator, things were put into train; so that he and the resident directors would, with the help of a power of attorney, arrange all the advertising and scrip printing without further aid from Valentine Blount.

There was not much need for pushing ahead the concerns of the Great Tasmanian Comstock, by which name it was chiefly known and designated. The whole island seemed to be in a ferment. The public and the share market only needed restraining. It was, of course, only in the hurry and crush of applications for scrip, in resemblance to the South Sea — well, we'll say, Excitement of old historic days. The blocks of silver ore, "native silver," malachite, and other specimens exhibited behind a huge plate glass window in Davey Street, had driven the city wild. Crowds collected around it, and a couple of stalwart policemen were specially stationed there by the inspector to prevent unseemly crushing and riot. In addition well-armed night watchmen were provided at the expense of the Comstock Company for the nocturnal safety of the precious deposits. The *Pateena* was to leave for her customary conflict with the rough waves of Bass's Straits at 12 a.m. So, after a hard night's work, the "popular director" took a parting smoke and retired for what sleep was likely to visit him by 8 a.m., when the two partners were to breakfast together. Mr. Blount had not a tranquil experience of "tired nature's sweet restorer." "Little-River-Jack," the Sergeant, and Sheila Maguire pursued one another through the Bunjil forest, accompanied by the doomed mail-boy and Mr. Bruce. Sergeant Dayrell had apparently come to life again, and was standing pistol in hand with the same devilish sneer on his lips, face to face with Kate Lawless and Ned. Then the melancholy *cortège* moved across the scene, with the police riding slowly, as they led the spare horses upon which was tied the dead inspector and the wounded trooper. All things seemed sad, funereal, and out of keeping with the enforced gaiety and cordial hospitality which he had lately enjoyed. It was a relief on awakening to find, all unrefreshed as he was, that he had ample time in which to recruit, by means of the shower bath and matutinal coffee, his hardly-taxed mental and physical energies. However, all was ready to respond to the breakfast bell, specially ordered and arranged for, and when Mr. Tregonwell, looking as if he had gone to bed early and was only anxious about the *Hobart Courier*, entered the breakfast room, all tokens of despondency vanished from Mr. Blount's countenance.

Then only he realised that a creditably early start was feasible — was actually in process of operation.

"Look here!" exclaimed that notoriously early bird, producing two copies of the *Courier*, of which he handed his friend one, "Read this as a preliminary, and keep the paper in your pocket for board-ship literature."

It was, indeed, something to look at, as the supplement displayed under gigantic headlines this portentous announcement —

"The Tasmanian Comstock and Associated
Silver Mines Company, Limited.

"Acting under legal advice, the Directors have decided to close the share list of this unparalleled mine, of which the ore bodies at greater depths are daily disclosing a state of *phenomenal richness*. All applications for shares not sent in by the fifteenth day of the present month will be returned. If over-applied for—of which information will be furnished by the incoming English mail—applicants will have shares allotted to them in the order of their priority."

This was to Mr. Blount sufficient information for the present. The future of the mine was assured, and he was merely nervously anxious that no malignant interference with the normal course of events should prevent his arriving in Melbourne on the following day, in time to take his berth in the Sydney Express that afternoon—which indeed he had telegraphed for the day before. The partners had arrived on board the *Pateena*, now puffing angrily, with full steam up, a full half hour before the advertised time, owing to Mr. Blount's anxiety not to be late, and were walking up and down the deck, Tregonwell in vain attempting to get his fellow director to listen to details, and Blount inwardly fuming at the delay and cursing the Tasmanian lack of punctuality and general slackness, when two shabbily-dressed men stepped on board, one of whom walked up to the friends, tapped Mr. Blount on the shoulder, and producing a much crumpled piece of paper, said shortly, "I arrest you in the Queen's name, by virtue of this Warrant!"

To describe Mr. Blount's state of mind at this moment is beyond the resources of the English language—perhaps beyond those of any language. Rage, mortification, surprise, despair almost, struggled together in his mind, until his heart seemed bursting.

For a moment it seemed, as he threw off his captor with violence, and faced the pair of myrmidons with murder in his eye, as if he intended resistance in spite of law, order, and all the forces of civilisation. But his companion, cooler in situations of absolute peril as he was more impetuous in those of lighter responsibility, restrained him forcibly.

"Nonsense! keep calm, for God's sake, and don't make a scene. Just allow me to look at the warrant," he said to the apprehending constable. "I wish to see if it is in order. I am a magistrate of the territory. I can answer for my friend, who, though naturally disgusted, is not likely to resist the law."

The men were placated by this reasonable treatment of the position.

"The warrant seems in order," said Tregonwell. "The strange part of it is that it should not have been cancelled all this time, as we know that no proceedings were taken by the police at Bunjil in consequence of the non-appearance of the prosecution for the Crown. How this warrant got here and has been forwarded for execution is the astonishing part of the affair. Do you know," he said, addressing the peace officer, "how this warrant came into the hands of the Department here?"

"Forwarded for execution here, sir," said the man civilly, "with a batch of New South Wales warrants, chiefly for absconders, false pretences men, and others who have a way of crossing the Straits. It oughtn't to have been allowed to run, as the case wasn't gone on with. The acting clerk of the bench there is a senior constable, not quite up in his work; he has made a mistake, and got it mixed up with others. Most likely it's a mistake, but all the same, the gentleman must come with us for the present."

"All right, constable, we'll go with you, and make no attempt to escape. Bail will be forthcoming—in thousands, if necessary."

The steamer's bell began to sound, and after a few minutes, and a hurried colloquy with the captain, who promised to see his unlucky passenger's luggage delivered at the Imperial Club, the friends descended into the boat, and Tregonwell read out the warrant in his hands. It was apparently in order:—

"To Senior Constable Evans and to all Police Officers and Constables in the Colony of Victoria.—You are hereby commanded to arrest Valentine Blount—known as 'Jack Blunt,' at present supposed to be working in the 'Lady Julia' claim, forty miles from Bunjil, on the Wild Horse Creek, in company with Phelim and Patrick O'Hara, also George Dixon (known as Lanky), and to bring him before me or any other Police Magistrate of Victoria. This warrant is issued on the sworn information of Edward Hamilton Bruce, J.P. of Marondah, on the Upper Sturt, and for such action this shall be your warrant.

"(*Signed*) H. Bayley, P.M."

The sorely-tried lover felt much more inclined to fling himself into the waters of the Derwent, and there remain, than to occupy for one moment longer this ignominious position at the hands of the myrmidons of the law. However, the next step, of course, was to interview the police magistrate of Hobart at his Court House, and after having explained the circumstances, to apply for bail, so that the period of detention might be shortened as much as possible. This process of alleviation was effected without unnecessary delay, the magistrate being a reasonable, experienced person, and as such inclined to sympathise with the victim of malign fate, obviously not of the class with which he had been for years judicially occupied.

The officer briefly stated the case, produced the warrant, and delivered up his prisoner, who was permitted to take a chair. Mr. Parker, P.M., scanned the warrant with keen and careful eye before committing himself to an opinion. After which he bestowed a searching glance upon Mr. Blount, and thus delivered himself:

"It appears," he said, "that this warrant was issued, with several others, upon the sworn information of Edward Hamilton Bruce, J.P., of Marondah, Upper Sturt, who had reason to believe that the person named—viz., Valentine Blount—generally known as 'Jack Blunt,' was concerned with Phelim O'Hara, Patrick O'Hara, George Dixon (otherwise Lanky), and John Carter, known as 'Little-River-Jack,' in stealing and disposing of certain fat cattle branded E.H.B., the property of the said Edward Hamilton Bruce. It is now the 20th of November," said the worthy P.M., "and I note that this warrant was signed on the 10th of September last. By a curious coincidence I have this morning received a communication from the Department of Justice in Victoria informing me that separate warrants were issued for the persons named in the information, but that, owing to deficiency of proof and difficulty of identification of the stock suspected to have been killed or otherwise disposed of, the Crown Solicitor has ordered a *Nolle Prosequi* to be entered. 'In accordance with which decision, notices of such action were signed by the bench of magistrates at Bunjil, Victoria, and the warrants, in the names of Phelim O'Hara, Patrick O'Hara, George Dixon (*alias* Lanky), and John Carter (*alias* Little-River-Jack), were cancelled. But through inadvertence, the warrant in the name of Valentine Blount (otherwise Jack Blunt) had been mislaid, and, with other documents, forwarded to James Parker, Esq., P.M., Hobart. He is requested to return the said warrant to the Department of Justice, and if the said warrant has been by misadventure executed, to release at once the said Valentine Blount, known as "Jack Blunt."

"'I remain, sir,

"'Your obedient servant,

"'George B. Harrison,

"'*Under Secretary of Justice.'*

"That being the case, I have the pleasure to congratulate you, sir, on your escape from a very unpleasant position, and to apologise on behalf of the Department with which I am connected, for the unfortunate mistake, as well as for all consequences to which it may have led in your case. Sergeant, let the accused be discharged."

Thus, after undergoing tortures, as to which the same time spent on a rack of the period—say in the time of His Most Christian Majesty, Philip of Spain—would have been a trifling inconvenience, was our unlucky *détenu* restored to liberty.

After bowing to the genial P.M., who had seen so many discomfitures, disasters, and disorders, that nothing was likely to cause him surprise or disturb his serenity, the friends returned to their club to lunch, as well as to make such arrangements for the morrow as might suffice for clearing out to Melbourne with the least possible delay and public disturbance. Fortunately, another steamer on a different line, just arrived from Callao and the Islands, was due for an early start in the morning. Mr. Blount resolved, after dining at the club, to spend the night on board of her so as to have no bother about getting ready before daylight, at which time the skipper promised departure. Frampton Tregonwell, the friend in need, would bear him company and help to keep up his spirits so rudely dashed until the time arrived for the partial oblivion of bed, which, indeed, it was long before he found.

Next morning, however, the excitement of a gale took him out of his self-consciousness for a few hours, and the unfamiliar companionship of the passengers aided the cure. He was only partially recovered from a state of shock and annoyance, but could not help being attracted by the men and women; they were of rare and striking types, such as were around him, in all directions.

They were certainly cosmopolitan—grizzled island traders, sea-captains, and mates out of employment at present. Adventurers of every kind, sort, and degree, with their wives and families of all shades of colour and complexion. Speaking all languages indifferently ill, Spanish and Portuguese, French, German and Italian, and, of course, English more or less undefiled. The men were fine specimens physically, bold, frank, hardy-looking, such as might be expected to reply with knife and revolver to adverse argument. Handsome dark women and girls, with flashing eyes and unrivalled teeth, who seemed perfectly at home, and regarded the wildest weather with curiosity rather than with apprehension. Sydney seemed familiar to many as their port of arrival and departure, which, having reached, they were more free to find passage to the ends of the earth.

Such a happy-go-lucky unconventional crowd of passengers, it had rarely been Mr. Blount's lot to encounter, far-travelled though he was. The captain, mates and ship's crew were, in their way, equally removed from ordinary personages. One could imagine the captain—a spare, saturnine American—a pirate, suddenly converted by a missionary bishop—bearing his captives of the lower hold, previously doomed to torture and spoliation, to a free port, there to be released, unharmed, with all their goods and chattels scrupulously returned. Here was an opportunity altogether unparalleled, presented to "an observer of human nature."

But it was like many other gifts of the gods, presented to the dealer in the souls and bodies of his fellow creatures (intellectually regarded), at the precise time and place, when, from circumstances, he could make no use of the situation. A banquet of the gods, and not the ghost of an appetite wherewith to savour it!

In his present mood, had Helen of Troy, accompanied by Paris and Achilles, with Briseis as "lady help," been one of the strangely assorted crowd (there *were* half a dozen modern Greeks on board, miners returning from an inspection of an alleged "mountain of tin")—even then he would not have listened with interest to their respectful cross-examination of the "goddess moulded" as to her adventures since the fall of Troy, or her well-grounded apprehension of her probable fate under adverse feminine rule.

All romance, sympathy, curiosity even were dead within him for the present. Fate had counter-checked him too often. He expected nothing, hoped nothing, but feared everything—until his arrival at the homestead on the Upper Sturt, when he could see Imogen, pale, perhaps, and more fragile than when last she turned her impatient horse's head homeward—but infinitely lovely and dearer than all, as having proved her loyalty to him, from their first meeting by the waters of the Great River, in despite of doubt, calumny, and unjust accusation.

All these were gone and disposed of; now was the season of faith and fruition—the reward of her love, and truth—of his constancy. Here his complacent feeling of perhaps scarcely justified self-laudation faltered somewhat. Yes! he *had* been true—he *had* been faithful—any other feeling was merely involuntary deflection from his ideal, and he was now going to claim his prize!

The wind stilled. The sea went down. The stars came out. The soft air of the Great South Land, hidden away from the restless sea-rover for centuries untold, until the keel of the great English captain floated into the peerless haven, enveloped the wave-worn bark, as with a mantle of peace and forgiveness; their voyage was practically, virtually, at an end. Mr. Blount remained on deck smoking with the more hardened of the foreign passengers, who apparently needed not sleep at all, until the midnight hour; then wearily sought his cabin. Cabin indeed, he had none, for, determined to get away at all hazards, he had expressed his total indifference to such a luxury, and his willingness to sleep under the cabin table, if necessary, only provided that he got a passage. The captain said if that were so he could come, taking his chance of a bed or sofa. However, he had been to sea before. A judicious *douceur* to the head steward procured him, after a certain hour, one of the saloon lounges, and the privilege of dressing in that important functionary's cabin. Awake with the dawn, he found himself just in time to witness the safe passage of the *Donna Inez* through the tumultuous harbour entrance of the "Rip," and after a decent interval, to arrive, undisturbed by anxiety about luggage, at the ever open door of the Imperial Club.

Here, with his property around him—apparently safe and uninjured— he began to find himself an independent traveller of means and position again. He had been relieved of the horrible uncertainty of delay—the doubt and fear connected with a trial for a criminal offence, and all the other disagreeables, if not dangers, of a discreditable position. His railway ticket had already been taken for Waronga, whence the coach on the ensuing morning, after a daylight breakfast, would take him on to Marondah.

All went well. He saw again the rippling river, the friendly face of Mrs. Bruce—he had always delighted in that dear woman—so refined, so ladylike, and yet practical and steadfast. The ideal wife and mother— remote from the metropolis, and the frivolous slaves of fashion—yet how infinitely superior to them all. He saw the fair Imogen coming to meet him, shyly repressing her joy and gratitude for the turn which their fortunes had taken, but only refraining on account of the spectators from throwing herself into his arms. This she confessed afterwards, after a decent interval of explanation, and full confessions on both sides. Neither of them would own to have been the most overjoyed at the meeting, delayed as it had been by an apparent conspiracy of all the powers of darkness.

Mr. Bruce had not as yet returned from the "Ultima Thule" of Western Queensland, where he had a share in an immense cattle station. His stay had been protracted and unsatisfactory. A dry season had set in—had followed several rainless years, in fact—nothing could exceed the frightful position of the squatters in that district.

The destruction of stock was awful, unparalleled. Never since the first white man's foot had touched Australia's shore, had there been such loss, and probable ruin (he wrote to his wife).

He should be glad to get back to Marondah, to see some decent grass again, and hear the river rippling through the calm still night, and the river-oaks murmuring to the stars. *That* was something like a country. He would take the first chance to sell out of Mount Trelawney, and never go out of Victoria for an investment again.

So Edward Bruce had written in a peaceable mood. He supposed a general amnesty must be declared, and all be forgiven and forgotten. By the way, he met Jack Carter (Little-River-Jack) at a place not a hundred miles from Roma (he wrote). "He was in a position to do me a service at a critical juncture, and did it heartily and effectively. So all scores are cleared between him and me. You mustn't suppose, however, that I am in danger of my life, or that bushranging, cattle-stealing, and an occasional interchange of revolver shots, is part of the order of the day. What I mention is exceptional, and I don't wish it to go further for several reasons.

"The Manager, Mackenzie, and I were riding along rather late one evening, and a good twelve or fifteen miles from home. The weather (of course) was fine, but the hour was late, and the sun, which had been glaring at us all day, only just about to set.

"'By George! that's a big mob of horses,' said Mac., 'going fast too. Coming from the back of Goornong and heading for Burnt Creek. Six men and a black boy. Depend upon it, there's something "cronk." They might see us yet. Yes, they do! They've halted. Left two men and the boy with the mob, and the rest, four men, are coming across the plains to us.'

"'Do you know who they are?'

"'I can pretty well guess,' he said. 'They're a part of that crowd that we broke up last year, a very dangerous lot! The big man with the beard is Joe Bradfield, the best bushman in all Queensland, and perhaps Australia, to boot. The chap alongside him is "Jerry the Nut." *He's* a double-dyed scoundrel, if you like, twice tried for murder, and ought to have been hanged years ago, if he'd got his rights. Supposed to have shot "Jack the Cook," who quarrelled with him, and started in for Springsure to give the lot away, but never got there. Found dead in the Oakey Creek with two bullets in him. Jerry was proved to have overtaken him on the road; was the last man seen with him alive. Put on his trial—a strong case against him, but not sufficient evidence. Here they come. We've seen them in possession of stolen horses. I expect they've duffed them from that Bank station, that was taken over last week. They may think it safer to "rub us out." They're villains enough for anything. You're armed, and my "navy, No. 1" is pretty sure at close quarters. Cut off by —! we may have to ride for it too—' As he spoke, three men emerged from a clump of brigalow at an angle from the line at which the 'horse thieves' were riding. They also made towards us, and riding at speed, seemed as if they desired to reach us at about the same time as the others. Such, it appeared, would be the case.

"The four men that had left the mob of horses, rode at the station overseer and me as if they would ride over us. Then pulled up with the stock-horses' sudden halt, not brought up on their haunches, like those of the gaucho of Chile or the cowboy of the Western States, by the merciless wrenching curb, but with the half pull of the plain snaffle, the only bit the bushman knows, when with loose rein, and lowered head, the Australian camp horse drives his fore-feet into the ground, and stops dead as if nailed to the earth.

"'What the h—l are you two doing here?' shouted the tall man, a Hercules in height and breadth of shoulder, yet sitting his horse with the ease and closeness of early boyhood, though his beard and coal-black hair were already streaked with grey. Tracking us down? My God! it's the worst lay you was ever on. Isn't a man to ride across a plain in the blasted squatters' country without he has a pass from a magistrate? That's what it's coming to. Well, you're on the wrong lay this trip. Come along back with us, or we'll make yer.

"'And look dashed quick about it, or ye'll not come back at all. Bring up the darbies, Joe! We'll see how the bloomin' swells like 'em.'

"As the last speaker uttered this threat, he and the other men raised their revolvers.

"'I'll see you d—d first,' I replied (excuse bad language). 'We're from Trelawney this morning, and on our lawful business.' Here I drew my revolver.

"The encounter looked doubtful, when the three new arrivals rode up, and, like the other bushmen, stopped dead, with their horses side by side.

"'No, yer don't!' said one of the new arrivals, a man as tall and massive as the first 'robber' (for such he seemed). 'I'm not goen' to stand by and see Mr. Bruce, of Marondah, double-banked by you Queensland duffers while I'm round. There's been trouble between him and our crowd; but he's a man and a gentleman, and I'm here to stand by him to the bitter end. It's five go four now, so fire away, and be d—d to you!'

"'Who the devil are you?'

"'I'm Phelim O'Hara, and this is Little-River-Jack, and my brother Pat. We've come up, like the Proosians at Waterloo, rather late in the day; but "better late than never." You're Joe Bradfield, that we've heard of, and Jerry the Nut that murdered his mate, I suppose. So you'd better go back to the French, and let the allies go their own way. No one's goen' to give you away, if your own foolishness doesn't. We're on our own ground, so hear reason and clear out. I heard a big lot of police, and Superintendent Gray, of Albany, was on yer track.'

"'When did you hear that?'

"'No later than yesterday. And you're ridin' straight into their bloomin' arms, if yer don't get back the way yer kem' in. Take a fool's advice, and get into the ranges again. This country's too open for your crowd, and you'll have to do the gully-raker's racket for a month or two, till the "derry's" toned down a bit.'

"This apparently reasonable advice seemed to have weight with the troop of highly irregular horse, as, after a short colloquy, they rode back to their companions in charge of the horses, and heading them towards the distant ranges, disappeared shortly from sight.

"'O'Hara!' said I, 'whatever you and your mates may have done in the past—at any rate, as far as I am concerned—is now past and gone. I freely forgive anything that there may have been to forgive, in consequence of your manly conduct to-day. If you will come back with me to the head station, I dare say Mr. Mackenzie can find you something to do in this bad season. Unfortunately, we have only too many vacancies for bushmen like yourselves and Jack Carter.'

"'We'll take your word for it, Mr. Bruce,' said Little-River-Jack; 'and, if we come to terms, there'll be no station on the Upper Sturt that'll lose fewer stock—barrin' from the season—while we're to the fore.'

"'All right,' said Mackenzie, 'you're just the chaps we want this awful season; and, now you're going straight, each of you will be worth half a dozen ordinary men.'"

The day was still warm, not much change from the 110° in the shade which the sunset-hour had registered, but a gradual coolness commenced to o'erspread the heated landscape. "The stars rush out, at one strike comes the dark," making an appearance of coolness, to which the abnormal dryness of the air in mid-Australia lends a perceptible relief. Confident of a welcome, and the hospitable reception of a head-station—always superior in comfort to the more casual arrangements of the out-stations—the five horsemen rode steadily forward in peace and amity; Mr. Mackenzie, as knowing every foot of the run, taking the lead with the two O'Haras, while Mr. Bruce and Little-River-Jack followed quietly in the rear.

CHAPTER IX

"'I'd like to tell you, sir,' said Carter, 'how we first got acquainted, me and Mr. Blount, to put him right with you, because I heard a whisper that you thought he must be in with us, in the "cross" butchering line.'

"'I don't deny,' I answered, 'that I thought it very suspicious that a man like him should be living with you fellows, and yet have no idea that dishonest work was going on?'

"'All right, Mr. Bruce, don't spare us. It *was* dishonest, there's no two ways about it, and we chaps ought to be ashamed of ourselves, as are well able to get a living straight and square, and under fear of no man. Now we've had a fright and been let off you'll never hear another word against us. But I wanted to have a word about Mr. Blount. If he had been copped along with us, it would have been a cruel shame, a regular murder, and him as innocent as the child unborn. His horse was knocked up, or next door to it, when I came across him a few miles from the "Lady Julia"; I'd a few cattle with me, and asked him to help me drive them. He stayed at our place that night. The man I was selling them to sent for them before daylight, and all he could hear was them being let out of the yard.'

"'He was a dividing mate after that, though?' said I, knowing that such mining agreements comprehend all knowledge in heaven and earth, and under the sea.

"Carter answered my unspoken thought when he said, 'He bought Tumberumba Dick's share, him as went to Coolgardie, and if he knew mullock from wash dirt, then, it's as much as he did. As for cattle, he hardly knew a cow from a steer. Then he lost his moke and went down the river to get word of him.'

"'Yes!' I said. 'I met him then; he came on me just as I was shooting a small mob of wild horses. I had been watching for them for months. They seldom came so far in; but I dropped the stallion first shot, a noted grey, said to be thoroughbred; the mares and foals wouldn't leave him, so I got them all, one by one.'

"'Mr. Blount was astonished, I suppose? Seems a pity, too, they were a well-bred lot. I've had many a gallop after the same lot, thinkin' to yard 'em, but they always got away. Anyhow, they're no blessed good, if you do yard 'em; mostly sulk and always clear the first chance. His cob, it seems, joined your horses, and was run in to the paddock. So you put him up for the night and sent him home on his own horse. Came part of the way with him, you and the ladies, and Black Paddy. Nigh hand to the "Lady Julia" you spotted your "E. H. B." bullock with a fresh brand on. And he never said nothen'. Next day Black Paddy ran our tracks to the claim and the stockyard, found where the last bullocks had been driven to the Back Creek slaughter yards. That was as plain as A B C, and we had to clear. Phelim waited on to get his horse back that he'd lent him, and start after Pat and Lanky, who were well on their way to Omeo.'

"'All quite correct,' I said; 'but why didn't he act straightforwardly and tell me like a man that he had been working in your claim?'

"'Because he didn't want to give us away, and if he said what he knew, but *didn't understand*, the police would have been up next day and collared the lot of us before we had a chance to cut it.'

"'But why was he so tender about your party?' I said. 'You had deceived him, and he might naturally have felt angry at being let in for aiding and abetting cattle stealers, and all the more anxious to see you punished.'

"'That's all right, Mr. Bruce; but you see there was another reason why he stood by us, though he didn't wait an hour after he knew we were on the cross; wouldn't take his share of the gold neither, which he'd worked as hard for as any of us.'

"'What *was* the other reason?'

"'Well, sir,' rather shamefacedly, 'he thought I'd *saved his life*, as it were.'

"'Saved his life? How could that be?'

"'It was this way, sir.' As he spoke, he looked quite sad and confused. 'You know that Razor Back ridge on the short track to Bunjil?'

"'Yes! I was over it once, and a brute of a track it was. That was where Paddy Farrell was killed.'

"'The same; well, when we was coming along it from Bunjil to the claim, that cob of his—a flat-country horse—got frightened, and had half a mind to back over the edge. I was thinkin' of somethin' else; when I looked back I saw Mr. Blount was confused-like, he didn't know how to stop him. I slipped off, and held the cob, while he did the same, and started old Keewah along the track, with the reins tied to the stirrup-iron. My old moke trotted on, and the cob after him, till they came to the trap-yard, where we found them when we came up, half an hour after. There wasn't much in it. Any man who'd lived in rangey country couldn't have helped doin' it; but he chose to believe I'd saved his life. So it was chiefly that that made him not let on to you about where he'd lived. Nothing might have come of it; but it was a close shave, and no mistake.'

"'I'm very glad to hear the explanation, Carter. I don't see how he could have acted differently, as a man or gentleman. I shall write and tell him so. And now, a word with you; which you can pass on to your mates. Make no mistake, you've got a fresh start in life! You three fellows are young. Anything there is against you, as far as I know, is over and done with. These warrants are just waste paper. But be careful for the future. If you stick to the Nundooroo station till the drought's over, you're made men. I'll let the Inspector-General of Police know how you behaved.'

"'All right, sir; we're on. We won't go back on you,' was his reply.

"'You may expect to see me at Marondah, within the month, though travelling through a desert, as this country is virtually now, is very slow and unsatisfactory. I must pick up a riding camel, a "heirie," such as I've seen in the East, warranted to keep going for twenty-four hours on end, without water or food. However, I suppose rain will come some time or other.'"

Thus fully exonerated, it may be believed that Blount made the best use of his time at Marondah, where he had the field all to himself with the advantage of the most considerate of chaperons, in the person of Mrs. Bruce, who had always been, as she told him, his staunch supporter, even in the dark days, when her husband forbade his name to be mentioned, and when from adverse circumstances no letters had arrived to clear his character.

"*I* never doubted you for a moment," murmured Imogen, "but it must be confessed, it was hard work holding to my trust in you, when so many rumours were flying through the country. I never could make out why you joined such people at all, or what you were to gain by it. If you wished to know what a miner's life was like, there are plenty of gentlemen glad enough to go into any venture of the sort, with the aid of a little capital — men such as you have described at the 'Comstock' or at Zeehan."

"But how was I to find them?"

"Just the same way in which you would have done in England, through introductions to men of mark out here. They would have advised you for your good. And there would have been no risk of your being compromised by any action of theirs."

"No doubt it was indiscreet of me, but I wanted to see for myself, and form my own opinion by personal experience of a society so different from any I had known before."

"That is where you conceited Englishmen" — here she held up a warning finger — "make a mistake, indeed tons of mistakes. In vain we tell you that there is no special difference here between the classes of society, or the laws which rule them, and those of your own beloved country, which we are proud to resemble."

"But are they not different?"

"Not radically, by any means. Any departure from English manners and customs is chiefly superficial. Your squire, or lord of the manor, says 'Mornin', Jones! crops doin' so-so, too dry for the roots,' and so on. 'Nice four year old of yours. Looks as if he'd grow into a hunter.' But there's no *real* equality, nor can there be. Jones doesn't expect it."

"Mr. Bruce, I suppose, has much the same feeling for the farmers here, and they meet on much the same terms. Except when the suspicion of 'duffing' comes in, eh? then — then — relations are strained, indeed, as between the same classes, if poaching was discovered, and brought home to the guilty ones."

They had these, with many other, talks and disquisitions, such as are interesting to lovers, and lovers only, in the long delicious evenings and unquestioned idlesse which are the prerogatives of the halcyon days which follow a declared engagement, and before the completed drama of marriage.

The soft, mild months of the southern spring were now heralding the less romantic season of the Australian summer. The sun god was daily strengthening his power, without as yet the fierce noonday glare or burning heat. Chiefly precious to them were the moonlight walks by the river side when the shadows of the great willows which fringed the river bank fell over the hurrying tide, when star sheen or moonrays glinted through the close foliage or sparkled diamond bright on the rippling bars. There was a winding path a few feet from the bank, accurately marked by the cattle and horses, which roved unchecked through the great meadows.

Here the lovers were at liberty to indulge in fullest confidences. He told her that he had loved her from the very first moment that his eyes fell upon her, when, not knowing that any other than Mrs. Bruce was in the house he had been almost unconventional in the surprise of the meeting and his instant admiration. "That moment sealed our destiny," he said, "or rather, would have left me a lifelong regret had I never set eyes on you again. And what was your feeling, Imogen?" looking suddenly into her eyes, which, lit up by a fairy moonray, seemed to his eager gaze to glow with unearthly radiance. So, in old days did the fabled Oread enthrall the heart of the doomed shepherd or woodsman, luring him to follow into her enchanted bower, which he was fated never again to discover, wasting life wandering through the forest aisles, wearing out health, youth and passion, in the ever-fleeting, illusory pursuit.

"I think," she answered softly, as her eyes fell before his ardent gaze, "that I must have been similarly affected, why, I cannot tell, but the fact remains that if you had never returned—and we had not much time for love-making, had we, between that day and your return to the 'Lady Julia' claim, and the fascinating society of Mr. Little-River-Jack?—I should have 'fallen into a sadness, then into a fast, thence into a weakness,' and so on. As it was, I was very melancholy and low for a while, and between that and influenza, very nearly 'went out,' as my maid, Josephine Macintyre, phrased it. Then, when I was coming round, and reaching the stage of 'the common air, the sea, the skies, to "her" are opening Paradise,' and would have written to you, we heard that you had become a millionaire or a 'silver king' in Tasmania. It was foolish, I know, but I thought it might look as if I wanted to recall you because of your wealth—a vulgar idea, but still one that works for good or evil in this silly life of ours. But now, all will be forgiven, 'if this should meet the eye,' &c., as the advertisements say. You will forgive me, and I will forgive you, and there will never be any more doubts or despair, will there?"

That Mr. Blount made a short but impressive reply to this query may be taken for granted. The river marge, the sighing, trailing willows, the rippling murmuring stream, the friendly moon, all these were conditions eminently favourable to "love's young dream." Nor did they fail in this instance to ratify the solemn, irrevocable vow, often lightly, rashly, falsely sworn, but in this instance repeated with all the passion of ardent manhood, responded to with the heart's best and truest affection, the sacred, intensely glowing flame of the maiden's love, imperishable, immortal.

"You told me, the last time we met," she whispered, "that some day I should know why you came here to lead an aimless, wandering life. I always thought there was some mystery about it. Will you tell me now? It is lovely and mild, there could not be a better time. How clearly you can hear the ripple in the shallows. Was there a woman in it?"

"Of course there was, but mind, it all happened seven years ago. So if what I say may be used against me on my trial, I shall be dumb."

"I've copied out depositions now and then, for Edward," replied the girl, archly. "Having heard the evidence, do you wish to say anything? comes next. So I'll promise not to take advantage of your voluntary confession, if you make a clean breast of it, once for all. I have no fear of the dear, dead women, whoever they were."

"You need not," said Blount, as he drew her more closely to him, "not if Helen of Troy were of the company."

On their return to the verandah, where they found Mrs. Bruce still occupied with the needlework, which took up (so she said), fortunately, so much of her time, Imogen pleaded fatigue and retired, leaving the field free to her sister and the guest, who thereupon commenced a long, and apparently serious conversation.

Mr. Blount spoke more unreservedly of his private affairs than he had hitherto thought it expedient to do. Independently of his share in the Great Comstock Company, for which he had already been offered a hundred thousand pounds—he had a handsome allowance from his father—as also, thinking it might be needed, a letter of credit upon the Imperial Bank for five thousand pounds.

"It will always be a puzzle to me and Imogen," said Mrs. Bruce, "how, with all that money at your disposal, you should ever have run the risks you did in this gipsy business, with the people we found you with, or would have done, if you had remained a few days longer with them. You didn't want to learn their language, like Borrow—what other reason *could* there be?"

"My dear Mrs. Bruce," he replied, "you have been so good, considerate, and friendly to me, that I must make a clean breast of it. I have already told Imogen all there is to tell of a by no means uncommon event in a man's life, when one of your adorable, yet fatal sex is mixed up with it."

"I see, I understand, the 'eternal feminine'; we have not many romances of the kind in these quiet hills, but of course they are not wholly unknown, even in our sequestered lives. You are going to tell me of your tragedy."

"It was not far removed from the ordinary run of such adventures, though there might easily have been a catastrophe. I was young, I said it was seven years ago, since which I have industriously wasted life's best gifts, in trying to forget her. Beautiful, yes, as a dream maiden! a recognised queen of society, flattered, worshipped, wherever her fairy footsteps trod; but vain, ambitious and false as the Lorelei, or the mermaiden, that lures the fated victim. More than one man had thrown life, character, or fortune at her feet, unavailingly. I had heard this, but with the reckless confidence of youth, I heeded not. I met her at the quiet country house of a relative; men being scarce, she condescended to play for so poor a stake as the heart of a younger son, an undistinguished lover's existence, and she won!

"How could it be otherwise? She turned the full battery of her charms upon the undefended fort. We rode together, we fished the trout stream, more dangerous still. We read in the old library, morning after morning, and here my not unmarked university career served me well, as I thought. I had been reading aloud from a novel of the hour, when, looking up suddenly I saw a light in her eyes, which gave me hope, more than hope. I took her hand, I poured out protestations, entreaties, vows of eternal love; whatever man has distilled from the inward fires of soul and sense, under the alembic of love at white heat, I found words for and poured into her not unwilling ear.

"She was visibly agitated. Her cold nature, serenely lovely as she always was, seemed to kindle into flame under the fire of my impetuous avowal. I gained her other hand, I threw myself on my knees before her, and drew her down to the level of my face. I clasped her yielding form, and kissed her lips with soul-consuming ardour. To my surprise, she made no resistance, her colour came and went, she might have been the veriest country milkmaid, surprised into consent by her rustic lover's eagerness. 'You are mine, say you are mine for ever!' I whispered into her shell-like ear as her loosened hair fell over her cheek.

"'Yours,' she said in a low intense murmur, 'now and for ever.' Then gently, disengaging herself from my arms, 'This is a foolish business. I confess to being rather unprepared, but I suppose we must consider it binding?'

"'Binding,' said I, shocked at the alteration of her tone and manner. 'To the end of world, and afterwards, in life, in death, my heart is yours unalterably—to wear in true love's circlet or to break and cast beneath your feet.'

"'Poor Val!' said she, smoothing my hair with her dainty jewelled fingers, 'yet women have played false before now to their promises, as fondly made, and men's hearts have not been broken. They have lived to smile, to wed, to enjoy life much as usual—or old tales are untrue.'

"'Do not jest,' said I, 'a man's life—a woman's heart, are treasures too precious to win—too perilous to lose; say you are not in earnest?'

"'Perhaps not,' she said, lightly. 'Yes! you may have your good-night kiss,' and we parted. You would not think it was for ever.

"The house-party was not large at Kingswood, but it was as much disturbed and excited when our engagement was given out, as if it had been a much more exalted gathering.

"My devotion had not been unmarked, but the betting had been against me. I was too young, too undistinguished—what had I done? not even in the army—in literature, beyond a few tentative minor successes, I was unknown. How had I presumed to propose to—indeed to win this belle of the last two seasons—the admitted star of the most aristocratic, exclusive, socially distinguished set? I was fairly good-looking—so much was admitted—my family was unimpeachable, old and honoured, but where is the money to come from to uphold the dignity and pay the bills of a queen of beauty and fashion such as Adeline Montresor?

"She had not come down from her room next morning when we men adjourned to the grounds for a smoke, and the usual after breakfast stroll.

"I was in the stable examining a strain which had lamed my hunter a few days since, and which had accounted for my presence in the library on the eventful afternoon, when my attention was attracted by an observation made by one man to another who held out a morning paper for his friend to see.

"'I thought there was something "by ordinar," as our Scotch gardener says.

"'Death of Sir Reginald Lutterworth, all his money and the lovely place left to his nephew, Valentine Blount, the younger son of Lord Fontenaye.'

"'By Jove!' said his friend. 'What a throw in! This accounts for the unaccountable, to put it mildly. The fair Adeline sees something beyond the personal merits of our enthusiastic young friend.

"'A house in town—a place in the country, etc., presented at Court, Marlborough House in the future—what girl of the period could say no to such a present—with a still more gorgeous perspective?'

"'Certainly not Miss Montresor, nor any of her set. But what about Colonel Delamere?'

"'He'll receive a neat, carefully worded note, which being interpreted, needs only one word of translation, "farewell."

"'Perhaps to soften the blow, as the phrase runs, something like "my people so badly off, pressure brought to bear—feelings unchanged—bow to Fate, etc."'

"'Wonder if she saw it?'

"'My man says it's in all the evening papers, but we were so hard at work at bridge, that no one thought of looking at them. She couldn't have seen it, unless the maid took it up to her room when she went to dress for dinner. Ha! didn't think of that.'

"On inquiry, I found that my enslaver and her maid had left for London by the early train. A note had been left for me, containing only a few words. 'Dearest, I feel I *must* go home. See you at Oldacres. Au revoir.'

"I felt disappointed. Still I had no rational ground for distrust. It was most natural that a girl under such circumstances should wish to go home to her mother, and relieve her heart, when such an important step had been decided upon. I sent a telegram in answer, and arranged to leave for London, having to make certain arrangements in accordance with what would doubtless be my altered position.

"We wrote to one another daily. The letters, though not particularly ardent on her side, were affectionate and apparently sincere. A few days passed in making necessary financial arrangements, in receiving congratulations, freely tendered by friends and acquaintances.

"By my own family, I was regarded as a Spanish galleon, laden with treasure, which had come to redeem the faded glories of the estate, and to aid the wearer of a title, unsupported by an adequate income. Life was roseate, radiant with dazzling splendour.

"What cared I for the wealth? Was I not the proud possessor of the heart of the loveliest girl in England? I was invited to her father's place in the Midlands, for the forthcoming hunting season.

"The kindest, semi-maternal letter informed me that 'darling Adeline' had overtaxed her nervous system, and not been quite herself for the last few days. I could understand *why*. However, she was looking her best once more, and all impatience to greet me at Oldacres, next week, when some of their more intimate neighbours would be able to pay their respects. I made rather a wry face at the extra week's delay, thus imposed upon me, but suppressed any impatience as much as was possible, while thinking of the rapturous delight awaiting me, at the end of the probation. On the morning of the day on which I was to leave London, I received another of the extra-legal, important-looking documents, with which I had been so familiar lately. I was on the point of throwing it into the drawer of my writing table to await my return when I should be able to settle all formal matters in one morning's work. Something, however, urged me to open the bothering thing, and have done with it, so as not to have it hanging over me when I was impatient of business of any sort or kind.

"I read over the first page twice before I fully grasped its purport.

"'My Dear Sir,—We regret deeply the unpleasant nature of the communication which we are reluctantly compelled to make. We cannot sufficiently express our surprise at the apparent carelessness of Messrs.

Steadman and Delve, who have been your uncle's trusted lawyers and agents for fifty years, and in point of fact acted in that capacity for your grandfather, the late Lord Fontenaye, and we apologise, with sincere regrets, for not having verified with greater care the precise nature of Sir Reginald's last will and testament.

"'It now appears that the testator made *another will* a year after the one by which you were to benefit so largely. That other will has been found in a secret drawer, and is now in the possession of Messrs. Steadman and Delve. By it *all former wills* are revoked, and there is a total omission of your name as a beneficiary. With the exception of comparatively trifling annuities and legacies, the whole of the testator's very large estates, together with the sum of £300,000 invested in the three per cents, is willed to your elder brother, the present Lord Fontenaye.'

"This was a thunderclap; indeed, apart from the natural distaste felt by most men at having been suddenly displaced from a position of wealth and importance, my chief regret arose from the feeling of disappointment which my change from wealth to moderate competence would cause to my beloved Adeline.

"No doubt of her loyalty and good faith troubled me. A legacy from my mother provided a sufficient, if not unusual income, as well as a fair estate, upon which we could live in something more than moderate comfort. Surely no girl would hesitate to declare her willingness to share the fortunes of a man to whom she had plighted her troth, though dissociated from the splendour which surrounded the former position. I lost no time in telegraphing to her father the change in our circumstances, at the same time writing a full explanation and requesting a day's delay before visiting Oldacres, on account of necessary arrangements. But little time was lost in telegraphing an answer to my communication. 'Much shocked by your news. Please to await letter. Miss Montresor much overcome.'

"The first news had been disastrous; the second intimation was unpleasant in tone and suggestion. I could not but regard it as showing a disposition to retreat from the engagement. But was this possible—even probable? Could I think my adored one guilty of withdrawing from her solemnly pledged troth-plight, *entirely* on account of the change in my fortunes from those of a rich man with an historic rent-roll and estates hardly exceeded by those of any English proprietor? Was it then the rents and the three per cents which this angel-seeming creature accepted without reference to the man? It would appear so. My youth and inexperience, how inferior in worldly wisdom had they shown me to be to this calculating worldling in the garb of an angel of light.

"If so, of course it was not fully decided so far. Let the end try the man. I trusted that I should be able to stand up to my fight, heavy and crushing as might be the blow Fate had dealt me. But all light and colour, all sympathy with and savour of pleasure, so-called, died out of my life. My premonition was but too accurate. Following the statement in my legal adviser's letter, every paper in England had a more or less sensational paragraph to the effect that the announcement of the late Sir Reginald Lutterworth's testamentary disposition was premature and incorrect. The bulk of that gentleman's property, his great estates, and large deposits in the funds, goes to Lord Fontenaye, the head of the house.

"Soon after this, through some channels of intelligence, came a harmless looking paragraph in the personal column of the *Court Circular*:—'We are authorised to contradict the report of the engagement of Miss Adeline Montresor to the Honourable Valentine Blount. The arrangement, if any, was terminated by mutual consent.' A note of studied politeness from her mother left no doubt on my mind that her daughter's engagement to me, too hastily entered into in the opinion of Mr. Montresor and herself, must now be regarded as finally terminated. 'Mr. Blount would understand that, as no good purpose would be served by an interchange of letters or an interview, he would consult the feelings of the family by refraining from requiring either.'

"Such, and so worded in effect, was my *congé*. It was a hard fall. In more than one instance within my knowledge a fatal one.

"Last week, *fortunatus nimium*, I had stood on the very apex of human happiness. Rich—more than rich, the possessor of historic estates, with a commensurate rent-roll, above all ecstatically happy as the *fiancé* of the loveliest girl in England—high-born, highly endowed, the envy of my compeers, the admired of the crowd—a few short days saw me bereft of all but a moderate fortune, reduced in position, socially disrated, discarded by the woman of my passionate adoration.

"What remained, but as was suggested to the victim of an earlier inrush of disasters? To curse God, and die? The teaching of my youth, combined with a substratum of philosophic disdain of the ills of life, forbade the ignominious surrender. I took counsel with my calmer self, with my best friends, made no sign, arranged for regular remittances, and took my passage for South America.

"How I lived among the wild people and wilder adventurers, whom debt and dishonour, or Bohemian love of freedom had driven from the headquarters of art, civilisation and luxury, may be told some day; sufficient to say that during the five years I lived abroad much of my unhappiness and despair of life wore off by the slow but sure attrition of new occupations amongst strange companions. From time to time I sent home articles to scientific societies which gave me a certain vogue in literary circles. At length, and not until the end of the sixth year of wandering had been reached, a desire arose to see England and my people once more. Six months after my departure, Adeline had married an elderly peer, when, as Lady Wandsborough, she gained the position and consideration which I had been unable to offer her. Two years afterwards another excitement was caused among the smart set by her elopement with Colonel Delamere, 'a distinguished military man,' said the *Court Circular*, concerning whom there had been a growing scandal. Socially condemned, dropped and disowned, what was to be the end of the brilliant woman, whose entertainments, dresses, jewels, and friendships, made up so large a part of English and Continental chit-chat?

"Lord Wandsborough without loss of time obtained a divorce. There was no appearance of the co-respondent. Since then, there had been no authentic information about the arrant pair — neither, though I searched the fashion journals with unusual industry, did I come across the marriage of Colonel Delamere to the heroine of so many historiettes in high life. It was not that I had any strong personal interest in her career, fallen as she was now from her high estate finally and irrevocably.

"But I couldn't attain to complete detachment from all human sympathy for the fallen idol of my youthful dreams, though perhaps my strongest sentiment connected with her was one of heartfelt gratitude for the brusque manner in which she had discarded me, and so saved me from the keenest — the most exquisitely cruel tortures to which the civilised man can be subjected.

"Of all people in the world she was the last whom I expected, or indeed desired, to see again; yet we were doomed to meet once more. I told you that I came from Hobart, the day after my arrest (save the mark!), in a vessel from Callao, of which the crew and passengers were strangely mixed, various in character as in colour and nationality; South Americans, Mexicans, Americans of the States, both Northerners and Southerners. Among them I noted, although I was far from troubling myself about their histories, a tall, handsome man, who bore on him the impress of British military service. It was Colonel Delamere! I could not be mistaken. I had formed a slight acquaintance with him in earlier days; had watched him at cards, with some of the least villanous-looking of the foreigners, to whose excitable manner and reckless language his own offered so marked a contrast. I did not intend to make myself known to him, but accident was stronger than inclination. Seeing a lady struggling up the companion (the weather was still rough),

I moved forward and helped her to a seat. She turned to thank me, and after an earnest surprised glance at my face—'But, no! it can't be! Am I so changed?' she said reproachfully, 'that you don't know Adeline Montresor?' She *was* changed, oh! how sadly, and I had *not* known her. The second time, of course, I recognised the object of my youthful adoration, the woman by whose heartless conduct I had been so rudely disillusioned. She glanced at the Colonel, who, engrossed in the game, had not observed her coming on deck, and motioned me to take a seat beside her, saying, 'How *you* have changed since we last met! I treated you shamefully—heartlessly, I confess, but it was all for your good, as people say to children. You would never have been the man you are if Fate and I had not sent you out into the world with a broken heart. Now tell me all about yourself?' she continued, with a glance which recalled the spell of former witchery, harmless however, *now*, as summer lightning. 'You don't wish to cut me, I hope?'

"'Far from it,' I replied, 'you will always find me a friend. Is there any way in which I can serve you? you have only to say. What is your address?' She looked over at the Colonel and his companions with a melancholy air, and replied in a low voice, 'We are travelling as "Captain and Mrs. Winchester." Poor fellow, he cannot marry me, though he would do so to-morrow, if he were free from his wife, as I am from my husband. But she will not go for a divorce, just to punish us; isn't it spiteful? You can see—' here she touched her dress which was strictly economical—'that it is low water with us. I have tried the stage, and we have been doing light comedy in Callao, and the coast towns. You have seen me in the amateur business?'

"'Yes,' I said, 'how I admired you!'

"'I know that,' and she smiled with a strangely mingled suggestion of amusement and sadness; 'you were a first-class lover in the proposal scene, though a little too much in earnest. I really *was* touched, and if—if indeed—everything had been different, my heart, my previous experiences, my insane love of society triumphs, dress, diamonds, etc. These I thought I had secured, and so accepted your honest adoration. But even then I was in love with poor Jack—never loved any one else in fact. I have been his ruin, and he mine. I see he has finished his game, and is coming over. You may as well know each other.' The Colonel looked at me fixedly, much wondering at our apparent friendly attitude, then bowed politely and formally. 'No, Jack, you don't know him, though you've seen him before. He's an old friend of mine, though, to whom I did a good turn, the best any one ever did him, when I broke our engagement short off, after hearing he'd lost his money. Now you know.'

"'You're a queer woman,' said he, putting out his hand in frank and manly fashion, which I shook warmly. 'I always said you treated him brutally. It didn't break his heart, though it might have suffered at the time. We're all fools; I nearly shot myself when I was just of age over Clara Westbrook.'

"'Yes, I know,' assented 'Mrs. Winchester,' good-humouredly; 'now she's eighteen stone and can hardly get into her carriage.'

"'She was dashed handsome then,' pleaded the Colonel; 'but hang the past, it's the future we've got to look at—not a gay prospect, either. Some people make money here, I suppose; we were nearly getting off the boat at Hobart and trying our luck at that new silver mine, the Cornstalk, or something like that. Do you know anything about it?'

"'I'm a part proprietor, and so on,' said I, trying vainly to divest my manner of any trace of importance, cruel as was the contrast between my position and that of this forlorn pair. 'It was a chance investment when I came out here.'

"'The devil! Tregonwell, Blount, Herbert and Clarke. Forgotten your name, you know. Why, they say you're all worth £100,000 each?'

"'At least!' I said; 'quite a fluke, though. My partner, Tregonwell, who is a good man of business, wanted to throw it up. I held on out of pure obstinacy, and it turned up a "bonanza."'

"'Your luck was in, and ours is dead out,' said 'Mrs. Winchester,' 'there's no denying that, but ours may turn again some day. Where are we going next, Jack?'

"'Checked through to Coolgardie, West Australia,' said the Colonel. 'Know some fellows. Believe there are immensely rich gold mines there. Saw some quartz specimens in a window in London, as much gold as quartz.'

"'Quite true. There have been wonderful yields there,' said I; 'it's an awful hot place, very primitive and rough. Still, the women—there are ladies, too—manage to live and keep up their spirits.'

"'What do you say, Addie, hadn't you better stay behind for a while, at any rate?'

"'All places are alike to me now,' said she wearily; 'but where you go I go. We'll see it out together, Jack.'

"'We're to be in Melbourne to-night, the steward told me,' said the Colonel; 'perhaps Mr. Blount will kindly recommend an hotel?'

"'I know a good one,' said I, 'handy to your boat. I'll see you on board to-morrow. The *Marloo* leaves in the afternoon. I can give you letters to some people on "the field" as they call it.'

"We went to 'Scott's,' where I arranged certain things with the management. So that when the Colonel paid his bill next day, and we left together in a cab for the *Marloo*, he told his wife that the charges were most reasonable. She looked at me with a meaning glance and wrung my hand as the Colonel hurried off with the luggage. 'You're a good fellow,' she said, 'though it's late in the day to find it out. You've had your revenge, haven't you? Are you going to get married?'

"'Yes,' said I, 'next week.'

"'I wish you joy, with all my heart, what there is of it, that is. Is she beautiful, innocent, devoted to you?'

"'All that,' said I, 'and more.'

"'Then tell her my story, and when for vanity, pleasure, or the tinsel trappings of society she is tempted to stray from the simple faith of her youth (I had it once, strange to say), let her think of *me* as I am now, poverty-stricken, degraded, and, except for poor Jack, whom I have dragged down to ruin with me, without a friend in the world.'

"'While I live,' said I, 'you must not say that.'

"'I know—I know,' and the tears fell from her eyes, changed as she was, from all that she had been in her day of pride. 'But we can take nothing from you, of all men. God bless you!'

"Here came the Colonel. 'Come along, Addie, we shall be left behind. Ta-ta, Blount, you're a dashed good fellow, too good altogether, if you ask me. We'll let you know how we get on.'

"As the coasting steamer churned the far from limpid waters of the Yarra, I waved my hand once and turned my head. They went their way. She and her companion to a rude life and a cheerless future, I to love and unclouded happiness, with fortune and social fame thrown in as makeweights. So there you have the whole of it. Last dying speech and confession of a sometime bachelor, but henceforth able to proudly describe himself 'as a mawwied man,' like the swell in the witness-box, 'faw-mally in the awmy!'"

Edward Bruce came back from Queensland, and for fear of accidents the wedding was solemnised quietly, but with all due form and observance, between Valentine FitzEustace Blount, bachelor, and Imogen Carrisforth, spinster, of Marondah, in the parish of Tallawatta, district of Upper Sturt, colony of Victoria, Australia. The day was one of those transcendant glories of a summer land, which, as combining warmth with the fresh dry air of the Great South Land, are absolutely peerless. The lightly-wooded downs, verdant as in spring in this exceptional year, were pleasing to the eye as they stretched away mile after mile to the base of the mountain range. The exotic trees, oaks and elms, with a few beeches, walnuts, and an ash-tree, hard by the back entrance were in fullest leaf, most brilliant greenery. The great willows hung their tresses over the river bank, swaying over the murmuring stream, while they almost covered the channel with their trailing wreaths.

The glory of the wattle gold had departed; the graceful tender fern-frond appearing chaplets were no longer intertwined with the lavish spring gold which, following the windings of every streamlet and ravine, seems to penetrate the dim grey woodlands with golden-threaded devices. Herald and earliest note in tone and tendril of that manifold, divinest harmony, the Voice of Spring. A souvenir of the ocean in the form of a gladsome, whispering breeze came through the woodland at noon, tempering the sun's potent influence, until all comments and criticisms united in one sincerest utterance, an absolutely perfect day, fitting, indeed, as the youngest bridesmaid asserted, for such an ideal marriage.

Nothing went wrong with train or coach this time. Fate had done her worst, and was minded to hold off from these persistent seekers after happiness. Edward Bruce had arrived from Queensland, sunbrowned, rather harder in condition than when he left home, but hale, strong, in good spirits, and even jubilant, having heard by wire of a six-inch rainfall since his departure.

Little-River-Jack and the O'Hara brothers had crowned themselves with glory on Crichel Downs since they had been employed there. Energetic, athletic, and miraculously learned in every department of bush lore, they had thrown themselves into the work of the drought-stricken district with an amount of enthusiasm that rejoiced the manager's heart, moving him to declare that they were worth their weight in gold, and had saved the lives of sheep and cattle to the value of their wages six times over. He was going to give Little-River-Jack the post of overseer at a back outstation, and felt certain that no one would get hold of calf, cow, or bullock with the Crichel Downs brand as long as he was in charge. Phelim and Pat O'Hara were kept on the home station, and for driving a weak flock of sheep at night, or "moonlighting" the outlying scrub cattle, no one in all Queensland, except Jim Bradfield, was fit to "hold a candle" to them.

It was for various reasons, the bride's recent illness and other considerations, that what is known as "a quiet wedding" took place, yet were there certain additions to the family circle.

Pastoral neighbours, such as the MacRimmons, the Grants, the MacAulays, the Chesters, the Waterdales, could not decently be left out. Besides the seniors, they included large families of young men and maidens born and reared among the forests and meadows of the Upper Sturt. The climatic conditions of this Highland region proved its adaptability for the development of the Anglo-Saxon and the Anglo-Celt, for finer specimens of the race than these young people who rode and drove so joyously to this popular function would have been difficult, if not impossible, to find. The men, tall, stalwart, adepts in every manly exercise; the girls, fresh-coloured, high-spirited, full of the joyous abandon of early youth, as yet unworn by care and with the instinctive confidence of all healthy minded young people in the continuance of the *joie de vivre*, of which they had inherited so large a share.

It was noticed by some of these whose eyes were sharp and general intelligence by no means limited, that at the breakfast there was a new damsel who assisted the waiting maid, Josephine Macintyre (chiefly known as Joe Mac), a smart soubrette of prepossessing appearance.

With her the bride and bridegroom shook hands warmly before they departed "for good." Well and becomingly dressed, she was an object of more than ordinary interest to some of the youthful squirearchy.

"Why, it's Sheila Maguire, from Bunjil!" said one youngster to his comrade. "Thought I'd seen her before, somewhere. Doesn't she look stunning?"

"My word," was the reply. "They say she's been left a lot of money by old Barney, her uncle."

"She's a fine, straight, jolly girl, with no nonsense about her," declared the first speaker, "a man might do worse than make up to her, if he had to live in the back blocks."

"Why don't you try the experiment?"

"Thanks, awfully! Hope I shall do as well—but I'm not 'on the marry' just yet. Want to see another Melbourne Cup or so first."

There was no "marriage bell," yet all went well without that obsolete summons. Every one turned up at the right time, not even the best man was absent. He came the evening before—a cool, unpretending person, very correctly dressed, and with "soldier" written all over him—in spite of the vain disguise of mufti. He was presented as Colonel Pelham Villiers, D.S.O., Royal Engineers, just down from Northern India. That he had "assisted" at such functions before was evident by the air of authority with which he put the bridegroom through his facings, and even ordered the bridesmaids about—"like a lot of chorus girls"—as Susie Allerton observed.

She had (she said) "a great mind to refuse to obey," but after once meeting the look in a pair of stern grey eyes—hers were hazel—she capitulated. He took her in to breakfast, it was noticed, where they seemed excellent friends.

Punctually at three p.m. the drag came round with Edward Bruce on the box—behind such a team as only one station on the Upper Sturt could turn out. The leaders—own brothers—cheap at a hundred apiece, were a "dream," as an enthusiastic girl observed, while the solid pair of dark bays in the wheel were scarcely behind them in value.

Out came the bride in travelling suit of grey, on the arm of "the happiest man in Australia," as he had that day professed himself to be. Black Paddy noiselessly relinquished the rein of the nearside leader, a fine tempered, but impatient animal, and like one horse, the well-broken, high-mettled team moved off. The road was level, and smooth for the first half mile, then came a long up grade pretty much against collar, the team, at a touch of the rein, broke into a hand gallop, which they kept up easily until the crown of the hill was reached. There on the long down-grade—high above the river bank on one side, and scooped out of the mountain side on the other, the powerful leg-brake was applied, and the laden vehicle rolled steadily, and well controlled, until the level track of the river meadow was reached. There was a full quarter of an hour to spare when the railway station was neared, and with the luggage checked through to Menzies Hotel, Melbourne, and an engaged carriage for Imogen and himself, Mr. Blount decided that the first stage of matrimonial happiness was reached.

CHAPTER X

Hobart, where it was decided to spend the honeymoon, from their joint experience of its unequalled summer climate, and picturesque beauty, was reached on the following day. A charming villa "by the sad sea waves" had been secured for them, by a friend, the all-potential personage who "ran," so to speak, the social, sporting, and residential affairs of the city, and whose dictum, at once suave and authoritative, no Tasmanian, whether foreign visitor or native born, was found bold enough to withstand. The bridegroom remembered driving there in a tandem cart, drawn by a refractory pair, which he had reduced to subjection, doing the twelve miles out, at a creditable pace, though not quite in time for dinner. But the view, the isolation and the forest paths of this ideal private paradise had imprinted themselves indelibly on his memory.

As it happened, the person in charge of the cottage was absent, but refreshment was sent in by the housekeeper, which they were in a mood thoroughly to enjoy, looking forward to the many divine repasts which they would share in this enchanting retreat.

From the open window of the morning room, looking eastward, they gazed over the south arm of the Derwent; a broad estuary having the cloud effects and much of the spacious grandeur of the ocean. The headland, on which the bungalow stood, commanded a wide and varied view, in which sea and crag, land and water were romantically mingled. Scrambling down the cliff by a precipitous path to the beach, they found to their great delight that a raspberry plantation had been formed on the cliff-sheltered slope, much of which was in full bearing. The modified English climate of Tasmania is eminently favourable to the production of the smaller fruits, such as the currant, strawberry, gooseberry, raspberry and blackberry—this last growing in wild profusion in hedges and over fences.

"Oh! how delightful," cried Imogen, as, seated on a large stone she applied herself to the consumption of an enticing raspberry feast spread upon a leaf platter, woven deftly by the hands of her husband. "Look at the calm water—the fishing boats, the gulls, the small waves breaking on the beach! Was there ever such an ideal honeymoon lodge? And these lovely raspberries. We can get cream at the house. And what a leaf platter! Where did you learn to make one, sir? you must have had practice."

"At Nuku-heva! I was stranded there for six months once. The girls taught me."

"Girls, indeed! That sounds very general and comprehensive. No savage maiden in particular. Quite sure, now? No photograph?"

"If there was, I've forgotten all about her. I don't keep photographs. There's only one damsel that is imperishably engraved upon heart and soul—memory, aye, this mortal frame—by a totally new process. It has the effect of destroying all former negatives—the best specimens of photography are put to shame, and obliterated.

"And that is called—?"

"The last love of the mature man—the answering fondness of *the* woman—the best love—the true love—the only love which survives the burden of care, the agony of grief, the chances and changes of life. The steady flame which burns even brighter in the dark depths of despair."

"Oh! I daresay—fascinating creatures, I suppose—were they not?"

"I have forgotten all about them. There is one fascination for me, henceforth, and one only. It will last me until my life ends or hers. I pray that mine may be the first summons."

"Men were deceivers, ever," hummed Imogen. "But I must make the best of it, now I have got you. The Fates were against us at first, were they not? What a strange thing is a girl's heart! How short a time it takes to cast itself at a man's feet. How long—long—endless, wretched, unendurable are the days of doubt, grief, anguish unutterable, if he prove faithless, or the girl has over-rated his attachment. It nearly killed me, when I thought you had gone away without caring."

"And suppose I *had* never returned? I began to believe you had decided not to answer my letters. That Edward had not relented. That *you* did not care—transient interest, and so on. It is so with many women."

"Transient interest!" cried Imogen, jumping up and scattering the raspberries in her excitement. "Why, there was not one single hour from the time you left Marondah till I saw you again, that my heart was not full of thoughts of you. Why should I not think of you? You told me you loved me—though it was so short a time since we had met, and my every sense cried out that your love was returned—redoubled in fervour and volume."

"How little we know of women and their deeper feelings," mused Blount. "How often you hear of a pair of lovers, that he or she has 'changed their mind.' The ordinary platitudes are rehearsed to friends and acquaintances. When they separate—perhaps for ever—the outside world murmurs cynically, 'better before marriage than after,' and the incident is closed."

"Closed, yes," answered Imogen, "because one heart is bleeding to death."

While rambling through the old house, which was handsomely furnished, though not in modern fashion, they came upon a morning room, which had evidently been regarded as a fitting apartment for treasures of art and literature, etchings, etc.

In it was a bookcase, containing old and choice editions. The dates, those of the last century, told a tale of the family fortunes, presumably at a higher level of position than in these later days. A "dower chest" of oak was rubbed over, and the inscription deciphered; a few rare etchings were noted and appreciated. Through these the lovers went carefully hand in hand, Blount, who was a connoisseur of experience, pointing out to Imogen any special value, or acknowledged excellence; when, suddenly letting go her hand, he rushed over to a dim corner of the room, where he stopped in front of an oil painting, evidently of greater age and value than the other pictures.

"Yes," he said, first carefully removing the dust from the left hand corner of the canvas, under which, though faint and indistinct, the name of a once famous artist, with a date, could be distinguished.

"I thought so, it is a Romney. He was famed for his portraits. But what a marvellous coincidence! Perfectly miraculous! I was told that in Tasmania I should fall across curious survivals, as at one time the emigration of retired military and naval officers was officially stimulated by the English Government. The promise of cheap land and labour (that of assigned servants, as they were called) in a British colony with a mild climate and fertile soil, attracted to a quasi-idyllic life those heads of families, whose moderate fortunes forbade enterprise in Britain. Special districts, such as Westbury and New Norfolk, were indicated as peculiarly adapted for fruit and dairy farms."

"I remember quite well," said Imogen, "when I was here at school in Hobart, that many of the girls belonged to families such as you mention. Such nice people, with grand old names, but so very, very poor. The parents were not the sort to get on in a new country, though the sons, as they grew up, mostly altered that state of affairs. But they did not remain in Tasmania. No! they went to Queensland, New Zealand, or Victoria till they made money. Then they generally returned to marry an old sweetheart and settle down for life near Launceston or Hobart. They were very patriotic, and awfully fond of their dear little island. But what is all this coincidence? You seem quite excited about it."

"Will you have the goodness to look at this picture, Mrs. Blount?"

"I am looking," said she. "It must be a very life-like portrait of somebody. And how beautifully painted! Quite a gem, evidently. The more you look at it the more life-like it appears. What lovely blue eyes! A girl in the glory of her youthful graces; I mustn't add airs, I suppose, for fear of being thought cynical. But the expression must have been caught with amazing fidelity. Stamped, as it were, for ever. I suppose it is very valuable?"

"If it is the portrait which I have reason to believe it is its value is great. The original was found in an old manor house belonging to the De Cliffords. The house—once a king's—though not untenanted, was let to people unacquainted with art, and had been so neglected as to be almost in ruins. The owner of the estate, an eccentric recluse, was a very old man. He refused to have any of the furniture removed, or the paintings taken down from the walls. At his death, people were permitted to view the place, which was afterwards sold. The heir-at-law turned everything he could into money, and emigrated to Tasmania."

"Quite the proper thing to do. We did something of the same sort, whereof the aforesaid Imogen (I was so described in my settlement) met with one Blount, and marrying him, became the happiest girl in Australia or out of it. Didn't she?"

Blount responded appropriately; it would seem convincingly, for the dialogue was resumed as they again went out. She desired to know why, and wherefore, this particular portrait was so very precious. Other young women, doubtless, in that long dead time, had had their portraits painted.

"Because this is the *very* picture, I am almost certain, which inspired Robert Montgomery with those lovely lines of his: 'To the Portrait of an Unknown Lady.' Have you never read them?"

"No! I have heard some one speak of them, though."

"Well, the picture disappeared before the sale. The family would never explain. There was evidently some mystery, painful or otherwise, connected with it. Montgomery's lines had made it famous. And it was a disappointment to intending buyers, many of whom came long distances to bid for it."

"Rather a long story, but wildly interesting. To think that we should have come across it on our wedding trip, and *here* of all places. Well, as a punishment for your taking so much interest in an unknown lady you shall repeat the lines. I daresay you know them by heart."

"I think I do. At any rate I know the leading ones. If there are more we can read them together afterwards.

> "'Image of one who lived of yore,
> Hail to that lovely mien!
> Once quick and conscious, now no more
> On land or ocean seen;
> Were all life's breathing forms to pass
> Before me in Agrippa's glass,
> Many as fair as thou might be,
> But oh! not one, not one *like thee!*'"

Here the girl's head sank on her lover's shoulder, and as her slender form reclined with the unconscious abandon of a child against his breast, while his arm wound closely and yet more closely around her yielding waist, "Oh! go on, go on, my darling! let me hear it all," she murmured:

> "'Thou art no child of fancy—thou
> The very look dost wear
> That gave enchantment to a brow,
> Wreathed with luxuriant hair—
> Lips of the morn, embalmed in dew,
> And eyes of evening's starry blue,
> Of all that e'er enjoyed the sun,
> Thou art the image of but *one!*
>
> "'And who was she in virgin prime
> And May of womanhood,
> Whose roses here, unplucked by time,
> In shadowy tints have stood?
> While many a winter's withering blast
> Hath o'er the dark cold chamber passed,
> In which her once resplendent form
> Slumbered to dust beneath the storm.
>
> "'Of gentle blood, upon her birth
> Consenting planets smiled,

And she had seen those days of mirth
Which frolic round the child:
To bridal bloom her youth had sprung,
Behold her beautiful and young;
Lives there a record which hath told
That she was wedded, widowed, old?

"'How long the date, 'twere vain to guess,
The pencil's cunning art
Can but one single glance express,
One motion of the heart,
A smile, a blush, a transient grace
Of air and attitude and face,
One passion's changing colour mix,
One moment's flight, for ages fix.

"'Where dwelt she? ask yon aged oak
Whose boughs embower the lawn,
Whether the bird's wild minstrelsy
Awoke her here at dawn?
Whether beneath its youthful shade
At noon, in infancy, she played?
If from the oak no answer come
Of her, all oracles are dumb!'

"There are more verses; I will show you the poem so that you may enjoy the spirit of it. It was a favourite of mine, since boyhood. And now I see the crests of the waves towards the southern skyline, rearing higher. The sea breeze is often chill. Suppose we scramble up the path and go inside?"

"What a lovely view! and what delicious verses," cried the girl. "Shall we always be as happy as we are now? I feel as if I did not deserve it."

"And I am lost in wonder and admiration at the supernatural state of bliss in which I find myself," answered Blount. "I ought to throw something of value into the deep, to avert the anger of Nemesis. Here goes," and before Imogen could prevent him, he had unfastened a bangle which he wore on his wrist, and hurled it far into the advancing tide. "Let us hope that no fish will swallow it, and return it, through the agency of the cookmaid."

"Now, I call that wasteful and superstitious," quoth Imogen, pretending to be angry. "You will need all the silver in the South Pacific Comstock, if you throw about jewellery in that reckless fashion. And who gave you that bangle, may I ask? You never showed it to me."

"I won it in a bet, long ago. The agreement was that whoever won was to wear the bangle till he or she was married. After that, they might dispose of it as they thought fit. I forgot all about it till to-day. So this seemed an auspicious hour, and I sacrificed it to the malign deities."

"And this is man's fidelity!" quoted Imogen. "For of course, it was a woman. Confess! Didn't your heart give a little throb, as you pitched away the poor thing's gift?"

"Hm! the poor thing, as you call her, is happily married 'to a first-class Earl, that keeps his carriage.' I daresay she's forgotten my name, as I nearly did that of the possessor of the bangle."

The allotted term of happiness passed at the Hermitage, for such had been the name given to it by the original owner, who lived there for the last remaining years of a long life, too quickly came to an end. For happiness, it surely was, of the too rare, exquisitely attempered quality, undisturbed by regrets for the past, or forebodings for the future. Such wounds and bruises of the heart, as he had encountered, though painful, even in a sense agonising, at the time, were of a nature to be cured by the subtle medicaments of the old established family physician, Time. They were not "his fault," so to speak. Such sorrows and smarts are not of the nature of incurable complaints. The agony abates. The healthful appetite in youth for variety, for change of scene, the solace of bodily exercise, and the competition with new intelligences, extinguish morbid imaginings: thus leaving free the immortal Genius of Youth to range amid the unexplored kingdoms of Romance, where in defiance of giants and goblins, he is yet fated to discover and carry off the fairy princess.

"And I did discover her, darling, didn't I?" said he, fondly pressing her hand which lay so lovingly surrendered to his own, as after a long stroll through the fern-shadowed glades of the still untouched primeval forest, they came in sight of the Hermitage, and halted to watch the breakers rolling on the beach below the verandah, where during their first delirium they had so often watched the moon rise over a summer sea.

"All very well, sir," replied Imogen, with the bright smile which irradiated her countenance like that of a joyous child, "but the 'carrying off' 'hung fire' (to return to the prose of daily life), until the princess became apprehensive, lest she might not be carried off at all, and was minded to set out to reverse the process, and carry off the knight. How would that have sounded? What a deathblow to all the legends of chivalry! The page's dress would be rather a difficulty, wouldn't it? Fancy me appearing amongst all those nice girls and men at Hollywood Hall! Inquiring, too, for 'a gentleman of the name of Blount!' I hardly *did* know your name then, which would have been a drawback. I am tall enough for a page, though, and could have arranged the 'clustering ringlets, rich and rare,' like poor Constance de Beverley. How I wept for her, when I was a school-girl, little thinking that I should have to weep bitter tears for myself in days to come."

"And did she weep, my heart's treasure, in her true knight's absence?"

"Weep?" cried she, while—in the midst of her mockery and simulated grief, the true tears filled her eyes at the remembrance, "'wept enough to extinguish a beacon light'—I took to reading dear Sir Walter Scott again in sheer desperation. *Ivanhoe* and *Rob Roy* saved my life, I really believe, when I was recovering from that—hm—'influenza.' Oh, how wretched I was! As the Sturt, that dear old river, flowed before my window, more than once I thought what a release it would be from all but unendurable pangs. I don't wonder that women drown or hang themselves in such a case. I knew of one—yes—two instances—poor things!"

"Any men?"

"Yes; two also. So the numbers are even. We don't seem to be growing cheerful, though, do we? I feel just a little tired; afternoon tea must be nearly ready. There's nothing left for us now (as Stevenson says), 'not even suicide, only to be good,' a fine resolve to finish up with."

"Let us seal the contract, those who are in favour, etc. Carried unanimously!"

The day's post brought a letter from Mr. Tregonwell, which, like a stone thrown into a pond, disturbed the smoothness of their idyllic life. An incursion of the emissaries of Fate was imminent.

"Mr. Blount's presence was absolutely, *urgently* necessary at the mine. There was industrial trouble brewing. The 'wages men'—as those labourers at a mine are called, who are not shareholders—had increased necessarily to a large number; *they* wanted higher pay, the weather being bad and the discomforts considerable. The British shareholders were in a majority on the London Board and were beginning to make their power felt. No serious dispute, but better to arrange in time. Would have come himself to Hobart, but thought it imprudent at present to leave the mine. Very rich ore body just opened out. Prospects absolutely wonderful. Sorry to bother him, but business urgent."

"What a terrible man!" moaned Imogen. "Wherever we are he will always be coming suddenly down upon us and destroying our peace of mind. I suppose, however, that he is a necessary evil."

"He is a first-rate worker and very prudent withal, but to show the element of luck in these matters it is to *my* decision, not his, that we retained the share which is now likely to become a fortune."

"Oh! but there must be some special quality among your bundle of qualities which you are so fond of decrying," said Imogen, with wifely partiality; "some quick insight into the real value of things, which is in so many cases superior to mere industry and perseverance."

"There must be," said Blount thoughtfully, accepting the compliment, "or how should I have secured *one* priceless treasure to which all the mines of Golconda are but as pebbles and withered leaves."

"What treasure? Oh, flatterer!" said the girl; "how you have capped my poor but honest belief in you. Well, time alone must tell how this particularly clever human investment is going to turn out. It won't do for this lady to 'protest too much.' Now where shall I stay until my knight returns from the war?"

"In Hobart, I should say, most decidedly. It is a cheerful city at this season of year. The coolness of the summer, the charm of the scenery, the cheerfulness of the society—this being the play-place of six other colonies. Any chance of Mrs. Bruce coming over? Suggest the idea."

"Perhaps she might."

"Tell her I have taken a cottage between Sandy Bay and Brown's River for her specially; one of the loveliest suburbs. If she'll come over and take care of you, I shall be eternally indebted to her for the *second* time. You remember the first? How good she was. But for her —, etc."

"She must come as our guest, and bring Black Paddy and Polly, and the babies, for offside groom and nurserymaid—(that's good Australian, isn't it? nearly equal to 'Banjo' Paterson)."

"Stuff and nonsense! Australians talk the purest English; rather better, in fact, than the home-grown article. But oh! how I should love to have her here and the dear chicks. Edward could come for her afterwards."

So that was settled. Mrs. Bruce, replying, wrote that Edward had given her leave to come for a couple of months. It was really getting very hot and baby was pale. He, Edward, not the baby, was going to Sydney on business; thought of selling out of Queensland, so would cross over and spend the end of the visit with them.

These arrangements were carried out. Mrs. Bruce, with her servants and children, were safely bestowed at the pretty villa at Sandy Bay, where Black Paddy, as groom and coachman, and Polly, as under-nursemaid, excited as much attention as Mrs. Huntingdon's ayah from Madras. Mr. Blount was free to depart for the South Pacific Comstock (Proprietary), which included a decided change from these Arcadian habitudes. Arrived at Strahan, he perceived various improvements, which he correctly attributed to Tregonwell's boundless energy and aroused imagination.

Long stretches of corduroy, regularly repaired, rendered the transit business comparatively free from difficulty. Great gangs of men were employed in clearing the track for the projected railway. The work of piercing the forest was tremendous. The great size of the trees (a scientist had measured one eighty feet in circumference), the density and confused nature of the jungle, through which the way had almost to be tunnelled, if such an expression can be applied to operations above ground, retarded progress. The masses of fallen timber at the sides of the track, the whole laborious task carried on under ceaseless rain, was sufficient to over-task the energies of all but the stubborn, resistless Anglo-Saxon.

But on the mining fields of Australasia, if but the precious metal, gold, silver, or copper, be visible, or even believed to be within reach in sufficient quantities, *no toil*, no hardship is sufficient to daunt the resolute miner; neither heat, nor cold, the burning dust storms of Broken Hill, the icy blasts that sweep from the solitudes of Cape Nome over the frozen soil of Klondyke, have power to stay the conquering march of the men, ay, of the women of our race, or slake the thirst for adventure which is as the breath of their nostrils.

So, by the time Mr. Blount arrived on the scene, after a single day's journey from the coast, the melodramatic action of a progressive mining town was "in full blast."

The hotels and stores were comparatively palatial. Tall weatherboard buildings with balconies, enabled the inmates to gaze over the waving ocean of tree-tops and to mark where the jungle had been invaded by the pioneer's axe, that primary weapon of civilisation. The streets, miry and deep-rutted, had yet side walks with wooden curbs, which provisionally, at any rate, preserved the foot passengers from the slough into which the ceaseless trampling of bullocks, horses and mules had worn the track. As in all such places in their earlier stages, money was plentiful. Wages were high, labour was scarce. The adventurers who came to inspect the "field" necessarily brought capital with them. Under the Mining Act and Regulations of the colony, allotments had been marked out in the principal streets to be acquired by purchase or lease. Legal occupation had succeeded the early scramble for possession. A Progress Committee had been formed, precursor of municipal action, of which Mr. Tregonwell, of course, was the elected President. Its members advised the Government of the day of urgently necessary reforms, or demanded such, with no lack of democratic earnestness. Behind all this life and movement there was the encouraging certainty of the still-increasing richness of the principal mine, the original shares in which rose to a height almost unprecedented.

Among other necessities of civilisation, a newspaper had, of course, been established. The *Comstock Clarion* subserved its purpose by clean type, smart local intelligence, and accurate reviews of all mining enterprises from Australia to the ends of the earth. Having been waited upon by the editor without loss of time, Mr. Blount found himself thus presented to an intelligent and enterprising public:—

"A Distinguished Visitor.

"Yesterday morning we had the honour of welcoming to our thriving township a gentleman, to whose courage and enterprise the public of Comstock are indebted for the inception of a great national industry, the founding of a city fated to rival, if not surpass, in wealth and population both Hobart and Launceston. Mr. Blount courteously supplied, in answer to our request, the following interesting notes of his original connection with the great mine in which he owns a controlling interest.

"Visiting Tasmania *en route* for England a few years since, he was offered shares in a newly-prospected silver mine. Mr. Tregonwell was then associated with him in mining ventures. The partners were offered a half share in the claim newly taken up of four men's ground, Messrs. Herbert and Clarke owning the remainder. Mr. Tregonwell, though experienced and sanguine—of which qualities we have ample proof before our eyes— advised the rejection of the 'show.' Mr. Blount, for a reason not stated, was firm in retaining it. He was in a position to find the cash for payment of lease application, rents, and working expenses until the discovery of the richest silver lode south of the line was an accomplished fact. 'Si monumentum queris, circumspice.'"

The Latin quotation was inappropriate, inasmuch as it was not proposed to erect any kind of memorial structure in honour of Mr. Blount, but it looked well, and few of the readers of the *Clarion* were critical. However, the article had the effect of directing all eyes to the visitor, unobtrusively dressed as he was, whenever he appeared. He was, of course, *fêted* and invited to banquets given by leading citizens or mining celebrities. The financial condition of the mine was eminently satisfactory, even brilliant. It held a high place among British investors and foreign syndicates. Members even of the British Parliament did not disdain to take passages in the "P. and O." or "Messageries'" boats for the special purpose of inspecting the wonderful mine. They returned laden with lumps of ore, being fragments of a silver mountain which they had seen with their eyes and driven a pick into when personally conducted by the American "mining Captain," who received £5,000 a year salary, and was promised another £1,000 should things continue to go well.

As the season had advanced the weather even in that austere and dreadful wilderness relaxed its icy grip. The forest trees, the giant eucalypts and towering pines, "had a tinge of softer green." The moss looked bright "touched by the footsteps of spring," haunting even that unlovely wild. Mr. Blount, though loyally impatient to return to his Imogen and the calm delights of Hobart, felt distinctly in better spirits. He even took a mild gratification in marking the heterogeneous element of the stranger hordes that arrived daily, gathered as they were from the ends of the earth, of all nations apparently, and several colours. "Gentle and simple," forlorn workers and wayfarers from many a distant land, mingled with derelicts of the classes akin to "Mr. and Mrs. Winchester." The men feverishly anxious to strike some lucky find or chance investment, the women poorly dressed, working at the humblest household tasks, all wearing the vague, yearning, half-despairing expression, which comes of the heart-sickness of "hope deferred." Theirs was the harder lot. Still, with but few exceptions, they faced the rude living and unaccustomed toil with the courage women invariably show when hard fortune makes a call on their nobler attributes.

Nowhere is the ascent of the "up grade" of mining prosperity, when the tide of fortune is flowing, and the financial barometer is "set fair," made easier than in Australasia. Rude as may be the earlier stages, the change from the mining camp, the collection of rude cabins, to the town, the city even, is magically rapid. To the gold or silver deposit, as the case may be, everything is attracted with resistless force as by the loadstone mountain of Sindbad. Time, distance, the rude approach by land travel, the stormy seas, all are defied. And though delays and dangers are so thickly strewn before the path of the adventurer, he and his like invariably arrive at their goal and would get there somehow, if behind every tree stood an armed robber, and were every trickling creek a turbulent river.

Mr. Tregonwell had proved himself capable of carrying out the rather extensive programme, financial and otherwise, which he had produced for the inspection of his partners on their first meeting at the mine. The manager of world-wide experience and unequalled reputation *had* been procured from America; had been paid the liberal salary; had proved himself more than worthy of his fame. The railway to Strahan was in process of completion. Contracts, let at many different points, were nearing one another with startling rapidity.

The price of provisions had fallen. Wages were high—yet the contractors were making as much money as the shareholders. With the exception of the very poor and the chronic cases of ill-luck from which no community is, ever has been, or ever will be free, the Great Silver Field was the modern exemplar of a place where every one had all that he wanted now, and was satisfied that such would be the case for the future.

The wages misunderstanding had been settled, an arrangement made with one of the most stable banks in Australia, by which the Directors agreed to cash Mr. Tregonwell's drafts for all reasonable, and, indeed, unreasonable, amounts, as some over-cautious, narrow-minded people considered. The predominant partner began to revolve the question of an early departure. The juniors, Charlie Herbert and Jack Clarke, had earned golden opinions from Tregonwell as cheerful workers and high-couraged comrades. He willingly agreed to their holidays at Christmas time, now drawing nigh, if one would remain with him for company, and perhaps assistance in time of need, while the other enjoyed himself among his relatives and friends in one of the charming country houses of his native land. As for himself, he did not require change or recreation, his duty was to the shareholders, who had entrusted him with such uncontrolled powers of dictatorship.

Mr. Blount would be within easy reach of telegrams at Hobart, whence he could come up for a week when a difficult point or question of further outlay needed to be settled. Comstock was not such a very uncomfortable place now, and would be less so in the near future, and Frampton Tregonwell had lived and thriven amid worse surroundings.

So, as the short summer of the West Coast crept slowly on towards the "great Festival" which heralds "Peace on Earth, and good will towards men," all things seemed moving in a tranquil orderly manner towards organised success and permanent prosperity. The big mill with the newest improvements, and a high-grade German scientist from Freiburg in command, had just been completed and was turning out unprecedented returns. Everything went smoothly, socially and otherwise. Although so near to what had once been an accumulation of the most desperate criminals the world could show, only kept under by the merciless uniformity of a severe administration—the present crime record was curiously low, and trifling in extent. Labour was well paid, well fed and lodged. All men had, moreover, the hope of even greater benefits, as results from their toil. Under these circumstances the list of offences is invariably light. The inducements to crime were so small, as almost to lead to an optimistic belief that incursions on the goods and persons of neighbours would at an early date cease and determine. The dream of the philanthropist would at last be fulfilled.

Perhaps, also, that other dream of a socialistic division of labour with equal partition of the fruits of the earth, and the partition of the fruits of labour (chiefly *other men's* labour) for the benefit of the poor but honest worker would be an accomplished fact.

So, in the ordering of things mundane, it came to pass that Mr. Blount, to his great contentment and satisfaction, had everything arranged and "fixed up," as Tregonwell expressed it (culling his phrases from all nations and many tongues), and departing via Strahan, bade farewell for the present to Macquarie Harbour, Hell's Gates, and the other lonely and more or less historic localities. The passage, for a wonder, was smooth, the wind fair, and it was with joy and satisfaction, which he could hardly forbear expressing in a shout of exultation, that he found himself once more in Hobart, within arm's length, so to speak, of Imogen and his "kingdom by the sea."

That young woman had kept herself well informed as to the time when the Strahan steamer might be expected, and appeared at the wharf driving the mail phaeton. Black Paddy was beside her on the box; in front was the bay mare, "Matchless," with her mate "Graceful," in top condition, and ready to jump out of their skins, with rest and good keep. This valuable animal, formerly hard worked, with but little rest, and far from luxurious fare, had been contented to rattle up and down the hills between Hobart and Brown's River and the Huon, without so much as a hint from the whip. Under present circumstances, she naturally took a little holding.

But Imogen and Mrs. Bruce had been accustomed to ride and drive almost as soon as they could walk. With great nerve and full experience, fine hands, an unequalled knowledge of the tempers and dispositions, management and control, of all sorts and conditions of horses, very few secrets of the noble animal, whether in saddle or harness, were hidden from them. So when Imogen drove up to the Tasmanian Club, where her husband had temporarily deposited himself, his specimens and belongings generally, he had no misgivings as to the competency of his charioteer, nor did he offer, as most men would have done, to take the reins himself.

"How well they look," he remarked, after the first greeting, "'Matchless' has fallen on her legs in coming to this establishment. Does she give any trouble in her altered condition?"

"Hardly any, only she doesn't like waiting, now there is no cab behind her. Burra burrai, Paddy! Mine thinkit mare plenty saucy direckaly."

That swart retainer understood the position, and helping the club servant with the heaviest trunk on to the back seat, stepped up beside it with noiseless agility, while at the same moment "Matchless" and "Graceful" moved off with regulated speed, which soon landed them at "home"—a word which Mr. Blount pleased himself by repeating more than once.

"Hilda looks just as she did," said he, "when I first saw her at Marondah. I admired her then. I admire her now—how little I thought that I should see her again, as a sister-in-law! or that a certain 'vision of delight was to burst upon my sight' so soon afterwards."

"I remember how you stared," said Imogen; "almost rudely, indeed. Didn't you?"

"First of all, I didn't know that Mrs. Bruce had a sister in the house. Secondly, when the girl aforesaid appeared, unexpectedly in all her fresh and smiling loveliness—pardon my partiality—I was completely knocked over, so to speak, and couldn't help a sort of rapt gaze—as at a wood nymph, which you unkindly call staring. I fell in love—at first sight as men say—deep, deeper, miles deep next morning, and so will remain till my life's end."

"I am afraid it goes rather like that with me, if I must confess," admitted Imogen, "though the heroine of a modern novel would never have behaved so badly, now would she?"

"All's well that ends well," said the returned voyager. "I'll hold the horses while you run in, Paddy!"

The luggage having been taken in, Paddy ascended nimbly, and drove soberly round to the stable.

Christmas having actually arrived, it was the commencement of the "season" in Hobart and Tasmania generally. The dear little island, so true an epitome of the ancestral isle in the climatic conditions, in the stubborn independence of the population, in the incurious, unambitious lives of the rural inhabitants, was filled with strangers and pilgrims from every colony in Australasia.

Persons in search of health, haggard men from the Queensland "Never Never" country, the far "Bulloo," and "The Gulf," where hostile blacks and fever decimated the pioneers! Outworn prospectors from West Australia—a rainless, red-hot, dust-tormented region, where, incredible as it may appear, the water is charged for separately as well as the whisky.

Commercial, pastoral and legal magnates, whose over-taxed brain craved little save rest and coolness—contented to lie about inhaling the evening breeze—to read, to fish, to muse, to think maybe, of a heaven, where lawyers' clerks, even with briefs, were not admitted. Sailors too, from the half dozen men of war from the South Pacific fleet, having a run ashore, and playing their part nobly, as is their wont on land, in all picnics, balls and cricket matches, even in drives to the Huon River nearly fifty miles out and back. This was rather an object lesson for British tourists, as to the capabilities of Australian horses, and Australian drivers, inasmuch as the leading drag with four horses, hired from a well-known livery stable proprietor, and driven by a native-born Tasmanian, negotiated the fifty-mile stage, allowing two hours for luncheon and boating on the river, between breakfast time and dusk, the whole being performed not only without distress to the well-bred team, but with "safety to the passenger, and satisfaction to the looker on." The road was by no means of average description, far from level, indeed, having shuddering deeps, where it wound along hillsides, and sudden turns, and twisted at right angles, when the leaders ran across a dip in the gully, which crossed the road, and the wheelers had their heads turned at right angles to the leaders. Then the down grade towards the sea, on the return trip, when the heavily laden coach rolled, lurching at times near the edge of the precipice, and the "boldest held their breath for a time." But through every change, and doubtful seeming adventure, in darksome forest, and ferny glade, where the light of heaven was obscured, the watchful eye and sure hand of the charioteer guided team and coach, with practised ease and assured safety.

Then the race meeting, to which you went by land or water, as taste inclined. The deep sea fishing in the harbour, or the streams so clear and cold in summer, where the trout lay under bridge or bank, and when skies were dull, took the fly much as in Britain.

The hunting with country packs, the shooting, the long walks over hill and dale—the halts, when a peep through the forest glades showed a distant view of the foam-crested ocean! What joyous days were those, when with Imogen by his side, who walked as well as she rode and drove, they started with a few picked friends for that exceptional piece of exercise, which includes the ascent of Mount Wellington. It is an Alpine feat, only to be attempted by the young and vigorous, in the springtime of life. "The way is long, the mountain steep," and if limbs and lungs are not in good order, the pedestrian is sure to tire half way, to collapse ingloriously before the summit is reached. Rough in some places is the track—over the ploughed field's (so called) painful march. A sprained ankle may easily result, from a slip, or worse even, a dislocated knee, most tedious and troublesome of the minor injuries, and which has lamed for life ere now the too confident pedestrian. Another danger to be feared, is the sudden envelopment by the mountain mist, under the confusing conditions of which more than one person has lost his way and his life, perishing in some unnamed retreat. No such dangers affrighted Imogen and her husband. They reached the summit, and standing there, hand in hand, beheld the unrivalled scene. High over forest and valley they gazed o'er the boundless ocean plain—so still and shining, three thousand feet below them. The forest, with apparently a level surface above its umbrageous eucalypts, looked like a toy shrubbery. The city nestled between the sea wall and the enormous mountain bulk, under whose shadow it lay.

The busy population looked small as the denizens of a populous anthill. "It is a still day, 'Grâce à Dieu,'" said Blount; "there's no tyrannous south wind from the ocean—coming apparently straight from the ice fields of the Pole, to chill us to the bone, and cause the poor forest trees to cry and groan aloud in their anguish. Wind has its good points, probably, but I confess to a prejudice against the Euroclydon variety. Especially when we are doing this Alpine business. By the way, there is Mr. Wendover's delightful woodland châlet—only a mile away. Suppose we make a call there."

"I scorn to acknowledge myself tired," said Imogen; "but raspberries and cream—this *is* the season—would be an appropriate incident on this day of days. They recall the Hermitage, do they not? I can't say more."

"And Mrs. Wendover is so charmingly hospitable," said a girl companion. "She has always the newest books, and music too, which, with the before-mentioned raspberries, takes one far in the pursuit of happiness."

"While youth, and the good digestion which waits on appetite, last," said a middle-aged person with a bright eye and generally alert expression. "Youth is the great secret. Heaven forbid that any of this good company should confess to a hint of middle age, but *I* have a haunting dread lest the world's best joys should be stealing away from me."

"Are there not compensations, Captain Warrender?" asked a lady, whose refined, intellectual cast of countenance suggested literature. "Think how delightful to hear of one's last new book being rushed for new editions, and simply being devoured all over the world."

"Success is pleasant in whatever state of life it comes to one, but were I allowed to choose between reading and writing, my vote would be distinctly in favour of the former. The delightful self-complacency with his task which the author of a successful book is supposed to feel is over-rated, I assure you. It becomes a task, like all other compulsory labour, and there are so many times and seasons when one would much rather do something else. The chief, almost the only valuable result to the producer (except the money, which, of course, is not despised) is, that the reputation of successful authorship brings with it a host of agreeable acquaintances, and even some true and lifelong friendships."

"Have you found other authors free from envy, malice, and so forth?" asked Mrs. Allendale.

"I can truly say that I have, with the rarest exceptions. Now and then a man writing on party lines will administer a dose of unkind, perhaps unfair, criticism which he calls 'slating' your book. But there is little real ill-nature in the article, however much you may feel annoyed at the time. And the freemasonry which exists among literary people, great and small, makes on the whole for friendly relations. A man says: 'Oh, you wrote *Cocoanuts and Cannibals*, didn't you? Had rather a run when it came out. Queer place to live in, I should think.' Then you foregather, and become, as it were, the honorary member of a club. Not that one volunteers this information, but it leaks out."

"Oh, here is the châlet gate, and I see Mrs. Wendover's pet Jersey cow, 'Lily Langtry,'" said Miss Chetwynde. "How nice she looks among the red and white clover. Puts one in mind of dear old England, doesn't it?"

"Where you never were," laughed another maiden of the happy isle.

"I know that, but I've read so much about the grand old country that I can fancy everything. Dear Miss Mitford! what a lovely touch she has! I shall go there some day if I live. In the meantime here comes Mrs. Wendover, all smiles, welcome, and a picture hat, dear creature! I wonder what Miss Mitford would have thought of this forest, which comes up so close to the house, if she had seen it. I should be afraid of a fire some day."

"Oh! our forests don't burn so badly, even when they are on fire; this place is safe enough. Sunburn is our worst danger just now, and there's the naval ball this evening. My cheeks *are* on fire, just feel them."

"Oh, certainly, Miss Chetwynd!" said a small middy, who was of the party. "Anything else I can do for you?"

"I was not speaking to you, Mr. Harcourt. I was replying to Clara Mildmay, and I shall cancel that dance I promised you this evening if you're not more respectful."

"Oh, here you are!" cried Mrs. Wendover, in accents of genuine welcome. "This is the most lucky chance. You must all positively stay to lunch. I was getting tired of my own company for once in a way. John had sent a messenger to say that he would not come out till the evening. So you are evidently sent by Allah to cheer my loneliness."

"We should all be charmed," replied Imogen, taking her place as chief chaperon, "but it is simply impossible. Captain Warrender will tell you that we are all going to the naval ball this evening, and by the time we get to Hobart we sha'n't have a minute to spare, to dress in time and get the sunburn off our faces."

"Then you must come in and have raspberries and cream. It's quite a charity to take them off our hands. Walter and Nora and I are going to the ball too, so I must insist."

Cooled and refreshed, indeed invigorated by the raspberries and Jersey cream, with suitable accompaniments, the jocund crew bade adieu to their hostess, and trooped off to the Fairy Bower, that fern-shaded trysting place in the heart of the forest, dear to so many generations of holiday folk, where the four-in-hand drag awaited them by the fountain, and bore them safely to their several destinations. The naval ball was a pronounced success. Could it be otherwise "manned" by the officers of the half-dozen men-of-war then in harbour? The band, the waiters at the buffet, the assistants who held the dividing line in the ball-room, the attendants at the doors of the supper-room, were all in uniform, while the epaulettes and profusion of gold lace lit up the mass of civilian costumes. It was a contention seriously debated at the time, and never satisfactorily settled, as to whom the honour of being the belle of the ball should be awarded. But all agreed that the crown of the Queen of Beauty, if there had been a tournament, as in the days of chivalry, at which to present it, should have been awarded either to Mrs. Blount (*née* Imogen Carrisforth) or to Miss Leslie, a native-born Tasmanian, whose complexion was held to be unapproachable south of the Line, and whose pre-eminence in loveliness had never before been disputed.

Each had their partisans, sworn admirers and liegemen. Each was declared to be the prettiest girl, or the handsomest woman in Australasia — for the New Zealand competitor "took a lot of beating," as an ardent youthful admirer phrased it. It remained, however, undecided, and will probably be revived, like other vexed questions from time to time, with similar lack of finality. As to one thing, however, the unanimity was pronounced and decisive — the success of the entertainment. When "God Save the Queen" was played, it was nearer three o'clock in the morning than two, and all but the most inveterate dancers had had enough of it. Some of the junior division indeed petitioned for just one more waltz and a galop; but discipline being the soul of the navy, as well as the army, the Admiral's fiat had decided the matter irrevocably. Carriages were ordered, shawls and wraps were donned by the matrons and maids who had "seen it out," as their partners expressed it, and the curtain fell upon one of the most successful comedies or melodramas, as the case may be, still popular, as in old historic days, on the mirthful, mournful, but ever mysterious stage of human life.

After this crowning joy came a succession of *fêtes*. Meetings of the Racing and Polo Clubs, with a gymkhana arranged by the latter society, also picnics and private parties, the Garden Party in the lovely grounds of Government House, where that befitting architectural ornament overlooks the broad winding reaches of the Derwent. All these had to be attended and availed of. The great events of the Polo Club, in "potato and bucket" race, when the competitors were compelled to dismount, pick up a potato from the ground and deposit the same in a bucket, placed for the purpose; as also the tandem race, when the aspirant riding one horse, had to drive another, with long reins, before him, also to negotiate a winding in and out course, before returning to the starting point, were both won by an active young squatter from the Upper Sturt, to the unconcealed joy of Mrs. Bruce and Imogen, the latter race, indeed, after a very close finish with a naval officer, who was the recognised champion at this and other gymkhana contests. But won it was, by the pastoral champion, though only by a nose. So after an inquiry meeting by the committee of the club, it was to him adjudged, and the trophy borne off in triumph. It is not to be supposed that the squirearchy of the land was unrepresented at these Isthmian Games, or that under such circumstances they left their wives and daughters, aunts and cousins behind; or, if such an unnatural piece of selfishness had been for a moment contemplated, that the women of the land would not have organised a revolt, declared a republic, elected a president, and marched down with banners flying to invest the capital, and make their own terms with the terrified Government of the day. No such Amazonian action was, happily, rendered necessary by sins of omission or commission on the part of their liege lords or legal protectors.

That they had sufficient courage and martial spirit for such an *émeute*, no one doubted. But with the exception of a quasi-warlike observation by a Tasmanian girl, on beholding the phalanx of alien beauty arrayed at the naval ball, that on the next occasion of the sort she intended to bring her gun and shoot a girl or two "from across the Straits" by way of warning, no specific action was taken.

So the old antagonism (veiled, of course, and conventional) that has existed between the home-grown and the imported feminine product, was conducted with discreet diplomacy, and the admirers of Helen or Briseis had to content themselves with displaying personal or conversational superiority in lieu of lethal weapons.

So on the ground in drags, mail phaetons, buggies and dogcarts of the period, the female contingent arrived, chiefly before the first gun of the engagement metaphorically aroused the echoes in the glens and forest glades around Mount Wellington. The Hollywood Hall family was fully represented, the Claremonts, the Bowyers. The magnate of Holmby, Mr. Dick Dereker, in all his glory, had deposited himself and his most intimate friend, John Hampden, a new arrival from England, at the club, and was daily to be viewed by the admiring population of Hobart in Davey or Macquarie Street in company with other stars of the social firmament. Mr. Blount noticed with interest the extraordinary popularity which encircled this favourite of fortune in the chief city of his native land. As he walked down the street it was a kind of royal progress. He was the people's idol, the uncrowned king of the happy isle. Men of note and standing crossed over to greet and shake hands with him. Even the shady characters had a soft spot in their hardened hearts for "Dicky Dereker." Why was this adulation? Other country gentlemen were handsome and chivalrous. All of them rode, drove, shot well; they, like him, had been born "in the island," and as such had the claims of a patriot for the suffrages of their countrymen.

But the difficulty was to find all these virtues, personal recommendations, gifts and graces, centred in one individual. The popular verdict so declared it. And if the "classes and the masses" in Tasmania had been polled as to his fitness for any post of eminence, from the vice-regal administrator of the government downward, every man, woman and child in the island would have gone "solid" for "Dicky Dereker."

Of this resistless, all-conquering sway, Mr. Blount was shortly to have proof and confirmation, had such been needed. Sooth to say, he felt more than slight misgivings; indeed, something near to what is called an accusing conscience, with respect to his marked attentions to and quasi-friendship for Laura Claremont on the occasion of his last visit to Hollywood Hall. He was then (it may be stated for the defence) in the somewhat perilous position of having been warned off, as he considered it, by the family at Marondah, and was thus unprovided with an attraction of counterbalancing interest. "Full many a heart is caught on the rebound," and doubtless the sympathetic manner and intellectual superiority of Laura Claremont, combined with her personal endowments, constituted a strong case for the unattached, unprotected stranger. When he returned to Tasmania, bringing his bride with him radiant with the overflowing happiness of the recent honeymoon, would the sympathetic "friend" in whose society he had so openly delighted look coldly upon him? Would *her* friends and compatriots combine to denounce him as an unworthy trifler, who, after paying compromising attentions, not only "rode away," but married a former flame, not even permitting a decent interval to elapse between his preference for the old love and desertion of the new?

Much troubled by these considerations he had even thought over an indirect way of breaking the news, in a non-committal way, to the young lady, and her (perhaps) justly incensed family and friends.

But *qui s'excuse s'accuse* recurred to his mind with painful promptitude. So, fortunately (as it turned out), he decided to trust to time and chance for extrication from the dilemma. For, as he was entering the hospitable portal of the Tasmanian Club, with a view to luncheon and the later news items, he was joined by Claude Clinton, who at once questioned him as to subscriptions for the forthcoming ball, given by the members and players of the polo club. "How many tickets shall I send you? They're a guinea for men and half as much for ladies; and have you heard the last engagement? No? It was only given out this morning. Laura Claremont has made up her mind at last; Dick Dereker is the happy man!"

"Send me a dozen tickets," said Mr. Blount, who felt like John Bunyan after his burden of sins had been removed. "They have my heartiest congratulations."

"All right," said the omnipotent Secretary for Home Affairs; "by the way, wasn't the fair Laura rather a friend of yours? The Tenby girls thought you were making strong running at the Hollywood Ball."

"Every man of sense and taste must admire Miss Claremont," he replied with diplomatic gravity, masking, however, emotions of such intensity that he had some difficulty in preserving calmness. "I was no exception to the rule, that was all."

"Perhaps it helped to bring Master Dick to the scratch—the affair has been going on for years; if so, you did her a service. Dick is a splendid fellow, but when a man has a whole island to pick from he feels inclined to dally with a decision. However, they are to be married at once—before the House meets—not to let the honeymoon interfere with his legislative duties."

"I am delighted to hear it," Mr. Blount affirmed, with such evident sincerity that Mr. Clinton departed to overtake his multifarious duties, with the conviction that he was a fine, large-hearted, generous personage, as well in the matter of ball subscriptions as in the more romantic passages of life's mystery. The young lady referred to had not come down to the naval ball for reasons of her own, or otherwise, the Squire's health requiring her attendance upon him at the Hall. Such, at any rate, was the explanation given by the family friends:—"Dear Laura was *so* attached to her father, and so self-denying and conscientious in the discharge of her duties."

Some of the frivolous division, perhaps a trifle impatient of perpetual proclamation of "Aristides the Just," hinted that there *is* such a device known to the female heart—inscrutable as are its myriad emotions and minor tendencies—as the encouragement of a fervent admirer, up to a certain point, for the stimulation of a laggard lover, the adorer No. 2 being known in the unstudied phrase as the "runner up." However that may have been, Mr. Blount took care to communicate the momentous intelligence to his wife and sister-in-law immediately upon his arrival at home. Mrs. Blount, with natural curiosity, expressed a wish to see this wonderful Laura Claremont—whom everybody praised and indeed referred to as one of the few girls in the island worthy of Dick Dereker. "I suspect *you* flirted with her on that driving tour—and at the ball too—you lost your card, I remember. Now confess!"

"She is a very fine girl—dark, and stately-looking. Every one admires her, but as for comparing her, *et cetera*, the idea is preposterous."

"He hadn't got our letters then, poor fellow!" said Imogen, who, fortunately, was not of a jealous disposition. "So if he made ever such a little swerve from what is called the path of duty I suppose I must forgive him. You won't do so again, sir, I'll see to that!"

"I hope you and Miss Claremont will be *great* friends. She is just the sort of woman you would like. I'll make a point of introducing you at the Polo Ball. Here are the tickets, and a few to spare."

"You have been most generous," said Mrs. Bruce. "I'll keep three for Edward, myself, and a friend, if one turns up. I daresay we shall find one or two."

"No, take half; I bought them for the family. Perhaps some of the Upper Sturt people may turn up."

"Quite likely," said Imogen; "perhaps even from Bunjil! Oh, dear! what fun that would be!"

"I know what you are laughing at," said her sister. "Do you see her joke, Val?"

"Not in the least. Let us share it, Mrs. Bruce."

"It is a good joke," said that merry matron, going off again into fits of laughter; "but I shall not tell you just yet. It is a secret."

The male relative looked puzzled, admitting that the solution was beyond him; at which stage it seemed destined to remain.

CHAPTER XI

A description of "the season" in Hobart, whether regarded as a summer land for tourists, a safe run ashore for the men and officers of the South Pacific "fleet in being" detailed at Hobart, or as an object lesson for untravelled inhabitants—would seem to consist mainly of a record of recreational events. A list of picnics and pleasure parties, driving and fishing excursions, with pedestrian rambles—chiefly by day, but occasionally *au clair de la lune*.

The rivers named after Messrs. Brown and Huon, long dead celebrities, received more than their share of patronage, it would seem, in the entertainment of reckless revellers, whose polo meets and gymkhanas alternated with the legitimate annual races and steeplechases.

There must have been business transactions, but they were eluded or postponed—the only exception being the Great Silver Bonanza, which kept its bond-slaves hard at work, by means of remuneration on the higher scale. Night and day, work proceeded with the regularity of one of its own steam-engines. The Hobart weather was delightful—occasionally threatening rain but chiefly relenting, and ending towards the close of day with soft and cooling sea breezes, which refreshed the pleasure-driven crowds to the inmost fibre of the nervous system.

In all these ingenious projects for lessening the strain upon the minds and bodies of ordinary humanity the officers and men of H.M. Royal Navy were conspicuously effective. At all aristocratic entertainments "Man-of-War Jack" was utilised to keep the gangways clear, to hold the rope of division in the ball-room, and otherwise, as "the handy man," in spotless array, to display his disciplined alertness. Even the naval Church parade was attended by the fair ones of perhaps the last night's entertainment. On each Sunday morning, therefore, boat-loads of worshippers, in silk or muslin, might be descried crossing the waters of the harbour, rowed by an ample crew, under the charge of an all-important middy, to the flag-ship or frigate, where divine service was celebrated by the Chaplain of the Fleet, or other amphibious clergyman, provided by the Lords of the Admiralty.

In this sense, perhaps, the gay season of Hobart constituted a social federation of the Australasian States, when other matters, not of ephemeral weight, might be suitably discussed. From the wave-beaten isles of New

Zealand, where the mountain-crested billows rolled on their stormy march from the ice-fields of the ultimate pole, to the mangrove-bordered marshes of Northern Queensland; from the "Never-Never country" and the "back blocks"; from "the Gulf" and the buffalo lands of Essington and Darwin, came languid, fever-stricken squatters, to breathe the cool air of this southern Lotus Land, differing among themselves in minor respects as to manner, accent, stature and ordinary habitude, but in heart and brain, British to the core. Roving sons of the Great Mother Land, holding God's Commission of the strong hand, the steadfast brain, to occupy the Waste Places of the earth and develop their inborn trend towards justice and mercy, law and order. With such inherited gifts, going forth conquering, and to conquer, to weld into one solid, enduring fabric, the Empire of Britain. Thus, handing down to their children's children lands of freedom "broad-based upon the people's will," where equal laws administered with moderation and mercy are to be the heritage of England's sons. The Greater Britains of the South, for all time; and whether in peace or war, loyal, self-contained, immovable, one and indivisible.

The great event of the season was to be the Polo Ball, looked forward to with almost feverish eagerness, not only by the young men and maidens of the Happy Isle, but by the large important contingents from abroad, which exceeded in number, and social value, those of any previous year. Hence applications for tickets were beyond all calculation.

Requests, even entreaties poured in, almost until the opening of the doors of the great hall secured for the function. Claude Clinton was, as he said, "walked off his legs," having indeed hardly time to dress and eat his dinner, while the committee, who had the onerous and responsible task of deciding upon the fitness of applicants, had to improvise a late sitting, so as not to disappoint the arrivals by the train from Launceston, just landed from the New Zealand Company's extra service boat, the *Rotorua*. The funds of the Club, however, would be benefited to such an extent, that the secretary and committee worked loyally till the last moment, and when Mr. Clinton had given a last authoritative order, and made a final inspection of the decorations, he sat down to his dinner at the Travellers' Club, and drank his pint of champagne with a conviction that everything had been done to deserve success, and that the issue lay with Fate.

Imogen had condescended to inform her relations that a friend of hers had arrived from Melbourne, who, having made up her mind at the last moment, would dress and join their party after dining at the Orient Hotel, where rooms had been secured for her previously.

She had written confidentially to Mr. Clinton and had her name properly submitted to and passed by the committee. All was arranged, and she would go under Imogen's chaperonage to the ball, and perhaps stay with them all night.

"What is her name? Do I know her, Imogen?" inquired her husband. "You are very mysterious, my dear!"

"You have seen her, she tells me, but I am not certain whether you will recognise her. She comes from some place near Adelong in New South Wales; her people used to live in Tumut."

"Then the probability is that she will be good-looking," said Mr. Blount. "Some of the handsomest girls I ever saw came from that sequestered spot. However, we must wait till she shows up. Was she a schoolfellow of yours?"

"No, not exactly, but I knew her when she was younger. You will know all about her when the time comes. I feel desperately hungry, after this exciting day. Oh, I hear the dinner gong."

The dinner was not unduly prolonged, as any one of experience in the anxieties and precautions which precede such an important function will understand. So that after an adjournment to the drawing-room, when, about nine o'clock, the maid delivered a message, *sotto voce*, to Mrs. Imogen, who forthwith left the room, everyone revolved great expectations. These were chiefly realised, when the hostess reappeared, accompanied by a tall, handsome, exceedingly well-dressed girl, who blushed and smiled, as she was introduced to the company as "Miss Maguire of Warranbeen." "Very pleased to meet you, Miss Maguire," began Blount, but, with a sudden alteration of tone and manner, "Why, it's Sheila! by all the Powers, what a transformation!" as Mrs. Bruce shook her warmly by the hand, while Imogen stood by her charge, apparently charmed with the metamorphosis which leisure, the use and reputation of "money" had effected in the unformed country girl, so lately the "maid of the Inn," at the secluded village of Bunjil, on the Upper Sturt.

"You didn't know me, Mr. Blount, I could see that. I had half a mind to ask you what you'd like for breakfast. I'm turned into a young lady, nowadays, you see! And Mrs. Blount, in her great kindness, persuaded me to come to the ball to-night, with her and Mrs. Bruce. I've been to the Show Ball at Wagga, and one or two in Tumut, by way of a start. But this is such a grand affair; I feel frightened."

"I am sure, Sheila, you have no cause to be," said Mrs. Bruce, reassuringly; "you native girls can all dance—it seems an instinct; your dress is charming, and you will gather confidence as the ball goes on—and your card is filled. You are a mysterious stranger, for the present. That alone will be an attraction. We'll see to your introductions; and there are naval men in profusion."

"I like sailors," said Sheila, "they are so unaffected and jolly, put on no side" (she had been at a country ball at the age of sixteen, to which the officers of a man-of-war, then in Sydney, had been bidden by a liberal-minded squatter, who had invited the whole of the "township" inhabitants, in one act, and a great success it was), for Sheila bore about with her for all time the memory of two polkas, a waltz, and a galop danced with the Honourable Mr. de Bracy, midshipman of the period, to their mutual satisfaction and enjoyment.

"I think you will have your share of partners, Sheila," said her hostess; "you certainly do credit to your dressmaker, and the Upper Sturt complexion will give you a chance with these Tasmanian girls, who are justly celebrated for theirs."

"What a transformation!" said Blount to his wife, before they put on their wraps. "I never could have believed it. Of course she has fined down since the Bunjil days. I believe old Barney sold a Queensland station, with 30,000 head of cattle, just before the seasons turned dry. So she and her sister are considerable heiresses. She has, as you see, self-possession, and sense enough to avoid anything *outré*."

"You'll see she'll get on quite well—make a success, indeed. People say money isn't everything; but it goes a long way in this, or any other country, especially combined with looks, and other good qualities. You had better dance the opening set of lancers with her for a start."

Mrs. Imogen's predictions were verified. There was a certain amount of romantic interest attached to the fresh-looking, handsome stranger, reputed wealthy, and who danced so well. "Came, too" (people said), "with that nice, high-bred-looking Mrs. Bruce and the bride." She danced the first lancers with Mr. Blount, and while exhibiting familiarity with the figures, moved with the graceful indifference which has succeeded the erstwhile precision with which the "steps" were anciently performed. Mr. Blount managed to secure an early waltz, and the naval men coming by shiploads, as it appeared to her, Sheila's programme was filled in no time.

That there could not have been a better ball, all the authorities combined to declare. The ever-successful secretary and plenipotentiary had once more covered himself with glory; the arrangements were perfect, the supper was "a dream," and when Sheila found herself taken in by the Captain of the flag-ship, the Admiral and the Governor being in the immediate vicinity, she wondered whether she was likely to fall down in a fit, or if some other kind of death would result from such an overflowing flood of triumphant, ecstatic bliss.

However, she did not die, or indeed was she likely to perish of nervous excitement consequent on pure, unadulterated pleasure; the early bush-training, together with a naturally good constitution, would always preserve her from such an untimely fate.

Imogen was carefully, prudently, introduced to Miss Laura Claremont, who prophesied that they would be great friends, and invited her and her sister to Hollywood. Both of which Imogen accepted conditionally on her husband's—she laid a slight emphasis upon that very possessive word—"on her husband's not being hurried away by Mr. Frampton to that horrid Zeehan." The Upper Sturt party, as we may for convenience describe them, got their full share of partners it may be believed, being all of the age when, if there be an ear for music, and a terpsichorean taste "what time the raving polka spins adown the rocking floor," with good music, suitable partners, and a smooth surface, nothing much better among the lighter enjoyments of life is to be found. With Miss Claremont Blount had danced before, when their steps appeared to suit extremely well. On this occasion, he saw no reason why he should deny himself the fleeting indulgence of once more gliding and sliding about with her in the accepted fashion.

She graciously acceded to his request for an after supper dance, and in one of the partly deserted side-rooms they came to a mutual understanding, which each felt was more or less needed.

"I owe you a few words," she said, "if our friendship is to continue—and I should be sorry for it to end abruptly. It appears to me that we were both in an exceptional state of mind when we met at Hollywood for the first time, and if something had not happened—which *did* happen—one of us would have felt a right to blame the other."

"You have stated the position most fairly," he said.

"I hope you don't think I am so logical," she replied, "as to be deficient in feeling. Believe me when I tell you"—and here her dark eyes glowed with a transient gleam of hidden fire, which he had never before noticed in them—"I don't exaggerate when I say that it was a fateful crisis, such as I had never before experienced."

"It was most truly a supreme moment in *my* destiny," he replied, as she faltered and then stopped, overcome by emotion.

"But, let me go on, I entreat, to make open and full confession, for I can never recur to the subject, and I trust you to make a similar promise."

"It is given," said Blount in all sincerity.

"Then," said Miss Claremont, "I will not deny that I was attracted to you at our first meeting, more, perhaps, than towards any man whom I had ever met, with one exception. You were different from any one with whom I had previously come into contact. This impression was confirmed as we saw more of each other. I recognised your mental qualities. I approved highly of your opinions, your personal attributes and general character appealed to me strongly. My heart was in an unsettled state; I was weary of waiting, and began to doubt whether Richard Dereker, with whom I had been in love ever since I could remember, intended to declare himself. I am not believed to be impulsive, but, under certain conditions, am very much so."

"All women are," interjected Blount.

"Possibly; but let me finish;" and she hurried on—her voice changed from the deliberate calmness with which she usually spoke, to a hurried monotone—"If you had proposed to me that night, I should have consented, I believe. But your departure next morning gave me time to reflect; saved me, most likely, both of us, from life-long incompleteness, which, to a woman at least, means settled unhappiness. Then, just after you left, my fairy prince 'made up his mind,' as people say, and I am the happiest girl in Tasmania. I need not ask about your feeling—it is written in large print over both of you, and—here she comes! I don't wonder."

"I was in a most forlorn and wretched state," said Blount, "when you took pity on me and healed my wounds by your sympathetic kindness. Never think you could have done me an injury—and you must let me say, even under our changed conditions, that *I* should not have been a life-long sufferer. But, as in your case, the fairy princess was persuaded of her knight's fidelity; the falsehoods set about by enemies were disproved, and the castle rang with troubadour ballads, and the usual merry-making, when the 'traitours and faitours' were put in their proper places; and so the incident is closed, and in all gratitude and enduring friendship it is a case of 'as you were.'"

"Yes; I know, I know," said the fair Laura; "no more protestations, or else your wife will require explanations, too. Who is the very handsome damsel she has with her?"

"Well; a great friend of mine, who stood by me staunchly in my tribulations and rendered me timely aid. She is a New South Wales heiress. I will tell you about her another time."

"We have been looking for you, Miss Claremont," said Imogen. "I was anxious to introduce my friend, Miss Maguire, a friend of my husband's, too, who did him important service at a critical juncture without which (between you and me) things might have turned out differently."

"Mr. Blount gave me to understand as much," said Miss Claremont, "and I am most happy to welcome any friend of yours or his to our island home. I hope you have enjoyed yourself, Miss Maguire?"

"More than I ever did in my life before," said Sheila, with such evident sincerity, that no one could help smiling. "I think the people here are the kindest and pleasantest I ever met. I have often heard of Hobart hospitality, but never expected to find it anything like this."

"I hope we shall continue to deserve such a good character. Strangers do generally approve of us, and there is no doubt we are always delighted to see them. I suppose we ought to make a move, Mrs. Blount, I see Richard looking out anxiously for me. We must all go and thank Claude Clinton if he isn't dead with fatigue. We owe a great deal to him."

"That we do," said Sheila, naïvely, "he told me he had been hard at work since daylight, arranging thousands of things. Poor fellow! I quite pitied him. I was nearly offering to help with the supper—I am supposed to be clever in that line."

"You might have come off as well as the girl who volunteered to take the parlourmaid's place when her sister was short of one at a big dinner, and afterwards married a baronet with ten thousand a year, who thought she said 'Sherry, sir?' so nicely!"

"I see Claude Clinton over there," interposed Blount, who thought the situation was becoming critical. "He'll be fast asleep if we don't go and pelt him with congratulations. Say something nice to him, Sheila!"

"That I will," said she, with effusion, "I quite love him for his kind-heartedness."

"You're not the only grateful one," said Miss Claremont, "but you'll have to wait your turn. Dick must make a speech, and we'll all say Amen."

"I'll do anything if you'll come home," said that gentleman. "You girls would stay till daylight, I believe. Claude, my boy! come here and be publicly thanked. These ladies have constituted themselves a deputation and wish to assure you that this is the best ball they ever were at in their lives; that it wouldn't have been half as good but for you; that they will be everlastingly grateful for the perfect arrangements you have made. Miss Maguire can't express her feelings in words, but is most anxious to—"

"Oh! Mr. Dereker!" cried Sheila, blushing to the roots of her hair, "pray don't—Oh!"

"Don't interrupt. She's most anxious to say 'Amen.'"

"Amen!" said Sheila, gravely, and evidently much relieved.

"For what we have received, etc., etc.," continued Mr. Dereker. "Now for shawls and the carriage. Can we set you down at the club, Claude? And you can make a suitable reply on the way."

Possibly he did, as he was wedged in, close to Sheila, and what he had to say was in a softly, murmurous tone; akin to that of the surges on the shore, which the silence of the summer night made clearly audible.

After the triumphant success of the ball, other entertainments followed in quick succession, in which the visitors, civil, naval and military, vied with each other in keeping up the excitement, so that the season of 18— was long known as the most successful, harmonious, and generally mirthful period recorded in Tasmanian annals. Races, regattas, picnics, gymkhanas, were in turn attended by crowds of visitors from all the colonies.

Of four-in-hand drags there was quite a procession. Agriculture was prospering. Stock was high in price and quality. Mining operations and investments not only in this, but in all the other colonies, were phenomenally payable. The financial glow shed by the ever increasing, almost fabulous yield of the Comstock, and of the great copper and tin mines, Mount Lyell and Mount Bischoff, gave a magical lustre to all monetary transactions. A kind of Arabian Nights' glamour was cast over the existence of the dwellers in the land, and of all the excited crowds who had hurried to the favoured isle, where Aladdin's Cave seemed suddenly to have opened its treasure chambers in real life and in broad day, to the favoured inhabitants of the Far South Isle.

Foremost among the gay throngs who seemed bent upon taking fullest advantage of the revelries of the period—so appropriate, so suitable, so thoroughly in harmony with the spirit of the hour, were the festive celebrities of the Victorian party, by which name they began to be known.

Mr. Blount had no notion of receiving all the benefits of his newly acquired possessions without doing something in requital. His liberality was unbounded. He subscribed generously to all charitable societies and local institutions. He gave picnics, dances and fishing parties. He even went the length of chartering a steamer and carrying off a large fashionable party to the weird, gloomy solitudes of Macquarie Harbour.

Here the frolic-minded crowd found their spirits lowered, and their imagination darkly disturbed, as they roamed amid the ruinous prison-houses, where rotting timbers told the tale of long neglect; of fast-fading memories of crime and suffering. They gazed on the immense, tenantless buildings, with hundreds of cubicles, the mouldering walls, roofless and ivy-grown, the church where it was deemed that the wretches whose lives were one long foretaste of hell, might be turned to hopes of Heaven, after completing a life of imprisonment, torture and despair. Vehicles were in attendance, besides saddle-horses and guides, under whose safe conduct the revellers made their way to the silent, deserted settlement, whence long ago the ghastly procession of chained men marched at morn to commence each day—a day in which they cursed their birth hour at dawn and eve, ending it by trusting that each night might be their last. The visitors trod the rotting planks of the stage, where fierce dogs had bayed and torn at their chains, as they scented the escaping convict—where more than one such desperate felon had been literally torn in pieces, or escaped the hounds to die a more terrible death amid the sharks which swarmed around the pier. These and other relics of the bad old days of mystery and fear, having been shudderingly regarded by the awed and whispering company, the *Albatross* departed with a fair wind, a smooth sea, and her much relieved visitors, who,

> "Ignorant of 'man's' cruelty,
>
> Marvelled such relics here should be."

Yet as the stars came out and sat upon thrones, looking with sleepless eyes upon the shadowy outlines of the darksome forest and the savage coast, a wailing nightwind arose sounding as a ghostly accompaniment to the dirge-like murmur of the great army of the dead—buried and unburied— around the accursed charnel-houses, which had polluted even that Dantean wilderness!

"Oh! let us get away from this dreadful place!" said Imogen, clinging to her husband's arm, "and I vote against seeing any other Chamber of Horrors. We come to Hobart for rest and pleasure while this halcyon season lasts. Let us not sadden our souls by one thought of the terrors in which this place is steeped. I should like to blot out their very memory and consume the relics off the face of the earth."

It must not be considered, either, that the "Truce of God" (as cessation of siege or battle was medievally termed), which the Happy Isle proclaimed to the war-worn denizens of other colonies, less happily situated for rest and recreation, was entirely devoted to Play. This year was the session, wisely ordained as fitting in with the general vacation, for the meeting of the Society for the Advancement of Science.

Hither came, therefore, to leaven the ordinary frivolities, learned professors from Australasian universities, legal luminaries, judges, the Q.C. and the rising barrister, mercantile magnates, statisticians of world-wide fame, even, indeed, Sir Gregory Gifford, also Sir Harold Harfager, an ex-Proconsul of our Indian empire. They were vice-regal guests. Minor luminaries, such as authors, war correspondents, politicians, home-grown and foreign—in fact almost all the men of "light and leading" were represented at this unique gathering. Missionaries from far Pacific Isles, who had faced cannibal hordes, and heard the yell from crowded war canoes, when poisoned arrows were in the air. They had their philological treasures and hard-won trophies to exhibit. The crowded lecture rooms testified to the interest taken in the soldiers of the Army of Peace. To add to the satisfaction with which the various excitements and entertainments were availed of by the party from the Upper Sturt, it so chanced that, in consequence of the favourable seasons Edward Bruce was enabled to join them a month earlier than he had expected. He was, moreover, in excellent spirits, openly avowing his intention to devote his stay in Hobart to pleasure unalloyed, as compensation for his late pastoral anxieties. He was not contented, however, after a fortnight's "idlesse," without organising a trip to The Mine, which had lately so developed in wealth, prestige, and reputation, that it was difficult to say whether it belonged to Tasmania or Tasmania belonged to it.

Everything and everybody appeared to be in a state of unprecedented prosperity in that happy and care-free *annus mirabilis* if ever there was one. Mrs. Bruce and Imogen mildly reproached Bruce for being in such a hurry to leave his family after so long an absence, and what was worse, carrying off Imogen's husband. However, he, a man of unresting energy and enterprise, declared that he could not stand any more of this lotus-eating life, and that if he did not get away out to the mine, he would have to return to Marondah.

At this dreadful threat Mrs. Bruce capitulated, fearing a premature departure from this land of Utopian delights, where the children were improving so fast, and gaining a reserve of vigour impossible in a hotter climate. This consideration, in the devoted mother's eyes, overbore all others, and caused her to look philosophically upon the proposed expedition—which was accordingly decided upon, and a day fixed for the start, the which came off without accident or delay.

It may be doubted whether, except in theatrical stage life, anything surpasses in rapidity of transformation the change from a fragment of the primeval wilderness into a thickly populated town, founded on a gold or silver field of proved richness. Macadamised streets and level footpaths take the place of miry dray tracks and sloughs of despond. So was it in the city of Comstock. Handsome hotels and shop fronts, with plate glass windows, had succeeded weatherboard and slab shanties with bark roofs. The electric light in globe and street lamps shed its searching radiance through main thoroughfare and alley.

The diurnal coach, by which our travellers arrived, was well horsed and punctual to a fault. The police magistrate and warden of goldfields, assisted by a strong body of police, preserved order and punished evil-doers with such deterrent strictness that offences against the laws were almost unknown. A municipality, with mayor, councillors, and aldermen had been formed after the British pattern. Thus the foundations of earliest English law had been laid, and as the erstwhile barren, hopeless lodge in the wilderness increased in wealth and population, so the State, "broad based upon the people's will," emerged ready made, only awaiting that gradual development which comes instinctively in Anglo-Saxon communities, to pass from the rude stage of the mining camp to the perfected organisation of the city. It was soon made apparent to the party that Hobart was not the only place where public entertainments and festive gatherings were to be found. The mayor and corporation of Comstock, waiting upon the distinguished visitors, whose arrival was duly chronicled in the *Clarion*, invited them to a formal banquet, where champagne in profusion was exhibited, and the health of their guests proposed by the mayor, Mr. Frampton Tregonwell, who made honourable mention of that distinguished pastoralist and explorer, Mr. Edward Hamilton Bruce.

Before this function they had been taken to the lower levels of the mine, when the "drives" being lighted up, and a few judiciously selected masses of "native silver" and malachite looked up for the occasion, Mr. Bruce formed the opinion that he stood in a "quarry" of one of the chief precious metals. Being a man of business habits, as well as of pastoral experience, he took the opportunity, under Mr. Tregonwell's authority, to inspect the accounts of the Company, and, after examining the astonishing values of crude and treated ore, he came to the conclusion that his sister-in-law (untoward as had been the early stages of their acquaintance) had displayed the unerring instinct with which her sex is credited in her venture in the matrimonial lottery. The audit demonstrated the cheering fact that an income of from ten to twenty thousand a year was assured to each of the four original shareholders in this most fortunate enterprise.

"I suppose you and Imogen will be taking a trip home in a few months?" he said. "With all this money, and the prospects of the season in London, Australia will lose some of its interest."

"Such is our intention; unless anything unforeseen comes in the way after the Hobart season has come to an end and you good folks have wended your way back to the Upper Sturt, I think of taking our passage by the first P. and O. steamer from Sydney."

"Won't it be rather cold to arrive in England so early in the year?"

"We propose to stay a month or two in Cairo on the way, refreshing our memories of the *Arabian Nights*; trans-shipping by the Brindisi route, and after a week or two in Paris, reaching London in May, in time for Imogen to hear her first nightingale."

"A very sensible programme, I wish we were going with you. However, later on, if the seasons and the stock keep up, we may come and stay at your country seat."

"It was the most fortunate day of my life when I stayed at yours, though appearances were against me, I confess. However, I look forward to seeing you and Hilda in my native county, which is not wholly without interest, especially in shooting, hunting, and fishing. However, I think it's drawing on to feeding time. Champagne goes better *after* subterranean experiences than before."

The banquet was a success. Blount found himself referred to, not only as the original capitalist in the formation of the great Mineral Property, which had advanced Tasmania by half a century, socially, commercially, and mineralogically (the last word a trifle slurred), but as "a patron of the fine arts, a generous supporter of local charities, and a citizen of whom they would all be proud, and would remember gratefully in days to come. They trusted that even in the splendid pageantry of the old and venerated society, in which he and his amiable wife were so soon to share, the humble, but heartfelt hospitality of the 'tight little island,' called Tasmania would not be wholly forgotten. Their honoured guests had accepted invitations to be present at a ball to be given that evening for the purpose of supplementing the funds of the local hospital, and all hoped to meet them there. They knew that there were several representative institutions, including the library, of which they were justly proud, to inspect. They would not detain the guests by making further remarks."

Mr. Blount had no hesitation in saying that he was never more genuinely surprised than by witnessing the astonishing, he might say unparalleled, progress made by the town and district since his last visit. In the formation of the streets, in the water service, in the installation of electric lighting, in the hospital and library, Comstock was ahead of many old-established country towns in Britain. Personally, he should always take a deep interest in the municipal, as well as the material, progress of the city, and feel genuine pride in having contributed to its inception and development.

A general inspection of the local institutions filled up the afternoon. The free library attracted much attention. It had been commenced by subscription, and with private donations, supplemented by books from tourists and visitors, who generally left any they brought to read by train or steamer on the journey up. It was a heterogenous collection, ranging from *very* light fiction to works on metallurgy, theology, and civil engineering. However, there was no lack of works of solid value, so that the miner who wished to improve or distract his mind had no difficulty in finding books to suit his taste. At the hospital, apart from typhoid fever and dysentery patients, the cases were mostly fractures and other injuries resulting from mining accidents. This establishment, as at all gold and silver fields, was most liberally supported, irrespective of race, creed, or colour. No working miner knew whose turn it might be the next to be carried there in agony or insensibility. Many were the gifts, unostentatiously bestowed, by former patients in the shape of necessaries or luxuries for convalescents. These duty visits performed, dinner was undertaken at the Palace Hotel, a stately three-storeyed building, with a verandah nearly twenty feet wide and balconies to match. After a more or less sumptuous repast in the *salle à manger*, electric lighted, where they were served by well-dressed waiters, with wines of undoubted excellence, and a *menu* almost extravagant in variety, and but sparingly partaken of; Messrs. Bruce, Blount, and Tregonwell sallied forth accompanied by a dozen dignitaries to the Town Hall. In this imposing building, a crowd of dancers in "plain or fancy" dress were already in the full swing of pleasurable excitement.

CHAPTER XII

A gold or silver field of decent rank and reputation must always compare favourably in its amusements with a town. In the wide range of his experiences, in war and peace, on land and water, British or foreign, the roving miner may challenge comparison with all sorts and conditions of men. Thus, he is never at a loss for a character to represent, a costume in which to disguise, or to heighten his personal attractions. The same rule applies to the women of the family, who have followed his wanderings, sharing in his privations or triumphs, as the case may be. Bearing with exemplary patience the inevitable hardships, they are none the less eager to recoup themselves when legitimate opportunities arise for amusement.

When Messrs. Bruce, Blount, and other magnates arrived on the scene, they were accommodated with seats on the daïs, where they sat proudly in full public view, reflecting how sharply contrasted was the scene before them with any possible gathering on the site of the "Comstock Claim" — "of four men's ground" — little more than a year ago! The great hall, seventy feet in length, by thirty in width, was brilliantly lighted, draped with flags of all nations, above which, surmounting the daïs, the Union Jack reigned supreme. Upon the satin-like Huon pine floor strolled a motley crowd. Pirates and princes, peasants and brigands, ballerinas and matadors, mingled with dairy maids and broom girls, flower sellers and fishwives (whose "caller herrin'" had the smack of the well-remembered cry), while dowagers and duchesses, grisettes, tricoteuses, shepherds and sundowners, jostled here and there, in the dance, with a Red Indian, a cow-boy, or even an aboriginal in his blanket.

"The distinguished visitors," so described in the morning's *Clarion*, paid due respect to their municipal and other entertainers. They stood high in the estimation of their partners, whose looks and enthusiasm for the dance they would have been indeed hypercritical to have criticised. Charlie Herbert and Jack Clarke, the latter having got rid of his unfortunate lameness, were habited as a bushranger and a stock-rider, respectively. They remained till supper was over, during which exceedingly festive refection, Mr. Blount's health, as a fearless explorer, was enthusiastically toasted, while Mr. Tregonwell was referred to as a world-renowned mining captain, and the father of the field. Charlie Herbert was eulogised as a worthy son of the soil, who, like Mr. Dereker—the speaker must say "Dick" Dereker (cheers)—was an honour to his native land, and like him, destined to make a name in the great world. Here every one rose, and cheered to the echo. The speeches in requital of this courtesy were brief but pointed; and long before the conclusion of the function, Messrs. Bruce and Blount quietly departed and soon after sunrise were on the way back to Hobart, accompanied by Charlie Herbert and Clarke, who deemed themselves to have a just claim to exceptional recreation after their pioneer experiences. Moreover, they explained that they could afford to enjoy themselves with a clear conscience, while Mr. Tregonwell remained on guard—a man never known to sleep on his post. So these young men chartered a four-in-hand drag, a few miles out of Hobart, and having borrowed a coach-horn, entered that city with all proper pomp and circumstance. When Charlie Herbert proceeded to "swing his reefing leaders," and pull up at the General Post-Office, quite a crowd had assembled, eager to gaze on, and to welcome the prospectors of the wondrous Comstock mine.

After depositing themselves and their belongings at the Tasmanian Club, the junior shareholders stated with decision that, having had a fair allowance of hard work and hard living, they were now going to enjoy themselves; also to make some return for the hospitality they had enjoyed in former years. As pleasant detrimentals, though suspiciously regarded by cautious matrons, they had always, on the whole, been popular, their want of capital being overlooked in favour of their engaging manners and family connections. Now, as original shareholders in the great mining property of the day, they were princes, paladins, long-lost brothers; in fact, most desirable and distinguished. Everybody, from the Supreme Court judges downward, called on and made much of them. Without them no party was complete. At the polo meets they were conspicuous; they rode splendidly, every one said, as indeed they did, but not having been able to keep ponies in former years, this was their first opportunity of exhibiting that accomplishment in public.

Of course, they were not long in letting people know that they wanted to give their friends, and more particularly the ladies of Hobart, some kind of entertainment; the question now being of what pattern and dimensions it should consist. To this end grave consultations were held; of balls and parties there had been nearly enough—the young people were, strange to say, beginning to be tired of dancing.

Laura Claremont talked of going home to Hollywood soon. If not earlier, certainly next week. Mr. Bruce was becoming impatient; he began to think about mustering those polled Angus bullocks in the river paddocks for the Melbourne market, when a chance remark by Mrs. Blount settled the matter, and decided the character of the entertainment.

"How would it be to have a picnic party to the Hermitage?" she inquired, with an air of much innocence and simplicity. "There is a lovely road by Brown's River, and such a view! No one is at the Bungalow now but a caretaker. There is one fine large room, and a grand verandah looking out to sea. The eatables, etc., could be arranged early in the day, and if we were a little late coming home, the nights are so lovely. We can have all the men-of-war people, and just in time, too; I heard they were to be off to the islands soon."

"Magnificent!" cried out Charlie Herbert and Jack Clarke in one breath. "Mrs. Blount, you have saved our lives. Jack and I were getting quite low-spirited and suicidal. We could think of nothing worth while. Balls are played out. The races at Elwick were about the last excitement. A picnic on a vast and comprehensive scale is the very thing. Miss Maguire, when does the Admiral give the order for Nukuheva?"

Sheila blushed, and seemed taken aback, but rallying, answered, "'The captain bold does not confide in any foremast hand, Matilda!' Isn't that in one of the Bab Ballads?"

"Oh! I thought Vernon Harcourt might have told you," said Charlie. "You and he seemed so confidential the other evening."

"Suppose you ask him yourself, Mr. Herbert? But, at any rate, it won't be till the week after next." Here everybody laughed, and the girl, seeing that she had "given herself away," looked confused.

"Tell him not to be rude, Sheila. What business is it of his? Say you won't go to his picnic, and then it will be a dismal failure." Mrs. Blount stood alongside her *protégée* and looked threateningly at Master Charlie, who pretended to be shocked at his *faux pas*, and went down on one knee to Sheila to implore forgiveness.

"I've a great mind to box your ears, Mr. Herbert!" she said, as her face lighted up with a smile of genuine mirth, "but I suppose I must forgive you this time. Now, what about this picnic? that's the real question, and where is it to be?"

"I vote for the Hermitage," said Imogen. "Don't you, Hilda? I drove you there one day with 'Matchless.'"

"A lovely spot," said Mrs. Bruce; "only I was afraid the mare would jump over the cliff once. The road is lovely; I feel sure all the world will come. We must have half-a-dozen four-in-hands—Imogen and I will be chaperons. I suppose you young men can forage up two more?"

"Miss Claremont!" suggested Jack Clarke. "She *is* so nice."

"Quite agree with you," said Imogen; "but she is not married yet. Suppose you ask Mrs. Wendover, of the Châlet, she is so kind, and, at the same time, capable of keeping order, which is necessary, Mr. Herbert, isn't it?"

"Now, don't be severe, Mrs. Blount! All you young married women get so dreadfully proper, and talk alarmingly about your husbands. I'll find security for good behaviour."

"Only my fun," said Imogen. "But I'm afraid you've hurt Sheila's feelings. Has she forgiven you?"

"Oh! Mrs. Blount, don't tease him any more," cried Sheila. "He looks really sorry. It was all my fault, for taking his chaff seriously."

"What do you think of Lady Wood?" said Mrs. Bruce, "from West Australia?"

"The very one," cried out all the council. "She has a habit of authority, as the wife of the Premier of the Golden West Colony—("and, though this is a silver mine, 'Shivoo,' the relationship is obvious," this interpolation was Mr. Jack Clarke's). Those who are in favour, hold up your hands! Against it, nobody. The resolution is carried."

"Now for ways and means," said Charles Herbert. "First of all, the four-in-hand drags—there mustn't be fewer than half-a-dozen, with power to add to their number; the men, too, must be able to drive. Claude Clinton and I will see to that. Of course we make him an honorary member of the committee of management. The affair wouldn't be complete without him."

"Of course not. (Chorus) 'For he's etc. etc.'"

"Isn't it rather early for a song?" queried Mrs. Bruce.

"Not at all, when two such voices as yours and Mrs. Blount's are available, and this is such a grand room to sing in. Music after breakfast—when you've nothing to do afterwards, is simply delicious."

"Well, only one verse—Sheila and I will join in," said Mrs. Bruce. "If Edward comes in, he'll think we're going out of our minds."

The tribute to Mr. Clinton's merits having been rendered with feeling, Sheila's fresh voice holding a good position, the council went on to strict business.

"The drags first," said Mr. Herbert, "the affair must be started properly—now, who are there? There's Gerald Branksome from W.A., *he* can drive, I know—he won the tandem race at the Polo Gymkhana, and the Victoria Cross race at Hurlingham last year. He can be guaranteed. There's Jim Allanson just down from Sydney, a well-known whip, I've seen him drive to Randwick from the Union Club. The Quorn Hall drag with its four greys will take some beating. I wired to Dick Dereker, he'll turn up. Jack, are you good for the brake, with that off leg of yours? It's a responsible position."

"Count me in," said that gentleman, who had been to San Francisco; "Joe Bowman will help with the brake business."

"That's good enough," said Herbert, "Joe will keep an eye on you going down hill. I'll have one, if I have to wire to Melbourne for a team, that makes the half-dozen, doesn't it? I daresay there'll be another or two by and by. Buggies, tandem carts, and private carriages may be left to their own discretion, or that of their owners—there'll be no lack of them, I daresay."

Once the great event was decided upon, neither difficulties nor delays were considered worthy of notice. The date was fixed: the invitations were sent out next morning. The social status of the entertainment being exceptional, no one dreamed of refusing. Rumours of the scale of magnificence upon which it was to be carried out commenced to circulate— for one of the conditions of unparalleled advantage in such affairs, an unrestricted bank balance, was in this case notorious.

Money being no object to these youthful Monte Christos, they were able to indulge, therefore, all the fancies of generous dispositions, with excited imaginations. No expense was spared; no thoughtful kindness omitted. A large proportion of the hackney carriages and other livery stable vehicles were secured. As at a contested election, they plied from the General Post-Office to the Hermitage, with free transit for all holders of invitation cards. The arrangements were complete and successful, beyond all previous holiday experiences, and when Charlie Herbert took the lead with an impressive team, and the belle of Hobart on the box seat of his drag, life, it may be confidently stated, had few richer moments, or more dazzling triumphs in store for *him*.

If he did not quote "let Fate do her worst," there could be no doubt that he felt, deep down in his heart, the delicious, ever new, ever fresh sentiment of the poet.

Next in order came Edward Bruce, with Sheila on the box beside him, wild with joy and the excitement of such a position, of which, except in a dream fairy tale, she had never realised the possibility. Imogen, beside her, had insisted on relinquishing the place of honour. "No, Sheila, my dear! My fortune is told, your turn has yet to come, and you have all our best wishes, you know."

"You are too good, Miss Imogen, Mrs. Blount, I mean! Really I don't know what I am saying."

"Well, you're looking your best to-day, Sheila! Your dress couldn't be better, and this lovely day has sent all the roses to your cheeks. Why, you might pass for a Tasmanian girl, really—and we know what that means."

"Now, you girls!" said Edward Bruce, in accents of veiled command, "keep your eyes about you, going down this hill. It's trying with a heavy load, and I've heard of accidents. Imogen, put your foot on the brake that side, and give me the least bit of help. Now, we're on the level again. Isn't that view of the sea lovely?"

Reginald Vernon Harcourt, R.N., Flag Lieutenant of H.M.S. *Orlando*, was understood to be of that opinion, as he leaned forward from his seat in the body of the coach, immediately behind the two young women aforesaid, and remarked as much. This was not the only statement he made before the procession pulled up at the Sandy Bay Hotel, at the base of the hill immediately below the Hermitage. And it did not go unnoted, that, being favourably situated for talking to Sheila over her right shoulder, he made prompt use of the position, as a naval strategist of experience, while Imogen and Jack Clarke similarly situated, did not appear to be quite so eager for conversation.

The enumeration of the drags and traps following would resemble that of the Greek ships at the siege of Troy. It will be sufficient to say that Mr. Dereker's grey team was held to be the best, as to matching and style; Dick Dereker, the most finished exponent of the coaching science—worthy of the great annual pageant in Hyde Park. There were a few dissentients, who thought the Quorn Hall team and drag faultless. But the opposition votes were too powerful. He was "Dick Dereker," therefore unapproachable in love, war, sport, and every other form of manly excellence. There was nothing more to be said. His name settled the matter.

As it happened, nothing could possibly have been more deliciously perfect than the weather. Warm, without oppressive heat or sultry feeling, the faint sea breeze, the murmuring lazy surge-roll, completed the magic spell, which invited to sensuous enjoyment, the happy possessors of unworn youth—in which class, the greater proportion of the guests were fortunately included.

The day, the season, the environment and attendant circumstances being propitious, so was the gathering, which was beyond all precedent successful. All the four-in-hands had turned up; there was such a crowd at the General Post-Office, that traffic was temporarily impeded. But that did not matter in Hobart, as it certainly would have done in Melbourne or Sydney—where indignation would have been aroused. The Tasmanian population is kindly and forbearing, especially to the stranger within their gates, through whom, in the season, it must be admitted, their revenues are substantially benefited. So, as the four-in-hands passed in single file down Davey Street, cheers rent the air, and hearty popular enthusiasm was evoked. The hill below the Hermitage was long and steep, so it was arranged that the drags and carriages were to be left at the hotel, where adequate accommodation had been provided, as well for the horses, as for the grooms and drivers to them appertaining. The walk up hill was neither long nor unduly fatiguing; providing also for reasonable deviations into the forest paths, whence more extended views might be enjoyed, or confidential communications exchanged. This arrangement seemed to suit the majority of the guests, who might, without loss of time, have been seen scattered over the sides and summit of the forest hill. At the sound of the great Chinese gong, a fragment of loot from the Summer Palace at Pekin, in the half-forgotten Chinese war, a strong converging force prepared to invest the Hermitage. Here were seen tables on trestles in the principal room, laden with all the good things which a very active, well-paid caterer had been able to collect. Haunches of venison, barons of beef, saddles of mutton, turkeys of great size and amplitude, wild fowl of all descriptions, lake trout, fresh salmon (frozen), grouse and pheasant, from the same miraculous arrangement, rendered the choice of viands difficult, and the taste of the most fastidious "gourmet," easy to satisfy. With the popping of the first champagne corks, the conversation began to strike the note of cheerfulness proper to the occasion, after which the "crescendo" was maintained at an uninterruptedly joyous, even vivacious level.

Speeches were sternly deprecated; an immediate adjournment to the beach was proposed and promptly carried out. The shining sands invited to every kind of game and dance suitable to an open air revel. Sets of lancers were formed; games such as "twos and threes," "oranges and lemons," "hide and seek," found enthusiastic supporters, while those pairs who had anything particular to say to each other found quiet paths and shady nooks in the forest fringe, which lay so conveniently close to the beaches and headlands.

There was, apparently, no lack of mutual entertainment, or necessity for the givers of the feast to invent fresh frolics, for, just as the low sun gave warning, and the last game of "rounders" came to an end—in which, by the way, Sheila, who was as active as a mountain colt, had particularly distinguished herself—the recall bugle was sounded. A late afternoon tea was served, and a descent made to the lower level, where the drags, carriages, buggies and dog-carts stood, with horses harnessed up, ready to start. Among these last-mentioned vehicles was one, a dog-cart, which was originally intended to accommodate more than one pair. The driver regretted his inability to take up a third person for want of room. It subsequently came out that, being a youth of foresight, he had removed the back seat before leaving Hobart, holding the ancient averment, "two's company, three's none," still to be in force and acceptation. However, after the inevitable amount of bustle and occasional contention of ostlers, all the teams were duly mustered and loaded up in the same order as before.

There were, of course, certain reconstructions, among which it was noted that Mrs. Blount had relinquished her seat next to Miss Maguire, in favour of the Flag-Lieutenant of the *Orlando*, alleging preference for the higher seat behind, as by this removal she commanded a more extensive view of the glorious landscape, spread out by sea and shore, below and around. Sheila and Lieutenant Harcourt did not appear to be so deeply interested in scenery—at least, on this occasion—as they kept their heads down mostly, and spoke, though uninterruptedly, in rather a low tone during the homeward drive.

On one occasion, however, they looked up suddenly as a fresh young voice commenced the opening verse of a well-known song, and before the magical couplet of "The ship is trim and ready, and the jolly days are done," was well over, the whole of the occupants of the drag, as well as those of the one immediately behind, joined in with tremendous enthusiasm, until, when the comprehensive statement that "They all love Jack" was reached, the very sea-gulls on the beach were startled, and flapped away with faint cries of remonstrance. Then, for one moment, the Flag-Lieutenant and Sheila looked into one another's eyes, and read there something not wholly subversive of the sentiment.

The moon had risen, illumining the broad estuary, over which, in shimmering gleams, lustrous lines of fairy pathways stretched to the silvery mist of the horizon; star-fretted patches of lambent flame traversed the wavelets, which ever and anon raised a glittering spray upward, while from time to time the low but distinct rhythmic roll of the surges fell on the ear. Higher and higher rose the moon in the dark blue, cloudless sky—the surroundings were distinctly favourable to those avowals which the moon has, from time immemorial, had under her immediate favour and protection. If some of the merry maidens of the day's *festa* listened to vows more ardent than are born of the prosaic duties of every-day life, what wonder? Next morning there was great excitement at the clubs, and among all the inner circles of Hobart society. Two engagements were "given out," one being that of Lieutenant Vernon Harcourt, of the *Orlando*, to Miss Sheila Maguire, of Tumut Park, New South Wales, and the other of Mr. Charles Herbert, and a young lady to whom he had long been attached, though circumstances had hitherto delayed his declaration. Suspicions had been aroused as to Mr. Jack Clarke and another fair maid, but nothing was as yet "known for a fact." Of course, little was done on the day following this stupendous entertainment. Everybody was too tired, or declared themselves to be so. The members of the Polo Club got up a scratch match, however, just to "shake off the effects of a late sitting at whist."

A few ladies rode out to this affair, the ground being situated picturesquely on the bank of the broad Derwent. Among these Dianas was Sheila, riding a handsome thoroughbred, and escorted by Mr. Bruce, also exceptionally well mounted. Mr. Harcourt was observed to join them from time to time, when his "quarter" was up at polo. He was the show player of the fleet; always in a foremost position at the gymkhana. In this particular match, Sheila was observed to take great interest, turning pale, indeed, on one occasion when he was knocked off his horse in a violent passage at arms.

His opponent was adjudged to have been in the wrong, and well scolded by the captain of his side; the game went on, and Sheila recovered her roses—her spirits also, sufficiently to join in the cheering when Lieutenant Harcourt's side won the match by a goal and two behinds.

Both of the engagements met with general approbation. The Tasmanian young lady and her lover belonged to (so to speak) "county" families, known from childhood to all the squirearchy of the island—always general favourites. So everybody congratulated sincerely and wished them luck. The over-sea couple were, of course, strangers, and under other circumstances, local jealousy might have been aroused by a girl from another colony carrying off a handsome naval officer, always a prize in colonial cities. But Sheila's simple, kindly, unaffected manner had commended her to even the severe critics of her own sex, the more sensible members excusing his invidious preference among so many good-looking, well-turned-out damsels, something after this fashion:

"You see, he's only a lieutenant; it may be years before he gets a ship. He couldn't afford to marry yet, without money. They say she has tons of it, and she is certainly very good-looking, and nice in her manner. So Mr. Harcourt hasn't done himself so badly." One person was slightly dissatisfied. That was his captain. "He is my sailing-master, and a very good one, too," he said, in an ill-used tone of voice. "He'll always be thinking of her now, and counting the days till he can leave the service. Suppose the ship runs on a rock, I get my promotion stopped, and all because of this confounded girl." Different point of view!

As for Sheila and her lieutenant, they were perfectly, genuinely, unmistakably happy. They were both young, she just twenty, he not quite arrived at thirty. He was a rising man in his profession, and Sheila's money, which was, very properly, to be settled upon herself, would allow them to live most comfortably while he was on shore; besides aiding—as money always does, directly or indirectly—in his promotion. So the immediate prospect was bright. Sheila declared that she had always loved sailors since that eventful ball, where she had joined in the dance on equal terms with the nobility of Britain. What a fortunate girl she was, to have such friends; and how much more fortunate she had become since!

This memorable picnic, often referred to in after years, was considered to be virtually, if not officially declared, the closing event of the season. The fleet was to sail in a week or ten days for "the islands," a comprehensive term for a general look round the lands and seas of the South Pacific, in the interests of British subjects. They would be back in Sydney in three or four months, at the end of which time—a terrifically long and wearisome period Sheila thought—she and her sailor were to be married. The Admiral's ship and officers would then return to England, after a month's stay in Hobart and Sydney—the time of his commission having expired—and another Admiral, with another flag-lieutenant, would replace them. Sheila would also go to England, but not in the *Orlando*, modern regulations having put a stop to that pleasing privilege. But she could take passage in a P. and O. steamer, leaving about the same time, and be in England ready to receive him in a pretty house of their own—their very own—where they would be as happy as princes—happier indeed than some! After the departure of the fleet, a certain calmness—not exactly a dullness, but bordering on something of that nature—began to settle upon the Isle of Rest and Recreation. The Queenslanders, the New South Wales division, the Victorians, South Australians, and New Zealanders were taking their passages. Edward Bruce began to get more and more fidgety—he was certain that he was wanted at the station; really, if his wife and Imogen could not make up their minds to leave, he must go home and leave them to follow.

Matters were in this unsettled state, when suddenly in the cable column appeared the startling announcement, "The Earl of Fontenaye died suddenly yesterday, at Lutterworth, soon after hearing the news of his eldest son's death at Malta from an accident at polo. The title and estates devolve upon the younger son, the Honourable Robert Valentine Blount, at present in Australia."

This news, it may well be imagined, was received with mingled feelings by the people most nearly concerned. The Earl had been in failing health for years past; but as a confirmed invalid, had not aroused apprehension of a sudden termination to his succession of ailments. Blount and his father had been on excellent terms; their only serious disagreement had been on the subject of the younger son's unreasonable wandering—as the old man termed it—to far countries and among strange people. He had not gone the length of prohibition, however, and his last letter had assured the errant cadet of his father's satisfaction at his marriage, and of his anxiety to welcome the bride to the home of their race. Now all this was over. Blount would never behold the kind face lighting up with the joy of recognition, or have the pride of presenting Imogen in all her grace and beauty to the head of his ancient house. His brother Falkland too, who used to laugh at his pilgrimages, as he called them, and ask to be shown his staff and scrip, with the last news of the Unholy Land, as he persisted in naming Australia. What good chums they were, and had always been! His brother had never married; in that respect only withstanding his father's admonitions, but promising an early compliance. Now, of course, in default of a baby heir Blount was Lord Fontenaye, the inheritor of one of the oldest historic titles and estates of the realm—a position to which he had never dreamed of succeeding; the thought of which, if it had ever crossed his mind, was dismissed as equivalent in probability to the proverbial "Château en Espagne." Perhaps his most powerful consolation, independently of the change involved in becoming an English nobleman, with historical titles and a seat in the House of Lords, was the contemplation of Imogen as Lady Fontenaye.

To her, the feeling at first was painful rather than otherwise. She sympathised too deeply in all her husband's mental conditions, not to share his grief for the sudden loss of a father and brother to whom he had been warmly attached. He would never be able to tell that father *now* how deeply he regretted the careless disregard of his feelings and opinions. Nor could he share with his brother, in the old home, those sports to which both had been so attached since boyhood's day. The pride of proving that in a far land, and among men of his own blood, he had been able to carve out a fortune for himself, and to acquire an income, far from inconsiderable even in that land of great fortunes: even this satisfaction was now denied him. Imogen too, dreading always an inevitable separation from her sister, felt now that their absences must necessarily be greater, more lengthened, until at last a correspondence by letter at intervals would be all that was left to them of the happy old days in which they had so delighted.

Why could not Fate indeed have left them where they were, provided with a good Australian fortune, which they could have spent, and enjoyed among their own people, where Valentine would have, in time, become an Australian country gentleman, bought a place on the Upper Sturt, and lived like a king, going of course to Hobart in the summer, and running down to Melbourne now and then? Why indeed should they have this greatness thrust upon them?

So when Imogen was called upon by various friends, ostensibly to inquire, but really to see "how she took it," and whether she showed any foreshadowing of the dignities, and calmness of exalted rank, they were surprised to see from red eyes, and other signs, that the young woman upon whom all these choice gifts had been showered had evidently been having what is known in feminine circles, as "a good cry," and was far from being uplifted by the rank and fame to which she had been promoted.

This state of matters was considered to be so unwise, unnatural, and in a sense ungrateful, to the Giver of all good gifts, that they set themselves to rate her for the improper state of depression into which she had allowed herself to fall. She was enjoined to think of her duty to society, her rank, her position among the aristocracy of the proudest nobility in the world. Of course it was natural for her husband to be grieved at the death of his father and his brother. But time would soften that sorrow, and as she had never seen them, it would not be expected of her to go into deep mourning or to wear it very long. In the face of these, and other practical considerations, Imogen felt that there would be a flavour of affectation in the appearance of settled grief, and allowed her friends to think that they had succeeded in clearing away shadows. But she confided to Mrs. Bruce, in the confidence of the retiring hour, that Val and she would always look back to their quiet days at Marondah, and their holiday, lotus-eating season in Hobart, as part of the *real* luxuries and enjoyments of their past life.

"However, you will have to come and see me at Fontenaye!—how strangely it sounds—with Edward and the dear children, and we must get Mr. Tregonwell to make something happen to the Tasmanian Comstock, so that *we* will come out like a shot. But, oh! my dear old Australia! how I shall grieve at parting with you for ever!"

Then the sisters kissed, and wept in each other's arms, and were comforted—so women are soothed in time of trial. On the next morning Imogen appeared at breakfast with an unruffled countenance, talking soberly to her husband and brother-in-law about the wonderful change in their future lives, and their departure by the next mail steamer.

This, of course, was imperative. The situation became urgent. Mr. Bruce agreed to remain until the P. and O. *Rome*, R.M.S. came for her load of so many thousand cases of Tasmanian apples, and with incidental passengers steamed away for Albany, Colombo, Aden, Cairo, and the East—that gorgeous, shadowy name of wonder and romance. Then would the Australian family return to their quiet home by the rippling, winding waters of the Sturt, and the English division return to become an integral portion of the rank and fashion, the "might, majesty and dominion" of the world-wide Empire which has stood so many assaults, and which still unfurls to every wind of Heaven the "flag that's braved a thousand years, the battle and the breeze."

It came to pass during one of the necessary conversations relative to the voyage, that Lord Fontenaye said to her ladyship, "Does anything occur to you, relative to Sheila Maguire, my dear Imogen?"

"Indeed, I have been thinking about her a great deal, lately," said the youthful countess. "She can't be married until Lieutenant Harcourt and the fleet return from the Islands. Till then, she will have to stay in Hobart."

"Won't that be a little awkward for her? She has no friends, that is to say, intimate friends, over here—though, of course, we could get her efficient chaperonage—eh?"

"I know what you are thinking of, Val! It would be the very thing—and oh! how kind of you."

"What am I thinking of, and why am I so kind—have I married a thought reader, my dear Imogen?"

"Why, of course, you are intending to ask her to go home with us, and to be married from Fontenaye. It is a splendid idea. It would be unspeakably nice for her, and she would be such a help and comfort to me, on our travels."

"The very thing! Do you think she will like the idea?"

"Like it? She will be charmed. He will come to England with the men of the *Orlando*, who are to be replaced, and they can be married as soon as she can get her trousseau together. We shall go to England much about the same time as the Admiral, so that Mr. Harcourt will be on full pay the whole time. I dare say it will be two or three months before he gets another ship. Poor dear Sheila, she never dreamed of being married from a castle, any more than I did of living in one after I was married."

"Or that I should give her away, as I suppose I shall have to do," rejoined her husband. "'Giving agreeable girls away,'" he hummed—"I shall feel like the Lord Chancellor in *Iolanthe*."

When this deep-laid plot was unfolded to Sheila, she entered into the spirit of it with enthusiasm, expressing the deepest gratitude, as with tears in her eyes, she thanked her tried friends for their thoughtful kindness. "I *was* rather down about being left alone here," she confessed. "It was all very well when I belonged to your party, but being here by myself till the fleet returned, and fancying all sorts of things in Mr. Harcourt's absence, was different."

"The advantage is not altogether on your side, Sheila. You will be company for me when my husband is away. We're both Australians, you see, and there are many things in common between us; old bush memories and adventures, that an English friend, however nice she was, wouldn't understand. Really I feel quite cheered up, now I know you're coming with us."

"And what do *I* feel?" cried Sheila—"but I won't describe it." Her colour deepened, and her dark grey eyes glowed, as she stood up and looked at her benefactress with passionate emotion in every line of her expressive face. "Yes! I feel that I could die for you"—she clasped Imogen's hand as she spoke, and kissing it again and again, rushed from the room.

"Her Irish blood came out there," said Blount; "how handsome the girl has grown, and what a figure she has! She'll rather astonish our untravelled friends in England. You're quite right, though, as to her being a comfort to you in foreign parts, and you can talk about the Upper Sturt, and dear old Marondah together, when you feel low-spirited."

"Dear Marondah!" said Imogen, softly; "I wonder when we shall see the old river again, and the willows, dipping their branches into its clear waters."

"Oh! you mustn't let yourself run down, that way. Bruce will be home next summer, if bullocks keep up and the price of wool. Think how they'll enjoy coming to stay with us, and what shooting and hunting he and I can have together. Sheila can hunt too. I'll smoke a cigar in the garden, and you'd better go to bed, my dear."

But little more remains to be told concerning the fortunes of Imogen and her husband, now Lord and Lady Fontenaye. They decided on a month's sojourn in Cairo, where they revelled in the mild climate, and the daily marvels and miraculous sights and sounds—the enchanted Arabian Nights' surroundings, the veiled women, the Arab horses, the balconies, almost touching across the narrow streets. The old-world presentment of the East was inexpressibly fascinating to Imogen and Sheila, seen for the first time.

They "did" Egypt more or less thoroughly, as they planned not to reach England before April—Imogen declaring that "the cold winds of March" would lay her in an early grave. So they went up the Nile as far as Philæ, filling their minds with such glories and marvels as might suffice for the mental digestion of a lifetime. They rode and explored to their hearts' content, "Royal Thebes, Egyptian treasure-house of boundless wealth, that boasts her hundred gates"; Luxor, with its labyrinth of courts, and superb colonnades; Karnak, that darkens the horizon with a world of portals, pyramids, and palaces.

"Perhaps we may never see these wonders again," said Imogen. "But I shall revel in their memories as long as I live. What do you say, Sheila?"

"I feel as if I was just born," said the excited damsel, "and was just opening my eyes on a new world. Awakening in Heaven, if it's not wrong to say so, must be something like this."

"What a charming way of getting over the winter," said Imogen. "One sees so much of the world in the process, besides meeting people of mark and distinction. Val tells me we may have a fortnight in Paris, for hats and dresses, before arriving in dear old England some time in April, which is a lovely month, if the spring is early. And this year they say it is."

"'Oh! to be in England, now that April's here'," quoted Lord Fontenaye, who now joined the party; "we shall be comfortably settled in Fontenaye, I hope, before the 'merry month of May,' when I shall have the honour of showing you two 'Cornstalks' what a London season is like."

"Oh! and shall we able to ride in the Park?" quoth Sheila, with great eagerness. "I do so long to see the wonderful English horses that one hears so much about—the Four-in-hand and Coaching Clubs too! What a sight it must be! I must have a horse worth looking at, price no object—new saddle, and habit too. Oh! what fun it will be! And you'll give Mrs. Bl—I mean, her ladyship—a horse too, won't you?"

"You're a true Australian, Sheila," said he. "I believe you all care more about horses, than anything else in the world. Now that the 'Comstock' is so encouraging in the way of dividends, I believe it will run to a hundred-and-fifty-guinea hackney or two—with a new landau, a brougham, and other suitable equipages."

These rose-coloured anticipations were duly realised. A wire was sent from Paris, and the "wandering heir" was duly received and welcomed in the halls of his ancestors. The time-honoured feasting of tenants and "fêting" of the whole countryside was transacted—a comprehensive programme having been arranged by the land steward, a man of great experience and organising faculty. The younger son of the house, it was explained, had always been the more popular one. And now that he had "come to his own," as the people said, their joy was unbounded. Everything was done on a most liberal scale. Correspondents came down "special" from the great

London dailies, by whom full and particular descriptions were sent through all Britain and her colonies, as well as to the ends of the earth generally.

The beauty and gracious demeanour of Lady Fontenaye, and her friend Miss Sheila Maguire, an Australian heiress of fabulous wealth, were descanted upon and set forth in glowing colours. Archives were ransacked for the ancestors of all the Marmions, from the days of Flodden and those earlier times when Robert de Marmion, Lord of Fontenaye in Normandy, followed the Conqueror to England, and after Hastings obtained a grant of the castle and town of Tamworth, and also the manor of Scrivelbaye, in Lincolnshire. Harry Blount, Marmion's attendant squire, was, according to the custom of the day, a cadet of the house, and being knighted with FitzEustace for gallantry at Flodden, attained to wealth and distinction; eventually through marriage with one of the co-heiresses of the house of Marmion, extinct in default of male heirs, became possessed of the title and estates. Hence, Robert Valentine Blount, the present Lord Fontenaye, has duly succeeded to the ancient tower and town, amid appropriate festivities and rejoicings. We are not aware that his Lordship presented a gold "chain of twelve mark weight" to the pursuivants, or the gentlemen of the press, but that the hospitality was thoughtful, delicate, and unbounded in liberality, no one honoured by its exercise will deny; while the beauty and gracious demeanour of the Lady of the Castle, so efficiently supported in her duties by her friend, the handsome Australian heiress, Miss Maguire of Tumut Park, lent additional lustre to the entertainment.

There for a while we may leave them, in the enjoyment of youth, health, and historic rank. If such gifts do not confer unclouded happiness, it must be admitted that but few of the elements of which it is supposed to be compounded were wanting.

Some delay in Sheila's marriage, however, took place. The *Orlando*, after having been ordered to China, to the dismay of the captain, and at least two of the senior officers, who had private reasons for not desiring to explore the Flowery Land, either in peace or war, was as suddenly recalled, and the cruiser *Candace* ordered to take her place. The *Orlando* was paid off, and the *Royal Alfred*, with a new crew and officers put into commission, and despatched to the Australian station at short notice. A telegram from Fontenaye caused Commander Harcourt, R.N., to betake himself to that vicinity at once. He had been promoted to the rank of Commander for a dashing exploit in bringing off a boat's crew at Guadalcanar, in the teeth of tremendous odds, and a shower of poisoned arrows. There was no need for delay now—Sheila had her trousseau ready weeks before, and the Lieutenant—I beg his pardon, the Captain—didn't require much time to make *his* preparations.

So there was another entertainment at Fontenaye, of comparative splendour and more true kindness and genuine friendship. All the neighbouring gentry were bidden to the feast, as well as the brother officers of the bridegroom. Lord Fontenaye gave away the bride, and made a feeling speech at the breakfast. When Commander Harcourt, R.N., and his lovely bride—for Sheila, in a "confection" from Paris, looked beautiful exceedingly—walked down the aisle of the old Abbey church, a girl of the period said "it put her in mind of Lord Marmion and Lady Clare, only that Marmion was a soldier, and not a sailor, and (now that she remembered) he turned out badly, didn't marry Clare after all, was killed, indeed, at Flodden, and ought to have married poor Clare, who did not do so badly, nor Lord Wilton either, after recovering his lands, his lady-love, and his position in society."

After this momentous function, Lord Fontenaye one fine morning looked up from the *Times*, which, after the fashion of secure husbands, he read during breakfast, with a sudden exclamation that caused Imogen to inquire what it was about.

"The death of Mrs. Delamere, poor thing! *That* will make a difference."

"Difference to whom?" inquired Imogen. "Oh! I see—now, those two can get married. Have you heard from them since they went to West Australia? Yes, I know, you showed me her letter."

"I heard *of* them later on, from a man I knew, that the Colonel had bought into the 'Golden Hoof,' or some such name, and was likely to make a big rise out of it, as he expressed it. What a turn of the wheel it would be, wouldn't it? He was 'dry-blowing' after they got to West Australia."

"What in the world's that?"

"A primitive way of extracting gold from auriferous earth, partly by sifting it, and then by blowing away the lighter dust particles, when the gold, if there is any, remains behind. Then, their tent caught fire one day, when she was away for an hour marketing (fancy Adeline buying soap and candles at a digging!), and everything they had in the world was burned, except what 'they stood up in,' as my informant phrased it."

"But you will send them something, poor things! How I pity them. Oh! how stupid I am! You *did*—I know you."

"Yes! and she sent it back—a decent cheque too."

"Quite right—they couldn't take it from you—*you* of all men. What did you do then?"

"I 'worked it,' as 'Tumbarumba Dick' would say. He was one of the partners in the Lady Julia claim. I sent Dick the cheque; told him to get the

diggers round about to form a relief committee, and to let them subscribe their share, then spread mine out in small amounts among the genuine ones. They couldn't refuse the honest miners' and their wives' assistance. No people are so generous in cases of accident or distress. Thus my money 'got there just the same,' and helped to give the forlorn ones a fresh start."

"Quite another romance—I suppose you have a slight *tendresse* in that direction still?"

"Not more than a man always has for a woman he has once loved, however badly she treated him; and that is a very mild, strictly rational sentiment; but *you* ought to have."

"Why, I should like to know?"

"Because, of course, when she broke my heart, and sent me out into the world drifting purposeless, I fell across one Imogen Carrisforth, who towed the derelict into port—made prize of him, indeed, for ever and ever."

"Well, I suppose she did shape our destiny, as you say—without the least intending it; and now I suspect she'll shape the Colonel's for good and all. They will be remarried quietly, live in the south of France, and the gay world will hear no more of them."

Fontenaye was always reasonably gay and truly hospitable; to the Australian division notably. Not unduly splendid, but comfortably and reasonably fine, on occasion. The nearest pack of hounds always met there on the first day of the season, when sometimes Lady Fontenaye, sometimes Mrs. Vernon Harcourt, appeared, superbly mounted and among the front rankers, after the throw off. Sheila was a frequent guest in her husband necessary absences at sea. Imogen was a little slow to accustom herself to addressed and referred to as "your ladyship" and "her ladyship" at e turn, but took to it by degrees.

"Now, what became of Kate Lawless and her brother Dick?" eager youthful patron of this veracious romance (not by any mear untrue, dear reader, though a little mixed up).

"And the roan pony mare 'Wallaby' that carried Kate nin a day to warn the police about Trevenna," screams a still you "You mustn't leave *her* out."

As might be expected, my dear boys, they came to and his sister disappeared after the fight at "the Ghost C rumoured to have been seen on the Georgina River, ir There were warrants out for both, yet they had not be day, word came to the police station at Monaro, th deserted hut between Omeo and the Running Creek

The Sergeant, taking one trooper who drove a light waggonette, rode to the spot. "This is where Mrs. Trevenna's child was buried, the little chap that was drowned," said the trooper, "under that swamp oak. I was stationed here then and went over. She *was* wild, poor thing! I wonder if that's her lying across the grave."

It was even so. A haggard woman, poorly dressed, showing signs of privation and far travel, lay face downward on the little mound. "Lift her up, Jackson!" said the Sergeant; "poor thing! I'd hardly have known her. She came *here* to shoot herself, look about for the revolver. Just on the temple, what a small hole it made! Shot the mare too! best thing for both of 'em, I expect. So that's the end of Kate Lawless! Who'd have thought it, when that flash crowd was at Ballarat! Handsome girl she was then, full of life and spirits too!"

"She never did no good after the boy was drowned," said the trooper.

"No! nor before, either. But it wasn't all *her* fault. Let's lift her into the trap. She don't weigh much. There'll be the inquest, and she'll have Christian burial. They can't prevent *that* in this country. And she's suffered enough to make a dozen women shoot themselves, or men either."

So the dead woman came into the little township, and after the coroner's jury had brought in their verdict that the deceased had died by her own hand, but that there was no evidence to show her state of mind at the time, poor Kate Trevenna (or Lawless) was buried among more or less respectable people.

There was a slight difference of opinion as to the identification of the woman's corpse, but none whatever as to that of the mare, among the horse-loving bystanders around the grave, which was several times visited during the following days. "That's old Wallaby, safe enough," deposed one grizzled stockrider. "Reg'lar mountain mare, skip over them rocks like a billy-goat; couldn't throw her down no ways. Ain't she dog-poor, too? Kate and she's 'ad hard times lately. What say, boys, s'pose we bury her? the ground's middlin' soft, and if she don't ought to be buried decent, no one does."

The idea caught on, and a pick and spade contingent driving out next , a grave was dug and a stone put up, on which was roughly chiselled—

"Wallaby—died——"